CUTTING
BLADES

Also by Victoria Blake

Bloodless Shadow

VICTORIA BLAKE

CUTTING
BLADES

ORION

First published in Great Britain in 2005 by Orion Books
an imprint of The Orion Publishing Group
Orion House, 5 Upper St Martin's Lane, London WC2H 9EA

All characters in this publication are fictitious and any resemblance
to real persons, living or dead, is purely coincidental.

A CIP catalogue record for this book
is available from the British Library.

ISBN (hardback) 0 75286 058 5
ISBN (trade paperback) 0 75286 813 6

Typeset by Deltatype Ltd, Birkenhead, Merseyside
Printed and bound in Great Britain by Clays Ltd, St Ives plc

www.orionbooks.co.uk

In memory of my parents,

Patricia Blake (1925–1995), a great storyteller and Robert Blake (1916–2003), a wonderful writer.

Acknowledgements

I would like to thank the following people: Maureen McEvoy, my first reader, for her love and support; Ivy Payne for inside information; Briony Young for keeping me in working order; Richard Collier, Rose Lamb, Keir Lusby, and Faith Noonan of the Whitton Writing Group for listening to early drafts; Teresa Chris, my agent, for encouragement and feedback; Kate Mills, my editor, for her enthusiasm and suggestions; Tim Waller, copy-editor, for spotting all the things I missed. Also at Orion, my thanks to Gaby Young and Genevieve Pegg. Finally, my source for the Wittgenstein quotation on rowing was a fascinating interview of Acer Nethercott of the OUBC by Matthew Syed in *The Times* on March 23 2004.

PROLOGUE

In the grey morning light, he looks like a giant standing on Putney Bridge in softly falling snow. Behind him a red London bus accelerates, sending a wave of brown slush across the pavement against the back of his trousers, but he barely notices.

He's six foot six, so tall he'd have to duck his head in the tube, but he stands up straight, not like some very tall people who seem to shy away from it. No, this man occupies his full height unapologetically. He is looking upriver towards the finish, four and a half miles away.

To the right of him is Bishop's Park, filled with plane trees whose black branches are now covered with a thick icing of snow. Further down on the right, at the end of the park, is Craven Cottage, the ground of Fulham Football Club. Clouds of chattering starlings hover in the air above the square heads of the floodlights and then settle.

He pulls up the hood of his dark blue sweatshirt, retreating out of the snow like a monk into his cowl, and lowers his eyes; he could almost be praying. *His whole life* . . . No, he stops that train of thought. That won't take him anywhere he wants to go. But the truth is that his whole life he's imagined this. Has he got this far just to throw it all away? He tries not to think of all the people he will let down: his mates, the coaches. Is he really going to do that? He places his hands flat on the stone parapet of the bridge. The snow soothes the blisters on his hands. He looks down at the snowflakes landing and melting on the black surface of the Thames. Maybe it won't take as long as he thinks.

When he first started rowing, they told him that his hands would harden, but they never have. They blister, then the blisters burst and then he gets new blisters on top of the old ones. He soaks them in white spirit every night, he does everything that's suggested to him, but still his hands are a torn-up mess. After every outing there's blood on the end of his oar, blood on his hands.

A flurry of snow blows into his face and a thought flashes through his mind. Is he running away because he's frightened of the race? He has to be certain it's not that. A knot is tightening and twisting in his stomach. Yes, that's fear, all right. But how can you not be afraid?

The race is four and a half miles long. Much longer than he's used to. At the point where most races finish he'll be expected to do that same distance twice over. The only certainty is how much it will hurt.

There's no race like it. That's what the coaches say.

That's why they have ambulances at the finish. And two years ago, with the crews neck and neck, someone in the Cambridge crew, an international rower of some repute, had blown up spectacularly, had just slumped over in his seat and started skying his blade, watched by seven million viewers in this country and a worldwide audience of four hundred million. He repeats the figure – four hundred million – and the knot twists and turns. Of course there's fear, fear of that very public exposure. Fear that he won't be able to hack it, that he'll catch a crab, that when the chips are down and the cox is calling for one last push he'll have nothing left to give.

And there are no silver or bronze medals in this race.

At the end there is a winner and a loser. It's a prizefight on the river and one of the crews gets knocked on its arse.

He straightens up and his coat falls open. OUBC is printed in white letters on his sweatshirt. Oxford University Boat Club. He hopes he can get all this sorted quickly. He hopes they'll have him back.

He looks at the place on the river where the boats line up for the start. Last year he'd climbed one of the plane trees in Bishop's Park for the start of the race. He'd dared to imagine himself in the stroke seat, the one closest to the cox, the most important seat in the boat.

He leans his head back and the hood, now covered in a white

cap of snow, falls back onto his shoulders. The light from one of the lamps strikes his face and for the first time you can see how very young he is – no more than a boy really, eighteen at the most.

Soft, white and impenetrable, the snowfall thickens. Put your hand in front of you and you'd have trouble seeing it. A bus grinds to a halt and the driver jumps out and, head ducked against the driving snow, struggles to unclog his frozen windscreen wipers.

The boy's gone now. Only the bloody imprints of his hands remain in the snow on the stone parapet of the bridge. But these are swiftly filled and soon there'll be no trace that he was ever there, standing on Putney Bridge looking upstream towards the finish of the Oxford and Cambridge Boat Race.

CHAPTER ONE

London in January – a city reeling from a million broken resolutions.

Sam Falconer, private investigator and occasional self-defence instructor, sat on the top deck of a number 220 bus, inching its way along the Fulham Palace Road in a swirling snowstorm. She was not thinking about resolutions, made or broken. She was too terrified to think of anything so mundane. She was thinking about the man she was sure had followed her through the snow from her flat in the New King's Road to the bus stop. She was thinking about her father, Geoffrey Falconer. Fear was having the same effect on her body as extreme cold – she was shivering but rooted to the spot.

Footsteps clattered up the stairs behind her. This must be him – she was sure of it. He had got on the bus behind her. She couldn't bring herself to look round. The footsteps drew closer and closer. Sam forced herself to take a look and sighed with relief as a young man wearing camouflage trousers and a parka threw himself into the seat across the aisle from her. He put a black-booted foot up on the metal bar that ran along under the window and began bobbing and weaving his head in time to the music hissing from his personal stereo. He was exuding teenage testosterone and aggression but given what Sam had been expecting, he seemed about as threatening as a Teletubby.

Sam stared out at the Christmas trees peppering the pavements and took some deep breaths in an attempt to steady her heart rate. The bus had reached Charing Cross Hospital and was beginning the slow crawl towards Hammersmith Broadway. Trying to divert her thoughts from her father, Sam opened an *Evening Standard* that had been left on the seat next to her. A poll had been completed which stated that if you smiled at a Londoner they were even less likely to smile back at you than a Glaswegian. Especially in January, Sam thought. Why would anyone want to smile in January? All she ever wanted to do was crawl under the duvet and stay there until an unknown benefactor had paid off her credit-card bills and until the crocuses were cracking the surface of the earth.

But tonight she had a self-defence class to teach. And she knew it would do her good. It would get her body moving and that should at least shift some of the fear.

The traffic hadn't moved for the last five minutes. It would be quicker to walk. Sam jumped off the back of the bus and, telling herself not to be paranoid and that she was not allowed to look behind her, not even once, she started trudging through the blizzard in the direction of the gym.

An hour later Sam looked up at the snow falling on the skylight of the gym where she was teaching and then back at the anxious faces of the fifteen women gathered in a ragged circle around her. There had been a funny atmosphere in the class that evening and it was all her fault.

Initially, Sam had thought it was just because this was the first class after Christmas and people were feeling stale and weighed down by too much turkey, but as the class continued and she caught sight of more and more of the women glancing surreptitiously at her face, she realised it had nothing to do with that: it had more to do with the fact that she was sporting a badly swollen black eye, a cut across the top of her nose, and another cut that ran from under her left eye down her cheek.

And *she* was teaching *them* self-defence.

'Look,' she said. 'I'm sorry, I should have said something about this before. Some of you may be wondering what on earth happened to me.' She gestured to her face. 'As well as teaching these classes, I'm a private investigator and someone pulled a gun on me. And then hit me with it. The truth is that if that happens there's not much you can do. Your only self-defence is a bulletproof vest. Guns are proliferating here but it's not nearly as bad as America – you're still pretty unlikely to come across them.

I survived. I may look a bit battered but I can still teach you things worth knowing about how to look after yourself. Any questions?'

No one said anything. Sam thought she'd got away with it. Then a small woman with auburn hair standing at the back of the group cleared her throat. 'Are you all right?' she asked.

Sam hadn't been expecting sympathy; she'd expected to be challenged.

'Yes,' she said, feeling the lump in her throat squeeze her vocal cords. 'Thank you, Eileen, I'm on the mend. Now, please find a partner and practise the moves I was demonstrating earlier.'

Sam gently patted the skin round her black eye and watched as the women split into pairs and began punching and parrying. Some of them had come via victim-support networks. The aim of the class was to make them feel physically more confident in their ability to take care of themselves, to empower them. Sam sighed. She'd considered covering up the bruises with a bit of make-up but since she rarely used it she was worried she might end up looking like Lily Savage, which would probably be even more terrifying.

Hubris, Sam thought. You think you're so damn shit-hot and then you are placed, looking like a panda, in front of a group of anxious and vulnerable women. Great. What a good way to start the year. Happy New Year to you too!

Sam began moving between the pairs of women and stopped to watch Eileen for a moment.

'The thing is, Eileen, really try and hit her. It's no good if you're too gentle about it.'

Sam stood in front of Eileen's partner, a tall woman with a mane of curly black hair, and looked her in the eye. 'So, Jane, are you ready? I'm really going to go for it.' The woman nodded. Sam punched. The woman parried the punch with her forearm. 'OK, great,' Sam said. 'Let's do it again. . . that's great.' She turned back to Eileen. 'Then Jane knows she can do it. She knows she can block a punch that has real intention behind it. Do you see? If you hold back it's not doing her any favours. You've got to mean it. Do it for real. So that if she gets in that situation she's confident she can protect herself.'

Jane nodded. 'It's more satisfying,' she said, rubbing her forearm.

'See,' Sam said. 'She wants you to go for it.'

Eileen smiled weakly. 'I find it hard even to pretend to hit someone.'

'You're doing great, Eileen,' Sam said and moved on to the next pair.

God, these women, Sam thought. She didn't understand it. Sam had leapt from the womb fighting and hadn't really stopped since. She had absolutely no problem with the idea of punching someone. She might be five foot one and under forty-eight kilograms but she was also a four-times judo World Champion. She knew all there was to know about fighting. She tried to be patient when she was teaching but sometimes she found it hard. What was the problem with hitting someone – especially in self-defence? She just didn't get it.

Washing her hands in the changing room toilets after the class had finished, Sam raised her eyes from the white enamel of the sink to her own reflection in the mirror in front of her. Even without the cuts and bruises, which obviously didn't help, she wasn't particularly happy with the face looking back at her. She was too short, her hair was too blonde and curly and to top it all she was way, way too pale. Her eyes were OK – very blue – but the rims were always pink. She sighed and, completely blind to her own prettiness, thought, not for the first time, that she looked like a white mouse with a perm.

She pulled a hand towel from a unit attached to the wall, dampened it and patted her face, then ran her hand through her unruly mop of blonde hair. Blondes were supposed to have more fun, weren't they? Well, not in Sam's experience they didn't – more like shorter necks from all the pats on the head they had to endure as children. She'd been a very cute kid. Even the most child-hating of individuals had been tempted to stretch out a hand and try their luck. Who knows how many inches she'd lost in the process?

She scrunched up the towel and threw it into the bin. She blamed the pallor of her skin on the fact that she'd been born three weeks premature. If she'd just managed to stay in the dark room of her mother's womb a bit longer then maybe she wouldn't have ended up looking so overexposed and maybe bright sunshine wouldn't have felt so much like a physical assault.

She wouldn't have ended up feeling so much happier in the shadows.

'Oh, get on with it, girl,' she said out loud. 'That's the face you've got.' And she walked back into the changing room.

As Sam was closing up the zip on her holdall, Eileen approached her tentatively.

'It's this,' she said, holding out a leaflet. 'We meet every week at St Mary's. I thought. . .'

Sam looked at the flyer. It was about a victim-support group. 'Thanks, Eileen, I'll bear it in mind. But, you know, I wasn't beaten up by my boyfriend or something – it was because of my work.'

'I know, but you've still been the victim of violence. The group's helped me a lot. Well, coming here does as well, of course.'

Sam smiled. 'Thanks.' She stuffed the leaflet into the pocket of her sheepskin jacket, picked up her holdall, hoisted it onto her shoulder and made for the door. She felt irritated. Victim? She was nobody's victim.

The pub was fairly empty and Sam spotted Alan straight away. He was sitting at a table, writing, and hadn't noticed her enter. She walked quietly up behind him and looked over his shoulder. Then she kissed him on the back of the neck, the width of which was a product of many hours working out, leaned over and tapped the paper he was writing on. 'I think you should add to that list: 5. Find alternative employment or at least a boss who has the good manners to pay me.'

He stood up and hugged her. 'Hello, darling. Happy New Year. Cheerful as ever, I see.'

Alan Knowles was an ex-policeman who worked for Sam at the Gentle Way Investigation Agency on a part-time basis. But as well as being her colleague he was also her best friend. He was a big bear of a man without a scrap of fat on him. He had a square face, brown eyes and black hair, cut close to his head. For a gay man he wasn't that much of a peacock, but one of the things he did insist upon was the maintenance of a year-round tan and he was completely resistant to Sam's jokes about Dale Winton and her dire warnings of the risks of skin cancer.

'Can I get you anything?' Sam said, pointing to the bar.

'No, I'm fine.' He pointed at a glass on the table in front of him. Sam grimaced. 'What the hell's that?'

'Mineral water.'

She turned round the piece of paper he was writing on. 'Oh, I see. "2. Drink less." I don't know why people do it. Why make resolutions in January? It's the most depressing time to do it. Now if it was the spring that would be a different matter. It's a more hopeful time of year. You look out of your window. The daffodils are blooming. You throw open the windows and walk out into your garden. Your cat throws itself onto the warm flagstones and rolls back and forth. You breathe in the blue sky and sunshine. You say to yourself, "Drink less", and then, you know, suddenly it all seems possible . . .'

'I haven't got a garden and neither have you. I live on the twenty-sixth floor of a high-rise and you live in a first-floor flat.'

'It's an imaginary garden, Alan. A garden of the mind.'

Alan made a shooing motion with his hand. 'Away with you and your gardens. Get that drink and leave me to my resolutions.'

Sam came back a few moments later, carrying a pint of Guinness. 'How was your Christmas?' she asked.

'My bloody brothers,' Alan said and shook his head.

'You go to the pub with them on Christmas Eve?'

'All eight of them.' Alan put his arm round Sam's shoulder and, assuming a gruff macho voice that in no way reflected his own, said, '"'E may be a poof but he's still our little Al, isn't he?" That's Bert's version of tolerance. He gets there after about four pints. Then he punches me in the upper arm, which hurts like hell but it's as close as he can get to showing physical affection towards his gay younger brother.'

'Was it Bert who hit you round the head when you were a kid and gave you tinnitus?'

'That was Johnny – he's up for parole next year – then God help us all.'

'What do you think upset them more? You being gay or you joining the police?'

Alan fiddled with the two earrings in his right ear lobe. 'Don't know.'

'Did you do it to annoy them?'

'Yeah, Sam, I thought, Why don't I fancy men? That'll really piss them off and make my life so much easier . . .'

Sam laughed. 'Joining the police, you idiot.'

'Well, it was my way of letting them know they couldn't keep dragging me into all their schemes. It got me out, that and the bodybuilding. Once I got big enough they couldn't keep putting me through windows any more.'

'So they don't talk to you about business?'

'No. Even though I'm no longer on the Job, I'm not to be trusted, which suits me fine. You should see the presents, though.'

'What about them?'

'Well, put it this way, Bert gave every one of us a DVD player.'

'Oh.'

'All the serial numbers had been filed off. It's all knocked-off stuff.'

'I remember the video.'

'That was fine until it burst into flames and melted *La Cage aux Folles*.'

'Look on the bright side. It could have been *Tootsie* or *Victor/Victoria*.'

'True.'

Sam swallowed a mouthful of beer. 'I steered clear of my family and stayed in my flat.'

'Was it all right?'

Sam stared at the table. 'I suppose. Edie came round from next door and we got pissed together and then argued over the Queen's speech.'

'Why?'

'She wanted to watch it. She told me the Queen was misunderstood.'

'Gawd. Red rag to a bull.'

'I'd had too much to drink. I told her she couldn't watch it. She flounced next door and we haven't spoken since.'

'How was the class tonight?'

'Hard going. I don't think this,' she pointed at her face, 'exactly filled them with much confidence.'

Alan cocked his head on one side and looked at her. 'It's getting better. It's good when the black starts to turn purple. Then you've only got from purple to green, from green to yellow and from yellow to pink and then you're all healed up.'

Sam reached into her pocket and brought out the flyer that Eileen had given her. 'I mean, it's come to a pretty pass when members of a self-defence class start handing out these to their teacher.'

Alan glanced at it and laughed. 'And you don't even look that bad, love. Never mind, you've got the boys soon and all they'll want to do is give you make-up hints about how to cover it up.' The boys that Alan was referring to were the members a self-defence class for gay men that Sam taught. 'They'll just think it's frightfully glamorous or gory or something.'

'Yes,' Sam said. 'Or, to put it another way, they won't give a toss.'

Alan smiled. 'So much easier to handle – especially for someone like you.'

'And who exactly is someone like me?'

He looked startled. 'God, I think that's a first, Sam Falconer displaying signs of introspection. Haven't you got a brand-new shrink to tell you that?'

Sam blushed. 'I've only been once. I'm not sure—'

'Should have started going in the spring, then. The sun is shining. The daffodils are blooming. You walk out into your garden and suddenly it all seems so possible.'

'You missed out the cat.'

'Oh yes. The cat's shitting in the window box . . . a light breeze is blowing the stench towards you . . .'

Sam laughed. 'Bastard.'

'Do you like him?'

'I've only been once. I'm not sure that liking comes into it. We argued.'

'Well, there's a surprise. Does he know what he's let himself in for?'

Sam ran her hand across her forehead and sighed. 'I think after that first session he was beginning to get the general idea.'

'Any work come into the office over Christmas?'

Sam shook her head.

'It's always quiet this time of year.'

'I know.'

'What are you going to do?'

Sam stared gloomily at the snow drifting slowly past the windows of the pub. 'Take anything. I'll do divorce. Everyone wants a divorce after Christmas. I do and I'm not even married.'

'Who do you want to divorce?'

'Frank – he's not the cat I married.'

'No, he's four times the size.'

Sam laughed.

'You still think your dad's following you everywhere?'

'Yup.'

'What are you going to do?'

'What can I do, if I can't even see him?'

Later that evening, walking to her flat in Fulham, Sam thought back to her first session with her therapist, Reg Ellison, a couple of weeks earlier. He lived in a house in Richmond in a road that ran north off the Lower Mortlake Road. After they had both sat down he had been the first to speak.

'And why do you want to enter therapy?'

'God, I don't *want* to – does anyone want to?'

Reg smiled. 'Well, what would you say has brought you here?'

'The bus.'

He didn't smile this time but looked at her impassively and waited.

'Headaches,' Sam said eventually. 'And flashbacks.' She paused. 'And nightmares.'

'When did these start?'

Sam felt pins and needles sparking in her hands. She squeezed them together, trying to stop the feeling from spreading into her arms. She cleared her throat. 'Er ... it was after Jenny.' She stopped. It was as if she could hear the blood pulsing round her body, pushing along the veins and arteries.

'Who's Jenny?'

'It was a case I was on. She'd been murdered by her father. I found her. They started after that.'

'How long ago was this?'

'About four months.'

'And you've been having them ever since?'

Sam nodded.

'Any recurring ones?'

'I'm drowning. I'm surrounded by clear blue water but in the nightmare I don't want to be rescued. Above me I can see this hand reaching down to grab me and I know that I have to get away, so I'm kicking and struggling to go deeper and deeper even though I know that if I do that I'll die.'

'Do you want to die?'

'In the dream?'

Reg blinked but didn't say anything.

'In the dream I want to escape. I know if the hand reaches me something terrible will happen.'

'And that will be worse than death?'

'Yes'

'Do you want to die?' he repeated.

Sam looked down at her hands. They were clasped together so tightly that the skin over her knuckles had turned white. Just a small cut and it would lay bare the bone. She brought her hand up to her neck and felt the ridge of a scar.

'Sam?'

She unclasped her hands and laid them palm-down on her thighs. 'No, of course not.'

'Did anything else happen round the time you found Jenny?'

'Yes, my father . . .'

Reg nodded.

'I thought he'd been a hero, killed in Oman in 1974.'

'Oman?'

'Yes.'

'SAS, then?'

'Yes. You see, that's what we were told. He was dead. I'd based my whole life on that, following in his footsteps. The judo, the drive to be the best – it was all about him. Then he wrote me this letter.'

'When was this?'

'About three months ago.'

'So he is alive?'

Sam nodded.

'Have you met up with him?'

Sam stared into the middle distance. She'd met up with him, all right. She rubbed her wrist. The bruises had gone but the memory remained. She could feel his hand gripping onto her, pulling her across the café table towards him. She could still feel his breath on her face and hear his words. *You're the only home I've got, Sam.*

'Sam?'

'Yes,' she said, 'I met up with him.'

'That's a lot to handle,' Reg said.

Sam didn't say anything, just sat staring down at her knuckles.

'Is there anything else you'd like to tell me?'

Sam looked up at him. 'I never learned to swim.'

'Well,' Reg said, 'we can start in the shallows.'

And that had been the polite part of the session. After that Sam had gone on the attack. She'd felt so vulnerable she needed to pick a fight.

Now, trudging through the snow towards home, hands plunged deep into the pockets of her sheepskin coat, Sam toyed with the idea of not going to tomorrow's session. Reg had suggested twice a week. She'd said once a week would be fine, thanks. No deal, he'd said. Twice a week or nothing. But that had seemed way too much to Sam. Not enough time between sessions to recover. She kicked at the snow in frustration. Why did revelation have to feel so like surrender? Why couldn't she cast the thing in some kind of framework that wasn't about him winning and her losing? Revelation felt unsafe but she was exhausted; too tired to do battle with him but too frightened by what was happening to her not to.

She came out of Buer Road into the New King's Road. Fulham was still blissfully empty. The schools hadn't gone back yet and the absence of cars parked in the side streets indicated that many people were still away. During the holidays London became an unusually civilised place to live because half the population left. Sam liked it like this. In the old days there'd been plague and fire to reduce the population; now there was only holidays.

She let herself into the mansion block she lived in and then into her flat and went into the kitchen to switch on the heating. She turned the dial to 'on' and nothing happened – no click, no whirr, no hum, nothing. Usually the boiler made arcane whirring noises to indicate it was working. This time it made absolutely no noise whatsoever.

Sam put her head in her hands and screamed.

There was a foot of snow outside and it was the coldest spell in the city for years. The weather forecasters had taken great pleasure in reporting that London was colder than Siberia; night-time temperatures of -10C had been mentioned. The flat was bitterly cold and damp. She didn't want the landlord, Crozier, to fix the boiler. His men were brutes that made the average gorilla look like a graduate from Lucie Clayton. Every time they set foot in the flat they made a point of breaking something.

All the rooms in the flat had fireplaces but they hadn't been lit in ages. Her gran had used fires before Crozier installed the central heating but that was years ago, and as far as Sam knew they hadn't been swept since. When it rained hard, the soot fell gently down the chimneys, sounding like the scampering feet of mice and making Sam sneeze.

Sam turned on the kettle and warmed her hands on it, wondering what to do next. Then she frowned and looked around her – something was missing. She walked out of the kitchen into each of the rooms in turn. Finally, she lay down flat on her stomach on the bedroom floor and carefully removed the board at the bottom of the wardrobe. Sometimes, when he had eaten something disgusting from the bins and was feeling off-colour or anti-social, Frank Cooper, her cat, hid here. But no green eyes gleamed at her from the darkness. Sam wheezed as dust balls rolled towards her.

She phoned Edie, her next-door neighbour, but there was no reply. Sam opened her front door and went out into the hall then lifted the letterbox of Edie's flat and whistled. No response. Maybe she was still pissed off with her. She went back into her own flat and stood in her hall, not knowing what to do.

She had let Frank out that morning. Usually Edie would have let him back into the block and then into Sam's flat. Sam had given her keys specifically for this purpose. When you lived in a first-floor flat, cat flaps didn't work, it was the front door or nothing, and Sam disapproved of cats that didn't go out. She wanted Frank to have an outside life but she didn't want him locked out all day if the weather was bad.

Sam left her flat again and walked along Cristowe Road, whistling for Frank. She peered into the bush he usually sat in and then ran down the steps that led to the back of the block and the dustbins. But there was no sign of him anywhere. Her boots squeaked in the snow but no fat orange cat ran to greet her. She gave up and went back inside.

No Frank and no Edie; that was downright weird. Edie went off on the boats tobacco-smuggling on Wednesdays and Saturdays, not Mondays. Sam opened the fridge but didn't feel the usual blast of cold air because the kitchen was at least as cold as the inside of the fridge. Empty shelves greeted her; it would have to be Nayaab's again. At least curry might warm her up. She had been such a good customer last year that they'd sent her a Christmas card – a particularly beautiful one of vibrant reds and pinks. She'd been strangely touched and then had burst into tears.

It was one of the reasons she'd started seeing Reg. If you were crying over a Christmas card sent to you by your local curry house, you knew you were in trouble. And then she'd been on the number 22 bus going down the King's Road and she'd seen the night lights and flowers against the wall of the fire station marking the place where a homeless man had always sat. A woman in front of her had turned round as the bus moved on. 'He was always there,' she said. 'What a shame.' And Sam, to her horror, had again felt the tears pouring down her face. And there was no way she was crying for the dead man. She'd never even spoken to him or given him money, only ever looked at him from the safe, sterile distance of the top floor of the bus.

She pulled the menu from the drawer of the kitchen table, walked back into the hall and picked up the phone.

Later that night as Sam slept, a noise outside the block tugged her into semi-consciousness. Sam was used to urban night-time noise. She lived on a main road within spitting distance of the bridge that crossed the New King's Road carrying the Wimbledon branch of the District Line. After three years of being woken by people working late at night on the track, night buses roaring past, drunken people getting out of taxis and crashing into the block and, of course, urban foxes, she was adept at rolling over and going straight back to sleep. So she pulled the duvet over her head and tried to do exactly that. But there it was again and this time she registered what the noise was – an ear-splitting howl, closer now and pitched high enough to penetrate the thickest of duvets.

God, Frank could hold a note; she should have named him Miles Davis.

Sam grabbed her alarm clock and held it in front of her sleep-blurred eyes. 'Well done, Frank. Four fucking thirty,' she said. She jumped out of bed and lifted the blind of her bedroom window. An immensely fat and shaggy marmalade cat was standing on the pavement up to his knees in snow, eyes staring up at the block. On seeing her, he let out an even more blood-curdling howl and began jumping through the snow towards the front door.

Sam was aware that by this time Frank had probably woken everyone on this side of the building – approximately twenty people. She threw open the door to her flat and bounded into the hall. She could hear the cat's yowls getting closer and closer. She ran down the stairs and flung open the main door and Frank shot through her legs and up the stairs. She turned just in time to see her flat door slam shut on his nose.

At that precise moment, the light came on in the hall and a woman appeared on the stairs. She had an angular face topped with spiky auburn hair and very pale skin; a red slash of lipstick covered a rather petulant mouth. She was wearing a long black raincoat and black leather boots and carrying a large leather bag slung across her body. She stood stock-still staring at Sam and Frank and gripped onto the strap that crossed her chest. Sam saw that every finger was encircled with a ring; the effect was of a very gaudy knuckle-duster. Frank stared back and then continued yowling at full throttle.

'Shhhh,' Sam said, running up the stairs towards him. The light, which was on a timer, went off. The woman backed away from them and punched the light on again. Sam grabbed the cat, clamped her hand over his mouth and, even though his fur was sodden, began to stroke him. 'I'm really sorry,' she whispered. 'I hope he didn't wake you. I think he got disorientated in the snow.'

The woman had obviously decided that Sam and Frank posed no threat because she released her grip on the bag and started down the stairs again.

'No, I was on my way out.'

'Oh, good,' Sam whispered. 'Usually I make sure he's in before I go to sleep but he disappeared on me last night.'

The woman nodded and continued down the stairs past Sam.

Sam stared at her closed front door. 'Excuse me . . .' she began. The woman stopped and turned round. 'The thing is, I've just locked myself out. The door slammed on me. Edie . . .' she nodded at Edie's flat, 'usually has my keys but she's not here at the moment and Spence – you know, in the basement flat – well, I'm not sure if he's back from his mum's, and even if he is back he takes sleeping pills, and even when he's awake he never opens his front door.'

Sam suspected Spence of taking all sorts of things, not just sleeping pills, but thought she should exert some neighbourly discretion. The woman didn't say anything and Sam continued.

'I was wondering if you'd let me use your flat.' She pointed to her sock-covered feet. 'It's not as if I can go anywhere. Then I could phone a locksmith and get myself sorted out.'

Sam didn't really expect the woman to agree. She wouldn't have been keen to leave a complete stranger alone in her flat, but she had no shoes, no money and no keys; it was bitterly cold and she was desperate. She didn't fancy trying to wake her neighbours and her only other option was to wait for them to get up and go to work.

'I don't know you from Adam,' the woman said firmly. 'That's not going to work for me.'

'But, I'm a woman of good character. I'm a private investigator. I'm one of the good guys.' Sam ground to a halt, not quite believing what had come from her mouth.

The woman laughed. 'Good character? You're joking, aren't you? Have you looked at your face recently?'

'Let me use your flat until I can get myself sorted out and I'll owe you a favour.'

The woman paused at the front door. 'Private detective, did you say?'

Sam was starting to shiver. 'Yup.'

She dug in her bag and brought out her mobile phone. She punched a few buttons, spoke into the phone and then handed it to Sam. 'Speak to Gerry; he's a twenty-four-hour locksmith.'

Sam had a brief conversation with the man on the end of the phone and then handed it back to the woman. 'Thanks.'

'How long did he say?'

'Said they were busy – an hour or an hour and a half.'

'I need to be going.' She put the phone in her bag and opened the front door. 'I may call in that favour.'

'What favour was that exactly? Leaving me on these stairs in the freezing cold for an hour and a half waiting for the locksmith to turn up with a yowling cat?'

The woman glanced at her watch and ran her tongue over the outside of her teeth, which were all crowded together at the front of her mouth, as if looking for an argument. 'I haven't got time for this. If I don't go now I'll never get a meter. You're a hell of a lot better off than if you didn't have a locksmith coming and that . . .' she gestured at Sam's clothing, 'looks pretty warm.'

Sam was wearing a baggy brown woollen jumper, which descended practically to her knees; covering her legs were frayed blue and white striped pyjama bottoms. Ex-boyfriends had their uses.

'I'll be in touch about the favour.' The main door of the block swung shut behind her before Sam could reply.

Sam sighed and squatted down with her back resting against her own front door. She tugged the jumper down over her knees and managed to stretch it far enough to tuck her toes underneath it. She closed her eyes and, despite the cold, she fell asleep. She was woken an hour later by someone tapping on the glass window in the front door. She got to her feet slowly, feeling stiff from the cold, and ran down the steps to open the door for the locksmith.

Gerry Doyle was tall and thin with shoulder-length curly brown hair tied back in a ponytail. He had the kind of face made romantic by long hair rather than seedy; more pirate on the high seas than computer nerd. He was handsome, he was missing three fingers of his left hand and he had Sam inside her flat in less than five minutes.

Sam was relieved and smitten and so was Frank, who wound in and out of his legs and flirted with him outrageously, rubbing his face on the silver steel toecaps protruding from the end of his boots. Frank could be a right slut when it came to men. Sam decided she could be as well, especially after Gerry tinkered away at her boiler and it roared into life.

Gerry sat at the kitchen table while Sam made them a cup of tea. 'It must be a fantastic job,' Sam said. 'Because people must be so grateful to you all the time.'

He shrugged his shoulders. 'People are people. Some are OK; others are right bastards. It's the way it goes. It's busy this time of year. There are lots of burglaries and break-ins in December and January, lots of presents to steal. People are stressed out after Christmas and then the cold gets them rushing and they lock themselves out.' He rubbed his eyes. 'I'm not complaining. It's good work.'

'How do you know my neighbour?'

'Jackie? I'm in and out of the market a bit and I've done some lock work for her.'

'Market?'

'Portobello.'

'What does she do?'

'Dealer.'

That description, Sam thought, could cover a whole multitude of sins.

'She wouldn't let me stay in her flat till you came.'

He laughed. 'It's like Fort Knox up there. I know – I've put half of them on.'

As he reached for his mug of tea, Sam couldn't help staring at his maimed hand. He saw her looking.

'I was working for a lumberjack business when the hurricane hit in October 1987 – when all those trees came down? We were contracted to the council to clear the roads and I did a solid stint of twenty-four hours straight through. I was up this tree cutting off a dangerous branch with a chain saw and the rope I was hanging from slipped. Not much, but enough to do this. I was only nineteen and thought it was the end of the world.'

Sam winced.

'Guy I was working with down on the pavement ended up combing my fingers out of his hair. I was lucky to be left with my thumb and first finger. At least I've got some grip with this hand, but I can't go up trees any more. You look like you've been in the wars yourself.'

Sam gently patted her black eye. 'Afraid so.'

His mobile rang. He spoke for a few minutes and then got wearily to his feet and stretched. 'Next call – Wandsworth. Thanks for the tea.'

'Do you have a direct line? In case this happens again.'

'There you go.' He handed her a card. As he made his way to the door, Frank ran backwards and forwards in front of him. He bent down and scratched Frank under the chin. 'There, there,' he said. 'It may never happen.' Then to Sam: 'See you.'

I hope so, Sam thought. She walked back into the kitchen and watched him getting into his van and driving away. Apart from the fact she found him attractive, Sam thought that there might be times when knowing a friendly locksmith, who also had a way with boilers, might have definite advantages.

CHAPTER TWO

'Oh.' Reg Ellison seemed surprised as he held open the door of his house and looked at Sam over the top of his round horn-rimmed glasses.

Sam frowned. 'Have I got the time wrong?'

A flurry of snow danced around her and then, spinning like a small tornado, moved through the doorway and did the same to Reg. He stepped backwards, brushing the flakes off his bald head and the front of his denim shirt.

'No, no, of course not. Come in.'

He stood aside and she walked past him into the hall and stood waiting for him to close the front door. He turned round and held out his arm, indicating that she should go into the room on the left.

'Didn't you think I'd turn up?' Sam asked when they had sat down.

'One never knows. First sessions are often difficult. People sometimes put their toe in the water and decide it's not for them. I'm glad you've come back, though.'

Sam remembered their final exchange a week ago.

REG: I'm not your opponent, Sam.

SAM: No.

REG: I'm not here to fight you. I mean, you were a World Champion – there'd be no point – but secondly this is only going to work if we can establish some sort of partnership.

SAM: I'm not good at that. I'm a loner.

REG: Well, that'll make it harder.

After that, it wasn't particularly surprising that he might doubt whether she'd turn up for the next session.

Reg's voice broke into Sam's thoughts. 'I'd like to talk to you about what happened leading up to the discovery of Jenny Hughes.'

'Why?'

'You said that's what triggered the flashbacks and nightmares. Could you tell me what you remember?'

Sam looked down at the floor. 'All I remember is looking down at the place she was buried.'

'And before?'

'I don't remember anything. How I got there. How I knew. I just came to, standing over where she was buried in the woods.'

'You don't remember?'

Sam bit her lip and shook her head.

'Has anything like that happened to you before?'

'What?'

'Periods of amnesia. Blanks.'

Sam stood up abruptly. 'I don't think I can do this. I'm sorry. I'll pay for the session but—'

'It's OK, Sam, it's OK.'

'But it isn't,' she said

'Please sit down. Tell me how you've been this week.'

She sat. On the way there she'd been thinking about what she wanted to talk about, but now, with Reg sitting in front of her waiting for her to speak, her mind had gone blank. She blurted out the first thing that came to her. 'I locked myself out – I liked the locksmith.'

'Every cloud.'

'He mended my boiler as well. I've got no work coming in . . . Actually, that's not really it.' Sam stopped for a second. It was her money. Was she really going to talk to him about her bloody boiler? 'No, I don't want to talk about any of that.'

'What do you want to talk about?'

Oh, God.

'I want to talk about my father. I want to talk about how I'm going to deal with the fact that I know he is out there somewhere and that there is nothing I can do about it. I want to talk about what the hell I'm going to do to make myself feel safe. And I want to talk about these.' She lifted a metal chain carrying two dog tags over her head. She used to keep them in her pocket but since his return she had started wearing them round her neck. The tags swung backwards and forwards between them.

Reg held out his hand. 'May I?'

Sam looked Reg in the eye. He had nice eyes – brown, steady eyes – and a solid, reassuring body. She was relieved that she found him in no way physically attractive. That was a cliché she was keen to avoid. He was too thick round the middle for her. She gathered the chain and tags into her own hand and then placed them in his.

He examined them carefully. 'Well,' he said, handing them back to her, 'that's something to get our teeth into. Why don't you tell me what happened when you met up with him?'

Sam placed the dog tags back round her neck. 'I went to a café and had tea with him and then . . .' As if it was the most normal thing in the world. She shook her head.

And then, looking at the greasy swirls on the café's formica table, she had remembered.

The water had looked so inviting – chlorine blue. She had cupped her hand and been disappointed that the water was the colour of tap water. It had looked so beautiful; why wasn't it like that in her hand? But it all changed so quickly. He threw her in. She remembered the shock of the cold water and the hot stream of urine against her legs, the plummet to the bottom, bursting lungs and clawing to the surface, gulping and gasping for air. She doesn't know how many times she sank and rose before he grabbed her. Maybe something about her struggling aroused him, because when she looked at his face, seeking reassurance, he had looked at her the way a cat looks at a bird it has decided to play with.

This is what she had remembered, but how can she be sure that this is what happened? How can she begin to talk about it with this man sitting opposite her?

'Sam . . .?' Reg's voice cut through her thoughts.

'I told him not to come near me but he grabbed hold of my wrist and dragged me across the table towards him.' Sam pulled up the sleeve of her jumper. 'I haven't got the bruises any more but after he'd done it you could see the individual marks where each of his fingers had dug into my skin.'

'So he hurt you?'

'Yes, mind you, I did the same to him. He will have had his own bruises, I can tell you. Just like mine. I know I hurt him as well.' She could hear the false bravado in her voice. What was she trying to prove? That she could be as violent as her father? How pathetic was that?

'Did he do that to your face?'

'No, he had nothing to do with this.'

'Do you feel threatened by him?'

'I believe he loves me. He saved my life. He killed for me.'

Reg cleared his throat. 'Killed?'

'This is all confidential, right?'

Reg nodded.

'I don't want to go into the details of it but, yes, he saved my life. I'm worried about him. He was a member of a four-man assassination squad based in Northern Ireland in the 1970s who were used to kill IRA suspects. He said that the three men in the squad with him are all dead. He implied they'd been killed.'

'You're worried for him?'

'I can't help it.'

'But do you feel threatened by him?' Reg repeated.

'He's SAS and a trained killer and he came looking for me. How do I not feel threatened? I feel him at my back all the time.'

'Have you told your family?'

'They know he's around.'

'But do they know you've met him?'

Sam shook her head.

'Why haven't you told them?'

'They wouldn't understand.'

'How do you think they'd respond?'

Sam puffed out her cheeks and shook her head. 'My brother, Mark, would go ballistic.'

'Why?'

'Betrayal. My father threw him headfirst into a glass cabinet when he was a child and almost blinded him. He'd think I'd betrayed him.' Her hand rose to touch the dog tags at her neck. 'And he'd probably be right.'

Later that morning, Sam entered the foyer of the Riverview building near Putney Bridge where she and Alan shared a fifth-floor office. She felt shaky, as if she needed to retrieve the bits of her she'd exposed to Reg, put them in a cupboard, cover them in dark cloths and allow the dust to settle.

Greg, the general manager of the building, was sitting at reception, listening to his personal stereo with his eyes closed and mouthing the words of whatever music was being pumped into his ears. His black, dyed hair and general coiffure indicated his night-time job of being an Elvis impersonator in the clubs and pubs of Fulham. Behind him the switchboard was lit up like Oxford Street on Christmas Eve.

Sam studied the movements of his mouth and, by the time he threw back his head and howled silently at an imaginary moon, had guessed what he was listening to. He opened his eyes, saw Sam, pulled out the earpieces and, sure enough, 'You ain't nothing but a hound dog' hissed into the air.

'How'd it go last night?' Sam asked. 'I'm sorry I couldn't make it.'

Greg shook his head. 'Snow's not good for business. People stay at home. So we only had a smattering, but the show must go on.' He ran his hand carefully over his perfect Elvis hair.

'That looks great. I think it's the best I've ever seen it.'

'Yes, indeed, girl. Stop the presses! I do believe I may be in the grip of a perfect hair day.'

Sam ran her hand through her own hair. 'I don't think I've ever had one of those. The closest I got was when I had a row with my mother and went out to the local barbers and got myself a Demi Moore in *GI Jane*. My mother almost had a heart attack – it was very gratifying.'

'So,' Greg said, 'you had a perfect practically-no-hair-at-all day.'

Sam laughed. 'Yes, and had to put up with everyone calling me sonny for the next couple of months.'

She walked across the foyer and punched the button for the lift.

When she entered her office, Alan was sitting with his feet on the table, reading the newspaper. He glanced up as Sam came into the room. 'You look all shrinkwrapped.'

'Give it a rest,' Sam said wearily. She took off her jacket, slung it over the back of her chair and sat down. She dug a thumb into the throbbing part of her right temple and screwed up her eyes.

'Your brother phoned.'

Sam's brother Mark was an English don at St Barnabas's College in Oxford, the town that the family had moved to after Sam's father had disappeared.

'What did he want?'

'Said some boy's gone missing – a rower. Didn't give me the details. Wanted you to phone him when you got in.' He handed Sam a piece of paper with a telephone number scrawled on it.

Sam looked at it and rubbed the end of her nose. 'Where is he?'

'Didn't say.'

She picked up the phone on her desk and dialled.

Mark answered. 'Hey, sis, you in your office?'

'Yes.'

'Can you see the boathouses from there?'

Sam swung round in her swivel chair and stood up. Now she was looking out of the floor-to-ceiling window down onto Putney Bridge. On the far side of the bridge was the usual mass of traffic clogging the bottom of Putney High Street; on the south bank of the Thames, a few hundred metres upstream from the bridge, were the boathouses.

'Are you looking?' Mark asked.

'Yup.'

'See the idiot bouncing up and down and waving like crazy?'

'Aha.'

'That's me.'

Sam laughed. 'Crazy bastard! What the hell are you doing here and why didn't you tell me you were coming?'

'Didn't know I was coming until the last minute. I'm helping them out for a few days. Tom King, the OUBC coach, asked me.'

'Alan said something about someone going missing.'

'Yes. Look, could you get yourself over here? Then I could fill you in and you could meet some of the people involved.'

'Sure. Just one thing, Mark. I can't do this for love – I'm too broke.'

'No, no, come and talk to the guys. You'll be paid, I promise.'

Sam put down the phone and repeated the last sentence to Alan. Alan grunted in amusement.

'Fancy a walk to the Land of the Brobdingnag?' Sam asked.

'Blow your nose, for God's sake.'

'Ha ha.'

Alan folded the paper in two, dropped it on his desk and stretched. 'There's no news in this bloody paper, so why not?'

It was no longer snowing as Alan and Sam stepped out of their building and began walking across Putney Bridge, but the clouds had a dirty-yellow, nicotine-type stain to them that suggested more snow was on its way. It was very still but the air was bitterly cold. Multiple footfalls had cleared the pavements and the roads were relatively accessible, but the bicycle lane was filled with brown slush.

Alan turned up his collar, pulled his blue wool hat down over the tips of his ears and then plunged his hands deep into the pockets of his coat.

'So, what's Mark doing in town? I thought he rarely ventured out of Oxford and hated London.' As he spoke, a small, white cloud appeared in the air in front of his mouth and then vanished.

'He's helping out with the Oxford rowing squad. They have a two-week pre-term selection camp in January. Four sessions a day and they see who's left standing at the end of it. When he was an undergraduate Mark was a Blue. He competed in the Boat Race in his second year. It was some achievement because he'd only been taught the year before. They'd taken one look at him, or rather his height, and dragged him down to the river to bank-tub him. The year he competed they won. It was great for him because he'd always been so bad at sport.'

Alan wiped a drip from the end of his nose and ducked around a stooped elderly man dragging a shopping basket on wheels behind him. 'Can't see what the fuss is about the Boat Race. They're not even the best university eights, are they? But there's always all this publicity for it.'

'It's the tradition,' Sam said. 'People like the tradition. They've been doing it since 1829.'

'So what?' Alan said. 'The royal family's been there since God knows when; doesn't mean I don't want their heads cut off and put on pikes and their estates turned into public parks.'

'I'm not defending it,' Sam lied. 'But nowadays they train like professionals – they go biking in the Alps in the summer, cross-country skiing in Switzerland before Christmas. It's a huge commitment; during term time they train twice a day. For every stroke of the race they've done two hours training. And it's not as if they get any prize money. It's one of the last truly amateur sporting events. The crews have their day in the spotlight and it's an excuse for a lot of undergraduates from Oxford and Cambridge to come up to London and get pissed and a lot of graduates to meet up with people they haven't seen for ages.'

'Well, *that* bit of it I can get my head around.'

Having reached the far side of the bridge, they turned right and walked along the embankment and past Putney Pier. The tide was out and the river was a muddy green trickle. A row of about a dozen boathouses faced the river and a concrete slope that ran down to the riverbed.

A tall man with a fringe of black hair hanging over his forehead, wearing green Wellingtons and a waxed green jacket, was standing outside one of the boathouses smoking. When he saw them he waved, threw the cigarette on the ground, stamped on it and loped towards them. He leaned down and hugged Sam with his left arm and managed at the same time to extend his right hand towards Alan.

Alan looked thoughtfully at Mark's hand for a second. 'You don't shake hands like your sister, do you?'

Mark laughed. 'Try me,' he said and Alan took hold of his hand. 'Thank God,' Alan said as he let go of Mark's hand.

'Keeping her in order?' Mark asked.

Sam punched her brother lightly in the ribs. 'Not a hope,' she said.

Alan smiled. 'It's a hell of a job, I tell you. She will go off and get into fights.'

Mark tilted Sam's head back and scrutinised her face. 'I can see – just like when she was a kid.'

Sam pushed Mark away. 'When you two have finished discussing me as if I wasn't here . . .'

Mark laughed and put his arm across the top of Sam's shoulders. 'Thanks for coming over so quickly. Come on in and meet the squad. They're upstairs.'

Sam stared at her brother and frowned. 'Why do you look different?'

Mark laughed. 'You really are hopeless. You're supposed to be a

29

private investigator and you never notice anything.' He tapped the skin under his right eye with his finger. 'Contacts.'

'Oh God, yes. Looks good.' She reached up and patted his cheeks, which were covered with a couple of days' growth. 'What's with the Grizzly Adams?'

He shrugged. 'I felt like a change.'

Although the hair on his head and his eyebrows was black, there were flecks of grey growing out in his beard. Sam frowned. Mark was forty years old, eight years older than Sam, but he had always looked extraordinarily boyish. The grey came as a shock; if he was getting older then she must be too.

Sam and Alan followed Mark up a staircase attached to the outside of one of the boathouses, which led into a large room occupying the whole of the top floor of the building. A group of twenty to thirty giants were milling around in various states of undress. There were whistles as they clapped eyes on Sam and several of them grabbed towels to cover themselves.

'Oh God,' Sam said. 'Crick-in-the-neck time.'

A slightly shorter man of about six foot detached himself from the group and strode towards them. He was in his early fifties, lean and fit-looking, with an energetic no-nonsense demeanour. He was wearing a dark blue tracksuit, trainers and a faded brown baseball hat. He had humorous blue eyes. Even with his face partly shaded by the brim of the hat, Sam could tell she was on the receiving end of an extremely direct gaze. But Sam liked coaches. She'd had a good relationship with her own coach, Tyler, so her immediate instinct was to like and trust this man. He held out his hand and Sam gripped it.

'Thanks for coming so quickly,' he said. 'I greatly appreciate it.'

Mark touched the man's arm. 'This is Tom King, our coach.'

'Shall we sit down?' King dragged four chairs into a rough circle.

'So,' Sam said. 'What's been going on?'

'A member of the squad, Harry Cameron, has gone missing.'

'When did you notice?'

'Yesterday morning. He didn't turn up for the first session and then he wasn't here today either. We thought we'd wait to see if he appeared this morning and he didn't.'

'He left no note, didn't tell anyone of his plans?'

'No, as far as we can gather he just packed up his gear and left.'

'Could he have just got fed up with it, decided to quit and not dared to tell anyone in case they tried to persuade him out of it?'

'Not Harry.'

'Why not?' Sam pressed.

'He's in his first year, right?'

Sam nodded.

'Well, before he'd even come up for his first term – so this was last summer – he phoned me up and asked me what sort of circuits he should be doing to give him the best chance to be in the final eight.

'Now Harry was barely eighteen, he'd not yet set foot in the university. I mean, I knew he was coming in our direction because his school coach, Eric Stiles, phoned me up to discuss him with me. He'd won everything you can win as a schoolboy – he was a junior international gold medal winner and National Schools champion – but he was taking nothing for granted. He impressed me. He was worried about the length of the race. It's much further than the races he'd been taking part in and he was concerned about the level of fitness required.'

'So it was very important to him?'

'He was utterly committed. Has been from the word go. He's a nice boy and a very special talent. He was one of the best schoolboy rowers this country's ever produced. If he was a footballer we'd be talking Wayne Rooney.'

'And what does disappearing at this stage do to his chances of getting a Blue?'

'Well, at the end of the two weeks we choose the squad and from that squad we choose the Blues and the Isis eights and a third eight.' Tom adjusted the baseball hat so that it sat on the back of his head, brim pointing towards the ceiling, and ran his hand across his forehead. 'If you're not in the squad . . .'

'So in walking out now he throws away his chance?'

'I think he would know that was the likely outcome.'

'Have you told the police?'

'We haven't done anything yet. We weren't certain that there were any grounds for telling them. I mean it's not as if he has to be here. He's over eighteen – just – he can do what he likes. And then Mark suggested we talk to you.'

'Been in touch with his family?'

Tom shook his head. 'There's no answer from his home.'

'But you *are* worried?'

'Yes,' Tom said. 'Him walking out just doesn't make sense. Others perhaps. Sometimes they know they're not going to make the cut and will walk away first. It makes them feel more in control, less rejected.'

'So what would you like me to do?'

Tom looked at Mark and raised his eyebrows.

'Well, find him,' Mark said. 'Or at least find out what's happened to him.'

'One thing you should know.'

Sam and Alan looked at Tom.

He lowered his voice. 'This kid is the best rower in the squad by a long way. The likelihood was that we would have him stroke the Blue boat.'

'Stroke?' Alan said.

'The stroke sits in the seat in front of the cox and sets the pace. The stroke is crucial.'

'So Harry's a bit of a star?'

Tom nodded. 'He's special. He's got an awesome physique, an eight-litre lung capacity that almost matches Matthew Pinsent's and fantastic technique. With him we've got a chance and without him ... I mean, obviously we want to know he's OK, but we also really want him back in the boat...' He left the sentence unfinished.

Sam leaned back in her chair. 'Oxford lost last year, didn't they?'

King nodded.

'Were you coaching them then?'

He shook his head. 'This is my first year.'

'OK, we'll need to interview the squad.' She pointed towards the group of men at the front of the boathouse and in the balcony. 'Alan can do half and I'll do the other. Was he sharing a room with anyone?'

'Brian Crawford.'

'Right, I'll start with him.'

Sam watched King walk over to the rowers and call them together. She stood up and wandered over to where a large chart was fixed to the wall. Across the top were mug shots of the rowers. Harry Cameron had short blond hair tufted at the front, blue eyes, a nice smile and a Kirk Douglas cleft in his large chin. Running down the left-hand side of the chart was a list: *5,000m Ergometer November, Circuit test 2 × 20 reps, Pairs head result, Fours head result, London Ergometer, Seat racing Dec 13-15 four and a half minutes.* Sam was trying unsuccessfully to decipher the list when a large hand reached over her head, unpinned Harry's photo from the wall and handed it to her.

'Thanks,' Sam said and turned round.

'I'm Brian Crawford,' the man said. He was roughly one and a half feet taller than Sam and had the ruddy face of a man used to spending hours outside in all temperatures and a black cap of hair cut close to his head.

'Do you mind if we sit down?' Sam said, gesturing towards the chairs recently vacated by Mark and Tom. 'Otherwise I may end up doing some permanent damage to my neck.'

Crawford smiled and sat down carefully, like a man who knew from experience what might happen if he threw his large frame at a folding wooden chair.

'So you share a room with Harry?'

'Yes.'

'Do you have any idea where he might be?'

'He keeps to himself. Not that he is unfriendly exactly, just isn't one of the lads. He isn't a mate or even someone I know particularly well.'

'At this stage you're all competing against each other for a place?'

'Well, yes, of course, but that generates a fairly friendly rivalry.'

'Has anything happened in the last few days that might explain his disappearance? Did he have any calls? Meet up with anyone?'

Crawford scratched his nose. 'He might have done. But he doesn't hang around with the rest of us in the evening. I don't know what he might have been doing. Basically, I saw him just before we went to bed and when we got up. That was it.'

'Did he talk to you about anything that was upsetting him? Arguments with a girlfriend, his family?'

'No, he's never mentioned anything like that. I don't think he has a girlfriend. If he does he certainly never talks about her.'

Sam fell silent and waited to see if he might come out with anything else.

'I'm afraid he isn't really my sort of bloke. Nice enough – just not my type. He's always reading his Bible first thing and to be honest it pisses me off. It's bad enough having to get up for early-morning outings, let alone him getting up an hour before that. We're doing four sessions a day and it's freezing out there.'

Sam laughed. 'Bit of a Bible-basher?'

'He doesn't bash exactly. In fact he's pretty quiet about it. But we all know he's a member of Christians in Sport.'

'Anyone he's particularly close to in the squad?'

'He's a first-year. This is only his second term. So, not really.'

'Anyone in the squad stand to benefit from his absence?'

Crawford laughed. 'He was a dead cert for the Blue boat. Everyone knew it. They try to keep you guessing but they couldn't with him, dead cert for stroke as well. He's an incredible oarsman. Put him in a pair with any other bloke in the squad and that boat goes the fastest. The scary thing is that they don't even think he's fully grown yet.'

'Who stroked the boat last year?'

'I did.'

'Were you expecting to keep your place?'

He rubbed the end of a jaw that wouldn't have looked out of place on Mount Rushmore. 'Place but not position. If it's not Harry it's likely to be Holden.'

'Who's Holden?'

'American – he was in their Olympic squad – he's only over for the year.'

'Do you mind?'

'I'd be lying if I said I wasn't disappointed, but the most important thing is to create the fastest boat we can with what we have available. If either of them makes the boat go faster – then no, I don't. I want the best possible crew on the river. I want to beat Cambridge.'

'Did he talk to you at all about his family?'

'No, not really, although my impression was he didn't have a very good Christmas and was relieved to be back with the squad – on the river. But then that could be said of lots of the guys.'

'OK, thanks.' Sam stood up. 'Anyone else you could recommend me talking to?'

'He gets on well with Briony Flint.'

'Could you send her over?'

'Sure.'

Sam watched Brian Crawford walk away from her and a woman whose head just about reached the level of his heart walk towards her. She had straight blonde hair tied back in a short ponytail.

'Cox, right?' Sam said.

Flint sat down opposite Sam. 'You psychic or something?'

Sam smiled. 'Are you the only woman in the squad?'

'Yup.'

'Anything you can tell me about Harry?'

'Not really, he's one of the newer ones in the squad. I coxed Isis last year so there are others I know better. I mean, I know who he is because everyone had heard about him, but—'

'Why?' Sam cut in.

'His reputation had preceded him, and it turned out the reality matched the hype. But he seems a nice man. Had his feet on the ground even when he was blowing them all away in the erg tests. He wasn't triumphalist about it. In fact, quite the opposite, he's very good but also very modest.'

'Can you think of anything he said or that happened in the last few days that might explain where he is?'

'Last session on the river he took part in he seemed distracted. Usually he's very quick to take instructions but he was a couple of beats off. It was nothing really, but I had noticed it because usually his concentration is so spot on. He apologised to me afterwards.'

'He say anything about why?'

'No – just said sorry.'

'Do you socialise with him?'

'He keeps himself pretty much to himself. He's a serious bloke, not like some of these.' She gestured to the front of the room where the noise levels of the rest of the squad were rising.

'Is it fun shouting instructions at them?' Sam asked.

'What do you think?'

'But you get thrown in the river at the end.'

'Yeah, that's not so much fun.'

'At least the rivers are cleaner these days.'

'So they say, but I reckon it's still basically one big rat latrine.'

'He have any particular friends or enemies in the squad?'

'Not really, he keeps himself to himself. This squad has a good feeling to it. They tease him about the religion but that's affectionate. Anyway, it's a good sign if they're teasing you.'

'Anyone tease him in particular?'

'Holden came up with his nickname. You've heard about that, right?'

Sam shook her head.

'Well, he has a problem with his hands. They get really torn up when he rows. Usually hands harden up but his never seem to, they are always a real mess.'

'So what did Holden call him?'

'Stig – short for stigmata.'

'Did Harry mind?'

'I think he did, although he had the good sense to try and cover it up; he's reading theology and very religious. The thing is, if you let on that you mind, it's even more likely to stick.'

'Anything else you could tell me?'

'Well, I thought I saw him.'

'When?'

'Yesterday, first outing of the day, the one he didn't turn up for. I thought I saw him standing on the bridge looking down at us in the snowstorm. We were rowing under the bridge and I looked up . . . anyway, that's not much use to you.'

'Did he wave or anything?'

'No, he was just standing in the snow, staring at the river.'

CHAPTER THREE

A couple of hours later Sam and Alan sat in a window seat in the Duke's Head, looking out at the river. It was the middle of the afternoon and the pub had emptied of lunchtime drinkers. Sam rubbed the condensation from the window and watched some of the men they'd just been interviewing climbing into two eights and taking to the water. She shivered in the draught of cold air seeping in round the window frame.

'I can't believe they actually send them out in this weather. You'd think their oars would ice up or their fingers'd drop off.'

'Tom said you never know what kind of weather there'll be on the day of the race. He said one year they rowed in a blizzard. So it's a way of preparing them for any conditions. Also he said you never know what they're made of until you send them out and they come back with ice in their hair.'

Sam laughed. 'It's the coxes I feel sorry for; they just get to sit there and freeze their arses off. Right then, do you want to go first?'

'OK.' Alan rubbed the palm of his hand over his face. 'He is popular. Couldn't find anyone to say a bad word about him. I mean, there was a bit of banter about this and that but he seems to be genuinely well liked. Everyone I talked to agrees on his status as star rower but said he wasn't a prima donna. He's a team player and buckles down with the rest of them and is very supportive of everyone in the squad.'

Sam nodded. 'The only criticism I got was from his room-mate, who didn't take to his early-morning Bible reading.'

'So we're looking at a serious person here.'

'Yes. Serious and well liked. Not someone to muck about with the lads. Very mature.'

'Unusually so, I'd say.'

'Any hint of girlfriend trouble?'

'No girlfriend, as far as my lot were concerned.'

'Mine neither.'

'Boyfriend?'

'No suggestion of that.'

'Drugs?'

Sam shook her head.

'Those boys are well muscled though, aren't they? And it is an endurance sport.'

'Yes, but they're also bright, Alan. They're not going to take anything that's going to shrivel their testicles to the size of dried peas, give them raging acne, weaken their heart muscles and kill them at the age of forty, are they?'

'Why not, if they want to win enough?'

'There's not the sort of money at stake to make people take that kind of risk. And it's not as if they don't have other options.' She tapped her forehead. 'They've got something between the ears. So, what about family? Any problems there?'

Alan frowned. 'No one seemed to know much about his family. You get anything on that?'

Sam shook her head. 'The trouble is, he just seems too good to be true. You know, the perfect sportsman, religious, hard working. He seems so squeaky clean it's unreal. Wouldn't even watch the dirty films the others got out.'

Alan nodded in agreement. 'No one can be that good, can they?'

'Maybe when they're eighteen they can,' Sam said.

There was a short silence.

'I wasn't,' Alan said.

'God, nor was I,' Sam agreed. 'What a stupid thing to say.' She sipped from her pint. 'Did you talk to a Holden Webster?'

'The American?'

Sam nodded.

'Yes. He was pretty laid back about everything.'

'Nothing to suggest his nose was put out of joint by Harry?'

'No, he seemed pretty made up with himself. It would take a lot to dent that sort of self-confidence. Although he did say he

38

thought the coaches were in danger of overrating Harry, that performing in tests wasn't the same as putting in a performance on the day.'

'I was looking at the training charts. Harry's got the better of him in every one. So I suppose he would say that.'

'So,' Alan said, 'what next?'

'The colleges open next week. He may just turn up for the beginning of term.'

'And if he doesn't?'

'We need to track down his family.'

'Tom said he's been phoning his home but with no luck. He's going to keep at it but they may well have gone away over Christmas.'

Sam pulled a piece of paper from her pocket. 'Tom gave me his parents' address. It's in Barnes. Let's pay it a visit.'

Half an hour later Sam and Alan stood looking up at the front of a large detached house. It looked thoroughly deserted but Sam had pressed the bell anyway. The only response was the upward flight of a couple of pigeons from the roof of the house and the consequent dislodging of a bit of snow.

'Not short of a bob or two, are they?' Alan said.

Sam scribbled a note asking his parents to phone Tom King as soon as they got home and pushed it through the letterbox.

'Let's try the neighbours – see if they know where they are or when they'll be back.'

The house to the left was also deserted, the one to the right was opened by a thin young girl with dark smudges under her eyes, holding a red-faced, bawling baby. Sam explained who they were and asked if she knew where the Camerons were.

'They all go away round here at this time of year,' she said.

'Leaving you holding the baby,' Alan said.

'It's not his fault,' she said wearily. 'He's teething.'

The baby had stopped screaming and was staring at Sam.

'Any idea when they're likely to be back?'

The baby reached forward and grabbed hold of Sam's hair, wrenching it hard enough to bring tears to her eyes. The girl apologised and began prising the child's fingers loose.

'I think I saw them leaving about three or four days ago. I don't know how long they'll be gone. I don't know them very well to be honest. They tend to keep themselves to themselves.'

The baby's grip had been loosened but it continued to make grabbing gestures towards Sam's head. Then its face turned puce. Its wails followed Sam and Alan as they made their way back to their car.

Mark stood in Sam's kitchen with a look of panic flashing across his face. 'You're not going to *cook*, are you?'

Sam glanced up from where she was squatting in front of her open fridge and with an expression of wide-eyed innocence replied, 'Yes, I was thinking of it.'

'Now, look,' Mark blustered, 'let me take you out for a meal.'

'No, it's fine. I think I've got a pot of pesto somewhere at the back.' She reached into the fridge. 'Yes, here we are. It's been opened but I'll just check the sell-by date . . .'

'Sam . . .'

Sam's shoulders were shaking with laughter. She closed the fridge, turned round and pointed at him. 'Got you.'

'You bastard.'

'I knew my generous offer of pasta and pesto would terrify you. We can get a curry from down the road.' Sam took a menu out of a drawer in the kitchen table and slapped it against her brother's ribs. 'Here. Choose what you want. You're paying.'

'Pig,' he said.

Three quarters of an hour later, Mark and Sam sat round the kitchen table picking at pilau rice, prawn korma, chicken wings and assorted vegetable dishes from the brown plastic cartons spread out in front of them. Outside, snowflakes danced against the glass like tiny ghostly moths seeking access to the light. Sam was feeling more and more anxious. She knew she had to tell him and that the longer she left it the worse it would be. Mark stretched across her and grabbed a chicken wing.

'I met up with him,' Sam said.

Mark munched on his wing. 'Sorry? Who?'

'Dad.'

The colour drained from Mark's face. He put down the chicken wing and stared at it as if it had just grown feathers and tried to fly. He opened his mouth to speak and then shut it again.

40

Oh God, Sam thought, this is going to be much worse than I feared.

'I told him not to come near me, to leave me alone,' she said.

Mark had gone so white Sam was afraid he might faint.

He pushed back his chair. 'How could you have gone ahead and done something like that without talking to me first?'

'I—'

'I just don't fucking believe you sometimes.'

'Mark—'

'Did he ask about me and Mum?'

Sam shook her head.

'What was he like?'

'Ordinary – you wouldn't notice him in a crowd.'

Mark nodded. 'He got in contact with you, right?'

'No.'

'*You* initiated the meeting?'

'Yes.'

Mark stared at her in disbelief.

'What?'

'*You* actually initiated contact with *him*?'

'So what?'

'You didn't think that you might discuss it with me or Mum first?'

Sam shook her head. 'I'm sorry, Mark. I just had to see him. I had to. I hardly thought either of you'd agree.'

'So bloody typical.'

'What is?'

'You, doing a lone ranger.'

Sam stood up and began stacking the empty containers and putting lids back onto the ones still holding food. She dumped the first lot in the bin and put the others in the fridge. She leaned against the sink.

'I told him I wanted nothing to do with him.'

'And what did he say? "Oh yes, that's fine"?'

She sighed. What he had said was: *It was time to come home.* What he had said was: *You're the only home I've got, Sam.* She turned away from Mark and pretended to do some washing-up. She pushed a green scourer half-heartedly round the inside of a once-white cup now dyed a permanent shade of brown from endless cups of tea, and blinked hard. If the tears didn't roll down your cheeks it didn't count as crying, did it? Too late – her tears splashed into the washing-up bowl, joining the bubbles floating on the surface of the water.

When she felt more in control of her feelings, she spoke.

'What he said was that he was part of a four-man assassination squad used to kill IRA suspects in the 1970s. He said the other three were all dead, having died in suspicious circumstances. He thinks he's going to be next.'

'So we're supposed to be worried for his safety? Well, fuck him. He wasn't concerned for my safety when I was a child and he was beating the shit out of me. Whatever he tells you, you mustn't get involved. You really mustn't.'

'It's OK, Mark. I'm not going to. I met him the one time. That was it.'

'"I met him the one time,"' Mark mimicked Sam's voice. 'Why did you do it, Sam? Why on earth did you want to meet him?'

Why *had* she done it? She wasn't altogether sure of the answer. Curiosity had definitely played its part. He was their father, for God's sake. Since she was four years old she'd thought he was dead. Her whole life had been dominated by the fact of his absence. Every fight she had fought, she imagined bringing him back to her. How was she not going to seek him out once she knew he was alive? How was she not going to want to find out what sort of man he was? She wasn't going to tell Mark about how her father had grabbed her wrist. It would just be more fodder for his argument. She sat back down at the table.

'I had to, Mark. My whole life's been dominated by the fantasy – the hero father. I needed to see the reality, to look him in the eye.'

'The last time I saw him he threw me into a glass-fronted cabinet. I nearly lost my eyes. He brutalised me as a child.' Mark ran his fingers lightly over the white mesh of scars on his forehead. 'How can you even think of meeting the man who did that to me? Let alone what he did to Mum.'

Sam folded her arms. 'I had to meet him, Mark – that's all I can say.'

'Did he hurt you?'

'Don't be silly.'

'I bet he did.'

Before she could stop herself, Sam touched her wrist. Mark grabbed her hand and pushed up her sleeve but there was nothing for him to see.

Sam didn't say anything.

'He did it to you, didn't he? He used to do that to me as a child. He used to grab hold of my wrist and pull me up close to him and then say, "Flesh of my flesh, bone of my bone", and he'd have a look of utter disgust on his face.'

Sam shook her head. 'How do you know he hasn't changed?'

'Well, you're not denying it happened, are you? And do you see what's happening? Already you're defending him. Do you see, Sam? You've already taken his side.'

Sam pulled her hand away from her brother. 'I'm not defending anyone,' she said. 'And I'm certainly not taking sides. I'm just telling you what I said. I told him to leave me alone and I have no intention of seeking him out again. I'm not taking anyone's side. I just had to see him the one time.'

Mark stared at her, disbelief etched across his face. 'My God, you still think he's a hero, don't you? Despite everything I've told you.'

'No,' Sam said. 'I know he isn't. Actually, I thought he was a rather sad and pathetic figure.'

Mark lightly touched her wrist. 'He's still violent. There's the proof he hasn't changed. He hasn't seen you since you were four years old and the first time he meets you, what does he do? Brand you as his.'

Sam pulled the sleeve of her shirt down over her wrist. She didn't tell Mark she had done the same to him. The violence had cut both ways.

She had branded him too; flesh of *her* flesh.

Sam filled the kettle at the sink. Neither of them spoke. No bad thing for them to have a bit of a cooling-off period, Sam thought, but by the time the kettle had clicked off the silence had become uncomfortable.

'No one had much to say about Harry that would explain him disappearing,' she said, putting a cup of tea in front of her brother. 'Have you got any ideas?'

Mark blew on the surface of his tea and sipped cautiously from the cup. 'It doesn't make sense at all. Not Harry. Some of the others, sure, especially the ones who know they're struggling to make the final cut, but he was a dead cert to be in the final squad and almost certain to make the Blue boat.'

'Had he been told that?'

'No. They keep them guessing because they don't want them becoming complacent. But I'd have thought he'd have a good idea himself.'

Sam nodded. 'No one had a bad thing to say about him.'

'He's a nice kid. Very unassuming and very talented.'

'Maybe he'll just turn up next week for the start of term and there'll be a perfectly natural explanation.'

'Maybe,' Mark said, but he didn't sound that convinced. He was hunched over his cup of tea, staring at the worn surface of the kitchen table, which had been scrubbed so many times it was practically white. He looked up suddenly and stared at Sam.

'What are we going to do about Mum? We need to tell her you met up with him She should be warned.'

Sam pulled a face. 'Do we have to?'

'No, Sam, just pulling a face won't do. We have to warn her.'

'Why? All I did was meet up with him once.'

'She has to be told.'

'You talk to her then.'

Mark stared at her. 'Jesus Christ, Sam. You're just like him. Such a fucking coward when it comes to the things that matter.'

'OK, OK, forget I said that. When shall we do it?'

'As soon as possible. Now that you've seen him, the whole thing feels closer to home.'

'I had to meet him,' Sam mumbled. 'I just had to. Don't make me feel guilty for wanting to meet my own father.'

'I don't think you know what you've done,' Mark said, 'how reckless you've been not just with yourself but with all of us. You've no idea.'

'You're still frightened of him.'

'And you're not?'

'No, I'm not.'

Mark stood up abruptly. 'You stupid little idiot, still playing the game of being daddy's favourite. You've no idea what you're getting yourself into. How dangerous he is.'

Sam felt the blood rush to her cheeks. 'I'm not getting myself into anything. I told him not to come near me.'

'And did you mean it?'

'Yes—'

'I don't believe you.' Mark pushed past her into the hall and Sam followed him. He grabbed his coat and opened the door. 'I don't think you believe it either.'

The slam of the door reverberated in Sam's fillings. She stood staring at her front door. She never argued with Mark. That wasn't part of their relationship. Mutual adoration, blind love – that was more the sort of thing. Slamming doors and walking out wasn't part of the deal, at any rate not until now, not until her father had come back from the dead. The letterbox clattered. Oh great, Sam thought, he's come back and we can sort it all out. But when she opened the door it wasn't Mark standing there but Jackie, her petulant mouth doing its best to twist itself into a smile.

'What do you want?'

'Gerry get you in OK?'

'No, that's why I'm still camping in the hall.'

'I was hoping to call in your offer.'

'Sorry?'

'You know – the favour.'

'Forget it,' Sam said wearily and began to close the door.

Jackie placed a ring-encrusted hand against the door. 'All right, I'll pay you.'

'Well, why didn't you say so in the first place?'

Sam led the way into the front room. Jackie stared hard at the cat hair on the sofa and decided to remain standing.

'So,' Sam said, 'what kind of thing were you wanting?'

'Well.' Jackie decided to risk perching on the arm of the sofa. 'I suppose you could say that what I'm looking for is a bodyguard.'

'Oh?'

'Yes. I stall out in Golding's Arcade in Portobello and one by one we're all being picked off.'

'What do you mean?'

'Robbed.'

'What of?'

She ran a finger across the top of the rings she was wearing. 'Jewellery.'

'Is that what you deal in?'

'Yes.'

'Is this happening in the arcade?'

Jackie shook her head impatiently. 'No, that's too public and there's security in there anyway. It's on the way there, in the car parks and even from a taxi.'

'How many so far?'

Jackie wafted her hand vaguely in the air. 'Enough to worry about.'

'Any idea why that arcade?'

Jackie held out her hand palm-down and rocked it from side to side. 'There are rumours.'

'And they are?'

'Danny who owns the arcade banned Alf from stalling out there. The rumour is Alf's a fence. That's why he banned him. They say he's exacting revenge. If he puts the frighteners on the other stallholders they'll go somewhere else. It damages the reputation of the arcade.'

'Has anyone told the police?'

Jackie snorted. 'Come on, they say Alf's in with the police.'

'But surely—'

'This is Portobello we're talking about.'

'I've never been.'

'Well, use your imagination.'

Sam tried. 'So what do you want?'

'Can you get me a bodyguard? Someone to come with me, escort me to the arcade and then come and pick me up and take me home?'

'Fine. This is for tomorrow, right?'

Jackie nodded.

'OK.'

'What's his name?'

'Sorry?'

'The bodyguard?'

'It's me.'

'Oh no, you're much too small.'

'Did no one ever tell you it's not the size that matters, it's what you do with it?'

'Yes, a man with a toothpick for one.'

Sam left the room and came back a few minutes later. She handed Jackie a large gold medal, which she'd won in the Judo World Championships in Paris in 1990.

Jackie looked at it for a few moments and handed it back. She looked Sam up and down. 'Very impressive, but you're still rather small.'

'Do you want me or not?'

'I leave at five-thirty in the morning.'

'So the other morning wasn't a one-off?'

'No, it all kicks off pretty early, I'm afraid.' She stood up. 'How much do you charge?'

'How many hours are involved?'

'Five-thirty to about one – eight hours.'

'A hundred pounds.'

'Seems a bit steep. And with the favour?'

Sam stared blankly at her. 'A hundred and fifty.'

'All right, all right . . . there's no reason to get snitty with me,' Jackie said, walking towards the front door. 'I'll knock in the morning.'

'Five fucking thirty,' Sam muttered as she closed the door behind her.

Sam drifted in and out of a restless sleep until three o'clock, when the phone rang. She lay in the darkness, waiting for her answerphone to take the call. The machine clicked on but no one left a message.

But then no one put down the phone either.

She dragged herself out of bed into the hall and stood over her phone. All she could hear was someone breathing. Not the exaggerated heavy breathing of a dirty caller, but someone was there all the same. It was quiet in the block and outside. Most late-night revellers were home by now. The only thing Sam could hear was the chatter of birds in the plane trees across the road and the roar of the occasional night bus. She stared at her phone, her heart thumping. It was him, she was sure. What did he want? Was he in trouble? Mark's words rang in her ears. *You stupid little idiot, still playing the game of being daddy's favourite.* As her hand closed over the receiver, the line went dead.

The call had woken Frank and she put some food down for him

47

in the kitchen and then threw herself back into bed. By the time her alarm went off at five o'clock she was so deeply asleep that waking up felt like dragging herself up through wet cement.

She pulled on thermal leggings and over the top of them a pair of jeans, then a thermal vest, an old Tintin T-shirt, the brown woollen jumper, a red hooded fleece and finally a blue raincoat. The raincoat had lost any waterproof qualities a long time ago but she loved it for its pale pink lining and its large poacher's pockets. She sat on the edge of the bed and pushed her feet into a pair of black caterpillar boots. Finally she grabbed a pair of brown furry gloves. She felt ashamed of these. Although the fur on the outside was synthetic they were lined with rabbit fur. Sam didn't approve of fur, but in the course of a long judo career she had managed to break almost every finger at least once and they ached like hell in the cold. She was sorry for the rabbits but every time she pulled on these gloves she thanked God for the warmth of their fur. There was a knock on the door and Sam opened it.

Jackie looked obscenely awake and this did nothing to improve Sam's mood as she followed her out of the block and along the road towards her car. The pavements were icy and treacherous and both women walked with the stiff-legged gait of people afraid they might slip.

Jackie stopped and looked around her. 'I'm not sure I can remember where I parked the car.'

Sam followed her down one road and then back again and off down another.

'Ah, here it is.

Sam didn't care. She got into the front seat, put on her seat belt and closed her eyes. 'Wake me up when we get there,' she said and, with the car heater puffing gently in her face, promptly fell fast asleep.

Sam reached out her hand to touch her father's arm. Her fingers passed straight through the flesh of his forearm as if it were soft cheese. Her fingers smoothed away the flesh and touched bone. This is what she was looking for. She gripped on, wanting to bruise him. Yet, as hard as she tried, no bruises would form. She couldn't hurt him; he was dead. She looked at her fingers covered in his flesh and blood and then felt his body move.

'What have you done to yourself?' he said and then she looked and saw that it was her own flesh and blood and her arm was dangling, ripped open and useless at her side. He reached out to touch her.

Sam woke with a start, feeling a hand on her arm. She had fallen asleep against it and it had pins and needles. She flexed her hand, trying to get the blood supply flowing. Had they arrived already? She rubbed her eyes. 'We here?' she asked.

Then she saw Jackie's face, a frozen mask of fear. It probably had something to do with the knife glinting at her throat.

'What the—?'

Then she saw the other one. Balaclavas covered their faces. Sam peered out of the window. They were in some sort of car park. Jackie's door was open and one man had his arm round her throat, the other stood in front of the car wielding a baseball bat. He tapped the bit of the windscreen Sam was looking through with the tip of the bat. 'Get out,' he shouted.

Jackie's eyes darted to where her bag rested between Sam's feet. Sam picked up the bag and tucked it inside her fleece.

'Let's do as the man says,' Sam said.

The man with the knife was already dragging Jackie from the car. Sam opened her door and got out.

'She hasn't got what you want,' she said. 'I have.'

The man with the baseball bat began to walk slowly towards her. Sam was sizing him up. Height. Weight. Balance. He was big, over six foot, but podgy round the middle and out of condition. His breathing was laboured, like a man who was carrying too much fat on his lungs.

'Steady,' Sam said, holding out her hand and backing away from him.

He was holding the bat in the middle and with a flick of his wrist he smashed it into the window of the door Sam had just opened. Sam kept backing away from him. She fancied her chances against him one on one, but there was the problem of the knife at Jackie's throat.

'If we just all keep calm,' she said, 'I'm sure this can be resolved amicably.'

She pulled the bag from her fleece and held it out. 'Let go of her,' she said, 'and it's yours.'

'Cut her,' the man with the baseball bat said to the other.

'Wait,' Sam shouted. By now she was just a couple of metres away from Jackie, with the other man closing in behind her. At that moment a car swung into the car park; its headlights were on full beam and for a second they were blinded.

It was all the time that Sam needed. She sprang at the man with Jackie. Her hands closed on the arm holding the knife and her foot kicked hard into the side of his knee. He grunted and his grip on Jackie weakened. As Jackie slipped out from under the man's arm, Sam kicked him hard between the legs and he doubled over. She heard a shouted warning and turned quickly, just in time to feel the baseball bat whistle over her head.

She pushed Jackie away from her. 'Get out of here. Phone the police,' she hissed and Jackie ran towards the car that had just turned off its headlights.

The man wielding the baseball bat paused.

'Time to cut your losses,' Sam said, backing away from him. 'Take your mate and go. The police'll be here any second.'

He glanced at the man still writhing in the snow then turned towards Jackie's car and swung the bat at the windscreen. It shattered. The two front headlamps were next. He helped his mate to his feet. 'Cunt,' he snarled at Sam, and the two men ran from the car park.

Jackie had phoned the police and five minutes later a police car swung up alongside Sam and Jackie, and two uniformed officers got out.

'Was it you who put in the call?'

Sam pointed at Jackie.

The policemen looked at her car. 'Could you tell me what happened here?'

'They ran off in that direction,' Sam said. 'I think they went through that hole in the fence.' She was about to continue when she caught sight of the expression on Jackie's face. 'Why don't you tell them?' Sam said to her.

Sam walked away from them and circled the car, crunching the pieces of broken glass into the snow. The car was well and truly trashed. She stamped her feet, trying to keep warm. One of the policemen called her back over.

'Did you get a look at them?'

'They were wearing balaclavas,' Sam said. 'So I didn't see their faces. The one with the baseball bat was about six foot and fat round the middle. He was wearing trainers, black jeans and a black jacket. The other one I'm not so sure. He was holding on to Jackie so I didn't get such a good look at him.'

The policeman nodded. 'You wouldn't be able to identify either of them if you saw them again?'

Sam shook her head.

'Sorry about the car,' Sam said, putting down her knife and fork.

It was a couple of hours later and Jackie and Sam were sitting in Freddy's Café surrounded by dealers pushing little plastic bags containing items of jewellery back and forth across the tables, and just about managing to keep Freddy off their backs by having one cup of tea after another.

For a woman who'd had a knife at her throat Jackie seemed remarkably calm. 'Insurance will cover the car,' she said phlegmatically. 'It wouldn't have covered this.' She gestured at the leather bag resting in her lap.

'How much?'

Jackie lowered her voice. 'Cash – five. Jewellery – nine or ten.'

Sam reached for her tea. 'Hundred?'

'Thousand.'

'You carry all that around on you?'

She nodded. 'Antique jewellery is expensive stuff. I can buy two items worth five hundred each and that's the thousand gone.'

'So, the stuff's very nickable?'

'Of course. It's worth a lot, easy to fence and very light to carry. If I were a thief I'd steal it.'

'So,' Sam said, 'I saved you fifteen thousand pounds and you got my services for a hundred. As a dealer, you must appreciate the bargain.'

'You fell asleep,' Jackie said. 'On duty.'

'You didn't wake me in time.'

'My no-claims bonus is fucked—'

'You've still got a throat.'

The two women paused, eyeing each other.

Sam tore up a piece of toast, stabbed it with a fork and wiped it round her plate. 'What did you tell the police? You didn't seem very keen for me to say anything to them.'

Jackie looked at her watch and stood up. 'So you'll meet me outside Golding's at one?'

'How are we going to get back to Fulham?'

'I'll order us a cab. The car will need to be towed.'

Sam nodded and watched her walking from the café.

Freddy loomed over Sam's table and swiped a dirty cloth over the table, sending crumbs tumbling into Sam's lap. 'Finished?'

Sam looked at a man who had just come in from the market; the end of his nose was lit up like a beacon from the cold and his hands looked like lumps of raw meat. No way was she going out in that.

'Same again,' she said.

'Huh?'

She picked up her plate and handed it to him. 'Same again – cooked breakfast. You know, everything – bacon, egg . . . all that stuff and a cup of tea.'

Freddy sniffed. 'You get fat.'

Sam shook her head. 'Grand Prix-style metabolic rate.'

'You still get fat.'

Sam reached over and grabbed a newspaper that someone had tucked behind the ketchup bottle. Freddy was still standing over her. 'You get fat, no one will love you.'

Sam looked at the exhausted bird-like woman behind the counter, who she presumed was Freddy's wife, and laughed. 'Well, that'll save me a whole load of grief then, won't it?'

CHAPTER FOUR

When Sam came back to the flat later that afternoon the answerphone was winking at her. First, Mark, saying that he had arranged to have lunch with their mother in Oxford the following day and that he expected Sam to be there. Second, Tom King, asking for an update. Sam groaned. She wasn't really sure there was a job as far as Harry was concerned. He was probably just some troubled kid who'd turn up of his own accord when he was good and ready.

As for lunch with her mother, she'd rather stick pins in her eyes.

A year after Sam's father's supposed 'death', when Sam was five years old, her mother, Jean, had moved the family from Hereford to Oxford. A few years later Jean had married Peter Goodman, a mathematician, who was the Warden of St Cuthbert's College and the family had moved in with him. Now her mother and stepfather lived in Park Town, North Oxford. Sam did not have an easy relationship with either of them. The fact that they had both disapproved of her judo career hadn't helped matters, neither had the fact that they didn't know what to make of Sam being a private investigator. She tried to avoid seeing them too often and in that way managed to keep things relatively civil, but Sam suspected that telling her mother she'd met up with her father would have about the same effect as lobbing a bomb into a fireworks factory. Her head throbbed at the prospect of it.

She threw herself into bed, tucked Frank Cooper under the duvet and crashed into a disturbed sleep. She woke at six feeling disorientated, as if it were three in the morning not six in the evening, and certain that she'd been woken by something, although the flat was quiet and there was no noise in the block or the street. She sat on the edge of her bed, her head in her hands, groaning. Sleeping during the day could make you feel even worse than before you went to bed.

As she walked through to the kitchen she saw a buff envelope lying on the hall floor. Maybe Edie was back. She always sorted through the post and put it through the letterboxes; it kept her up to date with what was going on in the flats.

The phone rang as Sam was filling the kettle. She stood in the doorway listening to see if it was a call she wanted to pick up. At first there was just silence like the call the night before. But then he spoke.

'Sam? Pick up. It's important.' The sound of his voice fixed Sam to the spot. 'I have to talk to you.' She slid down the wall until she was sitting on the floor, her chin resting on her knees. 'Sam, please ... you're the only one I can trust.' Her father's voice echoed in the darkness of her flat.

All Sam could hear was the blood pulsing in her head. She put her hands over her ears but that just made it worse: the sound increased from pulsing to roaring. She felt as if she was back in the swimming pool, unable to breathe. Mark was right. How could she have been so stupid? To make contact was to invite more contact. She had met up with him to tell him not to come near her. How ridiculous! Now here he was, wanting to talk to her. And it was all her fault. Pandora opened the box and then it was too late.

The Spites were let loose in the world forever.

His voice broke through the roaring in her ears. 'I need someone to look after it for me – to keep it safe. Sam, just keep it safe for me ...'

The phone went dead. Sam waited for her breathing to stabilise, then stood up slowly, walked along the hall and picked up the buff A4 envelope. *Don't open it. Don't look inside. All you have to do is hide it.* A voice spoke so clearly inside her head that for once Sam decided to listen to her own intuition.

She switched on a light, knelt down on the floor and rolled back one of her gran's rugs. Underneath was another rug and underneath that was a broken floorboard from when the landlord's thugs had installed the central heating. Sam folded the envelope lengthwise, lay down and pushed the envelope as far under the floorboards as it would go. No one would find it under here, under all these layers, pushed to the back and covered in dust. Even if they took the flat apart they'd be unlikely to get anywhere near it. Whatever it was.

The following day found Sam and Mark in Park Town, North Oxford. Park Town was situated just off the bottom of the Banbury Road and consisted of two elegant eighteenth-century, crescent-shaped parades, facing each other across a central garden. Sam was fond of the garden because it contained one of her favourite trees, a monkey-puzzle. Their stepfather, Peter, had rung to say his committee meeting was running over, so they had gone ahead without him and waded through chicken with all the trimmings. Now Mark and Sam were in the living room waiting for their mother to bring in the coffee.

Sickly winter light filtered through the large eighteenth-century windows and an artificial gas fire flickering in the grate gave a lame imitation of the real thing. Sam hated it – she wanted the smell of burning wood, she wanted to be able to prod it with a poker and see the wood and the coal resettle itself. Above all else she wanted embers, coiling and flickering like golden red caterpillars. She stared gloomily at the fraudulent fire and felt sick.

Her levels of anxiety had been rising steadily from the moment she first woke up that morning and contemplated the conversation that she and Mark were going to have. Her stomach had squeezed itself into a fist and she had only been able to pick at her food, much to her mother's disapproval.

Mark grabbed a magazine from the ottoman that stood between the fire and the sofa and threw himself into an armchair with cream-coloured cushions so plump and tight they looked as if they might explode into a cloud of feathers under his weight. Sam turned away from the fire and walked over to the windows, which looked out onto the back garden. A fat grey squirrel was chattering in a large snow-covered copper beech tree, its tail a furious, quivering S-shape curled tightly against its back. She heard a noise behind her and turned as her mother came into the room carrying the coffee.

Her mother was tall and dark like Mark, with a bob of straight black hair that fell to the level of her chin. She was fifty-nine now and Sam assumed she must dye her hair but she had never seen any trace of grey at her mother's parting; it wouldn't have dared show itself. A long elegant nose with a slight kink in the middle separated two almond-shaped brown eyes. She was wearing grey woollen trousers and a cream silk shirt. Everything about her mother, Sam thought, was tasteful and elegant, rather like this room. A huge painting of a seascape hung above the fire; to the right of the painting, lilies nodded from a vase in front of a circular gold-framed mirror; and on the silk rug under Sam's feet, blue Chinese dragons snarled against a golden background.

Sam was too short to be elegant and too indifferent to how things looked to be tasteful and whenever she came near her mother she ended up feeling like a scruffy troll.

Suddenly an image of Kenny Everett in drag came into her mind. He was wearing an obscenely short miniskirt, black tights and high heels. As he crossed one leg over the other with hip-dislocating vigour, flashing his crotch at the camera as he did so, he screamed: 'Of course everything is in the best paaaassible taste.'

Sam couldn't keep the smile from her face as she took the cup her mother offered her and tried to make up her mind where to sit. All the chairs looked comfortable but they were not designed for someone as short as Sam. It would have been all right if she could have taken off her shoes and curled up in one of them, but her mother wasn't really a shoes-off sort of a person. Sam decided the sofa was probably her best bet and sat down, perching on its edge.

'So,' her mother said, sitting down next to her, holding her coffee, 'there was something you wanted to talk to me about?'

Sam looked at Mark, who appeared to be just as ill at ease as she felt, and hoped he'd begin.

Mark dropped the magazine he was holding onto the ottoman and cleared his throat. 'You know that Dad wrote to Sam before Christmas.'

Her mother didn't say anything but her body froze. Her eyes darted from Mark to Sam and then back again.

Mark continued: 'I might as well spit it out. Sam met up with him.'

'What on earth do you mean?' Each word was enunciated clearly and separately and slowly; the effect was menacing.

'We told you he was back,' Sam said. 'It's like Mark said. I met up with him just before Christmas. You see, I wasn't sure if it was him. I wanted to be sure. I mean, I thought he was dead, Mum.'

'And you didn't think to discuss this with me beforehand?'

'We didn't want to upset you if it was nothing.'

Sam watched as her mother turned towards Mark; a smile that had nothing to do with anything humorous stretched across her face. 'You agreed to this?'

'Well, no, but it's done now and we have to talk about what—'

Her mother leaned forward and put down her cup and saucer. 'So you did this off your own back,' she said, glaring at Sam.

'I had to see him.'

'You had to see him,' she repeated, looking at Sam. '*You* met up with him.' She spoke the words very slowly and savagely.

Sam felt something in her snap. As a child she had been terrified by her mother's icy rages, rages that could go on for days and had to be tiptoed around cautiously, but now her own fury over-whelmed her.

'Yes, I met up with a father who I had been told by you had died when I was four years old. *My* father, who no one had ever talked to me about, who no one had ever told me the truth about. Yes, I met up with that man. So bloody what?'

'Sam,' Mark warned.

Her mother stood up. 'Get out,' she said.

Mark raised his hand in a pacifying gesture. 'Mum, hold on . . .'

She swung round. 'You too, Mark – both of you. Get out of my house.'

Sam got to her feet. 'You never told us the truth. Now we tell you the truth and you throw us out. He's back, Mum, and we need to discuss what to do.'

The slap caught Sam completely by surprise and stung like hell. Her coffee cup flew through the air and shattered against the white marble fireplace. The saucer remained in her hand. Tears rushed to her eyes as much from shock as from pain.

Her mother stood over her. 'How dare you tell me what to do? Why on earth do you presume that you can come to my house and tell me that you have met up with that . . .' She paused, her face contorting into a sneer. 'Murdering bastard.'

Sam put the saucer down on a small table next to the sofa and rubbed her cheek. 'I presumed nothing. I just knew I had to do it, that's all.'

'I suppose you never once stopped to consider how I might feel about it?'

'You won't talk about it,' Sam shouted. 'You never have. How are we supposed to know if you won't tell us?'

'Get out. Just get out – the pair of you.'

A few seconds later and Mark and Sam were standing on the steps outside their mother's house staring at the monkey-puzzle. Mark took a deep breath and then put his large warm hand against the side of Sam's face that had been slapped and winced in sympathy.

Sam put her own hand over his and patted it. 'Well, that was pretty scary,' Sam said. 'I haven't seen her like that since—'

'Since you told her you were going to train full time and not take up your college place.'

Sam smiled ruefully. 'God, yes, that was pretty terrifying.'

'I don't know why she slapped you and not me.'

'*I* met up with him, and anyway she likes you. It's always easier to blame the child you don't like. I'm sure I'd do that.'

'No you wouldn't,' Mark said. 'You're much too fair-minded.'

They began walking towards the Banbury Road. 'She needs to cool off,' Sam said. 'Then you get the task of phoning her and initiating the next conversation.'

'Thanks. I'll look forward to that.'

'I got slapped, so you get to make the phone call. Maybe you could talk to Peter first. At least he veers towards the rational.'

'I don't think he'll be much use. You know what his favourite quote is: *If in doubt, let it alone.* His policy is always to stand back and wait for it to blow over.'

They turned left off the Banbury Road into Parks Road.

'I can't believe she hit you,' Mark said. 'She never touched us – ever.'

'No, she didn't, did she?'

'She's going to feel terrible about that.'

'Well, good,' Sam said. 'Maybe that'll give us some leverage.'

They walked in silence along Parks Road towards the town centre. The snow lay thick over the University Parks and on the black railings that divided the parks from the pavement. In this weather Keble's lurid brickwork made it seem more like a fairy castle than a hideous taste mistake designed by someone tripping on acid. Sam's face stung from the slap and stung from the cold. She wiped her nose with the back of her hand. Oxford didn't seem so bad in the snow; even Sam couldn't fail to be moved by a sense of enchantment. A blackbird flew low to the ground across the white park, screaming for its mate. Oxford – maybe she'd been away long enough to feel some sense of affection for it.

'I suppose this place isn't so bad,' she said quietly.

'Steady on, love. That way madness lies.'

Sam laughed. 'You really love it, don't you?'

They had reached the bottom of Parks Road and were standing with their backs to the Indian Institute looking up the Broad. Mark gestured at the view in front of them. 'How can you not be affected by the sheer outrageous beauty of the place?'

'Because I was brought up here?'

'That's nonsense and you know it. I walk through Oxford every day and every day I think how lucky I am to live in one of the most beautiful cities on earth. Just because you're brought up somewhere doesn't make you immune to its beauty.'

'It's as if I need distance, a certain perspective to appreciate it again. I think that's been coming back recently. The snow certainly helps.'

'Look, it's Peter,' Mark said, gesturing towards a man cycling in their direction. He applied his brakes and stopped next to them. Mark shook hands and, after a second of not knowing what to do, Sam did the same. Their stepfather, Peter, was a distinguished-looking man good at balancing on more things than just a bicycle. Mark had always found him easier to deal with than Sam.

'I'm sorry I missed lunch. I'd hoped to be in time to see you both,' he said.

Sam looked at Mark, hoping he'd say something.

'I'm afraid we had some rather upsetting news for Mum,' Mark said. 'It's good you're on the way home.' Peter looked at him quizzically and Mark continued: 'I think it would be best if she talked to you about it. Perhaps I could phone you later to see how she is?'

'Of course.' He hooked his left pedal with his foot until it was at the top of the arc. 'Are you well?' he asked Sam, almost as an afterthought.

She shrugged. 'Mum slapped me. Other than that everything's hunky-dory.'

He frowned and looked at the ground and then pressed down on the pedal and moved swiftly past them in the direction of Park Town.

Sam shook her head. 'Unbelievable. Curiosity – zero. Emotion – sub-zero. If you put your hand inside that man's chest cavity it'd come out black with frostbite.'

'Come on, Sam. You know what he's like. You've always been too hard on him. He's not going to undergo some sudden conversion and become rampantly touchy-feely. Just because he doesn't express his emotions doesn't mean he doesn't have them.'

'I don't want him to be touchy-feely – God knows, I'm not. I just can't believe that man ever had an Italian mother.'

Mark laughed. Peter was the offspring of an Italian mother and an English naval officer father, who had met in Naples after the war. The English naval officer father was all too evident in Peter: in his formality, in his self-containment, in his ramrod posture. But as for the Italian mother, that was a complete mystery – and she was no longer alive to interrogate. Sam had spent a lot of her childhood poking away at Peter, trying to uncover even a glimpse of Italian temperament, with absolutely no success whatsoever. She had come to the conclusion that it had all been beaten out of him at the naval boarding school he'd been sent to at the age of seven.

There was only one sign of Italian in Peter – his dress sense. Somewhere along the line the importance of the *bella figura* had definitely filtered into him. He had always been a beautiful and careful dresser, favouring dramatic colours, which suited his dark Italian good looks. Sam had always appreciated the way he dressed. Some academics just didn't have a clue and scientists could be the worst of a sorry bunch. But Peter was by far the best-dressed mathematician in Oxford.

They had entered Radcliffe Square and were walking carefully over slippery snow-covered cobbles. The spire of St Mary's, the University Church that Mark and Sam had gone to as children, towered above them.

'Those services . . .' Sam said and shook her head.

Mark laughed. 'A touch dry. Do you remember that man who would never shake hands when it came to the Peace? He just stood there staring straight ahead, daring anyone to hold out their hand.'

'We didn't have a normal childhood, did we?'

'Come on, Sam, you were never a normal child. You were throwing yourself around on a judo mat from the age of seven onwards and you had pictures of Muhammad Ali stuck on your wall, not the Bay City Rollers or David Cassidy.'

'Oh please! Wrong era,' Sam said loftily. 'Annie Lennox, if you don't mind – much more transgressive.'

Later that evening, Sam sat in Mark's rooms in St Barnabas's College, sipping a glass of white wine. There had been no phone call from Peter or Jean and Mark had decided to wait until later in the week before initiating any contact.

There was something else Sam wanted to talk to Mark about.

'Has Mum ever talked to you about what happened?'

'When?'

'You know – about Dad.'

Mark frowned. 'What are you asking exactly?'

Sam drained her glass, reached for the bottle and poured herself some more wine. 'I had a conversation with my godfather, Max, before I met up with Dad.'

Max was a friend of her father's. The two men had joined the SAS at the same time. He ran a security firm in London.

Mark looked worried. 'And?'

'Well, you know that awful night when I was four and Dad threw you into the glass cabinet? He said Dad raped Mum and he didn't think it was the first time. Do you know anything about that?'

Mark had got up and was staring out of the window with his back to Sam.

'Mark?'

He turned round and Sam saw his cheeks were wet. Tears immediately sprang to Sam's eyes. It had always worked like this when they were children. It was as if they shared the same tear ducts. If one cried the other did.

'She never said anything to you?' Sam asked.

Mark slowly shook his head.

'I keep wondering—'

'What?'

'Well, if Dad did that before is that the reason she can't stand me? I keep thinking that would make sense of it.'

Mark shook his head again. 'You can't torture yourself with things like that. Even if . . . it's got nothing to do with you.'

'And at the same time it's got everything to do with me – do you see?'

'No.'

'She once said she had always tried not to blame me.'

'What do you mean?'

'I assumed she meant—'

'Stop it,' Mark said. 'I can't hear any more of this. I just can't deal with it. I don't want to talk about it any more.'

Sam saw how very upset he was and felt bad about bringing it up. They drank in silence for a while and then Sam decided a change of subject was in order.

'Are there any people you can suggest I talk to about Harry?'

'I've been doing some asking around. There's his college tutor, Colin Harding, the chaplain, Justin Burke, and apparently he also went to St Silas's.'

Sam winced. St Silas's was one of the evangelical churches most popular with students. Mark had gone there for a while as an undergraduate and she had tagged along. 'Oh God,' she said. 'I vowed I'd never go back there.'

Mark smiled. 'Time to dust off those tambourines.'

'Any non-rowing friends I could talk to?'

'Sure – there'll be people who have rooms next to him. He's a first-year, so he has rooms in college. I'll see if I can dig out any people who are close to him, who've had tutorials with him, that sort of thing.'

'Any mucking-about sort of friends?'

'I don't think he's that kind of bloke, Sam. The rowing training on top of the work is a huge commitment. It doesn't give them much time to muck about.'

'Poor bugger,' Sam said. 'Anyway, I'll see what I can find out tomorrow.'

CHAPTER FIVE

The following morning Sam stood in St Barnabas's chapel. Light shone through the stained-glass window, casting coloured patches on the uneven flagstones of the floor. Justin Burke, the chaplain, had the kind of cheeks produced either by days of skiing or by steady years of drinking. Given that he was elderly, had the width of a walrus and one of the best cellars in Oxford at his disposal, Sam decided that it was probably the latter that had resulted in their red, broken surface. She waited while Burke wrestled himself out of the white surplice he had been wearing for morning service and hung it up. He smoothed his hand across the top of his head, trying to create some sort of covering from the thin shreds of hair clinging to the scalp above his ears.

'How can I help you?' he asked.

Sam ran her hand over the golden breast of the highly polished bronze eagle that held a huge Bible on its outstretched wings. 'Mark spoke to you about Harry Cameron?'

He nodded.

'Did he attend chapel regularly last term?'

'Yes.'

'What was your impression of him?'

'Serious. Studious. Took his studies and his rowing very seriously. He came to chapel from his first week here.'

Sam sniffed the air of the chapel; it smelled of wood polish and old prayer books. As children they had been taken to chapel every Sunday evening during term time. Peter was a dutiful man who believed in supporting the institutions of college life and the chapel was one of those. He said it was hard work for the chaplains if the head of the college showed no interest. Sam could see other attractions for Peter. The main one being that he got to sit in something that looked suspiciously like a red velvet throne, looking up the chapel towards the altar. Unfortunately the Warden's family were expected to sit tucked away from the main body of the congregation and stare straight at, well, the Warden. And that wasn't nearly so much fun.

Sam remembered the tricky kneeler. Everyone had to land on it at the same time or it had a tendency to behave like a child's see-saw and drop someone to the floor while sending someone else up in the air. The service, unlike in St Mary's, had used the King James Version of the Bible. The poetry of the language was ingrained in Sam; she could still find the repetition of the words soothing, like a mantra, even if she was uncertain about her belief in God. She saw from the quizzical expression on the chaplain's face that he must have said something.

'Sorry. I was miles away.'

His overgrown eyebrows rippled across his face. If he could have transplanted them to the top of his head he would have had quite a good head of hair.

'You're Peter Goodman's daughter, aren't you?'

'Step-daughter.'

He nodded.

'We were always taken to chapel as children.' Sam ran her finger over the heavy gold leaf that edged the pages of the Bible. 'I haven't been in one for a long time. It brings back memories.'

'Good ones?'

'Mixed. I was rather a hyperactive child and found it difficult to sit still for any length of time. It probably did me good, although I found the sermons torturous.'

He laughed. 'Lots of adults might say the same.'

'But I liked the lessons. A few good tales in here.' She patted the Bible.

'Yes. Harry was interested in going into the church, you know.'

'Did he talk to you about that?'

'Yes – he wanted to find out how one goes about it.'

'Did he talk to you at all about his family?'

Burke shook his head. 'Although my impression was that they would not be supportive.'

'Can you think of any reason he might have gone missing?'

'There are all kinds of pressures on undergraduates during their first term. It amazes me they generally manage to survive it relatively intact. You may have better luck at St Silas's. He was a regular attendee there and I think their form of worship was generally more to his liking.'

Sam didn't quite manage to keep the distaste she felt from showing on her face. 'It's my next port of call,' she said.

'Not your type of thing?' he asked.

'Not really. I prefer the kind of religion where you can slide in and out and no one knows who you are,' Sam said. 'I don't like it when people wave their hands around and say "Praise the Lord". I feel panicked by it.'

Justin Burke laughed. 'Well, if your early introduction to religion was the chapel of an Oxford college that's not really very surprising.'

It was a short walk from St Barnabas's to St Silas's. The sun was shining as Sam cut up Market Street past the vans unloading fruit and vegetables, and meat and fish for the stalls in the covered market and turned left into the Cornmarket. One of the more bizarre aspects of Oxford was how two such beautiful streets as the Broad and the High came to be linked by this monstrosity, a street that would not have looked out of place in the middle of Swindon, a street stuffed with the usual depressing mish-mash of chain stores and whose complete lack of charm could not be disguised even under a thick covering of snow.

Sam pulled the collar of her coat up round her ears, crossed Carfax and headed down St Aldates to where St Silas's stood, set back from the road. Sam rang on the bell of a modern house attached to the side of the church and waited.

The Reverend Hodge was a very different sort of cleric to Justin Burke. For a start she was a woman, secondly she was wearing a jean shirt and chinos and thirdly she was approximately half his width. Sam preferred her clerics to be dog-collared and black-robed. Even when they were Low Church, she liked them to have a whiff of incense around them. She did not like them looking or behaving like normal folk, because then you might let your guard down and forget that they were after your soul. She certainly did not like them to be good-looking and charming, because that just seemed an added complication. And Emma Hodge seemed to be both those things. She took Sam into the kitchen, made her a cup of tea and ushered her into her study.

The walls of the room were painted white and bare other than for a plain wooden cross. In front of it was a kneeler and a lectern holding an open Bible. There was a desk piled with papers, and two beaten-up old armchairs. Hodge sat down in one of these and Sam took the other.

'How well do you know Harry?' Sam asked.

'He stood out,' Hodge said, 'because of his height. I always knew when he was in the congregation.'

'Do you know if he was experiencing any difficulties? Did you talk to him individually?'

'A bit – he introduced himself when he first started coming to the services. He was involved in some prayer groups attached to the church. But this was going to be only his second term here, so there hadn't been much time to get to know him well.'

'Anything at all that you can think of that would explain him disappearing?'

'The workload for new students is enormous. Within three or four days they're expected to have their first essays ready to read out to tutors who are often world experts in their field. That's a scary business. They're under a spotlight from the word go. Some of them think that they've done all the hard work at school to get here and so now they can relax, but they can't. It's very easy for people to end up with feelings of inadequacy, wondering what on earth they're doing here. Meanwhile, their parents are telling everyone how proud they are and how wonderful it is that they've got here. They are also expected to enjoy it and if they don't they can feel cheated.'

Sam smiled. 'I bet you don't get that version of Oxford life in the prospectus.'

'No, but I think you should. There are also a lot of opportunities here as well, of course. A large part of our role is pastoral. We pick up the ones who are struggling.'

'But as far as you know he wasn't one of those?'

She shook her head. 'He didn't seem to be but sometimes there are no signs that people are in trouble. The first you know about it is when they try to kill themselves or have breakdowns.'

'Or disappear.'

'Yes.'

Sam drained her cup and stood up. 'Thank you for your time,' she said.

'Can I invite you to one of our services while you're down?'

Hodge had helped her out so Sam felt she should do her best to be polite. 'I don't think so, thank you.'

'You're local, aren't you?'

'Was. I live in London now.'

'Did you ever come to St Silas's?'

'My brother went through an evangelical phase and I tagged along for a while.'

'And what happened?'

Emma was beginning to get on Sam's nerves; suddenly she felt like someone trapped on her own doorstep by a Jehovah's Witness. 'My brother realised he was bisexual and discovered that according to your version of religion he was unacceptable,' Sam snapped, 'and then I sat through a sermon in which a man actually tried to justify St Paul's opinions on women with long hair and how it should be covered up during services.'

'And then you both left?'

'We came to our senses.'

Emma Hodge opened her mouth to speak.

Sam held out a warning hand and stood up. 'Please don't. I hate it when people wave their hands in the air and beat tambourines. It really doesn't suit my personality and I have an abiding distrust of people who appear to have no doubts.'

Sam sat opposite Colin Harding in his rooms in St Barnabas's College. The theological tutor was tall and thin with the ascetic demeanour and pallid skin of a man who had just crawled out of a cave after many years' residence. But, Sam thought, for a religious man, he had alarmingly sensual lips. A freestanding, two-bar electric heater seemed to be the only heat source in the room and Harding had it angled towards himself. He crossed his legs and picked at some invisible fluff on the knee of his green corduroy trousers and looked at Sam with the kind of lugubrious eyes that any basset hound would have envied.

'How was Harry managing with the work?' Sam asked, rubbing her hands together in an attempt to generate some warmth.

'Passably.'

'What do you mean?'

'He was a hard worker. He wasn't likely to set the world on fire but he was thorough and could put together a well-argued essay.'

'So you wouldn't say he appeared to be struggling?'

'If they work hard they tend not to struggle. He certainly didn't give the appearance of struggling.'

'Did he mention anything that might have been worrying him? Anything that might explain his disappearance?'

'He came here with his essay. That was the limit of our communication – his work. And his work was perfectly adequate.'

'Did he miss any tutorials?'

He frowned, got up and took a file out of a bookcase then sat back down with it on his knees. He opened it and ran his finger down a page. 'One,' he said. 'Mid-term on 18 November.'

'Did he say why?'

'Some sort of family difficulty, I think. He didn't go into details and I didn't press him. We rescheduled for later that week.'

'Did you mind him rowing?'

'Provided the rowing didn't interfere with his studies, of course not. If he was still intending to row in his third year that might be a different matter, but it's his first year so ... there is, of course, prestige in having a rowing Blue at the college.'

He slid the tip of his tongue over his upper lip like a lizard and Sam, having a sudden and alarming image of herself as a juicy bluebottle, decided it was time to leave.

A morning filled with too much religion, theology and God delivered Sam, after a short walk through a maze of medieval alleyways, into the warm and smoky arms of the Turf Tavern. Oxford always had the effect of making Sam feel as if her head had disconnected from her body; she needed to focus on something she felt passionate about, and sport would do. She sat with the sports pages of *The Times* spread out in front of her, reading Simon Barnes, her favourite sports reporter, a man who wrote about sport in a way that no other person did. The only time she'd disagreed with him was when he'd compared David Seaman to Sybil Fawlty. That, she thought, had been pushing it.

After that morning's work, Sam felt as if the dust from the prayer books in the chapel had lodged in her throat. She picked up her pint, drank about a quarter of it and looked around her. Mark hated this pub. He said it was an Oxford cliché and more often than not stuffed with tourists, but Sam felt affectionate towards it.

Over the years generations of drunken undergraduates had poured out of this pub down Queen's Lane back to Teddy Hall and past the house where Sam had been brought up. Lying in her bedroom, Sam had been woken innumerable times by renditions of 'Jerusalem' and much more interestingly, endless obscene rugby songs. Interrogating Mark the following morning had been how she had increased her swearing vocabulary.

The pub was dark and poky and steamed up. Sam looked at two students sitting at the table next to her, who didn't seem old enough to have ordered the pints in front of them, and felt her age. Her mobile rang.

'Where are you?' Mark asked.

'Liquid lunch,' Sam replied, not mentioning the Turf and hence avoiding a stream of invective.

'I've spoken to Mum.'

'And?'

'Well, she's still very upset. You see, for her you meeting up with him is a betrayal—'

That word again. Sam cut across him. 'And how about lying to us for twenty-eight years and telling us that he was dead? How about that for betrayal?'

'I'm not defending her, Sam.'

Silence.

Mark continued: 'She doesn't want you to have any more contact with him.'

Sam thought of the A4 envelope stuffed under her floorboards. It was already too late for that. 'I don't intend to,' she lied. 'Did she apologise for slapping me?'

'I'm sure she regrets it.'

'I'll take that as a no, then.'

'She's not going to apologise to me, is she, for something she did to you?'

'Oh, I don't know. Why not? It involves less loss of face.'

'I think you should give her some space.'

'Give – her – some – space?' Sam weighted each word with a hefty dollop of sarcasm. 'I presume what you mean is that she is not over-eager for me to darken her door.'

'Stop being so melodramatic, Sam,' Mark snapped. 'It's difficult for all of us. We all need to take some time to calm down.'

'Has she told Peter that Dad's still alive?'

'Apparently he knew.'

'So now I have the perfect excuse not to be in touch with my mother – hallelujah. Praise the Lord.'

She heard him sigh. 'Sam, for God's sake, what are you babbling about?'

'Never mind, Mark, just ignore me. I've spent all morning with clerics and it's made me tetchy.'

'She knows she behaved badly.'

Sam decided to let it drop. 'Any luck in tracking down Harry's friends?'

'Yes – his tutorial partner. Her name's Lorna Marshall. I've arranged to meet her in the Grand Café at three.'

'The what?'

'Where Mum used to send us for milk.'

'What – the Co-op on the High?'

'That's the one, although it doesn't look much like a Co-op these days. We can get a coffee or something.'

'OK. I'll see you then.'

Sam closed her phone and looked at her watch; she had about an hour to go. Good – *Blackwell's*.

An hour later, clutching a bag of books that she could ill afford, Sam stood in the doorway of the Grand Café gazing around her in amazement. The Co-op had been transformed into the set of a Cocteau film. Golden muscular arms made of papier-mâché extended out of the walls, holding thick white candles. Enormous palms tickled the sides of marble pillars and a mirror attached to the back wall made the place look twice its actual size and reflected the traffic travelling up the High. She tried to remember the layout of the old shop and couldn't. The place had been run by a fat woman squeezed into a blue nylon overall, who had always watched her like a hawk through Dame Edna-type spectacles. But today she was greeted by a slim, dark-haired young man with square sideburns, wearing a pristinely white apron – a remarkable improvement.

Mark and a young woman were sitting at a table against the wall under one of the palms. Lorna Marshall had a sharp chin, a broad smile and short brown curly hair and was giving the piece of cake in front of her her undivided attention.

Sam kissed Mark, shook hands with Lorna and sat down. She stared around her. 'Bloody hell, bit of a change.'

Mark laughed. 'Just a bit.'

Sam ordered herself a cappuccino.

Mark picked up the bag of books, peered inside and laughed. 'What a surprise! Alex Ferguson's autobiography, a book on football by Sven-Goran Eriksson . . .' He rummaged a bit further. 'Yet another book on Muhammad Ali, although I can't believe there's a single one out there you haven't read, and John McEnroe's autobiography.'

Sam smiled shamefacedly and shrugged. 'The football's crept up on me since I've lived in Fulham. I never used to be that interested but then I kept being caught out by Chelsea playing. The whole of west London grinds to a halt. You can't get on a train because it's stuffed with fat men in blue shirts, so all the tubes are delayed. If you're on a bus, the traffic moves about one inch every half hour and if you're in a car the same applies. So I started checking the fixtures to see when they were playing at home, and then I started reading the football reports, and then Beckham put that goal in against Greece and England qualified for the World Cup and now I read all the football and am obsessed with Wayne Rooney and think Sven is God.'

Mark shook his head. 'It's a short road to perdition.'

'Edie likes it as well. Edie's my neighbour,' Sam said to Lorna. 'I have her over sometimes, especially when Manchester United are playing. Her husband used to support them.'

'Edie – likes football?'

'She likes the company, really. I cook fishfingers and chips and if there's a match she has to sit down and watch it, otherwise she brings in her Frank Sinatra CDs and dances round my front room. I never know what to do with her when she does that. I mean, I can't dance with her, can I? And it panics Frank.'

Mark smiled. 'God forbid the cat should be panicked.'

Lorna Marshall put down her spoon and wiped her mouth on a napkin. 'Do you think Sven—?'

'No, hang on a minute here,' Mark said. 'Shouldn't we be talking about Harry?'

'Well, you're no fun,' Sam said and smiled at Lorna. 'How well do you know him?'

'Same college, same subject – and that's quite a lot in the first term. They say you spend your second term getting rid of all the friends you made in your first term, but he isn't one I would want to get rid of.'

'What's he like?'

'Nice bloke. Easy with women and you can't say that about many of them,' Lorna said dismissively. 'You know, he could talk to you not just look at you like a piece of meat. A lot of them are very young and not very good company. They know how to drink and have a laugh with their mates but women . . . terrify them . . . they go around in packs getting drunk and throwing up and then wonder why they're still virgins.'

Mark laughed. 'Probably quite a good description of me at that age.'

'Rubbish,' Sam said firmly. 'You didn't have a problem with women, you'd been trained by me.'

Mark rolled his eyes. 'Oh yes, of course, that was a big help.'

Sam smiled at him and then directed her attention towards Lorna. 'So he seemed happy to you?'

'He was very busy. There was all the rowing he did and then there was the studying and the religion . . .'

'Was there anything that was worrying him, as far as you knew?'

'He was anxious about whether he'd get a Blue. He really wanted that.'

'But from what I can gather he was almost certain to.'

'Well, he wasn't taking that for granted.'

'So there was nothing unusual last term that might have made you think he'd be in difficulties?'

72

She shook her head. 'Not really, no . . .'

Sam sensed a reluctance to say something. 'If there's anything you can tell us, it's not going to land him in trouble or anything. You see, they're worried because they can't imagine what would make him walk out of the trials. We just want to make sure he's safe.'

'Well, there was this rather odd episode at the end of term. I mean it turned out to be nothing, but . . .' She picked up a spoon and stirred her coffee, obviously weighing up whether to tell them. 'We were walking along Cornmarket in the direction of the High. It was the last Wednesday of term and this woman started shouting at him in the street. She just went ballistic really. Started screaming at him . . .' She shook her head.

'What did he do?'

'He seemed really shocked. He kept saying, "I don't know what you're talking about. It wasn't me. You must be mistaken." We walked on a bit further and then, next thing we know, this police car has screeched to a halt and he's being taken off to the station.'

'He was arrested?'

'Yes. In the end they released him and he said it had been a case of mistaken identity. He had an alibi.'

'For what?'

She dropped the spoon into her saucer. 'Date rape. The woman said he drugged her and assaulted her.'

'You've got to be joking?' Mark said.

Lorna shook her head.

Sam stirred the top of her cappuccino into the liquid underneath. 'Who or what was his alibi?'

'*I* was. They wanted to know what he'd been doing on the evening she said it happened – and he'd been with me. The police got pretty heavy about it, suggested I was lying to protect him, but I wasn't. I wouldn't have done anyway, not over something like that.'

'What were you doing with him?'

'It was the day before our tutorial and from ten o'clock that night we were both working on an essay for the following morning. We were both knackered and behind with the work. We decided to split the reading list between us, and then meet up to swap notes. We were together in my room from about ten o'clock in the evening and we worked through the night. The tutorial was the following morning.'

'It was definitely that evening?'

'Yes, I'd written it down in my diary.'

'Could you see him doing something like that?'

'Absolutely not. He's a sweetheart. You couldn't imagine a gentler man if you tried.'

'Did you talk to him about it? How did he explain it?'

She shrugged. 'Some form of mistaken identity?'

Sam frowned. 'But he's not your average sort of bloke, is he? I mean, his height makes him stand out apart from anything else.'

'I know. But all I can say is that there's no way Harry would be involved in anything like that.'

'And he didn't mention it at all again?'

'Well, he didn't have much time, did he? It was the end of term and we were all heading home for Christmas. He thanked me for the alibi . . .' Lorna looked at her watch. 'God, I need to be going.' She wiped her mouth and picked up her bag. 'Thanks for tea,' she said to Mark.

'Can you think of anyone else we should talk to?' Sam asked.

'Not really. Have you spoken to his family?'

Sam nodded. 'His parents are away at the moment. Do you know if he had any siblings?'

'He didn't talk much about his family. I don't think he was particularly looking forward to going home for Christmas, but that's not uncommon, is it?'

No, it isn't, Sam thought, thinking of the blissful family-free Christmas she had just spent.

After Lorna had gone, Sam ordered herself another cappuccino.

'Any leads this morning?' Mark asked.

She shook her head. 'There's nothing to indicate that his disappearance has anything to do with the rowing, his studies, or problems adjusting to life here. Nothing like that.'

'What about this thing with the girl?'

'That's the only thing we have that suggests he's been in any sort of trouble. I did learn that he missed a tutorial in the middle of term for family reasons, but his tutor didn't enquire further. Mind you, Colin Harding's the kind of man who wouldn't ask any questions if you turned up with your own severed head under your arm. As long as the head could read out an essay.'

'But we've got nothing on the family?'

'I need to phone Tom and see if he's had any luck getting hold of the parents.'

'What'll you do about this thing at the end of term?'

'I'll talk to Phil about that and see what his take on it is.'

Phil Howard was Sam's ex-boyfriend and a DS in the Thames Valley police force.

'Why don't you arrange to see him and go back tomorrow?' Mark said.

'No, I need to get back to London today.'

'Phil's one of the good guys, you know, Sam.'

'Oh please! What's that supposed to mean?' Mark opened his mouth to speak but Sam held out her hand to stop him. 'He was my boyfriend, Mark. I know that.'

'I'm just saying.'

'I have to get back.'

'What for?'

She had therapy the following morning. For a minute she considered telling him and then changed her mind. God, the hard time she'd given him when he'd told her he'd had counselling. She'd been a right bastard about it.

She couldn't bear the teasing.

'Oh this and that,' she said and waved at the waiter for the bill.

CHAPTER SIX

As Sam opened the front door of her mansion block later that evening, she heard a car pull up behind her. She turned and watched a squat elderly lady wearing a black curly wig struggle out of a black cab. The cab driver got out and took a large suitcase from the front of the cab and deposited it on the pavement next to where Sam was standing.

'Edie!' Sam said. 'Where have you been?'

Edie handed over some money to the cabbie and dropped her purse into her voluminous bag.

'All right, babes?'

Sam noted that her face was the same colour as that of the walrus she had encountered in Oxford. Edie was seventy-nine, so she doubted she'd been skiing.

'Where have you been?' Sam repeated.

Edie patted her wig. 'Benalmádena – seventy-five degrees. For a week.' And then, noticing Sam's blank face, added. 'Spain, babes.'

Sam frowned. To her knowledge Edie had only ever been on day trips to France and Belgium before.

'Been stocking up, haven't I? The day trips are getting trickier. Keep getting stopped and last time they started taking addresses and marking the passports. French have upped their baccy prices by twenty per cent. I'm having to go further afield.'

'I'll give you a hand,' Sam said and then made the mistake of trying to pick up Edie's suitcase with one hand. 'God,' she said, quickly putting it down again. 'What on earth have you got in here?'

Edie cackled. 'There's nothing I haven't got in there, babes. Had to pay thirty-six pounds excess baggage.'

Sam picked it up again, this time using two hands, and began hauling the case to the front door. Edie held it open for her and Sam lugged the case up the first flight of stairs to their landing.

'I'll bring you in something later,' Edie said, putting her key in the door.

'Have you been to Spain before?' Sam asked.

Edie shook her head. 'But it's a piece of piss, travel.'

'Frank missed you,' Sam said.

'Course he did,' Edie replied, pushing her front door open. 'I've got some food for him.'

'From Spain?'

Edie nodded.

Sam laughed. Edie could be tricky but Sam admired her. After Edie's husband had died Edie had developed a new career as a tobacco smuggler. Sam wasn't sure she would have made her first trip abroad at that age. At that age, Sam thought, she would probably be being fed mashed banana through a straw. She put her key in her door and pushed it open.

For a second she could not take in what she was seeing.

It was a scene of utter devastation.

Her desk, which had stood in the hall, had been turned over and all its contents had been scattered over the floor. Paintings had been pulled off the wall, books pulled out of the bookcases and that was just the hall.

In the front room the dresser that contained all her gran's ornaments had been toppled over and the rugs were crunchy with broken glass and china. Nothing remained on the walls and every drawer was open with the contents tipped out. The mantel-piece, every inch of which had been covered with stuff, had been swept clean. Everywhere Sam looked she saw something broken.

There was a knock on the door. Sam moved towards it like an automaton. It was Edie, holding a bottle of white wine and some pouches of cat food.

'Don't know if this foreign stuff's any good—' Edie began pointing to the cat food. Then she saw Sam's face. 'What is it?'

Sam stepped to one side so that Edie could see what had happened. Edie's eyes widened as she stepped into the flat. 'You been done over?'

Edie followed her into the front room. When she saw the destruction she sucked on her teeth. 'All Rose's things.'

Sam picked up a piece of paper and then put it down again. Edie's eyes were darting around the flat. 'They left you the telly and the CD player and the CDs, didn't they?' She frowned. 'What *have* they taken?'

Sam shook her head. She had absolutely no idea. How could you tell in all this chaos? She knew what was broken – everything.

'How'd they get in? Wasn't the front door, was it?'

Sam walked out of the front room, down the hall and into the kitchen. One of the windows was open, not even broken. That was obviously the point of entry. A cold wind sliced through the kitchen. Someone had picked up the cat tray and emptied its contents all over the kitchen table. A miasma of cat's piss hung in the air.

Edie came into the kitchen behind her. 'Filthy bastards,' she said, staring at the excrement that covered the table

'It's Frank's.'

'Well, that's a blessing – of sorts.'

'The lock on the window was dodgy,' Sam said. 'It has been for ages. Ever since last summer, when Crozier's cowboys replaced the window frames with ones that didn't fit and none of the locks worked properly.'

Edie nodded. 'All those draughts sent my bills up no end.'

'Why'd they have to smash everything?' Sam said, sweeping some broken glass off a chair and sitting down.

Edie surveyed the chaos. 'It's like they were looking for something that they couldn't find and then got pissed off about it. They haven't nabbed the obvious things, have they?'

'I can't even tell,' Sam said.

The kettle was one of the few things that looked undamaged. She picked it up, felt the weight of water it contained, put it back down and clicked it on. She knew she should be doing something, but for now she felt paralysed. All she could manage was clicking on the kettle and staring at the mess.

'Shall I phone someone for you, babes?' Edie suggested.

Sam shook her head. 'It's OK, Edie. I just need a cup of tea and then I'll phone Alan.'

She remembered that she needed to check something; she also

knew she wasn't going to do that until Edie was safely back in her own flat.

'I'd give you a hand, babes, but I'm that knackered from the flight I can barely keep my eyes open.'

'Don't worry, Edie, that's fine.'

After Edie had finished her tea and gone back to her own flat Sam rolled back the rugs in the hall, lay flat on her front and felt as far as she could under the floorboards. Her fingers touched paper and she pulled out the envelope. She sat with it in her lap, staring at it. This, she presumed, was the cause of all this destruction. Should she go to the police? She couldn't make up her mind. She knew that if she called them in she shouldn't start to clear up. They would want to take fingerprints, but had anything actually been stolen?

Looking around, Sam saw that a hell of a lot of things had been smashed, but as Edie had said, the obvious things did not seem to have been taken. She found her phone under a pile of bank statements, plugged it back into the wall and phoned Alan. He would tell her what to do.

Twenty minutes later Alan stood in Sam's front room. Sam was kneeling down, throwing bits of broken china into a cardboard box.

'What do you think you're doing?' Alan said. 'You know you shouldn't touch anything.'

'I'm not going to report it.'

'Why on earth not? You'll need to in order to claim on the insurance.'

'For God's sake, Alan, do I look like a woman who has insurance? And even if I had it, what am I going to do? Claim for – a lifetime of knick-knacks lovingly collected by my gran? How can I replace those?'

Sam suddenly felt very upset. She'd adored her gran and had always been her favourite; it was because Sam looked so like Geoffrey, the son Rose thought she'd lost. Tears sprang to her eyes and a lump rose up in her throat. It was ridiculous, but these days everything was making her cry. It was as if the switch marked 'repression' was permanently switched to 'off'. She blamed Reg.

'You did need to get rid of some of those things,' Alan said gently. 'It's a long time since she died.'

'I know, Alan,' Sam said testily. 'But I would have preferred wrapping them up in newspaper and putting them in a cupboard rather than having them smashed all over my flat.' Sam held a piece of blue and white china in her hand that had once been part of a spaniel. 'These were my last connection with her.' She looked up suddenly. 'And if you say anything like your last connection with her is in your heart and that can never be broken, I'll cut out your tongue.'

Alan smiled. 'I wouldn't dare.'

'Anyway, I know what they were looking for and they didn't find it.'

'What do you mean?'

Sam tapped the buff envelope where it lay on the ground next to her.

Alan reached down to pick it up.

'No,' Sam said, putting her hand over the top of it. 'I don't think that's a good idea.'

'Well, fine, but you should consider that if they didn't find it this time round they may well come back and try again.'

'I know,' Sam said, placing another piece of china dog next to the previous bit.

'You sure about the police?'

'Absolutely,' Sam said. 'I don't want them involved. Now, are you going to give me a hand tidying up or what?'

Alan picked up another bit of blue china and put it next to the other two pieces. 'I presume you're thinking of gluing that back together.'

'Well, I can't pretend it hadn't crossed my mind.'

'Thought so.'

He nudged the envelope with his foot. 'You going to tell me about that?'

Sam sighed. 'I am, but you're not to shout.' She held two pieces of china together. 'These'll go back fine together.'

Alan was sweeping the floor gently with a broom, creating a pile of broken glass and crockery. 'Here,' he said, 'there's another piece.' He bent down and picked up a large ball of fluff. 'What on earth's this?'

'Frank's under fur.'

'You could knit socks with it.'

Sam picked up another piece of china. 'Shit,' she said and squeezed her finger. Blood ran across the palm of her hand and down her wrist. 'I thought I was being so careful as well.' She stood up and walked through to the bathroom and came back with a plaster.

'Do you mind?' She handed it to Alan.

He unpeeled it and wrapped it round her finger. The outside of the plaster immediately soaked with blood. 'Thanks.'

Alan picked up the broom. 'So . . .' he said.

'OK, now don't shout, Alan.'

'Of course not.'

'My father pushed it through the letterbox and then left a message on my answerphone asking me to look after it for him.'

'He *what*?' Alan shouted.

'What could I do? I hid it under the floorboards.'

'You should never have met up with him.'

'Why is it that everyone seems so certain of that? Suppose you had believed that your father was dead all your life and then you found he wasn't and then there was a chance of meeting him. Can you honestly tell me that you wouldn't have? It's easier fucking said than done, Alan.' She looked down at the pieces of blue china and pushed her hands through her hair. 'Jesus, what the hell am I going to do with these?'

'Have you talked to the shrink about this?'

'He's got a name, Alan. He's not "The Shrink". His name's Reg.'

Alan started to laugh. 'Your therapist's name is Reg?'

'I like it,' Sam said. 'It's a down-to-earth sort of name. Like him.'

Alan was shaking his head. 'Yes, but Reg . . . it just doesn't sound very, well, therapeutic, does it? Sounds like a bloke who'd come round and see to the drains.'

'Well, sometimes I think that's what I need – mental drainage.'

There was a knock on the door. Sam stood up, brushed the knees of her trousers and opened the door. It was Jackie.

'Look, it's not a good time right now,' Sam said.

'I'll only be a second. I'd like to employ you again.'

'You better come in then.'

'God, what happened here?' Jackie asked, stepping gingerly over a splintered drawer that belonged in Sam's desk.

'I got burgled.'

'How did they get in?'

'Window in the kitchen.'

Jackie looked relieved. 'Not the main entrance then?'

'No.'

'Well, I hope you can take better care of my property than you do of your own.'

Sam stared at her in stony silence.

'Was much taken?'

'No, but they smashed the place up looking.'

Jackie looked around the room.

'This is my colleague, Alan.'

Alan and Jackie nodded at each other.

'So . . .' Sam said. 'What can we do for you?'

'Well, what you did the other morning. I'd like that tomorrow and Saturday. And then I'll review it on a weekly basis.'

'What happens tomorrow?' Sam asked.

'Another antiques market – in Kempton.'

'I thought you were only likely to be done round Portobello.'

'They can try it on anywhere.'

'Same time?'

'Yes.'

'Well, that counts me out, I'm afraid. I've got an appointment tomorrow morning.'

'But I want you to do it.'

'Well, I can't. Anyway, before you said I was too small. Alan isn't.'

'That was before.'

'Before I saved your arse?'

'If you like.'

The two women looked at Alan.

He raised his eyebrows. 'What's involved exactly?'

Sam filled him in.

'Five-thirty!' He looked at his watch. 'I should be in bed now if I'm going to do that.'

'Is that a yes?' Sam asked.

'OK, but I don't want the Saturday as well.'

'I can do the Saturday,' Sam said.

'I'm not being funny, but can you handle yourself?' Jackie said to Alan.

Seeing Alan bristle, Sam jumped in. 'Alan is an ex-policeman and highly trained in self-defence. Look at him – of course he can handle himself.'

'Police?'

'It didn't do much for me either, lady,' Alan said. 'That's why I left.'

'OK,' Jackie said. 'Just for God's sake don't tell anyone we meet. Now, the price.'

'A hundred pounds, cash in hand.'

'For both days.'

Sam laughed. 'You're joking. For each day.'

'Well, I thought if I was going to use you on an ongoing basis perhaps you could do something on the price.'

'I don't think so,' Sam said.

'How about eighty pounds per day?'

Sam addressed Alan. 'What do you think?'

'Eighty pounds to get out of bed at five-thirty. You're joking, aren't you?'

'Ninety, then.'

Sam was a hopeless negotiator; she always ended up losing her temper and never at a strategic point. 'Oh fucking forget it,' she said, walking towards the front door and throwing it open. 'Find yourself someone else.'

'OK, OK – calm down. So, I'll see you tomorrow at five-thirty,' Jackie said to Alan.

'Seems so,' Alan said, staring hard at Sam.

Sam closed the door behind Jackie and walked back into the front room. 'Look, I know it's not great but it's not as if we've got work lined up and marching through our doors at the moment, is it? Maybe if we do this we'll get other stuff from the markets. You never know.'

'But they're dealers, Sam. They'll want to knock you on the price every time.'

'I know. I'm not stupid, but at least it's work.'

*

83

Sam and Alan spent the next few hours returning her flat to some kind of order.

'We can stop now,' Sam said, standing up with a full dustpan in her hand.

'It's still a terrible mess.'

'I know, but it's actually tidier now than before it was done over.'

Alan laughed and leaned the broom he was holding against the wall. 'I'll take you out for a pizza. It'll do you good to get out of here for a while and you can tell me what happened in Oxford.'

The walk to Pizza Express took about fifteen minutes of doglegging along the streets that ran between the New King's Road and Fulham Road. These side streets had not been cleared of snow as effectively as the main roads and the cars that passed them moved cautiously, as did Alan and Sam. Sam pushed open the door of the restaurant and welcomed the blast of hot air from the heater above her head.

'There's something I need to tell you before you go to Kempton with Jackie,' Sam said, shrugging off her coat and hanging it over the back of her chair.

'I don't like the sound of that,' Alan said.

'When I went out with her last time we were jumped by two thugs in the car park. One had a baseball bat, the other a knife.'

'Nice of you to mention it.'

'Sorry – but I didn't want to go into it with her there. When I was with her she was carrying fifteen thousand pounds in jewellery and cash, so it would be best to carry her bag.'

'And park somewhere other than the car park.'

'You're going to Kempton with her tomorrow, not Portobello, so that won't apply. She says they've been robbing all the stallholders in Golding's Arcade – something to do with a feud going on between a fence and the owners of the arcade. Perhaps you could check if your brothers know anything about it.'

Alan scowled. 'Could do. Truth is, I don't mind the knife and the baseball bat. I'm more worried about having to get out of bed at that time in the morning.'

Sam laughed. 'Especially in this weather.'

'Mind you, they say it's going to thaw,' Alan said.

'I know, but they've been saying that for the last three days.'

'If they keep saying it they'll get it right eventually.'

Their pizzas arrived. Sam speared a black olive off the top and popped it in her mouth. They ate quickly and in silence.

'So,' Alan said, wiping the last slice of pizza around his plate, 'you want to tell me about your father?'

'I just had to meet him,' Sam said.

Alan nodded. 'I can understand that.'

'Can you? Mark doesn't and my mother's gone bonkers about it.'

'Whatever he's done, he is your father. Did you like him?'

Sam remembered her father's hand around her wrist, dragging her towards him, towards those intense-blue, red-rimmed eyes. She felt his breath on her face. She felt her own fingers digging into the flesh of his wrist. She had felt her boundaries blurring even as she fought him.

Alan was staring at her. 'Sam?'

She looked up. 'Sorry, Alan. What did you say?'

'Did it settle anything for you, meeting him?'

She shook her head. 'He told me I was the only home he had. I told him I never wanted to see him again.'

'So that's all nicely resolved then. Is it true you don't want to see him?'

'Mark doesn't think so.'

'I'm not asking Mark.'

'The trouble is, I spent years believing he was a hero. Now I have to get clear about who he really is – I can't spin round on it that quickly.'

'So what are you saying? That you do want to see him again?'

'What I'm saying is that I don't know.'

'What are you going to do about the envelope? Aren't you even a tiny bit curious to know what's in it?'

The waiter removed their plates and asked them if they wanted to see the dessert menu. They both said 'yes' in unison. He brought the menu and both of them ordered the cheesecake.

'If I open it I just get dragged further in.'

'Don't you want to know what you're dealing with?'

'Of course, but there's another part of me that just wants to stick my head in the sand.'

Alan shook his head. 'I couldn't just sit there with something in my flat and not know what was in it, when I knew someone was so desperate to get it they'd turned my flat upside down.'

Their desserts arrived. Sam picked up her fork, cut off a piece of lemon cheesecake and slid it into her mouth.

'How about Oxford? Did you find out anything about the Cameron boy?'

'The only lead we got was from another student who had tutorials with him, who said that he'd been arrested at the very end of last term for date rape. But she provided him with an alibi, they let him go and she doesn't think he was charged with anything.'

'Rape? Come on! He wouldn't even watch a dirty film. That doesn't make any sense at all.'

'I know. It didn't make any sense to his friend either. I need to check it out with Phil.'

'Still no contact from his parents?'

'No.'

Alan insisted on walking Sam home.

'Are you going to be all right?' he asked as she pushed open her front door.

'I'll be fine and good luck tomorrow.'

Alan groaned and looked at his watch. 'It's already way past my bedtime.'

'Will you come into the office afterwards?'

'Probably.'

Sam watched Alan retracing his steps towards the Fulham Palace Road and then let herself into the block. Her flat felt alien. Someone had been in here touching all her things. Not just touching them. Smashing them. She felt smashed. She looked at the pathetic pile of broken blue and white china pieces she had saved. It had once been a King Charles spaniel, one of her gran's favourites. It wasn't worth anything – she'd probably bought it on a trip to the seaside – but she had loved it. Why did they have to smash that? She walked round the flat putting on all the lights that hadn't been broken. As she was taking off her coat, the plaster on her finger got caught in the zip and came off and the cut was torn open again. Sam stared into the cut, watching it fill with blood.

The next time she looked at her watch, two hours had passed and the blood had run out of the cut into the palm of her hand and congealed. She couldn't understand what had happened. In the bathroom she ran her hand under the tap, dried it and applied another plaster. Then, with all the lights blazing, she threw off her clothes, got into bed, pulled the duvet over her head and, after an hour of listening to her heart thumping in her ears, finally fell asleep.

CHAPTER SEVEN

'My mother slapped me and Mark's furious with me.'

Reg prodded his glasses back up his nose. 'And how do you feel about that?'

Sam resisted the temptation to be facetious. 'I don't like Mark being angry with me. I don't really like any disruption to our relationship. I feel as if my security's being threatened, like a house that's got subsidence. As for my mother, well, in some ways it was almost a relief.'

Reg frowned. 'Why?'

'I've known my whole life that she doesn't really like or approve of me. I don't think she ever has. And there's been absolutely nothing I can do about it. So, her slapping me, it's as if it's all out in the open now. The pretence is over.'

'Do you understand why they feel the way they do?'

'Sure I do. They feel betrayed by me. Mark looked frightened when I told him. As if I'd done something irrevocable, like Pandora opening the box.'

'What do you think he's frightened of?'

'He doesn't believe me when I say I never want to see my father again. He thinks I'm lying to myself. And now it's too late. I'm going to end up being dragged back in and if I am then he will be.'

'And are you?'

'What?'

'Lying to yourself.'

'I honestly don't know.'

'And why *did* you want to meet him?'

'I wanted to see him.'

'And what made you change your mind?'

'I just did.'

'You just did?' Reg repeated.

'Yes,' Sam said slowly, failing to keep the irritation from her voice. 'I just did.'

'You don't know why?'

Sam heard the clock ticking on the table between them. How much longer to go? Blood pulsed in her ears. *He had thrown her into the water and then pulled her out onto his lap. She had heard his heart beating faster and faster. And then . . .*

What had happened? She thought she knew but had she remembered correctly? Suppose she was wrong. There was a name for it, wasn't there? False memory syndrome. She'd only been four. How would she ever know the truth of what had happened? The flashback had first happened when she met her father in the café. But since then the doubts had been creeping in, since then, whenever she had the flashbacks, the perpetrator was faceless. How would she ever know whose hand was reaching down through the water?

'Sam?'

'What?'

'Where did you go just now?'

Her mouth was dry. 'I want to stop.'

Reg opened his mouth to speak but Sam was on her feet. 'I pay you. This is my time. I can do with it what I want.'

A car backfired. Reg looked startled. He took off his glasses and Sam noticed that his hands were shaking. 'Do you want to sit down and discuss it?'

Sam felt furious. 'Don't take this personally but this whole thing is a fake. How am I supposed to trust you when an imbalance of power is built into the relationship? You take my money. I reveal everything about myself and you tell me absolutely nothing. You just sit there all fucking safe and cosy and judge me. You peer at me over the top of your glasses, set all the bloody parameters and I'm just supposed to go along with it. You get to take your six-week holiday in the summer. Well, what happens if I have a bloody nervous breakdown when you're off in Barbados? Then I'm just fucked, aren't I? Well, fuck you. It's all designed to suit you and stuff me.' Sam started for the door.

'What do you want to know about me?'

His response took her completely by surprise. She stopped and turned round. 'I didn't think you were supposed to reveal anything about yourself.'

'You can't have it both ways. Accuse me of not saying anything about myself and then accuse me if I offer it. What do you want to know?'

'Why do you do this?'

'Sit down and I'll tell you.'

Reluctantly Sam sat down.

'I fought in the Falklands, 2 Para – Goose Green, 1982. Got shot up and shipped back here, had a breakdown. Army didn't want to know. They patched me up physically, then chucked me out on civvy street. Started drinking, lost my wife and kids. Lots of ex-services do. Tried to kill myself. Got some help, got some counselling and started going to AA. Did my ninety meetings in ninety days. Then began to train as a therapist.

'I specialise in ex-services and post traumatic stress disorder. Soldiers generally make terrible clients, of course, because they equate expressing emotion with weakness – it's the way we're trained. I broke down rather than admit I needed help. I saw that as shameful so I went mad instead. I try and show my clients that there's another route available to them if they're brave enough to take it.' He held out his hands, which were still trembling. 'Cars backfiring, sudden unexpected noises, I still find very difficult.'

'Why are you seeing me, then?'

'You're a fighter, aren't you?'

At that precise moment Sam felt far from a fighter. She felt slightly sick and as if two demons were sitting in her brain and pushing daggers out through her eyeballs.

'Do you still want to finish?'

Sam nodded and stood up.

'One thing, Sam. You mentioned Pandora's Box?'

'Yes.'

'It wasn't just the Spites Pandora let loose in the world. It was also the Star of Hope. Perhaps you could look at what you were hoping for when you met your father.'

Sam sat at the bus stop outside Reg's house huddled against a wind that seemed to blow directly into her face whichever way she turned. She tore off the plaster and picked at the cut, squeezed it till it bled. Holding her hand down she watched the dripping blood pockmarking the snow. Felt relief. Someone walked past her but she didn't care; she wanted them to see her bleeding. Blood was a relief, a release from the numbness and chaos, from disintegration.

Hope?

There was none.

Not now, anyway. Not now she had met him. Before that, of course, there had been the fantasy. A double sheet of newspaper wrapped itself around her legs and she kicked it away. Yes, there was always the fantasy. The warrior hero killed in action. Sam was hardly original in the kind of father she had wanted as a child. Wasn't that the kind of father that every little girl wanted? The one who swung you on his shoulders and told you how great you were. Who explained the world to you and believed in you. Wasn't that how it was supposed to work?

Instead Sam had her stepfather, Peter, a man not really of the world at all. She had wanted a man of action because that was the father she had lost but instead she had got an academic and, even worse than that, she had got a mathematician. Sam knew mathematicians could be heroes. Look at Alan Turing and the cracking of the Enigma codes. If that wasn't heroism, she didn't know what was. Didn't they say that he had done more to win the war than any other single individual? But as a child Sam did not want this kind of invisible, quiet, intellectual heroism; she wanted a more gung ho, blood-and-guts variety. Peter was about as far away from a man of action as you could get.

Sam wrapped a tissue round her finger and took the buff A4 envelope out of her bag. She was carrying it with her because she didn't know what else to do with it. Leaving it in the flat was no longer an option. It was only a matter of time. Who did she think she was kidding? She would have to open it and read it eventually and then she would be even more involved, even more dragged in. She would be entangled in her father's life and never be able to escape. Death, she thought, is the only thing that's going to free me from him. Suddenly death didn't seem such a bad thing. She put the envelope back in her bag.

She hadn't even talked to Reg about the burglary. That was the problem with therapy. Before she went she'd prepared herself to talk about one thing, but when she got there she found herself gibbering on about something else completely. Then the minutes ticked by, she was handing over the money and she was gone. A bus drew up and Sam jumped on board.

Back at her office in Putney Sam felt calmer. At least there was work to do – thank God for Harry, without that she didn't know what would become of her. She put in a phone call to Phil Howard. As she waited for him to come on the line, Sam thought about the last time they'd slept together. It was the last time she'd had sex and that was . . . She was just flicking through the calendar on her desk, trying to work that out, when his voice broke into that somewhat depressing line of thought.

'Sam?'

'Oh hi. How are you?'

'Yeah, fine, what can I do for you?'

A bit quick with the pleasantries, Sam thought. He's probably got a new girlfriend.

'I wonder if you know anything about a Harry Cameron, a student who was arrested at the end of last term. He was accused of date rape.'

'I might. How are you involved?'

'He went missing from an OUBC training squad last week and they've asked me to look into it.'

'I remember the case. A woman called Siobhan Clarke accused him of spiking her drink and rape.'

'Did you believe her?'

'She was adamant it was Harry but he had a cast-iron alibi. The woman who provided his alibi – Lorna Marshall, wasn't it? – said he'd been with her late that evening and she came across as convincing. When we checked up on him, we couldn't find anyone to say a bad word about him. Cameron was so clean-cut it wasn't true. Everyone we spoke to was willing to swear it wasn't him.'

'What did you make of it?'

'Looked like mistaken identity to me.'

'But Harry's pretty difficult to mistake, isn't he? He's so tall for one thing and—'

'I know. To be honest, the whole thing didn't hold together. We believed the girl and we believed him but the alibi was solid. Lorna Marshall had only known him since the beginning of term so it wasn't as if she had much reason to lie to protect him. So you haven't been able to track down the Cameron boy yet?'

'We were waiting to see if he'd turn up at the start of term but he hasn't.'

'Another thing, Sam, the custody sergeant said he asked for a Bible. And when they took him some breakfast he was praying. I mean, unless he was a really good actor or had some severe Jekyll and Hyde thing going on, there was no way he was involved.'

'So who did it?'

'We're still investigating.'

'Would you let me know of any developments?'

'I'll see what I can do.'

'Thanks. So, everything OK with you, Phil?'

'Yeah, great. Drop in next time you're in town.' He hung up.

Sam put down the phone and sighed. He's happy, she thought, or at any rate happily indifferent to me. She had resisted the temptation to pry or reel him in. She thought again of the last time they had slept together. On that occasion he'd said he wanted them to get back together. He'd said he'd move to London, even though he'd sworn he'd never work for the Met.

She sat staring into space and then dug in the pocket of her jacket for her wallet. She flicked through it until she found the card she wanted, dropped it on her table and stared at it for a few moments before picking up the phone. She got an answerphone.

'Oh hi,' she said. 'It's Sam Falconer. You probably don't remember me. You let me into my flat a few days ago when I was locked out and fixed my boiler. I've got a very fat cat. Anyway, that's beside the point. I was wondering if you do window locks. I've been burgled and I've got one that needs fixing. Could you give me a call?'

Alan came into the office at about midday looking as if he'd just arrived from Australia. He threw his coat at the coat stand and slumped down in the chair on the other side of Sam's desk. Sam had been doing paperwork, which involved picking up pieces of paper, reading them, groaning loudly and then putting them in another pile.

'How'd it go?'

Alan rubbed his eyes. 'Five fucking thirty is how it went.'

'Why don't you go home and get some sleep?'

'I thought I'd treat it like jet lag, you know, try and stay awake as long as possible.'

'What, torture me with your grumpiness all afternoon, you mean?'

'Sure sounds good to me. Those dealers – you should see them. It's frightening the way they behave. I'm surprised any of that jewellery stays intact the way they snatch and tear at it.'

'Any trouble?'

He shook his head.

'You get paid?'

He nodded. 'Cash.'

The phone on Sam's desk rang. It was the OUBC coach, Tom King.

'Hi, Sam. Got any news about Harry?'

'Well, I've spoken to his tutor, the chaplain of St Barnabas's and the vicar at St Silas's and they said nothing to suggest there was any reason for him to go missing. The only thing we found out was that he was arrested at the end of last term on suspicion of date rape.'

'Harry! You're joking. He was unreal – he'd walk out of a room if there was too much swearing on the TV. No way would he be involved in anything like that. My impression of him was that he disagreed with sex before marriage.'

'Well, it makes no sense to me either. All the people I spoke to had similar views but apparently the girl was adamant that it was Harry. The police let him go because he had an alibi, but suppose he *was* involved in some way and was frightened that it would all come out.'

'No – that can't be it. Not that boy. I tell you. It would be like suggesting Mother Teresa was turning tricks at King's Cross.'

Sam laughed.

'I finally managed to get hold of his dad today. He's just come back from holiday.'

'What did he say?'

'Frankly his attitude surprised me. He seemed very unconcerned. Said they were used to him disappearing for a few days at a time. He's done it since he was a boy. My impression is that his father's used to not knowing where he is.'

'But what did he make of the rowing thing? The fact that he's walked out during the trials?'

'Not much is the short answer. He didn't seem concerned at all. Just said they thought he'd turn up eventually. That he always does. I filled him in about you and said you'd go and see him. He wasn't that keen but I managed to persuade him. Is that all right?'

'Sure,' Sam said.

'Watch out for him,' King said. 'He's not a particularly nice man.'

'Thanks for the warning.'

'We really need Harry back, Sam. From the first moment I clapped eyes on him I wanted him as stroke. With him we've got a chance. Without him . . .'

'What about Holden?'

'It's not the same. The boat doesn't run the same way as when Harry strokes it. Holden's a really good oarsman but that's not enough, you have to share the same vision as the rest of the crew.'

Sam thought that the whole thing was becoming much more important than a Boat Race. 'Maybe his father will give us some leads,' she said and put down the phone.

'Father's back,' she said to Alan. 'Fancy another trip to Barnes?'

The man who opened his front door to Alan and Sam had his son's height combined with the physique of a heavyweight boxer. He was wearing a blue, long-sleeved button-down shirt open at the neck, brown corduroys and highly polished brown shoes, which looked as if they'd last a hundred years. His manner was not at all welcoming.

'Come in, come in,' he said brusquely, standing to one side.

He led them into a large living room and stood with his back to the fireplace above which hung an enormous glass-framed, Venetian mirror. He didn't invite them to sit or offer them anything to drink. Sam walked over to French windows which looked out onto the garden. Snow lay inches thick on the windowsills. It was cold and grey and the light was starting to fade. Sam noticed that the glass round the door handle had been smashed and replaced with some hardboard.

She turned round. 'What happened here?'

'Bit of trouble with some local kids trying their luck when I was away.'

'Anything taken?'

He ignored her question. 'I'm busy, so this'll have to be brief.'

Sam nodded. 'I understand you're just back from holiday.'

'Yes. I'm not sure what all the fuss is about Harry. He's done this before, you know. It's no big deal.'

'Under what circumstances?'

'No particular ones. It's as the fancy takes him.'

Sam frowned. 'So – he just wanders off without telling you?'

'Pretty much.'

'But it seems very out of character.'

'What do you know about the character of my son, Miss . . .?'

'Sam Falconer,' Sam said slowly. 'Ms.'

A silence bristling with antagonism filled the room. Sam glanced at Alan, indicating he could take over the questioning, and turned away to look at the garden again. They'd get nowhere if she got into some sort of stand-off with the man.

'What we know about your son,' Alan began, 'is that he is a very talented rower, liked by his contemporaries and of a religious disposition. We can find nothing to indicate why he would have walked out of the OUBC rowing trials. It seems that he was very keen to row in the Blue boat and must have realised that disappearing would affect his chances of being selected. They are extremely eager to know where he is, not only for his own safety but also because he makes the boat go faster.'

'Rowing!' Cameron spat the word out. 'I don't give a damn about his bloody rowing. Or his degree. What's he doing wasting his time at university? I told him he could come and work for me as soon as he left school. That he could start earning some serious money. But he wants to go to university and study theology. What's the use of theology? He might just as well be studying English. It equips you for nothing. Now law or economics or politics, that I could understand, but theology . . .'

'You didn't want him to go?'

'No. I was dead against it. I didn't go to university and it never did me any harm. You just put your career on hold and idle away

96

three years. At the end of it, you're three years behind the other man and your parents are out of pocket.'

'Oxford is not a load of rich kids running around hugging teddy bears and getting drunk,' Sam said. 'They have to work bloody hard or they're kicked out. That's not a particularly glamorous part of it, so the media don't give it much coverage. Your son was not only working hard he was rowing hard as well.'

'What makes you such an expert?'

'My brother and my stepfather are Oxford dons. My brother's an old rowing Blue.'

Cameron emitted a dismissive snort. 'And what does that make you – the village idiot?'

Alan shot Sam an anxious look but all she did was laugh.

'I'd have thought you'd have been proud of him,' she said.

'Well, I left that to his mother.'

Nothing in life is ever simple, Sam thought. 'Can we speak to her?'

'Who?'

'His mother.'

He shrugged. 'Up to you.'

'Is she here now?'

'I should bloody well hope not, we're divorced.'

'Well, could you tell us where we could reach her? Perhaps Harry's with her.'

'All too bloody likely. He always was a mummy's boy.'

'How long have you been divorced?'

'None of your business.'

'Did he live with you or his mother?'

'Time for you to leave. I haven't hired you to look for him and I don't have to answer these kinds of questions.' He strode over to the living room door and held it open.

Neither Sam or Alan moved.

'Did you know that Harry had been arrested on suspicion of a serious sexual assault at the end of last term?'

Cameron looked startled. 'You're lying.'

'Didn't he tell you?'

'I don't believe you.'

'You can check with Thames Valley police. Do you think he could have gone missing because of that?'

Cameron didn't say anything.

'Look, something might have happened to Harry. Could you let us know where his mother lives or at least pass on our details to her?'

'Get out.'

As Sam and Alan began to move towards the door Sam said. 'However much you disapprove of what he's doing, you must want to know that he's safe?' As she drew level with him she handed him her card and when he refused to take it she threw it down on a table near the door.

Alan and Sam stood on the pavement outside the house.

'It's ironic, isn't it?' Sam said, zipping up her fleece. 'That man would prefer to have a son who left school at sixteen, who's shagging everything in sight and earning shitloads of money. Instead he's got a son who's at Oxford studying theology and probably going to get a Blue and become a priest and he disapproves of all of it.'

Alan ducked his chin into the collar of his coat. 'How much do you think a house like this in Barnes is worth?'

'Chelsea footballers live here, don't they? Says it all.'

'So he's rolling in it?'

Sam nodded.

They began walking to where Alan's car was parked. 'No photos of Harry. Did you notice?'

Sam shook her head. 'No, I didn't. What about all those ones on the mantelpiece?'

'None of him.'

'So, who could we talk to who'd know where Harry's mum lives?'

'The kid rowed at school, right?'

Sam nodded.

'Well, maybe his teachers or rowing coach would know something. Didn't Tom King mention an Eric Stiles?'

'Good idea,' Sam said. 'Also could you check out whether Cameron reported a burglary? Maybe that's got something to do with Harry. Maybe he knew his dad was away and broke in.'

'Surely he'd have a key?'

'The man doesn't seem on such good terms with his son, does he? Maybe they argued. Maybe Harry stole something...'

'Harry seems an unlikely thief.'

'I know, but we haven't got anything at the moment, Alan, other than an accusation of sexual assault that makes no sense even to his hostile father, and a broken pane of glass. That's why I'm in the land of the "maybes".'

Back in the office Sam phoned Tom King.

'The guy was not Mr Charm,' Sam said. 'Wouldn't help us at all. Wouldn't even give us the mother's address. Do you know it?'

'No – it was just that address and telephone number we had.'

'I was wondering if you could put me in touch with Eric Stiles. I thought he might be able to fill in a few gaps.'

A few minutes later Tom phoned back with the number.

When Sam rang it, a gruff voice answered, obviously from a mobile, as there was background noise that sounded like an engine. Before she could say anything a voice boomed down the phone. 'Four, you're late on the catch.'

'Mr Stiles, my name's Sam Falconer. I'm a private investigator. Tom King gave me your number.'

'This some sort of joke?'

'No, it isn't.'

'What the hell do you want with me?'

'Harry Cameron's gone missing and I'm trying to track him down. I was hoping I could meet up with you—'

'Four – take your head out of your arse and listen to me. You're LATE.'

Sam winced and moved the receiver away from her ear.

'Harry, you say?'

'Yes. Would it be possible to talk to you?'

'Where are you?'

'In my office near Putney Bridge.'

He barked a short sharp laugh. 'Just going under it now. I'll be off the water in an hour. You want to talk to me, I'll be in the third boathouse up on the left.'

Sam put down the phone and looked across at Alan. His head was resting on his folded arms and soft snores were emanating from the bundle of his arms and head. Sam picked up a piece of

99

paper, groaned and put it on another pile then picked up the next . . .

An hour later, having left Alan still snoring at his desk, Sam ducked into the bottom of the boathouse Stiles had mentioned. There was no one there. She walked to the back and shouted up the stairs. 'Hello there.'

A voice shouted. 'Come on up.'

Upstairs Eric Stiles was sitting, rubbing oil over a small metal strut. He stood up as Sam reached the top of the stairs and wiped his hands on a dirty rag. He was a short, wiry man with white, wavy hair, chewing gum with the ferocity of Alex Ferguson on the touchline. A scar ran from under his left eyebrow straight up to his hairline, cutting through the furrows of a deeply lined forehead. Next to his chair stood some rubber boots; a pair of blue and white flecked fishermen's socks were draped across the top of them. His feet were bare with blue veins burrowing their way under the surface of exceptionally white hairless skin.

'Take a seat,' he said, gesturing to the chair opposite him. 'Sorry I was a bit short on the phone.' He pointed to his chewing mouth. 'Trying to quit.'

Sam nodded sympathetically. 'How many were you on?'

'Twenty or thirty – depending on the day. Doctor told me I had to, so now I'm chewing gum and covered in patches but there's still these.' He held out a leathery pair of hands. 'No one tells you what the hell you're supposed to do with them.' A brutal, racking cough stopped him talking and brought tears to his eyes.

Sam nodded at the cloth he'd picked up again. 'Stripping down the boats should keep you busy.'

He nodded. 'So what's this you were saying about Harry? Gone missing?'

'Yes.'

'And how can I help you?'

'Could you tell me a bit about him?'

'Fantastic rower. Best boy I ever trained. Absolute natural talent. Like God had designed him for it. The right physique, the right attitude. He's an incredible natural athlete *and* he worked at it. Took nothing for granted. That's what you want as a coach, talent combined with hard work, and that's what I got with Harry.

It's a once-in-a-lifetime thing. If you get one in your coaching career you're lucky. You just have to hope you handle them right. It's a big responsibility.'

Sam nodded. 'Tom King said much the same thing.'

'I phoned Tom before Harry arrived in Oxford and had a word with him about the boy. Told him he didn't need pushing because he did that himself. If anything, he needed to be calmed down sometimes. King spoke to me at the end of last term and told me how he was doing. I appreciated it. You know, sometimes it's hard to let the real gems go, but I had him from the age of thirteen. I was lucky. We won everything we entered.'

'Was the Boat Race important to him?'

'He was obsessed with it, knew all the statistics. We used to tease him that he should go on *Mastermind* and have it as his specialist subject. He knew I'd competed in the race. Used to ask me about it all the time.'

Sam frowned. 'You competed in the race?' She'd have thought Stiles was much too short.

'Cox.'

'Ah.'

'It's how I got this.' He ran a finger along the line of the scar. 'The eights clashed and their stroke caught me with his blade.'

'Ouch.'

'I was taken to the hospital after the race with concussion.'

'Did you win?'

A slow smile formed across his face. 'Oh yes.' He rubbed one foot with the toes of the other.

'Have you any idea where Harry might be? We spoke to his father, who was obstructive rather than anything else. He wouldn't even give us details of Harry's mother. Wouldn't tell us much, really.'

'That man! The boy didn't deserve him, I tell you. Didn't want him rowing at all. Couldn't see the point of it, he said. Wouldn't pay anything towards the costs of it. And he's rich as Croesus. Some big-shot antiques dealer who started out working for one of the large auction houses. I went over there one time, to that big pile in Barnes, to try and get some money out of him for kit for the boy and to pay for him to travel to the schoolboy World Championships. Wouldn't give anything. Not one penny. I couldn't believe it. Ended up having an almighty row with him. I told him he didn't know what he had on his hands with Harry. He told me not to tell him about his own son and then the whole thing descended into a slanging match.'

'Much the same happened with us,' Sam said.

The last of the evening light was filtering through from the windows at the front of the boathouse. Sam stood up, walked over to the windows and looked down onto the river.

'Sometimes family support doesn't matter,' she said. 'It can make you even more determined to succeed. Having the right team around you is what matters.'

'Was that how it was for you?'

Sam was surprised. 'Sorry?'

'I'm a black belt. A friend's son was competing in the European Championships in Prague in 1998. I saw you fighting in the final.'

'Christ,' Sam groaned. 'I lost.'

'You dislocated your shoulder.'

'And then I lost.'

'I sometimes use the film of your fights to motivate my crews. I ask them how much they want it, do they want it as much as you did?'

Sam's face was stony. 'You use my failure to motivate them?'

'No, I use your fighting spirit to motivate them, your desire to win. You refused to accept you were beaten. You got up and tried to continue.'

'And failed,' Sam said drily.

'There are defeats more triumphant than victories.'

'You don't tell that rubbish to your crews, do you?'

He laughed. 'In Berlin in 1992 you won the World Championships with a fractured leg. I show them that one as well. You still fight?'

Sam rotated her right shoulder and shook her head. 'It kept popping out. Prague was the end of the road for me.'

'Find it hard to quit?'

Sam thought of her blue *judogi* hanging in her wardrobe. The one she'd been wearing when she first became World Champion at the age of twenty. The one the moths would be tearing into soon. She had an image of the suit, empty of her body, fighting invisible opponents. Grief rose up in her stomach. The suit twisted and turned and threw. She could feel the texture of the suit in her hands. She knew she should get rid of it. Next time she was in Oxford she'd visit Tyler, her old coach. Maybe he could suggest someone she could give it to. She sighed. 'Still coming to terms with it.'

'How long ago did you retire?'

'Three or four years now.'

'Give yourself time. It gets easier.'

'It better had.'

'Is there anything else I can tell you about Harry?'

'What was his family situation?'

'His parents divorced when he was in his early teens. He had been a dayboy but at that point he became a boarder. Boarding school can be good for the ones from broken homes because they don't have to deal with all the aggro on a day-to-day basis. It can get tricky in the holidays but—'

'Who got custody?'

'Well, that was the thing – the father did. The mother had health problems. Heart, I think it was – and she was always a very fragile person. She was in and out of hospital for a while. So he got them.'

'There were other siblings then?'

'No, just Harry and David.'

'David?'

'Yes, just the twins.'

'Sorry?'

Eric looked up from the metal strut he was holding. 'Harry has a twin brother David.'

'You're joking?'

'You didn't know?'

Sam shook her head. 'No one's mentioned a twin.'

Eric shrugged. 'Well, he's got one.'

'Did they go to the same school?'

'No. David didn't pass the eleven-plus and there were rumours that he was always getting into trouble at school.'

'What sort of twins were they?'

'Oh, identical, apparently. I heard it was impossible to tell them apart. I was always telling Harry he should get his brother to row but he said David wasn't interested in anything like that. That he couldn't see the point of it.'

'Why do you think no one knows about him?'

Eric shrugged. 'Maybe they weren't that close.'

Sam thought about the missed tutorial and wondered if David had had anything to do with that. If he'd had anything to do with the rape.

'So you never met his brother?'

Eric shook his head.

'Do you know where their mother lives?'

'Grace? She lives in one of the boats moored against Cheyne Walk. She's a nice woman. A bit alternative, if you know what I mean, but nice. She used to come and watch Harry row. At least she showed an interest. Very non-pushy. She said the great thing was that he was happy doing it. That's what she wanted for him.'

'Is that down by Chelsea Wharf?'

'Yes, that's right. Her boat's the wooden one tucked practically under Battersea Bridge.'

'Do you think he could be with her?'

'Maybe – her more likely than the father.'

'Thank you,' Sam said. 'You've been really helpful.'

'Will you let me know if you find him? Let me know that everything's all right?'

'Of course.'

He stood up to shake hands with her.

'Have you ever thought of coxing? You're the right size and every now and again I need someone.'

She shook her head. 'Too cold for me.'

'In the summer it's beautiful. The early mornings on the river – you can't beat it. The peace and quiet ...'

'Yeah, right.' Then Sam shouted as loudly as she could: 'Four! Pull your head out of your arse.'

Eric laughed and looked down at his feet. 'It's the fags speaking, or rather the lack of them. Get in touch if you change your mind.'

'My brother was a rowing Blue. He used to say: "Show me a first-class oarsman and I'll show you a first-class lunatic."'

Eric laughed. 'I wouldn't deny it. But you could apply that to any sport. To get really good you've got to be obsessive. You could apply it to judo.'

Sam nodded and started down the steps. Prague! She'd been so full of adrenaline she hadn't really felt the dislocation. Tyler had

had to pull her off the mat. She'd screamed at him and insisted she could keep going but he'd told her she couldn't. She'd pushed him away with her good arm and insisted on going back onto the mat to bow to her opponent. Only then had she dropped to her knees, clutching her shoulder, teeth clenched in agony. And, although she hadn't known it at the time, that had been the end of her competitive career.

She stood on Putney Bridge. Even though she had ambiguous feelings about Oxford she liked to think that the water flowing under this bridge had flowed under Magdalen Bridge further upstream. It was sentimental but she liked that link to her old home. The tide was out and herons were fishing in the shallows. A sleek head flashed towards the water and came up with something silver and wriggling. What was it with the English that they turned failures into heroes? Sam was no Eddie the Eagle. She despised such thinking. She saw nothing to admire in her loss in Prague. She'd been careless and that was it, her career was over. All because of one stupid mistake. Sam's sporting heroes were the likes of John McEnroe, Roy Keane, Steve Waugh and Martin Johnson – all of them winners, all of them ferocious competitors.

She looked back down at the water and shivered. Deep water still terrified her. Ever since her father had thrown her in the water, she'd refused to go near it. As a child she'd had a panic attack the first time she'd had a swimming lesson at school. Her mother had taken her to the doctor, who had diagnosed an asthmatic condition triggered by an allergy to chlorine. Sam had known it wasn't that but didn't care as long as she could skip the lessons. Jean hadn't pried, it wasn't her style and perhaps she'd suspected something she didn't want to be told. Sam had been too embarrassed to tell Eric but there was no way she'd ever be a cox.

She looked up at her office window. No lights were on. Alan was probably long gone and sleeping off his five-thirty start. Sam dug her chin into her scarf and headed for home.

CHAPTER EIGHT

The following morning Sam paced up and down her flat waiting until it was nine-thirty before phoning Alan.

'Sorry, did I wake you?' she said disingenuously.

'Oh God, woman, what the hell is it? Can't you let a man get his rest?'

She laughed. 'Sorry, Alan, I spoke to Eric Stiles, Harry's rowing coach, yesterday and I need you to find out something for me. Apparently Harry's got an identical twin brother called David.'

'Is this one of your sick jokes? Let's wind up Alan when he's barely awake?'

'No, I'm afraid not. Eric wasn't certain but he suggested David had been in trouble at school. It's a bit of a long shot but could you see if he's got a criminal record? Maybe he attacked the woman in Oxford. It would explain why she was so adamant it was Harry.'

'Why wouldn't Harry have told the police?'

'Loyalty. He'd have landed his brother straight in it.'

'OK, I'll see what I can rustle up.'

'Also you were going to check to see if Cameron reported a burglary.'

'I know I was,' Alan said. 'And I would have done if I hadn't been forced out of my bed at five-thirty yesterday morning and had to stand in the freezing fog watching a group of antiques dealers tearing at piles of jewellery like a pack of jackals.'

Before Sam could reply he slammed down the phone. She had forgotten how grumpy he could be when he didn't get enough sleep.

*

The weather forecasters had finally got it right – the snow had melted away during the night. From the top deck of the number 22, Sam stared at the wet black pavements and mourned the snow's passing. What with the dire warnings of global warming, she wondered if that was the last heavy fall of snow she'd ever see in London. It was bright today. A brisk wind had torn up the clouds and was blowing them swiftly across a startlingly blue sky. Sam got off the bus at the top of Beaufort Street and walked down towards the river. She crossed Cheyne Walk and leaned on the parapet of Battersea Bridge, looking along the line of boats moored between the bridge and Chelsea Wharf. The pagoda-like roof of Chelsea Tower was gleaming golden in the sun. A helicopter buzzed over Sam's head, its engine barely audible above the roar of traffic from the bridge behind her.

Sam looked down onto the creosoted roof of a dark brown wooden boat. Smoke was pouring from a metal chimney and being picked up by the wind and whisked along under the bridge. The tide was out and the boats looked forlorn and stranded on their flat bottoms. String slapping against masts and ragged flags and pennants flapping in the wind reminded Sam of seaside ports and childhood holidays in Cornwall, as did the seagulls mewing and wheeling overhead.

Her train of thought was interrupted by a woman coming out onto the deck of the boat carrying a red gas canister, which she placed carefully alongside four others. She was dressed in a crimson chunky-knit cardigan with a huge golden sun on the back; loose black cotton trousers flapped against the top of her Doc Martens boots. Her long blonde hair whipped around her shoulders and she swept it away and looked up at the sky. For a moment she closed her eyes, angling her face towards the sun and Sam saw her features in repose. She was a striking woman, statuesque with fine cheekbones and a good strong jaw. Harry had obviously taken after his mother. As Sam was observing her, the woman opened her eyes, looked directly up at Sam and smiled.

'Could I have a word?' Sam shouted.

The woman nodded and pointed to the gate and a series of green painted walkways that led from the street to her boat. Sam made her way along them and stepped onto the wooden deck of the boat.

'My name's Sam Falconer. I'm a private investigator and I've been asked by the Oxford University Boat Club to look into the whereabouts of your son, Harry.'

She frowned. 'I don't understand. I thought he was at college. The term's just started, hasn't it?'

'It has, but he's not there – he disappeared a week ago from the OUBC trials at Putney and he hasn't turned up at college.'

Grace Cameron didn't seem very concerned. 'Maybe he's gone off on one of his walks.'

'Walks?'

'He does it periodically. Pilgrimages, he calls them. Do you know my son, Sam?'

'No, I've not met him.'

'He's an extraordinary boy. Always was – completely unlike other children. He's always been profoundly spiritual and he wasn't brought up that way. His father . . .'

'I've met him,' Sam said.

She smiled. 'Ah, well, then you'll understand.'

'He definitely seemed more interested in mammon.'

'Yes,' she said. She seemed about to say something else but then changed her mind. 'Would you like some tea?'

Sam nodded and followed her into the boat. The living room was on the top of the boat, filled with two large squashy sofas with floral covers, wicker chairs and side tables and a multitude of plants – palms, weeping figs and a couple of exuberant spider plants in severe need of contraceptive advice. Steps led down to the lower level of the boat, where there was an open kitchen area and Sam presumed the bedrooms. Grace picked a newspaper off a chair and dropped it onto the table and gestured to Sam to sit down. Then she cleared the table of several dirty plates and cups, dumped them in the sink and switched on the kettle.

'I won't be a second,' Grace said and walked through to the front of the boat.

Sam pulled the paper Grace had placed on the table, the *Antiques Gazette*, towards her. What attracted her attention wasn't the headline but what the paper had been covering, a tray of jewellery. Even Sam, who knew nothing about jewellery, could see that this was extraordinary. One particular piece caught her eye. It was a curved triangular gold brooch on which three enamelled goldfish swam among engraved water plants; it was inset with two blood-red stones. She realised that something she had taken as a casual gesture, the picking of a paper off a chair, hadn't been. Grace had been intending to cover these up. Quickly she put the paper back over the tray.

Grace returned, threw two tea bags into a bright red teapot and followed them with boiling water.

'So, Grace, when was the last time you saw Harry?' Sam asked.

'He spent Christmas with me. His father went abroad. I wasn't expecting to see him after the trials because he said he'd go straight from there to Oxford. He wanted a few days to do some reading before term began.'

'How did he seem the last time you saw him?'

'Oh, his usual self. He's a very cheerful boy. When you have such faith, such certainty, it helps. I envy him.'

'I've spoken to Eric Stiles.'

'Oh, isn't he a nice man? He was so good for Harry. He realised it wasn't just a sport for him. It was about something much bigger.'

No, Sam thought. It's never just about the sport. 'So when he goes on these "pilgrimages" how long is it usually before he turns up again?'

Grace shrugged. 'The longest time he was missing – I think was about ten days.'

'Does he visit particular places – religious sites . . .?'

She laughed. 'He says he goes where God guides him.'

'Could he be with David?'

'Oh, I don't think so, no. Do you have milk and sugar?'

'Just milk.'

Grace put the cups and teapot on the table, poured the milk into the cups and shook the teapot from side to side before pouring out the tea. 'What you have to realise about my son is that the rowing, the studying, all of that's nothing to him. His life is about God and it has been since he was little. Everything else is of little significance. And it's growing stronger in him.'

'So you're not worried about his absence?'

She closed both hands around her cup. 'Do you think I should be, Sam?'

'I don't really know. Tom King, the OUBC coach is. He said

Harry was so motivated to be in the Blue Boat that he just couldn't understand him walking out with only a day of training left, and without telling anyone anything. But if he has a history of disappearing then maybe there's no cause for alarm. Did he tell you about what happened at the end of last term?'

Grace looked puzzled. 'No.'

'Apparently there was a case of mistaken identity. A woman accused him of date rape. But he had an alibi.'

'Harry!' She laughed. 'That's ridiculous.'

'So he didn't mention it?'

She shook her head.

'I was wondering if Harry could have been having some difficulties with David. Do you think David could have followed him to Oxford, for example? If it was David the girl had seen that would make sense of it.'

'Oh, God . . .' Grace leaned her elbows on the table and put her face in her hands; her hair fell forward, covering both hands and face. 'Poor Harry . . .' She was silent for a few seconds before sweeping her hair back. 'You so hope that it's all over, and then when it starts again . . .'

'What's over?'

'The worry, I suppose . . .'

Sam waited for her to continue but she didn't.

'Are you in the same line of business as your ex-husband?'

'Yes, we're both antiques dealers. David's been round the markets with us since he was little. It's a shame he won't stick with it, because he has a good eye.'

'Do you know if David visited Harry in Oxford last term?'

'No.'

'Would Harry have told you?'

'Not necessarily. He's very protective of me. There are times when I'm more robust than others. Recently, I . . .' She petered off. 'I've not been well . . . not at my best. He might well have kept things from me that he thought might upset me.'

'Does Harry have any particularly favourite places that he visits when he goes wandering?'

'I'm sorry I really don't know. He never says. He always tells me not to worry and that he'll be back before long.'

'Could I look at the room he uses when he stays with you?'

'Of course. It's that one there.' She pointed to a door at the front of the boat. 'What are you looking for?'

'Anything that might give us an idea where he is.'

The room was cramped and would have been exceptionally small for a man over six feet in height. On the side table was a Bible. Sam sat on the bed and flicked through it. There was a yellow Post-it note sticking out of the book and she turned to the page it was marking. Genesis 4 – the story of Cain and Abel. Sam knew the story, or thought she did. She read through the chapter.

Abel became a shepherd, but Cain was a farmer. After some time, Cain brought some of his harvest and gave it as an offering to the Lord. Then Abel brought the first lamb born to one of his sheep, killed it, and gave the best parts of it as an offering. The Lord was pleased with Abel and his offering, but he rejected Cain and his offering.

Sam felt sorry for Cain. What was the matter with his harvest? What were you supposed to offer God if you were a farmer? Also God was pleased with Abel, but that didn't stop him being murdered by his brother. So, if God were pleased with you, you'd be murdered and if he wasn't you'd go through life with a mark on you that meant no one would kill you. Basically, it didn't add up. All in all, it seemed to Sam that the God of the Old Testament was a tricky fellow. The following sentences had been underlined:

Your brother's blood is crying out to me from the ground, like a voice calling for revenge ... You will be a homeless wanderer on the earth ... Cain went away from the Lord's presence and lived in a land called 'Wandering', which is east of Eden.

Sam closed the book, put it back on the bedside table and remembered a verse from *King Lear* that Mark had a tendency to quote: *As flies to wanton boys, are we to the gods; They kill us for their sport.* Yes, Sam thought, that made more sense of it. She opened a cupboard. A green fleece was the only thing hanging there. She unzipped the pockets and found a white packet of matches with a black line drawing of the Mad Hatter from *Alice in*

Wonderland. She turned it over and read the address: *The Mad Hatter Cocktail Bar – 23, Walton Street, Oxford.* She put it in her own pocket, picked up the Bible and walked back to the kitchen.

'He's underlined these passages,' Sam said.

Grace took the Bible from her and looked at them. 'It doesn't particularly surprise me. Harry was always interested in brothers – brothers in the Bible and literature and real life. They look exactly alike. It's quite uncanny. And yet they are so different. It's been hard for Harry. For both of them.'

'Disturbing, I would think.'

'Yes. Will you let me know if he turns up?'

'Of course. Is David staying with you?'

She shook her head. 'They were both here at Christmas. We had a lovely Christmas.' Suddenly she put her face in her hands and began to weep.

Sam waited until Grace had regained her composure. 'Do you know where David is now?'

'Sometimes he turns up here. I keep clothes for him. He's not at his father's at the moment?'

'I suppose he might have been. Your ex-husband wasn't exactly forthcoming.'

She smiled. 'No, that's not his style I'm afraid.'

'Anywhere else he could be? At friends?'

Grace's eyes filled with tears again and she shook her head.

As Sam stood up to go, there was a noise from the front of the boat. She stopped and turned her head in that direction and then looked back at Grace.

'It's the boat moving against the moorings,' Grace explained. 'At high tide it floats free from the riverbed and when the wind gets up it grinds against the mooring posts.'

Perhaps, Sam thought. But what it had sounded like was someone moving around behind the closed door.

Grace followed Sam upstairs and onto the deck. 'You'll get in touch if you find out anything?'

Sam nodded.

'Do you have children?'

Sam shook her head.

'A blessing and a curse,' Grace said.

'Harry being the blessing and David the curse?'

'I try not to look at it in that way.'

Sam shook hands with Grace and then negotiated the series of walkways to get back onto the bridge. The wind had dropped but the tide was rising, as Grace had said. The curtains of the room at the back of the boat were drawn. Sam waited for a while on the bridge to see if anyone came out of the boat but then, growing bored by the lack of activity, set off up Beaufort Street.

Back in the office Sam phoned Alan again.

'Any luck?'

'David was done for possession,' he said. 'They were going to do him for dealing, which is much more serious, but the father hired a fancy QC who got him off that charge. All the same, he got six months. Came out on November 18. Before that he had the usual sheet you'd associate with a junkie – petty theft, stealing from shops, mugging a kid for a mobile, drunk and disorderly outside a club on the King's Road.'

'Well, that explains the missed tutorial. Was he dealing?'

'Yes, definitely – probably to fund his own habit.'

'Has he got a probation officer?'

'Yup, but apparently he missed their last appointment. He said David wasn't in good shape. He's not surprised he failed to turn up. Drugs are so easily available in prison it's not the place to be if you want to keep clean.'

'So, if he came out before Christmas I suppose he could have decided to give his brother a visit and got himself into some trouble with that girl – and then Harry ends up being mistaken for his brother.'

'Surely Harry would have told the police.'

'It's a tricky situation to be in though, isn't it? Especially if you feel any sense of loyalty towards your brother. If Harry had turned round and said, "Look, I've got an identical twin brother with a criminal record who's just come out of prison", the police would have trotted off and looked for him. If you keep quiet and stick to your story and wait for your alibi to come through then you hold a more neutral position. The police have to find it out for themselves and you buy your brother some time.'

'Poor bloke . . .'

'Which one?'

'Harry. There he is in his first term at university, wanting to impress, and what happens? His brother turns up and starts really fucking things up for him. Suppose he hadn't had an alibi. He'd really be in the shit.'

'Maybe the sexual assault thing was just a taster to bring Harry into line, to get him to do what David wanted. Maybe he was jealous of his brother.'

'But he'd be relying on Harry not to shop him to the police.'

'Perhaps he knows his brother well enough to know he won't do that. Any luck with the burglary at the father's house?'

'He didn't report it.'

'Maybe nothing was stolen.'

'Or maybe something was stolen and he didn't want to tell the police about it. Mr Cameron is also known to the police and not just because of his son.'

'What do you mean?'

'He's got a shop in Camden Passage in Islington. Stolen stuff's turned up there a few times. He's always claimed to know nothing about it and they haven't managed to make anything stick. Also he slapped Grace around a bit before they finally separated. Police were called out a couple of times to the house.'

'Why doesn't that surprise me?'

'He looks the type.'

'Maybe David broke in.'

'Surely he'd have a key.'

'Suppose he wanted to make it look like a burglary. He knew his father was away and he needed some money or wanted to steal something. If he'd just taken it, it would have been obvious who it was, whereas if he broke a window it could be anyone.'

'I can't see his father falling for that kind of thing.'

'No, nor can I.'

'But suppose he stole something from his father that he knew he wouldn't want the police to know about.'

'Something that was already stolen, you mean?'

'Yes.'

After chewing over a few more possibilities Sam ended the call with Alan, spun round in her chair and stared out of the window. Twins: one good, one bad. Both missing. Sam wondered what it would have been like if she and Mark had been twins. The thought didn't bear contemplating. They were as different as you could get: different sex, height, hair colouring, disposition, sexual orientation. When Sam wondered about her capacity to love, she only had to consider her feelings for her brother to know how strongly and deeply she could do it. She knew all about the bone and marrow of love.

She looked again at the photo she had of Harry: the blond hair, the Kirk Douglas cleft and the broad smile. She wondered if he had been in his mother's boat when she was there and if so why he was hiding. She wondered whether either of the boys had been involved with the broken pane of glass in the door that looked out into their father's garden in Barnes. The quotation from Genesis came back to her. *Your brother's blood is crying out to me from the ground.* She wondered if they were both still alive and if so where the hell they were. Sam had liked Grace Cameron but it was clear she'd not wanted to discuss David. Also, she'd been vague to the point of obscurity on a number of points and Sam wasn't sure she could necessarily rely on anything she'd told her.

And then there'd been the jewellery Grace had covered up, the brooch with the three intertwined fish and the blood-red stones.

The phone interrupted her train of thought. It was Mark.

'Sam?' Her brother sounded as if someone had him by the throat.

'What's the matter?' Sam said immediately.

'It's—'

'What is it?'

'He's here . . .'

Sam heard Mark swallow. She was on her feet, her knuckles white against the receiver. 'Mark, for God's sake tell me what the hell's happened.'

'It's Dad—'

'What's he done? Are you all right?'

'He's turned up here.'

'What's he done?' she repeated.

'It's nothing he's done, Sam. It's the fact that he's come here.'

'Has he approached you?'

'Mum's convinced she's seen him out in the garden in Park Town just standing and watching the house.'

'He hasn't approached her?'

'No, nothing like that.'

'Are you all right, Mark?'

'No, I'm not, Sam. I'm not all right at all.'

Sam imagined herself rushing to Victoria coach station, getting on a bus, arriving in Oxford, running across St Barnabas's front quad and up the uneven wooden stairs, banging on Mark's door and throwing her arms around him and never letting go. Bone and marrow – this is what it was all about.

She looked at her watch. 'I'll get there as soon as I can. It'll be all right, Mark.'

'I don't see how it can be,' he said. 'I don't see how it can ever be all right again. Mum's in a terrible state. I've never seen her like it.'

'Mark, listen to me. It's going to be fine. You're not a child any more. He can't hurt you in the way that he did.' She didn't believe what she was saying, was only saying it to reassure him.

'It's the old feelings, Sam. The old feelings get triggered.'

'Oh, Christ.' Sam looked at her watch. 'I should be there in about three hours. We'll go to the pub. We'll talk it all through. Mark?'

'Aha.' He sounded defeated. 'We'll go to the pub . . .'

'Wait for me,' Sam said. 'I promise you, it's all going to be fine.'

Sam put the phone down and stood for a few moments staring at her desk, knowing that was a promise she couldn't possibly keep. Then she picked up the receiver and phoned her godfather, Max. Before, when she'd wanted to get in touch with her father, she'd gone through Max to arrange it.

'Max?'

'Yes.'

'It's Sam. Where is he?'

'Who?'

'Come on, Max. Don't give me that shit,' Sam shouted. 'Who the hell do you think?'

'Calm down.'

'Is he working for you?'

Max coughed. 'I can't—'

'OK, have you seen him – last couple of days? You can tell me that, can't you?'

'No.'

'No, you can't tell me? No, you haven't seen him?'

'Haven't seen him.'

'For how long?'

'Few weeks. Why? What's happened?'

'He's turned up in Oxford. Mark says he's stalking Mum. Why's he doing that, Max?'

Max remained silent.

'OK. Listen. If you speak to him, tell him to cut it out. Mark's really upset.'

'Has he done anything?'

'Terrifying my mother and brother amounts to doing something in my book, Max.'

'But—'

'I have to go.' She slammed down the receiver.

Sam was shaking as she threw on her coat, grabbed her bag and rushed for the door. She should never have met him. Mark was right. This was all her fault. She had put her family in danger and now it was up to her to sort it out. Mark had sounded defeated, devoid of hope. She couldn't bear to hear him sound that way. It terrified her. What had Reg said about that? That Pandora let the Star of Hope out of the box as well as the Spites.

Well, Mark was surrounded by Spites.

Sam jumped as a cyclist, who she'd been about to step out in front of, screamed at the top of his voice and whipped past her. 'Sorry,' she said, but he was already gone in a flash of green helmet and pumping lycra. Her heart was racing as she ran up the steps onto the platform at Putney Bridge station and swore as she saw the destination announcer flashing *Edgware Road – 12 minutes*.

CHAPTER NINE

Sam knocked on the door to Mark's rooms in St Barnabas's and waited. There was no reply. Sweat prickled the surface of her hands. She hammered on the door again and shouted. Oh God, what had happened to him? Why hadn't he waited for her? Still there was no reply, only the noise of a door opening on the staircase below her and a man's voice shouting, 'Please be quiet, I'm trying to teach in here.'

Sam bounded down the stairs. 'I'm sorry,' she said to a fair-haired man with bulbous blue eyes, who looked as if he should be the pupil not the teacher. 'I'm Mark Falconer's sister. Have you any idea where he might be?'

'I passed him in the quad about an hour ago heading towards the lodge.'

'Was he with anyone?'

The man shook his head. 'Please keep the noise down.'

'Sorry.' Sam ran past him down the stairs and out into the quad. At the lodge she asked the porter, a solemn young man with the reverse triangle-shaped face of a Vladimir Putin, if Mark had left her a message and was told that he hadn't

Sam stepped out into the Turl. What should she do now? There was no point in getting the porter to let her into Mark's rooms, because he'd been seen leaving the college. Sam's mind was filling up with images of Mark – all involving him being in trouble. She ran through the conversation she'd had with him on the phone and felt panic rising. She was trying to wrestle herself into a somewhat calmer state and failing hopelessly when her mobile rang. She fumbled in her bag for it and snapped, 'Hello?'

'It's Jackie.'

Sam put her fist to her forehead and screamed silently into the street.

'I was phoning about tomorrow.'

Sam had completely forgotten. Alan had done the market during the week. She was down for Portobello – tomorrow morning. 'I'm sorry, something's come up at my end and I'm not going to be able to make it.'

On the other end of the phone, Jackie maintained a resolute, emotionally blackmailing silence. Sam's mother had a tendency to do this and it always pissed her off. The best response was to meet silence with silence but that took more patience than Sam had today.

'Are you there?' Sam shouted. 'I can't hear you.'

'We had a deal.'

'I know, it's just I can't do it. I've been called out of town on an emergency. I'm sure Alan will be able to. I'll phone him and get him to call you.'

'The deal was with you.'

'Look, Alan came with you before and it was perfectly fine. Do you want me to ask him? Otherwise I won't waste my time making the call.'

Silence again.

Oh, fuck that, Sam thought, and cut her off. She left the phone on and waited. It rang again almost immediately.

'Oh, hello,' Sam said. 'Did you cut me off?'

'Make the call,' Jackie said.

'Fine.'

Sam phoned Alan with her fingers crossed.

'Now look, Alan, don't be angry,' she began.

'Why should I be angry?'

'I'm in Oxford.'

'So.'

'Jackie's in Fulham.'

'Yes.'

'She wants protection in Portobello tomorrow morning at five-thirty.'

'No.'

'Please, Alan.'

'I'm going out – it's Simon's birthday.'

'I'm really sorry, Alan, but something came up in Oxford. I had to come here – it's Mark.'

'Listen to me, Sam. I'm not getting up at five-thirty on a Saturday morning. I've only just recovered from last time.'

'Couldn't you just go out and then stay awake until five-thirty, do the thing with Jackie and sleep after that? It'd pay for your night out.'

Alan sighed and said nothing.

'Pleeeeease, Alan. I'll owe you one. Like you said, we might get other work from it.'

'I'll do it – but this is the last Saturday I'll ever do.'

'Fine. No problem. Will you phone her?'

'No. You can phone her and tell her I'll be there.'

'Thanks, Alan,' but the phone had already gone dead in her hand.

Sam phoned Jackie and then stood watching undergraduates locking up their bikes and walking through the main entrance of the college. The smell of over-cooked meat drifted across the quad, indicating that food was being served in hall. She didn't know what to do next. Wait for Mark to come back? Where the hell was he? He'd known that she was coming. Perhaps she should go to her mother's. Almost as soon as she had the thought, she dismissed it. What – turn up at home and be her mother's punch bag? She didn't think so, no. She would need the mediation skills of Mark before she contemplated that course of action. In the meantime she had some time to kill. She looked at the phone in her hand and punched the buttons.

'Phil,' she said. 'It's me. I'm in town – fancy a drink or some supper?'

They had agreed to meet in Brown's in St Giles because the service was quick and the food was reasonable in price and always reliable. Sam was already seated when Phil arrived. He looked in pretty good nick, Sam thought, watching him walk towards her – thinner, not so blurred round the edges, altogether more sharply defined. His hair was longer than last time she'd seen him and it softened his features. He wasn't a hard man but the skinhead haircut he often wore could make the gentlest of men look as if they might nut you. Attraction flickered in her, as it always did with Phil. Stop it, she said to herself. Don't pry. Don't ask any questions. Don't mess about with him. You were the one who said you didn't want to get back together. You can't have it both ways.

But she still wished that she could.

She wished they could have had a conversation in which they'd agreed to occasional sex. But they hadn't. Anyway, there was no getting away from the fact that he looked as if someone had taken him in hand. Why was it, Sam thought, that when you suspected someone else of loving them, they immediately became about ten times more attractive? She stood up and kissed him on both cheeks and he took off his leather jacket, slung it on the back of the chair and sat down.

'I've ordered this,' Sam said, tapping the bottle of white wine in front of her.

Phil shook his head. 'Not for me, thanks.'

The waiter came over and Phil ordered a tomato juice.

Sam considered saying something about the drink, or lack of one, and then decided against it. 'You're looking very well,' she said. 'You've lost weight since I saw you last.'

'I've taken up running. I'm working up to the London marathon in the spring. You still looking for Harry Cameron?'

Sam sipped her wine. 'Yes, and I just found out something that I thought might interest you. He's got a brother – identical twin. Did you know that?'

He frowned. 'No, I didn't.'

'His brother's name's David and he's got a record. He was sent down for possession and came out of prison in November and has failed to turn up for the last meeting with his probation officer.'

'Identical?'

'Peas in a pod, apparently.'

'He was out before the assault happened?'

Sam nodded.

'Why didn't Harry tell us, then? It would have let him off the hook.'

'If he tells you, he betrays his brother. Maybe he's loyal to his brother even if the brother doesn't deserve it. If he stays silent you have to work it out for yourself and he gets to feel better about himself.'

'But the brother's record isn't for sexually related crimes?'

'No, that's true, but there's always a first time.'

'Do you know where David is?'

'I don't know where either of them are and nor do their parents, or at any rate if they do they're not letting on.'

Phil grunted.

'The father's a monster and the mother's in bad health. She doesn't seem quite with it. If a small nuclear device went off next to her, she'd probably just turn round and ask you if you said something.'

Phil's phone rang and Sam listened to his side of the conversation. 'Yes . . . yes, I do . . . how bad . . . oh, I see . . .' His eyes fixed on Sam, as if the conversation he was having had something to do with her. 'I've got Sam here, as it happens . . . yes, thanks a lot, George. We'll be right over.' He closed up his phone. 'That was George Ryan at the Red Lion. He says he's got Mark in his bar there and he's completely out of it.'

'What do you mean?'

'Drinking to get drunk.'

'What other reason is there?' Sam said, glancing at Phil's tomato juice.

'No, Sam, this is serious, apparently he's *really* drunk. George was doing him a favour by phoning me. He's worried about him leaving the pub in the condition he's in. He wants me to come and get him.'

'Shit, he hasn't done that in ages.' Sam grabbed her coat, picked up her bag and went to find the waiter to pay.

When she got back to the table, Phil was holding the almost-full bottle of wine. 'What shall we do with this?'

Sam saw a young couple sitting a few tables away, took the bottle from Phil and walked over and put it on their table. They looked up in surprise.

'Enjoy it,' she said.

'That was kind of you,' Phil said as they walked out of the restaurant.

By the time Sam and Phil got to the Red Lion, Mark was folded up in a corner seat like a rag doll. Sam looked at him and remembered what he had said on the phone: *It's the old feelings, Sam. The old feelings get triggered.* Yes, she thought, the fucking feelings. Well, one way to get rid of the feelings was to numb them with alcohol.

'He's a quiet drunk, I'll say that for him,' George said after he'd patted Sam's cheek by way of welcome. 'But the stuff he's put away and the speed . . .' He shook his head. 'He started off gently enough but once the bloke he was drinking with left, he really let rip. Started lining up doubles. I've never seen him drink like that. I don't like to think of him going home alone with that lot inside him.'

'Bloke?' Sam said.

'Yeah, he came in here with some bloke I've never seen before.'

'What did he look like?'

'Short, fair, late fifties, early sixties – ex-con or maybe ex-services. Not the usual type I see him with.'

Fear gripped hold of Sam. She felt the colour drain from her face.

'You all right, love?' George asked.

'Yes, I'm fine. Look, thanks for watching out for him, George. I really appreciate it.'

'Something happen?' George asked. 'Girlfriend trouble? That's usually what gets them into this kind of state.'

In Mark's case it was more likely to be boyfriend trouble but Sam didn't really want to go there with George. Maybe he'd be fine. But maybe he wouldn't. 'Family stuff going on at the moment, George. It's all got too much for him.'

'But not for you, love?'

'Oh well, yes – for me too, George. It just takes people different ways, doesn't it?'

'Want me to order you a cab? You won't get him far walking.'

'Can you drive us?' Sam asked Phil.

He shook his head. 'I'm leaving the car at the station these days because I run into work in the mornings.'

'I'll call a cab,' George said.

'Can we go to your place?' Sam asked Phil. 'I don't want to take him into college like this, people might see him, and I certainly can't take him to my parents.'

Phil sighed. 'Why not?'

'I know this sounds pathetic but last time my mother saw me she slapped me and I haven't spoken to her since.'

He laughed. 'OK – mine it is, then. I just need to make a call.'

Sam watched him walk outside the pub, taking his phone out of his pocket as he went, and wondered who he was talking to.

When the cab came and the driver saw the state Mark was in, he was extremely reluctant to take them, and the fact that Phil was a police officer didn't placate him.

'Someone's sick in my cab, that's a night's earning's down the drain for me and I can't afford it.'

'Might never happen, mate,' Phil said. 'And you might get a big tip for your trouble.'

And Phil had been right on both counts. Mark hadn't stirred, hadn't said a word. He'd allowed himself to be helped into Phil's house and had folded up on the sofa in much the same way as he had in the pub.

Sam and Phil stood looking down at Mark's sleeping form now spread out at their feet. They'd thrown the sofa cushions onto the floor and stretched him out there with a duvet over him and a pillow under his head.

'Do you know what this is about?' Phil asked.

'I'll tell you later. Would you mind watching him for the next hour or so?'

'Come on, Sam! Do I look like a bloody babysitter?'

'No, of course not, but there's something I need to do. It won't take long.'

'Where the hell are you going?'

'I've got another lead on the brothers I want to follow up. I promise I won't be gone long.'

Phil looked at his watch. 'I'll watch him until eleven. Then you need to be back here. I'm on an early shift tomorrow morning.'

'Thanks a lot.'

Letting herself out of Phil's house into Walton Street, Sam welcomed the cold night air on her face. Mark was safe but she'd get no sense out of him until he was sober. She crossed the road, turned left and walked along past the cinema. Five minutes later she was looking up at the sign bearing the same image as the packet of matches in her pocket – the Mad Hatter. She went down the steps into the basement and pushed open the door. Hot, smoke-filled air caught in her throat. The club was crammed to the gills. Behind a small bar to the left of the door stood a tall man wearing a battered top hat pushed to the back of his large head. He had podgy features and small beady eyes buried inside swollen caves of flesh. A yellow felt waistcoat with mother-of-pearl buttons covered his substantial stomach. On the wall behind the bar, Sam saw an old sepia-coloured photo of a man who looked remarkably similar to the man behind the bar, standing in the doorway of a shop. Across the front of the shop ran the words *Theophilus Carter – Furniture.*

The man looked at Sam briefly before concentrating on the silver cocktail shaker in his hand. As he shook, the inch-long ash on the end of his cigarette broke off and drifted into a glass. He stopped shaking, picked up the glass and blew on the ash until it fluttered out onto the floor. He then poured the white liquid into the same glass, stuck a piece of pineapple onto its rim and threw a cocktail umbrella into the drink, as if he were throwing a dart at a board.

Sam pushed her way to the bar and took out a twenty-pound note. A few minutes later he reached her.

'Yes?' he barked.

Sam, thinking it might be diplomatic to buy something, asked for a margarita.

'Don't know what you're talking about,' he said before moving off to the other end of the bar.

A woman next to Sam giggled and passed her the menu. There wasn't a piña colada or a margarita to be seen. Instead there was a Dormouse, an Alice, a Red Queen, a Tweedledum and Tweedle-dee, a Lion and Unicorn . . .

Sam scoured the list of ingredients for tequila and decided that the Jabberwock With Eyes of Flame was in fact what she wanted, although she was also tempted by the Slithy Tove. She followed the man down to the end of the bar and tried again.

'Jabberwock.'

'Well, why didn't you say so in the first place? How do you want it?'

'What are the choices?'

He sighed. 'Lime, strawberry, on ice . . .?'

'Lime,' Sam said. 'On ice.'

'Salt on the rim?'

She nodded.

'Sure you wouldn't like a Long Hard Screw Against the Wall, love?'

Sam smiled. 'According to this, that's a Dormouse, so he'd probably be short, soft and furry and fall asleep on my shoulder.'

He glared at her and with tremendous theatricality and some violence began to prepare the drink. A few minutes later the corpses of several limes were scattered across the bar and Sam had her cocktail. 'Thanks,' she said as he put it down in front of her. 'I was wondering if you could help me out.'

He flicked a dirty white cloth over his shoulder. 'I doubt it.'

'I'm looking for a friend. I wondered if you'd seen him around.' She showed him the photo of Harry. He took a pair of glasses out of his waistcoat pocket, placed them on his nose and peered at the photo. Not a muscle of his face moved.

'Why d'you want to know?'

'Like I say, he's a mate. Haven't seen him around for a while and I think he used to hang out here.'

'Little young for you, isn't he?' He handed the photo back to her, placed his right hand in an arched position against his waistcoat and said, 'I have never set eyes on him.'

Sam sipped her drink (surprisingly good – extraordinarily cheap) and considered her options: truth, lie, half-lie. The man took a drag on his cigarette, blew the smoke at Sam and wiped the bar cursorily with a cloth.

Sam inhaled and said, 'You're sure you've never seen him?'

The man didn't reply.

'OK, look. I'm a private investigator. He's disappeared and I've been asked by his family to try and find him. They're very worried about him, so anything you could tell me would be welcome.'

The Mad Hatter leaned across the bar. 'Never – seen – him – before.' He flicked her glass with a long, nicotine-stained fingernail. 'Which of those words don't you understand? Now drink up and piss off.'

'All right, all right.' Sam made calming gestures with her hand. She drained her glass and then under the pretence of needing the toilet walked deeper into the club. In the Ladies a girl with spiky, dyed black hair was wiping the mascara from under her eyes. Sam showed her the photo and received an apologetic shake of the head and a shrug.

'Man behind the bar wasn't very helpful,' Sam said.

'Ever since the end of last term, the police have been crawling all over him. It's bad for his nerves.'

'Why are the police interested in this place?'

'A woman was attacked.'

'What was her name?'

'Siobhan.'

'Siobhan Clarke?'

'Yes, she started the evening here.'

'Were you there that night?'

The girl shook her head.

'Why's this place so popular?'

'Have you seen the size of the drinks?'

Sam nodded. 'Generous proportions.'

'And they're cheap – cheapest cocktails in Oxford by a long way. Students appreciate cheap.'

'Anything else being sold here?'

The girl smiled and began to push her way past Sam.

'Just one more thing. What does Siobhan do?'

'She works behind the bar.'

Sam came out of the toilets and tried a few of the tables with the photo but got no response. She felt a hand on her arm and turned to see the Mad Hatter towering above her. 'Out,' he said, pointing to the door. 'Stop bothering the customers.'

She held up her hands in mock surrender. 'I'm going, I'm going . . .'

He escorted her to the door.

'What's with the Mad Hatter theme anyway?' Sam asked.

He pointed at the old photo behind the bar. 'My great, great grandfather Theophilus Carter – the original Mad Hatter.'

Sam peered at the photo. 'But he sold furniture by the looks of things.'

'Yes, but he wore a hat and . . .' He bent down until his face was level with Sam's and she could smell the onion on his breath and see teeth that any American would have fainted at the sight of. '. . . if I'm anything to go by, he was quite, quite mad.'

The door of the club crashed shut on her heels. The trouble with growing up in an Oxford college, Sam thought as she trudged up the steps to street level and began walking back to Phil's, was that it had given her an unnatural tolerance for rude eccentrics. In fact, the madder they were the more disposed she was to like them.

Sam woke at six the following morning on the sofa in Phil's front room. She swung her feet onto the floor and waggled her neck backwards and forwards, trying to relieve the stiffness. When she opened the curtains a couple of inches light from the street lamp shone through the window, striping Mark's face and the red washing-up bowl sitting on the ground next to his head. It was a long time since she'd watched him sleeping. People talked about the love they experienced for their child being the strongest love they had ever experienced. Well, Sam didn't think she was likely to have children and she reckoned Mark was it for her. He was her strongest love. At any rate, at this point in her life he was. He had never been an angry drunk, not even as a teenager, when God knows there were always enough things to feel angry about. When he got really drunk he just faded away like a ghost. It was like watching someone turn from colour to black and white. There was never any *Sturm und Drang,* no violence or aggression. In that way he was completely unlike Sam.

When Sam drank heavily she turned nasty.

Mark groaned in his sleep and turned over. His hair fell away from his forehead to reveal the mesh of scars on his forehead. Sam felt tears sliding out of her eyes and down her cheeks. Emotion choked her. What had their father wanted with him? Why couldn't he have stayed away? How could you pick up your own son and throw him through a glass cabinet? It was a miracle he hadn't lost his sight on the splintered wood or the broken pieces of glass. It was a miracle he'd grown up so sweet-natured. He was a miracle, really. The miracle groaned, lifted himself onto his elbow and threw up violently into the washing-up bowl. Thank God for that, Sam thought. At least he's not going to choke on his own vomit. He spat, wiped his mouth and then collapsed back onto the cushions. Soon his snores were reverberating around the room. Sam wrinkled her nose as the acidic smell filled the room. She picked up the bowl and dumped the contents in the lavatory, then sluiced the bowl clean and put it back next to him. He had rolled onto his back, so she grabbed hold of his arm and pulled him into the recovery position before going into the kitchen.

She switched on the kettle and opened the fridge to see if there was any milk. She heard someone come into the kitchen and turned. Phil was standing in the doorway yawning.

'You're up early,' Sam said.

Phil tightened the belt of his blue towelling dressing gown. 'I'm due in at seven. Did you manage to get any sleep?'

'Couple of hours. Mark's still sleeping but at least he's been sick.'

'You making some tea?'

Sam nodded. The kettle clicked off and Sam took the cups out of the cupboard above her head. With the familiarity of an ex-partner, Sam began to make them tea. For Phil, she half filled the cup with water, squashed a tea bag against the side of the mug until the water turned almost black, filled it to the brim with milk and stirred three sugars into it. For herself, she put in about a quarter of the amount of milk and no sugar. They stood in silence, inhaling the steam rising from their mugs. Birds were starting to sing in the garden despite the grey misery of the morning.

'Are you going to tell me what you got up to last night?'

'OK, but don't shout.'

Phil put down his cup and folded his arms. 'Would I?'

'Well, yes, you would.'

He smiled.

'I went to the Mad Hatter.'

He rubbed the palm of his hand over his face. 'Oh, for God's sake, Sam.'

'Look, I'm worried about Harry, Phil. What the hell's happened to him?'

'What made you go there?'

Sam took the packet of matches from her pocket and dropped them next to Phil's mug. 'I found these in a coat on his mother's boat.'

'Whose coat?'

'Could have been either of them.'

'What did you find out?'

'Nothing much – the owner's a mad old bastard who doesn't like being asked questions. Siobhan Clarke works behind the bar there.'

Phil nodded. 'I could have told you that.'

'I know, but I fancied sniffing around a bit myself.'

'You should watch yourself there,' Phil said. 'That place doesn't have a good reputation. This case with Siobhan isn't the first that's originated there.'

'I'll bear it in mind.'

'Do you know what got into Mark?' Phil asked.

'My father.'

He frowned. 'What?'

'You know I told you I got that letter?'

He nodded.

'Turns out it was him. I met up with him – it's definitely him. Now Mark says he's been standing outside Mum's house, staring.'

'Christ!'

'And George said Mark was in the pub with someone who sounded like him.'

'Can he handle it?'

Sam shrugged. 'I'm not sure any of us can.'

Phil put down his cup and wrote down a number on a piece of paper. 'You could give him this.'

'What is it?'

'Number of AA.'

Sam snorted. 'He hasn't got a drink problem, Phil. He's got a father problem.'

Phil shrugged. 'Fine – whatever. It's up to you. It may not be appropriate. But he's made himself life-threateningly drunk and you've had to sit up all night with him. He's not a teenager. If that's not a problem for a forty-year-old man, I don't know what is.'

'It's a one-off.'

'Good.'

'You don't think so?'

Phil held up his arms in a gesture of surrender. 'Sam, what the hell do I know? He's not my brother. Give it to him if you think it'll help, don't if you don't. I'm going to get dressed.' He picked up his mug and walked out of the kitchen.

Sam sipped her tea and listened to him moving around upstairs. When she had been going out with him she had always been keen to be off as soon as possible in the morning. The most she'd been able to stand was a weekend (well, one night, to be precise) before she needed to be away from him, needed to be alone. 'For God's sake go,' he used to say, unable to bear her restlessness. 'I'm not stopping you.' Now, standing in his kitchen, listening to him getting ready to leave, she wondered why she'd always been in such a hurry to go and what it was exactly she'd been running away from.

Sam had just finished washing the mugs when Mark appeared in the doorway.

'Well, well,' Sam said. 'The Kraken Awakes.'

He moved cautiously towards the table and sat down, hugging his stomach.

Phil appeared in the doorway dressed in a blue tracksuit and trainers.

'Morning, Mark.'

Mark didn't reply. He leaned his elbows on the table and put his head in his hands.

'I'm off,' Phil said. 'I'll see you when you're next in town.'

Sam followed Phil to the front door. 'Thanks so much, Phil, you've been great.'

'I'll see you, Sam.' He kissed her on the cheek, adjusted the rucksack on his back and set off jogging towards the centre of town.

Back inside, Mark was still hunched over his stomach like a swan protecting its nest.

'So,' Sam said quietly.

'There's no need to shout.'

'Clean up and I'll take you to the market for breakfast.'

Mark stood up, clamped his hand over his mouth and rushed out of the room.

An hour later, Mark, still looking ashen-faced, sat opposite Sam in a café in the covered market. They had walked. Sam told Mark it would do him good and the truth was it had brought a bit of colour back into his cheeks. Mark sat staring at a full cooked breakfast as if the sausage was holding a knife and might jump off the plate and stab him. Sam was tucking into hers. Mark picked up a heavily sugared cup of tea and sipped cautiously. Smoke from the two men sitting at the next table drifted over them.

Sam looked at him. 'Come on, Mark, at least try to eat. You know it'll make you feel better.'

Mark picked up his knife and fork, poised them over the plate as if he was about to engage them with the food but then swallowed and dropped them on the table.

Sam reached for the tomato ketchup bottle and squeezed some onto the side of her plate.

'So,' she said, 'do you want to tell me what happened?'

Mark shook his head.

'George said you were drinking with someone. Was it Dad?'

Mark didn't say anything.

'What did he want?'

Mark picked up his tea, raised it to his lips, winced as the smell hit his nostrils and put it back down again.

'Mark?' Sam's tone was sharper.

He looked up at her. 'Forgiveness.'

'What?'

'He asked for my forgiveness.'

Sam reached out and touched her brother's hand.

'In a way it was the worst thing he could possibly have said to me. After he'd gone I just sat there thinking how impossible it was, that I ought to be able to, but I couldn't. I've never felt more hopeless in my entire life.'

'How dare he?' Sam said. 'How dare he play games with you like that?'

'But what if he means it, Sam?'

'He has no right to ask that of you. He can't just absolve himself of what he did by throwing the onus onto you to forgive him.'

Mark didn't say anything. He just sat there, hunched over and miserable.

'Do you think you should talk to someone else about this?' Sam said.

Mark didn't reply.

'I've started seeing someone.'

Mark looked puzzled. 'Phil? Is that why we were at his place?'

Sam laughed. 'No – what I mean is . . . well, I've started seeing a therapist.'

The look on Mark's face was one of complete and utter amazement.

Sam blushed. 'Oh, come on – it's not that much of a shock, is it?'

'Well, excuse me, yes it bloody is.' He groaned and grabbed his head.

'I know pot and kettle come to mind, Mark, but the truth is I changed my mind.' This actually wasn't quite true. She'd started getting terrible headaches and flashbacks, she'd felt as if she was disintegrating and *then* she'd changed her mind, but . . .

Mark was still shaking his head in disbelief. 'Well, good for you.'

'And you?'

'And me what?'

'Are you still seeing someone?'

'You put O'Connor in prison, if you remember.'

'Well, that's true, but there must be others. The whole of North Oxford is hopping with therapists.'

'Well, I'm not, Sam, no.'

'Don't you think—?'

Mark cut across her. 'I don't want to talk about it, Sam. Not now.'

'Well, fine,' Sam said. 'But I spent last night watching over you to make sure you didn't choke on your own vomit. If that's not a cry for help I don't know what is.'

'I just went out and got drunk, Sam. Isn't a man allowed to do that without having a whole load of cod psychology flung at him by his younger sister who has always been completely resistant to any sort of self-analysis but has now undergone some fucking conversion on the road to fucking Damascus and is lecturing me about it?' The volume of his voice rose steadily while he was speaking; by the time he hit Damascus he was shouting.

Sam looked around and saw that everyone in the café was staring at them. She stabbed at a chip with her fork and poked it savagely into the puddle of tomato sauce on the side of her plate. They were silent for a while until the babble of voices had resumed. Sam finished her breakfast and Mark watched her. The silence was broken by both of them starting to speak at once.

'Sorry,' Sam said.

Mark spread both hands flat on the red formica table top. 'Look, Sam. I'm glad you're seeing someone. It's not that—'

'No, I know.'

'It's just you've always been so anti—'

'Yes, I know.'

'So, you, telling me to see someone—'

'Yes?'

'Well, it just really pisses me off.'

'I understand.'

'And also, I don't know if it does any good. Dredging over the past, bringing it all back, feeling the fucking feelings. What good does it do in the end? It just makes me feel terrible all over again and, you know, now there's this research that's been done after September 11 and they're saying that repression of memory and traumatic events might be better for you than reliving it. That you actually get over it faster.'

'I know, I saw that. Stiff upper lip is best. Mum would approve of that.'

'So how the fuck do you know what the best thing to do is?'

'But hangovers make you feel terrible as well.'

Mark ignored her comment. 'Do you like him or her?'

'Reg? Yes he's OK. He's an ex-Para, he fought at Goose Green.'

Mark laughed. 'You giving him hell?'

'I don't know why everyone automatically assumes that.'

'I wonder.' Mark picked up his knife and fork again. 'Maybe I'll give this a go. The tea's settled my stomach a bit.'

In the short walk from the market to St Barnabas's, Sam updated Mark about David and also her visit to the Mad Hatter. Half an hour later Sam was sitting in Mark's rooms in college listening to him splashing around in the bath when the phone on his desk rang.

'Will you get it?' Mark shouted.

Sam picked up the phone. 'Hello, Mark Falconer's phone.'

There was a pause. 'Is that you, Sam?'

Oh God, it was her mother. 'Oh,' Sam said.

'Is Mark there?'

'He's in the bath.'

Silence.

She heard her mother swallow. 'You know that your father's been here?'

'Yes, Mark told me – that's why I'm down.'

'I see.'

Sam heard the tremor in her mother's voice and, despite the slap, despite her mother and her never having really got on, she felt a wave of something that felt uncannily like love or perhaps protectiveness towards her. 'How dare he do this to us?' Sam snapped.

Silence again. Then: 'Why has he come back now, Sam? What do you think he wants?'

He wanted a home from Sam, forgiveness from Mark. God knows what he wanted from Jean. Maybe it was her mother's fear transferring to her down the phone, maybe it was the draught created by Mark opening the bathroom door; whatever it was, Sam felt the hairs rise up on the back of her neck. She didn't know what to say.

'It's Mum,' she said, handing the phone to Mark, who stood with a towel tied round his waist, dripping onto the carpet beside her.

As Mark started to speak to their mother, Sam's mobile rang. She dug in the pocket of her jacket and answered it.

'Sam?' Jackie said.

'Yes.'

'Oh God . . .' She sounded breathless. 'Thank goodness I've managed to get hold of you.'

'What is it? Didn't Alan turn up?'

'No, no, that was fine, he turned up like you said he would. Look, Sam, he's been stabbed.'

'What the hell are you talking about?'

'They've taken him to St Mary's, Paddington.'

'Is he all right? What happened?'

'They came back.'

'Who?'

'The same ones.'

'Where are you?'

'At the hospital but I don't know his details like next-of-kin . . . does he have a wife or—'

'Wife? Of course not,' Sam snapped irritably. 'He's gay.'

'Look – I don't know him. Why should I know that?'

'Spend two seconds with him and I'd think it'd be blindingly obvious he doesn't have a wife.'

'They're operating on him now.'

'Operating?'

'To stop the bleeding.'

'Where's he bleeding from?'

'They stabbed him in the stomach.'

'Oh, Christ, is he going to be all right?

'They haven't said.'

'I'll be there as soon as I can. Are you all right?'

'Yes.'

Sam closed her phone and looked up to see Mark staring at her. She had been so absorbed in the call she'd been having with Jackie that she'd completely forgotten the other conversation taking place between Mark and her mother.

'You're going?' Mark said.

'I have to, Mark. Alan's been stabbed. He's in hospital.'

'How did that happen?'

'We've been looking after this dealer in Portobello—'

'Doesn't he have family?'

Sam didn't understand what he was saying. 'What do you mean? Alan? Yes, eight brothers.'

'Can't they look after him?'

'I'm family too.'

'So am I, Sam. So's Mum. I told her we'd go there this afternoon and discuss what to do about Dad.'

'I'm sorry, Mark, but I can't. I would have, but not now. I have to go. The whole thing is my fault. Don't you see? It should have been me. Alan was doing me a favour. I can't . . .'

Mark turned away from her, walked back into the bathroom and quietly closed the door. Sam would have felt better if he'd slammed it.

CHAPTER TEN

Bert, Alan's brother, stood up and for the third time in the last half hour jangled an enormous amount of change noisily in the pocket of his leather jacket and told Sam he was going to take a stroll outside. Sam nodded. She understood all too well. A stroll outside seemed a damn good idea to her too. No one in his right mind enjoyed hanging around in a hospital. Sam hated hospitals for the simple reason that the last time she'd been in one was when her gran was dying: the smell, the white coats, the sensible, cheerful people. She shuddered. It had been fucking awful, a horrible, undignified death. She drained a can of Coke, scrunched it in two, walked over to a metal bin and threw it noisily inside. When she turned round, a woman was standing in the doorway.

'Are you Alan Knowles's sister?'

'Yes,' Sam lied. 'How is he?'

'Well, we're pleased with how the operation went. The stab wound perforated his intestine. He's lost quite a lot of blood so we'll be keeping him in intensive care, probably for a couple of days.'

'Is he going to be all right?'

'We're very pleased with how the operation went,' the woman repeated.

Why did doctors never answer your questions properly? They relied on you being so grateful that you couldn't bring yourself to be rude. Sam was just about to cast gratitude to the winds and be very rude when Bert came through the door. He saw the doctor and looked terrified.

'It's good news,' Sam said quickly.

The doctor repeated what she'd already said to Sam, told them that they would be able to visit Alan tomorrow and left.

'So the little feller's going to be OK,' Bert said.

Sam smiled. Alan was six foot two and worked out, but he was still little in Bert's eyes, being the youngest of eight extraordinarily burly brothers.

'I need to phone the others. I'll do it outside.' He brandished his mobile. 'These things can fuck up the machines, can't they?'

Sam followed Bert out onto the pavement. It was dark and starting to drizzle. Bert pointed to the pub across the road. 'Pint?'

Sam nodded and under the wing of Bert's arm ran across the road, ducking between the cars and bikes hissing on the wet tarmac.

'What'll it be?' Bert asked when they were inside.

'I'll get them,' Sam said. 'Why don't you start making the calls?'

'OK, love, ta.'

Sam watched him walk over to a table. He was a big man and his gait was more from side to side than forwards. Sam ordered the pints and carried them over to the table where Bert was sitting, talking into his mobile. She put the pint in front of him and sipped from her own.

A man was sitting at the table next to them, wearing what looked like pyjamas and a dressing gown. He was small, about sixty, with thick grey hair sticking out in tufts from his head. He was staring intently at the pint in front of him. He moved a shaking hand towards it and as he picked up the pint, Sam saw the plastic tube taped to the back of his hand. He turned his head sideways, feeling Sam's eyes on him.

He raised the glass to her. 'Don't let the bastards grind you down,' he said and took a big gulp of beer. Sam raised her own glass in reply and then returned her attention to Bert, who appeared to have made his final call and was picking up his pint.

'Cheers,' he said. 'Here's to Little Al.'

Sam lifted her glass a second time.

'Little Al,' the man to her right said, lifting a chaser to his lips.

'Who's he?' Bert asked.

Sam shrugged. 'He's not allowing the bastards to grind him down.'

Bert laughed. 'It's odd, you know, when he was in the police force I was always worried about what might happen to him, especially the areas he was working in, but I never thought he'd get stabbed working for you.'

Sam couldn't hold his eye. She stared at her pint. 'No,' she said eventually. 'Neither did I.'

'What was he doing?'

'Protecting an antiques dealer in Portobello Road.'

Bert shook his head. 'Shit, that complicates things.'

'Why?'

'It's our patch – can't just let that go by.'

The beer was going to Sam's head. She'd come straight up to London from Oxford and gone directly to the hospital. Up to now she'd been so worried about Alan she hadn't felt tired, but now the crisis was over she felt shaky and exhausted and a bit pissed. She also felt guilty as hell.

'It should have been me, Bert,' she blurted out. 'I got called away to Oxford and couldn't do it. He was doing me a favour.'

'Well, he's going to be OK. He's a tough little shit. Always was. Had to be, growing up with us lot.'

'But he didn't want to do it, Bert. Said he was going out. I said he should just stay awake, do it and then sleep it off later. Maybe he was too tired, maybe—'

Bert ran his finger across his top lip. 'Come on, Sammy, he's a grown man. You couldn't make him do something he really didn't want to.'

'We've been short of work since Christmas. We were hoping to get more work on the basis of this one dealer.'

'Was the dealer hurt?'

'No.'

He grunted. 'Well then, maybe you will.'

Sam's mobile rang and she gave Bert an apologetic look and took the call.

It was Grace Cameron. 'I was wondering if I could see you?'

'Sure. Has anything happened?'

There was a pause 'I'd rather not talk on the phone if that's all right. Could you come here? I'm looking after a dog and I can't leave him because he barks all the time and my neighbours complain.'

Sam glanced at her watch. Ten o'clock. 'Can it wait till the morning? It's just a friend of mine's in hospital and to be honest it's been one hell of a day.'

'Of course, tomorrow's fine.'

Sam arranged a time to go over and closed her phone. She picked up her pint and drained it. 'I need to get home.' She got to her feet.

Bert looked up at her. 'I'll stay a bit – maybe they'll let me see him. I'd feel better if I could see him.'

'I'm *so* sorry, Bert.'

'Not your fault, love. Thanks for waiting with me.'

He stood up and hugged her awkwardly but emotionally. Sam inhaled enough smoke-infused leather and aftershave to make her hair stand on end. She'd always liked Bert. He was dodgy, of course, but he wasn't full of bullshit and it was obvious he cared about Alan.

Outside the rain was coming down even harder now. As she stepped out into it, a saying floated into her mind: *Some people walk in the rain, others are rained upon.* Bert would have thought that was pretentious crap, but as she sprinted for the cover of the tube, Sam had to admit that tonight she was definitely the rained upon.

An hour later, Sam knocked on Jackie's door. No answer. She tried again. She was about to give up and go back downstairs when the door opened and a bleary-eyed Jackie stood scowling at her.

'I was asleep.'

'Can I come in?'

'Well, you've woken me up now.' She stood back from the door to allow Sam to enter.

'I've just come from the hospital.'

'How is he?'

'They operated. Seem to think the operation went OK. He lost a lot of blood.'

Jackie ushered Sam into her living room. It was very different to Sam's in that it was clean, uncluttered and not scarred by cat claws. For a second, Sam wondered what it would be like to lead a tidy, minimalist life, including a cream-coloured carpet, but then, deciding her imagination couldn't stretch that far, she turned her attention back to Jackie, who had curled up in a large armchair.

'Could you tell me what happened?'

Jackie yawned. 'I've just done all this with the police.'

'So it should be fresh in your mind.'

'We avoided the car park for obvious reasons. We parked on a meter. They jumped us as we were walking out of Ladbroke Square.'

'Same people?'

'I don't know.'

'Fat men in balaclavas?'

'Yes, I wouldn't be able to identify them.'

'Then what?'

'Alan was carrying my bag.'

'Yes.'

'If he'd handed it over I think it would have been fine. But he decided to put up a fight.'

'It was his job to put up a fight.'

'Next thing, he was doubled over on the pavement and they were sprinting down the road.'

'What did they get?'

'The bag I gave him didn't have much in it.'

'What do you mean?'

'I was carrying most of it in a body belt.'

'Had you told Alan that?'

'No.'

'So he was stabbed protecting something that was worth nothing?'

Jackie held out her hand. 'I know, I know. You don't have to tell me, I should have told him.'

'It's amazing, isn't it,' Sam said, 'how you always seem to land on your feet?'

Exhaustion poured over her; she didn't even have the energy to shout. She stood up and walked to the door. 'Whatever you do, don't tell him,' she said.

'Wait – I didn't pay him.'

Jackie searched in her bag and came up with two fifty-pound notes and handed them to Sam.

Sam took it. 'What's this – blood money?'

'If you don't want it . . .' Jackie reached to take it back.

Sam pocketed the money and made her way down to her own flat.

As she came through the door, Frank threw his flank against her leg and then, howling, followed Sam into the kitchen. She opened a packet of cat food that Edie had brought back from Spain, which she thought was some sort of fish, and watched Frank guzzling it down.

After the cleanliness and order of Jackie's flat Sam felt depressed by her own. It was actually getting beyond a joke. She walked through the flat picking up clothes and bundled them into the washing machine. She then did the same with plates and mugs and dumped those in the sink to soak.

Then she opened the cupboard in the kitchen and looked at the hoover.

And the hoover looked back.

Last time she'd used it there'd been a weird burning smell and it had started to scream.

It had been like a scene from *The Exorcist*.

Sam closed the cupboard door, picked up the broom and decided a little light sweeping was all she was up to. She swept the hall and the front room, trying to get rid of the cat litter, which got stuck between Frank's toes and then scattered throughout the flat.

Alan had been telling her for months that she should get a cleaner. He knew a nice young man, gay, a resting actor, very good-looking, very tactful, who lived locally and needed the money.

'How tactful?' Sam said.

'Very,' Alan said.

'I can't have a gay man looking down my lavatory. I'd die of shame.'

Then she'd told Alan that she felt that she had a moral duty to clean up after herself and it was good for her soul, and he had replied, 'But you don't. You live like a pig.'

'I know,' she said.

And that had been the end of that conversation.

Dust rose from the carpet and caught in the back of Sam's throat; she tried to disentangle the end of the broom from Frank's mighty orange paws, failed and sat down on the sofa. Frank lost interest in the broom and came and climbed onto her lap. He didn't want her to clean either. Exhaustion overwhelmed her. Suddenly she remembered that Gerry hadn't returned her call about the window lock. Weird. Perhaps he was away. The thought flashed across her mind that maybe he'd been involved in some way in her burglary. But then she dismissed it. That was ridiculous, he'd been in the flat and seen there was nothing to take. She closed her eyes. No sign of Harry and no sign of her father. Mark so upset and Alan stabbed. Her head hurt. The plaster on her finger was wet from when she'd poured water into the washing-up bowl. She took off the plaster and looked at the cut – it had closed up. Sam felt disappointed but before she had time to think why, she was asleep.

Mark and Alan are standing side by side. Sam looks down at Mark's stomach and sees a snake protruding from his shirt. She grabs hold of its head and pulls. When she looks up at his face she sees that he has turned into Alan. She pulls harder and a pile of glistening entrails tumbles out of his body onto the ground. Alan doubles over, holding his stomach.

'What have you done to me?' he says.

'But I thought it was a snake,' Sam says. 'It was a snake. I was trying to save you.'

'You've killed me,' Alan says.

As they both look down at the piles of intestines, they transform themselves into a heap of snakes, which begin to slowly slide towards Sam . . . a lime-green one with ruby red eyes detaches itself from the others and begins to climb up Sam's leg. As it reaches her waist, she holds its head in her hands and sees that its eyes are drops of blood; it blinks and the blood rolls out of its eyes into Sam's hands . . .

The following morning, sitting on the top of the number 22 bus as it negotiated the bends of the World's End, Sam thought that under no circumstances would she ever talk to Reg about any dreams that contained snakes. Snakes, she thought, were just too embarrassing and dreams generally were out of the question. She'd phoned the hospital first thing and got a suitably bland, reassuring answer from a tired-sounding nurse. Yes, Alan was OK. Yes, he'd had a good night. Yes, they were pleased with his progress. Sam thought about sending him flowers but then, remembering how quickly the flowers her gran had been sent had died in the stifling heat of the hospital, decided against it. She would bring him something when she visited.

The bus stopped and Sam jumped off and walked down Beaufort Street towards the river. It was hard to believe that only a week ago the snow had been lying thick on the roofs and pavements. Now you could almost smell spring in the air and observe it in the frenzied actions of the pigeons. A thin black cat sloped ahead of Sam as she made her way along the pontoon to Grace's boat and above her head a single magpie screamed a warning from a large plane tree. Nothing like starting the day with a double whammy of bad luck. A man was walking towards her. As he drew level, Sam glanced across and saw that it was Gerry.

'Hi,' she said and they both stopped.

'Oh hi. Sorry, I was miles away. I've been meaning to call you.'

'What are you doing here?'

He pointed to the boat next to Grace's. 'Home sweet home.'

'You live here?'

He nodded. 'How about you?'

Sam pointed to Grace's boat. 'I've come to see Grace.'

'How do you know her?'

'Through work.'

'She's not in by the way. I just tried.'

'That's weird. I'd arranged to meet her.'

'Maybe she's walking the dog. Haven't noticed him barking and he's a yappy thing.'

'When did you last see her?'

He shrugged. 'I saw lights on there last night.' He stretched his arms behind his head and twisted his hair into the back of a green sweater that the moths had obviously enjoyed.

Sam frowned. 'She knew I was coming. I made the appointment last night and she was keen to see me.'

'You want to wait for her? Have some coffee?'

'Aren't you working?'

'Day off,' he said. 'No plans and the whole day ahead of me.'

Sam picked her way across the gangplanks onto Gerry's boat. 'Do you own it?' she asked.

'I'm boat-sitting for a friend. Mind you, have been for the last year.'

'Where is he?'

'Last card I got was from Thailand but that was three months ago. I pay the rent into his account. That way I get somewhere to live and he has the money to travel. With any luck he won't be back for a few years yet.'

The boat was much smaller than Grace's. Grace's had felt spacious and light, a bit like a flat, but this boat was cramped and dark and filled with damp heat from a gas fire. Sam squeezed her way onto the seating behind a fixed wooden table and watched Gerry move his large angular frame elegantly around the small interior spaces of the boat. He opened a tin of Illy coffee and spooned some into a cafetiere. When the coffee was ready, Gerry asked if Sam wanted to take it outside. It was a nice day but chilly. Sam agreed. She didn't like the damp heat of the boat, didn't feel as if she could breathe properly; there wasn't enough light and air.

They sat on deckchairs made of wood and faded navy blue canvas and sipped their coffee. Sam was facing Grace's boat and Gerry was looking along the line of the boats moored against the embankment. A seagull landed between them and strutted backwards and forwards begging for food, its yellow eye snapping from one to the other. In the end, bored with the lack of result, it flew down and landed in the water next to Grace's boat, ducking its head up and down next to a blue plastic bottle that was bumping against the hull.

'So are you an antiques dealer like Grace?' Gerry asked.

'No – her son's gone missing and I've been hired to find him.'

'David?'

Sam frowned. 'No, actually – Harry.'

'So what do you do exactly?'

'I'm a private investigator.'

He didn't say anything but couldn't stop a smile from spreading across his face.

'What?' Sam said.

'No, nothing.' He took out a pouch of tobacco and started a roll-up. Once it was finished he lit it, inhaled and closed his eyes. 'Have you found him?'

'No, not yet.'

'Have you talked to David?'

'No.'

Sam wondered whether she should mention that she could get him cheap tobacco from Edie. Mind you, Edie would probably want him to buy hundreds of pouches at a time.

Sam nodded at his cigarette. 'I know someone who gets that cheap. I can ask her what price she wants for it.'

He shrugged. 'Thanks, but I don't pay full price for it as it is.'

'Well, keep it in mind if your source falls through. She's seventy-nine, lives next door to me and she's always on the look-out. Finding new customers for her is my contribution to Help the Aged.'

Gerry laughed.

The gull was continuing to duck its head under the water near the side of Grace's boat.

Sam frowned. 'I suppose it's ducking for fish, is it?'

A gust of wind swept along the line of boats and the door to Grace's boat crashed back on its hinges and then swung shut.

Sam stood up. 'Are you sure she isn't in? The door's open. Maybe I should—'

Gerry twisted in his chair and looked to where the seagull sat bobbing on the surface of the river. 'Jesus...' He threw his cigarette overboard and jumped to his feet, sending his chair crashing to the ground behind him.

'What?' Sam asked, but he was already sprinting towards Grace's boat. Sam followed him. Gerry lay flat on his stomach and reached into the water at the side of the boat. The gull flew into the air above them with an irritated cry. That was when Sam saw the cloud of blonde hair floating near the surface of the water.

'Shit.' Gerry had let go of the body and was standing up now, staring down into the water. 'Call the police.'

'My phone's in my bag,' Sam said, starting towards Gerry's boat.

He grabbed hold of her arm. 'No, I'll go. Wait here.'

Sam stared into the water and immediately realised why Gerry hadn't tried to get the body out of the water. There was no doubt that Grace Cameron was dead. The back of her head had been smashed like an egg. As Sam was watching, the body rolled over and Sam saw her face – although it could no longer really be described as a face – there were no features left, just red pulp. The seagull landed on it. Sam screamed and as it rose into the air she saw something red in its beak. Sam doubled over and was violently sick. When she had brought up everything there was in her stomach, she straightened up and saw Gerry on the deck of his boat bent over her bag.

He looked up and saw her watching him. 'Sorry,' he said. 'I can't find my mobile.'

Sam glanced inside Grace's boat; it had been completely turned over. Gerry joined her, his jumper had become snagged on his belt and his mobile phone was visible, attached to it.

Sam pointed to it. 'It's there,' she said.

He looked down at it. 'Oh shit, I'm always doing that. I've only just got the cover for it with the belt clip.'

Soon, in the distance, the whine of a police siren could be heard drawing closer and closer.

Sam sat in a police interview room trying to keep what she had seen an hour earlier out of her mind. She and Gerry had watched Grace Cameron's body being pulled from the river and zipped into a blue body bag. Sam tried not to think about the seagull. A white tent had been erected over the boat and SOC officers in white overalls and blue overshoes had started crawling everywhere.

Sam sat forward in her chair, put her face in her hands and tried to quell the nausea in her stomach. The door opened and a man with a zigzag nose came in, followed by a younger woman in uniform holding a cup of tea, which she put down in front of Sam. They both sat down opposite her.

'DI Skinner,' he said, holding out his hand.

Sam nodded and took it. Skinner was in his fifties, wearing a blue suit, a black shirt and a tie so disgusting that Sam imagined the only reason he must be wearing it was as some kind of dare. The black leather belt round his waist was having a hard time holding his trousers up under his paunch. At some point in his life he must have suffered from very bad skin, because his cheeks and neck looked as if someone had dripped acid on him.

'I understand you had an appointment to see Grace Cameron, is that right?'

'Yes.'

'When was that appointment made?'

'Yesterday evening at about ten o'clock.'

'You're sure of the time?'

'Yes – I remember looking at my watch a couple of minutes after she made the call.'

'What was your connection with the dead woman?'

'I'm a private investigator and I was looking into the disappearance of her son, Harry.'

'Had it been reported to the police?'

'He went missing relatively recently – about nine days ago – and neither she nor her husband seemed very concerned.'

Skinner scratched an ear flattened and devoid of cartilage. 'Why were you involved, then?'

'He's a rower in the Oxford University rowing squad – the coach had asked me to make some enquiries. He was worried about him.'

'But his parents weren't? That's a bit odd, isn't it?'

Sam shrugged. 'That's the way it was.'

'Why did she want to talk to you?'

'I don't know. She said she didn't want to talk on the phone and that she couldn't leave the boat because she was looking after a dog which barked if it was left alone.'

'Dog?'

'Yes.'

'There was no dog on the boat.'

'No?'

'Was it hers?'

'I don't think so, no. She gave the impression she was looking after it for someone.'

'Any idea whose it was?'

Sam shook her head.

'Had you met up with her before this?'

'Yes, two days ago.'

'And what had you talked about?'

'Her son, Harry. She said he had a tendency to go walkabout, so she wasn't worried by him going missing.'

'How did she seem to you?'

'A bit vague.' Sam tapped her forehead. 'Like she wasn't quite

148

all there. She said she hadn't been at her best recently and I think she had a heart condition.'

'Did she seem suicidal?'

'No, no, nothing like that – just a bit woolly-headed and upset.'

'Was the dog with her?'

'No.'

'Can you think of anyone who'd want to kill her?'

Sam shook her head. 'Look, I've only met her once. I barely knew the woman.'

'So this Harry – did he get on with his mum?'

'I haven't found him to ask but everyone I've talked to about Harry has said that he's religious and serious.'

'What did his mum say?'

'She said the same.'

'Who else have you talked to in the course of your inquiry?'

'The father – Grace and he were divorced. Not much love lost there.'

'Do you have his address?'

Sam nodded and he pushed a pad of paper across the table towards her and she wrote down the address in Barnes. He tore it off the pad, walked to the door and handed it to someone outside.

'Is he wearing that tie for a dare?' Sam said to the woman officer.

She smiled but didn't reply.

Skinner sat back down. 'Anything else you can think of that would be helpful for us?'

'Harry's got a twin brother David — you should run him through your computer and talk to Phil Howard at Thames Valley.'

'Why?'

'Kid's got a record.'

'What sort?'

'Drugs, petty crime – he went inside for possession and came out last November. He missed his last meeting with his probation officer.'

Skinner nodded at the policewoman who got up and left the room.

'You realise we need to talk to both her sons?'

Sam didn't say anything.

'Are you going to keep looking for Harry?'

'I need to speak to the OUBC. If they want me to I will.'

'We will also be looking for him, of course. Both of them.'

Sam wasn't quite sure what Skinner was saying to her. Was he warning her off? Warning her about them? She remained silent and waited.

He sighed. 'Look, love, let us know if you catch up with them before us, will you?'

Sam nodded. But in fact she wasn't sure what she would do. With the kind of resources the police had, she thought it was much more likely to be the other way round.

He handed her his card and Sam followed him out of the room.

She made her way back to the river, hoping to find Gerry there, but there was a policeman blocking the way to his boat and when she asked him he said that Gerry was still at the police station. The sun was beginning to disappear and the wind was picking up, ruffling the surface of the river. Grace's boat was still covered by a white tent and lit up with several powerful searchlights. A number of police had fanned out along the green walkways that linked the boats to each other and were going in and out interviewing the other boat owners. A small crowd had gathered on top of the bridge looking down onto the area where the police were working and Sam joined them. Who on earth would want to hurt, let alone kill, someone as harmless as Grace Cameron? She wondered if the jewellery had something to do with it. Sam saw Grace holding her face to the sun, her blonde hair swirling around her in a golden mane. Poor woman. Sam suddenly felt completely exhausted. She had to get home.

Chelsea were playing at Stamford Bridge so the traffic in the King's Road was nose to tail. After standing at a bus stop for fifteen minutes facing into a biting wind and watching a car move about an inch, Sam decided it would be far less stressful to walk. As she set off, she put in another call to the hospital and received the same bland assurances about Alan. Then she left a message for Mark to call her. She needed to talk to him about what had happened to Grace as well as about her father. It took her roughly thirty minutes to get home.

She threw her bag on the chair in the hall and walked into the kitchen to feed Frank and put on the kettle for a cup of tea. The wind had got up and was slamming against the side of the building and making one of the windows rattle like hell. Sam knew which one it was; the wedge of paper she usually stuffed into the crack must have become dislodged. She tore a piece of newspaper from the knee-high pile of recycling in her kitchen and walked down the hall, folding it in her hands. When she turned on the light in the front room, she saw a man huddled on her sofa. He was curled up with his back towards her, but as the light came on he rolled over and his face became visible. It was her father and his face was contorted in pain.

CHAPTER ELEVEN

'What the fuck are you doing here?' she snapped.
But her father didn't reply; he moaned and curled tighter around his stomach. Sam walked over to the sofa and looked down at him. He was shivering uncontrollably, his teeth were clenched and his face was grey and sweaty. What was the matter with him? Overcoming her reluctance to touch him, she took hold of the front of his coat and pulled him into a sitting position. As she let go of him, she realised her hands were wet with blood and that the sofa underneath him was also sodden. She pulled open his coat and saw dark bloodstains on his shirt. She ripped it open and saw a torn-up mess on the upper right-hand side of his chest from which blood was leaking. She ran into the bathroom, grabbed a towel, folded it and placed it against the wound and applied pressure. As she leaned over him, the dog tags she was wearing round her neck dislodged and swung against him.

He grabbed them, pulling her head down towards him. 'You've got to help me, Sam. You're the only one I can trust . . .'

His hand slid off them and he lapsed into unconsciousness. Sam reached into her pocket, got out her mobile and phoned 999. To the question 'Which service do you want?' she replied: 'Ambulance.' But before she could give any more details, her father had roused himself from the sofa and knocked the phone out of her hand.

'Don't be fucking stupid. They'll be looking for me in the hospitals.'

They, Sam thought, who the hell are 'they'?

'But you'll bleed to death.'

He shook his head. 'No hospitals.'

'Hold this,' Sam said, taking his hand and placing it on top of the towel. She retrieved the phone from the floor and put in another call, this time to Max. Sam was shaking as she waited for Max to pick up the call. What was she going to do if he didn't answer?

'Max Johnson Security,' a gruff voice replied.

'Oh, thank God you're there, it's Sam.'

'Sam, what—?'

She cut across him. 'You've got to come over. It's my father – he's been shot. He's losing blood but he doesn't want to go to a hospital. Do you know anyone who could treat him?'

'Shot? What do—?'

'Shot, shot!' Sam shouted. 'He's got a bloody great hole in his shoulder. Tell me what the fuck to do.'

'Apply pressure to the wound.'

'Yes, yes, I'm doing that . . .'

'And don't let him lose consciousness, Sam. It's very important you keep him awake and warm. I'll be there as fast as I can.'

Sam closed up her phone and looked at her father. He was shivering and his lips were turning blue. She went into her bedroom and got the duvet; as she came back into the front room she saw his head had rolled back on his shoulders.

'Dad,' she shouted. It was the first time she had called him that and she felt a wave of emotion rise up her throat. Geoffrey Falconer's eyes opened. 'Dad, you mustn't fall asleep.' She sat down, put the duvet over him and took hold of his hand, which was slippery with blood. Again she pulled him into an upright position. She didn't know if it was the best thing to do but she thought it would be easier to keep him awake. He groaned as she moved him and gritted his teeth. 'Max is on his way. He'll be here soon but you must stay awake.' She racked her brain to think of something to get him talking. 'Tell me about the envelope, Dad. What's in the envelope?' His eyes closed again. 'Dad?' She patted him gently on the face, feeling the stubble on his cheek, and he opened his eyes. 'What's in the envelope?'

'Envelope?'

'The one you wanted me to look after.'

'Names . . . places . . . dates . . .'

Sam didn't know what he was talking about but it didn't matter. 'Tell me the names. Come on, we've got to keep you awake.'

'Roddy Brennan . . .'

'Yes, go on.'

'All the names – go on, Dad. Concentrate.'

He continued in a low voice, listing name after name, and whenever he stopped and seemed to be sliding into unconsciousness, Sam gently shook him.

He grimaced. 'Let go of my fucking hand, will you, you're crushing it.'

'Sorry.'

About twenty minutes later Max was ringing on her doorbell.

He pulled up Sam's father's jacket and shirt and looked at his back. 'Bullet's gone straight through,' he said. 'There's an exit wound and it missed his lung. All good news but, from the way it's bleeding, it probably clipped an artery.'

'How do you know all that?' Sam asked.

'In the SAS some of us get medical training. Have to. Places we end up in can be a long way from any medics. I phoned around and we've got some boys working in casualty at Charing Cross at the moment. They know we're on our way. Casualty's the best place to train soldiers. If we can get him there they'll take a look at him, no questions asked. If it's official and they find out it's a bullet wound it has to be reported to the police.'

Sam's father was now shivering uncontrollably.

'He's in shock. We need to hurry. Help me get him up.'

Half an hour later, Max and Sam stood outside a room in the Charing Cross Hospital, where Geoffrey Falconer was being seen to by two doctors.

'Do you know what happened?' Max asked.

Sam shook her head. 'Just came home and found him there.' She folded her arms. 'Is he working for you?'

Max sighed.

'Come on, spit it out.'

'I owe him my life, Sam. You know that. He asked me for a bit of work and I gave it to him. Nothing too troublesome. He just had to baby-sit a couple of minor celebrities for a day. Nothing very taxing for him but enough to keep him ticking over.'

'Is that how this happened?'

He shook his head. 'This didn't have anything to do with what he's doing for me.'

'Is he going to be all right?'

'He's been lucky. Any lower and he could have been hit in the lung. On the other side and you've got the heart involved and although there was a lot of blood, really it's just a flesh wound. It's not as if he's broken anything or the bullet's still in there.'

'I want you to talk to him, Max.'

'Why? What's going on?'

'He turned up in Oxford and frightened my mother half to death. He didn't approach her or anything, just stood outside their house watching. Then he met up with Mark and asked him to forgive him.'

Max drew in his breath sharply. 'Shouldn't be doing stuff like that.'

'He asked me to look after some papers for him and I got burgled.'

'Did they find what they were looking for?'

'No.'

'Do you know what it was?'

Sam didn't say anything.

'Have they been back?'

'No.'

'And you've still got it?'

'Yes.'

Max sighed and ran a finger over an orange moustache flecked with grey. 'If it was Special Branch they'll be back and they'll be keeping an eye on you.'

'He told me that he'd been involved in assassination squads in Northern Ireland, that the three other men who had been involved were all dead. He implied that they'd been murdered.'

'People do die in our business, Sam. You don't join the SAS if you're not interested in high-risk situations. These are not people who want to retire, grow old gracefully, put on their slippers, potter in their garden and watch *Countdown*. People die in training, car crashes, parachuting. You name a dangerous pastime, you'll find a fair number of special forces people interested or involved.'

'Of course, but presumably you could use that fact to cover over murders as accidental deaths. Especially if they were people who knew things you didn't want coming out.'

Max shrugged his shoulders. 'Maybe.'

'Anyway, someone shot him, Max. That's not a bloody accident.'

'They must be getting desperate.'

The door behind them opened and a young man in a white coat spattered in blood came out. He looked from Sam to Max. 'We've got the bleeding under control – the axillary artery was clipped. We need to get his fluids regulated and we've given him an injection against infection. Then he'll need somewhere to rest up and recuperate.' He looked enquiringly at her.

And Sam in turn looked at Max.

'Anyway,' the man said, 'he needs somewhere to go.' Then he went back into the room.

'I'm not having him, Max. I can't.'

'Sam—'

'He saved your life,' Sam said. 'You owe him.'

'Don't tell me what I do or do not owe him. That's between me and him and has absolutely nothing to do with you.'

'Sorry,' Sam said. 'But I can't have him at mine, Max. You don't understand.'

'No,' Max said. 'I don't. He's your father, Sam, whatever he may have done in the past.'

'I owe him nothing,' Sam shouted. 'He went away when I was four. Since he's been back there's been nothing but trouble. You've no idea how much effort it takes to stop this fucking up my life completely. Yesterday I was looking at Mark lying on the floor pissed out of his skull because my father got it into his head to ask him for forgiveness. I will not have him in my house. I will not look after him. I will not do any of those things.'

'He came to you, Sam, not me.'

'I don't care. This is the end of it for me, Max. If he doesn't go with you he goes out on the street. I'm going home now.'

Max grabbed hold of Sam's upper arms. 'You're just going to walk away from him?'

Sam shook herself free of him. 'Just fucking watch me. That's exactly what I'm going to do. It's what he did to me when I was four. How dare he even come to me?' Sam turned away from Max and walked towards the hospital exit.

Behind her she heard him shout. 'But he did come to you, Sam. Why's that?'

Outside she inhaled great breaths of air. Nursemaid her father? No, she didn't think so. No fucking way. He'd come to her – she'd got him sorted out and that was an end to it. She was clear about what she owed him. Absolutely nothing. But then why did she feel so guilty? She felt the dog tags against her skin. Why the hell was she still wearing these? What did they symbolise? Safety? The protection of her father's ghost? But he wasn't a ghost and never had been. He was alive and dangerous and not to be trusted. What was the matter with her? It was just weakness, the guilt of the weak. She ran out of the hospital and set off along the Fulham Palace Road towards home. What she needed was a good drink. A bottle of vodka swam into her mind. Yes, that would do it. But then she thought of Mark, lying dead drunk on the floor next to a red washing-up bowl. Keep passing the open doors of the off-licences, she thought, as she marched towards home. Don't let the bastard turn you into a drunk. Keep moving, keep moving, and she was home in double-quick time.

Reg crossed his legs. Sam didn't know what to say. She didn't know how to start. She could barely remember what she'd just been saying. She didn't want to recall last night. She sat in silence feeling sick, her whole body aching. She should have just drunk the vodka and been done with it, it surely couldn't have made her feel any worse than she was already feeling.

Reg scratched his eyebrow. 'Sam?'

She looked up at him.

'You've been sitting in silence for the last ten minutes. Could you try and put some words on where you are?'

She stared at him. How to start? How to get in there when it was all mess and fear and sickness?

To begin at the beginning. But where was that exactly?

'He'd been shot. He turned up in my flat.'

Reg frowned. 'Is this a dream?'

'No. It happened yesterday evening.'

'Who?'

'My father.'

Reg blinked in surprise.

Sam felt a jolt of anger. 'How dare he even come near me? Max said he should stay with me but I couldn't . . . I couldn't have him in my flat . . .' Anger gave way to tears. An overwhelming feeling of hopelessness poured through her. She covered her face with her hands, feeling the tears seeping from her eyes. Reg pushed a box of tissues across the table towards her.

'He came to you for help?'

'Fucking bastard,' Sam shouted. 'How dare he ask me for anything?'

'You feel very angry.'

'No shit.'

'Tell me about the anger.'

'He disappears when I'm four and I'm told he's been killed. I worship him as a hero my whole life. He comes back from the dead and I discover that he was never a hero. That he beat up my mother and that he bullied my brother mercilessly. The man was a vicious bastard.'

'And what did he do to you?'

'What do you mean? Isn't that enough? I don't want the man near me.'

'Of course it's enough. You have every reason not to want him near you. I can see that what he did to your family was horrific but I'm trying to get clear in my mind what you feel he has done to you.'

'If he hurts my brother and my mother he hurts me.'

'You were four when he went missing?'

'Yes.'

'What do you remember of him?'

Sam felt dizzy. Oh no, she thought, not this. 'I'm not sure what I remember. How can you be sure of what you remember?' Sam placed her hands over her face again. Behind them was darkness and safety, a safe cave where no one could reach her.

Reg didn't say anything. The half-truth hung in the air.

Sam wasn't sure how long she remained like that, with her hands covering her face.

From far away she heard Reg's voice. 'It's time.'

Sam took her hands away from her face, feeling dazed and nauseous. 'Sorry?'

'The session's over.'

'Oh, right.' She stood up, grabbed her coat off the back of her chair and headed for the door in a rush.

Reg stood up. 'You haven't paid.'

Sam turned round. 'Oh...' She fumbled in her jacket and handed over the money. 'You know last time you asked me what I was hoping for by meeting up with him?'

He nodded.

'Without wishing to sound too much like a bad song, I was hoping for a hero.'

'Ah.'

Sam shook her head. 'How foolish can you be?'

Reg had taken off his glasses and slipped them into his top pocket. 'You can phone me, Sam, any time.'

Sam felt flustered. 'What?'

'You can phone me.'

'How does that work?'

'You pick up the phone, you punch in the numbers and you speak to me.'

'Oh, I see, sorry. OK, thanks.'

Sam stood on Reg's doorstep, gulping in the cold winter air, wanting to get as far away from Reg and as far away from being four years old as possible.

Sam went straight from Reg's to St Mary's. Alan had been transferred into a general ward. There were eight beds altogether, all occupied, with about two feet between the beds. Guests were the focus of everyone's attention and private conversation was impossible.

'You look terrible,' Alan said.

'I thought that was my line,' Sam said.

He smiled. 'I want you to know this is all your fault,' Alan said and then, looking at Sam's stricken face, burst out laughing. The laughter was quickly followed by a yelp of pain. 'Shit,' he said, clutching his stomach. 'Belly-laughing with a recently perforated intestine is obviously not a good idea.'

'I had this dream about you,' Sam said.

Alan poured himself some water from a plastic jug sitting on the table next to his bed. 'Glad to know I'm haunting your every guilt-ridden moment.'

'This snake was coming out of your stomach.'

'Very Freudian.'

'Really?'

'Come on, Sam!'

'Anyway, I pulled it and all your intestines fell out on the floor.'

Alan stared at her. 'What on earth made you think that was a good dream to tell me about?'

'I thought it might make you laugh.'

'Laugh? It sounds as if you were trying to castrate me.'

Sam looked down and realised somewhat to her own disbelief that she was actually in the histrionic act of wringing her hands. She unlocked her fingers and placed them palm-down on her thighs. 'I am *so* sorry, Alan.' She shook her head. 'I couldn't feel more guilty if I tried.'

'Oh try a little more. Just for me,' Alan said. 'Just a tiny bit more – please.'

Sam laughed.

'That's better,' Alan said. 'But for God's sake don't tell me any more dreams.' He held out his hand to her.

She took it in both of hers.

'Easy, girl, easy,' he said. 'Sick man here.'

'Sorry,' she said relinquishing her grip a little.

'If you say the words "It should have been me", I'll send you off to the next scriptwriters' seminar.'

'How much longer are you going to be here?'

'Until I die of malnutrition,' Alan said. 'The food is—'

'Slop,' the man said in the bed next to him.

'Meet John,' Alan said. 'Known to the inmates as Appendicitis.'

Sam nodded.

'John is a chef so he is more traumatised by the food than most of us.'

'It makes you want to get out,' John said quietly. 'It makes you *so so* desperate to get out.'

'Have they said when you can leave?' Sam asked Alan.

He shrugged. 'No, not yet. I suppose they want to make sure I'm not filled with pus and all that sort of thing.'

'You're fit, though. You should heal fast.'

He nodded. 'I should.'

'Can you remember what happened?'

'At first I thought he'd just punched me in the guts. It was only when I put my hand there and saw the blood I realised I'd been stabbed.'

'Could you ID them?'

'Two fat blokes in balaclavas – they're two-a-penny in Portobello on a Saturday morning.' He laughed. 'Could be a couple of my brothers.'

They both turned to watch an enormous bunch of flowers walk into the ward. It was so huge you couldn't see the face of the person carrying them. The flowers – long-stemmed, red amaryllis – wobbled towards Sam and Alan and were then lowered to reveal Jackie.

'Now that's what I call a bunch of flowers,' Alan said.

Jackie smiled and rested the large rustling bunch on the end of the bed. 'How are you?'

'Perforated,' Alan said.

'Yes, of course.'

'Stabbed,' Alan said.

'Yes.' Jackie was looking increasingly panicky.

'Punctured.'

'Alan . . .?' Sam said.

Alan smiled. 'Just my little joke. Guilt is such a lovely way to make people suffer.'

He wiggled his toes and the flowers on the end of the bed rustled. 'Those'll give the nurses hell, their vases are about two inches high and those are the really tall ones. I think they want people bringing in nothing higher than a daisy. We'll have only short flowers in this hospital. Short and regulation-size, like your turds.'

'I think I should be going,' Sam said.

Jackie looked alarmed at the idea of being left alone with Alan. 'Yes, me too.'

'Not so soon,' Alan said. 'You've only just arrived and I want to make you suffer much, much more.'

'I'll come again in a couple of days,' Sam said.

'Next time, for God's sake bring me something I can eat,' Alan said. He rustled the flowers again with his feet. 'I suppose I could try these . . .'

Sam and Jackie said goodbye and walked out of the ward together.

'He's angry, isn't he?' Jackie said.

'I'd say so,' Sam replied. 'And tired and irritable . . .'

'It's not our fault,' Jackie said.

'No,' Sam said 'It's your fault.'

'Thanks for that.'

'Look, we both know he hasn't got the fat bloke in the balaclava in front of him so we're the next best thing.'

'I do feel guilty,' Jackie said.

'Oh God, so do I,' Sam said. 'So do I.'

They had left the hospital and were standing in Praed Street.

'Do you have a minute?' Sam said, nodding at the café across the road. 'I'd like to talk to you about something.'

Jackie glanced at her watch. 'It'll have to be quick. I've got an appointment in Antiquarius in the King's Road at three.'

A few minutes later Sam and Jackie were sitting opposite each other stirring their coffees.

'Do you know Grace Cameron?' Sam asked.

'Everyone knows Grace; she's been around in the market for donkey's years. First she was in business with her husband. They ran the shop in Camden Passage together but after the divorce she specialised in jewellery and began building up her own business. And she was better off without him. He had a reputation in the market – he's a bastard to deal with and a womaniser. She's done all right for herself. Anyway, what's your interest in Grace?'

'I've been hired to look for her son.'

Jackie tapped her nose and sniffed loudly. 'Trouble there.'

'No, not that one. I'm looking for Harry.'

'David's the one I know about. Wasn't the kind of lad you wanted anywhere near your goods.'

'What do you mean?'

'He had a drug habit and everyone knew he was light-fingered. Also he's been around the market since he could walk so he knows what to steal. I saw him in Portobello before Christmas but he didn't look right, he was still using.'

'Grace is dead.'

'Poor woman. Was it her heart? I know she'd had problems.'

'No, I'm afraid not – she was killed yesterday.'

'What – you're saying she was murdered?'

Sam nodded. 'Looks like that. Can you think of anyone who'd have a reason to do that?'

All the colour had drained out of Jackie's face. She stared into her cup of coffee.

'Jackie?'

She looked up. 'The rumour was that when David went into prison he owed money. I presume it was still owed when he came out. And it was to the wrong sort of people.'

'But why would they have come after Grace?'

'Everyone knows she's a dealer – that she's got the goods. If David didn't come up with the money, she would have been a relatively soft target to settle the debt.'

'But why kill her?'

'Maybe she wouldn't tell them where her stuff was.' Jackie shook her head. 'Poor Grace.' She looked at her watch and stood up. 'Shit, I'll be late. I have to go.'

Sam stood up as well. 'You said Cameron was a bastard. Do you know if he was ever violent towards her?'

Jackie frowned. 'Hit her, you mean? Maybe, but that was years ago, before they were divorced.'

Back home, Sam phoned Mark. She wasn't sure what she was going to tell him but she knew she had to be in contact.

'Mark? It's Sam.'

Silence.

'Alan's going to be all right,' Sam continued.

She heard him sigh. 'Good.'

'He's still in hospital—'

'What do you want, Sam?'

'I just wanted to touch base. See how you were. Did you talk to Mum?'

'Yes.'

'And?'

'What do you care?'

'Alan got stabbed – what was I supposed to do?'

163

'And you were so relieved to get out of here.'

'This whole thing isn't easy for any of us, Mark.'

He sighed. 'No, it isn't.'

'At any rate, Dad shouldn't be troubling Mum for a while.'

'You haven't seen him again?'

Sam immediately regretted telling him but it was too late so she battled on. 'He turned up at my place. He'd been shot. We got him to a hospital and Max is looking after him.'

'I don't believe you.'

'He turned up, Mark. I did not invite him. What was I supposed to do? He was practically unconscious. Anyway, he's not going to be around in Oxford for a bit.'

'Who shot him?'

'I've no idea.'

'Why did they shoot him?'

'He's got information about what the security forces were up to in Northern Ireland during the seventies. The assembly's just been suspended again and there's all the stuff in the papers about military intelligence running double agents – Nelson in the UDA and Scappaticci in the IRA – and innocent people being killed to protect their identities. Also the Bloody Sunday inquiry is going on. Someone, somewhere doesn't want the information he has out in the public domain.' Sam thought of the envelope. 'And they're prepared to kill to prevent it.'

'You must be careful, Sam,' Mark said. 'If they tried to shoot him, what else will they do?'

'Max will look after him. He owes him one.'

'That's not the point.'

'And there's more bad news, Mark. Grace, Harry's mother, has been killed.'

'Oh, no.'

'I'm afraid so. So now the police will be looking for the two boys, not just me. They'll be especially interested in David, given his history.'

'Surely they don't think he'd kill his own mother?'

'Who knows? Maybe he came to his mum's looking for money. According to another dealer I know, he owed money when he came out of prison and was still using. He knows that both his mum and his dad have thousands of pounds in stock and he knows how much it's worth because he's been around the markets since he was a child. If they won't give it to him maybe it's a relatively easy way to discharge the debt. Either he steals it or tells whoever he owes to do it. Grace would have been an easier target than the father. The thing is, she'd phoned me the night before, asking me to come over.'

'What did she want to talk to you about?'

'I don't know and I never got to find out. Maybe someone knew what she was going to tell me and decided they'd get rid of her before she could talk to me. I'm going to come down to Oxford again. I want to go back to the Mad Hatter and talk to Siobhan, the woman who accused Harry of assault.'

'You think Harry and David are together?'

'November 18 – the day Harry missed a tutorial, was the day David came out of prison. I bet he went to meet him. He seems like the sort of man who would. If his brother called on him, he'd drop everything – including his dreams of taking part in the Boat Race – and go.'

'Do you think they know she's dead?'

'They do if they killed her.'

'Harry couldn't have been involved with that.'

'If Harry knows I bet he gets in contact with Emma Hodge.'

'Why her?'

'Out of the people I spoke to, she's the one I'd go to.'

After Sam had finished the call with Mark, she pulled the buff envelope out of her bag. Time to read it. She had to. She was on the point of tearing it open when the doorbell rang. She picked up the intercom phone.

'Hello.'

'It's DI Skinner. We spoke yesterday. I have a few more questions I'd like to ask you.'

Sam buzzed him in and ushered him into her front room. Skinner glanced round and frowned. 'Sorry about the mess,' Sam said. 'Housework's not my thing.'

'Something happen here?'

'Me and the cat. You know – everyday life.'

'Cat must have bad habits.'

'Complete slut,' Sam said amiably. 'Still makes him about a hundred per cent better than me.'

Sam watched Skinner staring at the stains on her sofa. She hadn't got round to stripping the covers off. The colour of the sofa was muddy red anyway but the blood had created large brown marks on the fabric.

'Tipped a whole pot of coffee over it. Come into the kitchen and I'll try and make you some that stays in your cup.'

Skinner followed her along the hall.

'Keep to the right,' Sam said. 'There are broken floorboards in the middle.'

In the kitchen Skinner perched carefully on a rickety wooden stool while Sam filled the kettle and washed up two cups.

'What can I help you with?'

'You mentioned something about a dog.'

'Sorry?'

'You said the reason Grace Cameron wanted to see you the following morning and at her place was because she was looking after a dog which she couldn't leave. Is that right?'

'Yes.'

'Did she say who the dog belonged to?'

Sam shook her head. 'She just said it barked a lot if it was left alone and she didn't want to bother the neighbours. Noise travels faster over water, doesn't it?'

'We have reason to believe the dog was her son David's.'

'Who told you that?'

'His father. We wondered if she said anything like that to you?'

Sam frowned. 'No, she didn't.'

'You're sure?'

'Yes – absolutely sure. I'd have remembered something like that. I'm looking for Harry so if she'd said it was David's dog, I would have asked her where he was, on the assumption that they might well be together.'

'Did she tell you when she'd last seen David?'

'Christmas, I think.'

'You're absolutely sure?'

'Yes.'

'Did you hear the dog barking when she phoned you?'

Sam shook her head. 'No – there was no dog in that call.'

'How do you know Gerry Doyle?'

'Gerry? I don't really know him. He's a locksmith. I locked

166

myself out a while back and he came and let me back in. When I turned up to speak to Grace, I bumped into him and he asked me if I wanted to wait for her and have coffee.'

'A locksmith?' Skinner grunted in amusement.

Sam frowned. 'Well, what would you call him?'

'Locksmith will do.'

'Who saw the body first?'

Sam ran a hand over her face. Oh shit, she didn't want to remember. 'There was the gull,' she said. She felt sick and sweaty again. She saw the yellow eye of the gull observing her and Gerry from the railings of his boat. She saw it ducking its head in the water next to the blue plastic bottle. She sat down and put her head between her knees. Everything in front of her eyes went black.

'Are you all right, love?' She heard Skinner's voice but couldn't see him. She felt his hand on her arm then heard him walk out of the kitchen.

Next thing she felt was cold water running over her neck and trickling down her back. She opened her eyes and waited for the stars to clear. Skinner was standing next to her, holding a flannel in his hand. Sam tried to sit up but her head spun.

'Keep your head down, love.' He placed the flannel against the back of her neck and squeezed. She remembered his broken nose and wondered how many times he'd done this with boxers.

'Sorry,' Sam said, feeling her stomach heave.

'It's all right. She was in a terrible mess.' He handed her a glass of water. 'I'm sorry to press you on this but we do need to know the exact order of things. Where was Doyle when you first arrived at the boats?'

'I was walking along the pontoon towards Grace's boat and he was walking towards me.'

'Did you see him coming off her boat?'

'No – he was already on the pontoon.'

'But the direction you were heading in, that only leads to Grace Cameron's boat, doesn't it? If he was walking towards you he must have been coming from her boat?'

'I suppose so.'

'Who stopped who?'

'I stopped him. He came level with me and I looked across and realised I knew him.'

'You're sure?'

'Yes – I don't think he'd noticed me. He said she wasn't in and asked me if I wanted to have some coffee and wait for her.'

'Did he seem agitated?'

Sam frowned trying to remember. 'Not particularly.'

'Then what happened?'

'We sat outside drinking coffee and I was watching the gull and then the door blew open and I made some comment about was he sure she wasn't there because surely she'd have locked the door and then he turned round and saw her under the water and ran over to the boat.'

'You're certain that's what happened?'

'Yes.'

'*He* was the one to see her first and *he* ran to the boat?'

'Yes.'

'Did he seem upset?'

'You couldn't see her – the state she was in – and not feel upset.'

'And you've no idea what she wanted to tell you?'

Sam shook her head.

'She didn't hint at anything in the call?'

'No.'

He drained his cup and put it down on the kitchen table. 'It still gets to me, you know, the bad ones. And I've been on the job twenty years. They take the piss out of me for it, but if it didn't I'd start to worry.'

Sam stood up unsteadily.

'Are you all right now?'

Sam nodded. 'Yes, I'll be fine. Thanks.'

From her front window, Sam watched Skinner drive away and breathed a sigh of relief. She looked at the sofa and set about tearing the cover and then did the same to the cushions. She doubted her coffee explanation had impressed him. As she tugged the material free she heard something fall onto the floor. Sam frowned and picked up a black leather wallet. It must have fallen out of her father's pocket when he was curled up on the sofa. It was still sticky from his blood.

CHAPTER TWELVE

Sam dropped the wallet and stared at the palms of her hands, now covered with her father's blood. A shudder of revulsion ran through her. She walked to the bathroom and began to wash her hands, running the bar of soap down the inside and the outside of each finger, and repeating it again and again, as if she were a surgeon preparing for an operation. Then she held them under the hot tap until they were the colour of lobster.

Who would have thought the old man to have had so much blood in him?

The trouble with having an English don for a brother was that you ended up with a head full of quotations and half the time you had no idea where they came from. She shook her hands into the sink and picked up a towel. Well, at least that was a quotation she knew. Everyone should be allowed one Lady Macbeth moment in their lives. Mark had once told her that the word 'blood' and variants of it appeared forty-five times in *Macbeth*. That was when he was a teenager and had become obsessed with Shakespeare after seeing Derek Jacobi in *Hamlet*.

Sam looked at her hands. As if water could make any difference. His blood ran in her veins and there was nothing she could do about it. She couldn't purge it from inside her body. She couldn't get rid of it that easily.

She took a roll of kitchen towel into the front room, ripped off several sheets, folded them and picked up the wallet from the floor. When she was sure it was as dry as she could make it, she carefully flicked it open. Credit cards were the first thing she saw. She levered one out, but it wasn't in her father's name – it belonged to a James Parker, as did all the others. In the back of the wallet was a wedge of fifty-pound notes. She counted them – a thousand pounds. But who the hell was James Parker and why did her father have his wallet? Had he stolen it? Had he killed him?

Then behind the notes Sam found a newspaper cutting. It was yellow and slightly crumbly at the folds. She opened it – and a picture of herself at twenty years old, a gold medal hanging round her neck, smiled back at her. Paris 1990, the Judo World Championships. Sam sat staring at it for a long time. Now it was absolutely clear to her what she held in her hands. He must have had this in his wallet for twelve years.

The final pocket in the wallet yielded another photo: a woman and two children. The photo had been taken at the seaside. A small, dark-haired woman stood on the beach, her shoulder-length hair tangled and tugged by the wind. Behind her was a blue sea and white-topped waves; on either side of her were a boy and a girl. The girl stood holding her mother's hand, staring straight into the camera, the boy squatted at her feet, fingers dug into the sand. She stared at the photo and the faces of the two children. She heard her father's words. *It was time to come home. You're the only home I've got, Sam.* If she was right, this photo said something very different. She stared and she stared until she was absolutely clear about what she was looking at – her father's second family.

Sam felt an intense surge of jealousy. All the years that she had mourned her father's death, they had had him. She knew it made no sense to envy them. After all, it depended on what he had been like. Why envy them a violent and destructive man? But what ate away at Sam was the thought that he might have changed. Suppose he had been a proper father to them? Suppose he had fathered them in a way that Sam had never had, in a way she had longed for? If that was the case, she wanted them all to rot in hell. She wanted them wiped from the surface of the earth. She wished that she had never opened this wallet and never set eyes on them. The final thing she found was a driving licence in the name of James Parker giving an address in Norfolk. She put everything back in the wallet and sat for a while staring into space, only dimly aware of the noise of the traffic outside and the rumble of the tube crossing the bridge over the New King's Road.

Then she opened the envelope. Inside was a sheaf of A4 paper. The first sheet was covered with the same writing as in the letter she had first received from her father telling her that he wasn't dead. It was the writing of a person who didn't do it all that often. Sam settled down to decipher the spider's crawl.

My name is Geoffrey Falconer. I was a sergeant in the SAS serving first in Oman and then in Northern Ireland. I am not proud of the things I have done. None of it. And I will not use an excuse that I was just following orders, that I had no choice. I know I had a choice. I know I could have refused, refused from the start, but once the thing was in motion it became more and more difficult to get off. The thing moved faster and faster and the longer you leave it the harder you know you will fall. This is my attempt to set the record straight. They had truth and reconciliation in South Africa; this is what I would say to such a body if one is ever set up to deal with Northern Ireland. They don't want me to tell it. I am the only one left to tell it. I know they will try to silence me. They've killed all the others.

Between 1974 and 1975 I was involved with a four-man troop of SAS soldiers who were used to abduct and assassinate members of the IRA caught crossing the border into Northern Ireland. The people involved were captured by other troops operating on the border and handed over to us for killing. All in all, I was involved in the killing of around forty people during this time. I was also involved in the unlawful killing of Catholics at random on the streets of Belfast to stir up sectarian hatreds and divisions. The three other men I worked with were Johnny Nichols, Dave Smith, and Jo Dodds. Dodds was our leader and he reported to 39th Brigade headquarters at Thiepval barracks in Lisburn. All of them are now dead.

I do not know the names of all those I killed. The names I do remember I've listed below. We used two burial grounds. I attach maps showing the burial grounds of the people we killed. Each one contains approximately twenty bodies. One site was on the edge of forest land. Conifers will have been planted over the bodies, making it difficult to identify. The burial site is now quite deep in

*the forest. The other was in a bog. The bodies were pushed
beneath the surface of the vegetation that covered the bog.
This prevented the bodies from floating to the surface,
allowing them to decompose.*

Sam flicked through the rest of the paper. There were two maps
attached, both with a large black cross and a map reference. One of
the maps had 'Antrim Borough LGD' written across it. And then
there was a list of names. She turned back to her father's writing.

*I did not join the SAS to do this sort of work. None of us
who were involved will ever be able to forget. The
memories and nightmares will stay with me for the rest of
my life. They have almost destroyed me. My aim in
making this information known is that the bodies of those
people who were killed may be recovered and given the
dignity of a proper burial. The graves need to be
excavated by experts. But for that to happen the
government has to admit to what they were authorising in
Northern Ireland. We were not a rogue unit, as the
government will try to suggest. We were run out of
Lisburn with the full knowledge of the commanding
authorities and the Ministry of Defence. They wish that I
did not exist and they are frightened of what I know and
what I will say. Three of my colleagues are no longer alive
and I doubt I will be much longer. There have already
been attempts on my life. I wish to make it clear that
money is not my motive. I want to set the record straight.
I want the bodies properly buried. The IRA have shown
that they are willing to disclose to the media the graves of
twenty known victims of Republican murder squads on the
Black Mountains on the outskirts of Belfast. It is time for
the British government to show the same openness. I am
also calling for a public inquiry into the deaths of Johnny
Nichols, Dave Smith and Jo Dodds.*

Sam stared again at the list of names in her hand. Each name had
a family, wives, children, brothers and sisters, mothers and fathers.
One disappearance – how many lives destroyed? How much grief?

She specialised in finding missing persons; her father had specialised in making them go missing. Maybe the guilt, the responsibility had transferred to her in some way – the sins of her father had
become her burden. How many times had he pulled the trigger?
How many had he actually killed? What had that done to him?
What had her father been intending to do with the contents of the
envelope? What on earth should she do with it? She had absolutely
no idea.

She picked up her mobile and called Max. 'How is he?'

Max sounded pissed off. 'Sleeping a lot. Keeps going on about
having left something at your place. Maybe he's feverish. Wound
doesn't look infected. They shot him up with enough antibiotics to
kill a horse.'

'No one knows he's with you?'

'Only Paula.' Paula was Max's receptionist and girlfriend. 'She
has to know. I can't stay here all the time. We take it in turns.'

'Look, Max, I know you're pissed off with me but I just
couldn't do it. You don't understand.'

'One thing I understand. Blood's thicker than water. He *is* your
father.'

'And he *is* your friend.'

'You can't forgive him.'

'Don't talk to me about fucking forgiveness,' Sam snapped.
'You haven't got a fucking clue.'

'Why don't you tell me?'

Sam was shaking. 'Because it's absolutely none of your
business.'

Silence.

'Well, if you can't tell me, how do you expect me to
understand?'

Sam ignored him. 'Has he told you who shot him?'

Max sighed. 'He hasn't said much really. Like I say, he's been
sleeping most of the time.'

'I'm worried about him, Max. I just read the contents of an
envelope he asked me to look after for him. You need to be really
careful. Don't leave Paula alone with him.'

'I have to, Sam. I can't just stop my life and my business.'

'I think he should be moved.'

'He'll move himself when he's ready. At the moment he's too weak. What was in the envelope?'

'Details of operations he was involved with in Northern Ireland in the seventies, burial sites, names . . .'

Sam heard a sharp intake of breath on the end of the line.

'What was he intending to do with it?'

'I don't know – it's a sworn affidavit.'

'Oh, Christ . . .'

'The thing is, Max, what about the doctors at the hospital? Do they know where you live?'

'No.'

'But they know that you took him?'

'Yes, they know that.'

'Well, they could trace you, couldn't they?'

'As soon as he's up to it, he's going to want to move himself, but until then he has to have somewhere to hole up.'

'I just wanted to warn you, Max, that's all.'

'OK, well count me as warned.' The line went dead.

Nightmares weaved their way in and out of Sam's sleep as she tossed and turned. Prague. Again. The split second before she dislocated her shoulder, the moment when it could have gone either way. The moment she went back to and tried to alter more than any other in her life. Sam woke with her shoulder throbbing. She rotated it round and round, trying to ease the pain. Prague! Would she never be rid of it? Tyler had once suggested that she watch the film of the fight. He'd said that she might be surprised at what she saw there. At the time she had been furious with him and told him not to be so stupid. Did he want to rub her nose in her failure? No, he'd said, that wasn't what he meant at all, but he hadn't pushed it any further. Prague had been the end of the road for her. She could never go back.

Sam stared into the darkness. The only thing that was holding her together at the moment was the search for Harry Cameron. Thank God for that. Without work there'd be nothing, nowhere to go where she could shut out her family, her father. No place to hide. And she knew that was exactly what she did. She hid in other people's pain like a parasite in its host – anything not to feel her own. She felt the scar on her finger with her thumb but, however much she pulled at it, the cut wouldn't open. It wouldn't bleed.

Sam came to in the kitchen standing in front of the sink. How had she got here? She didn't remember walking down the hall. She looked down at her hands. In the right one she was holding a bread knife. She looked at her left hand.

Now the cut was open.

Much deeper than the first one.

Blood clouded the water in the washing-up bowl. She dropped the knife and clutched her finger, applied pressure. Felt herself starting to shake. Felt relief. Then shame.

Reg had said that she could call him any time. But wasn't that a bit like inviting a politician to tell you the truth? You'd be safe in the knowledge that they'd never do it. Walking back to the bedroom she paused and stared at the phone. She wondered how bad things would have to get before she allowed herself to take up his offer.

Worse, she thought, so much worse.

She woke with a low-level headache that a cup of tea and an overripe banana did nothing to shift. She sat at the kitchen table with a piece of paper and a pen, trying to organise her day and failing.

She flexed her finger; it throbbed. Sam knew she should go and get it stitched. She also knew she was going to do no such thing. What was happening to her? She couldn't remember actually doing it. Memory. Sam knew she couldn't rely on it. The three years immediately after her father disappeared were a blank. Occasionally, feelings and images from that time emerged but nothing she could put together in a reliable narrative. It was as if her life had only really begun when she was seven years old and first set foot on a *tatami*, when she started to fight. She ran her finger over the scar in her neck. That was from the blank time.

The doorbell went and she walked through to the front of the flat. It was probably the postman; he often rang round this time to get into the block. He usually rang Edie's bell but today was pensions day and Edie was at the post office. Sam didn't really listen to the woman's voice on the end of the phone, buzzed her in and began walking back to the kitchen. She'd only taken a couple of paces when someone knocked on the door. Maybe it was a parcel.

When Sam opened the door, it was to a cloud of cigarette smoke, standing inside of which was a woman a couple of inches taller than her but about three times the width. The woman held out a cigarette stub that she was holding upright to stop the two inches of ash on the end toppling to the ground.

'Sorry,' she said, pointing at the carpet-covered hall. 'Would you mind? I should have got rid of it outside but I was in need of every centimetre.'

She had thin black hair that just about managed to straggle to her shoulders and an exceptionally pasty face. Her voice had a soft Scottish burr to it; it was the kind of voice that could have made a fortune from phone sex or reading the news on Radio 4. Sam, who had had some experience of tough women during her fighting career, knew that this woman was the genuine article.

'What do you want?'

'Could we do something with this? I wouldn't like to put holes in the carpet.'

Sam turned round to get her bin but when she turned back it was to find the woman had come into the flat and was standing directly behind her. She took the metal bin from Sam and stubbed out the fag end. 'Thanks.'

'Out,' Sam said.

'Keep your hair on.'

'Now.'

The woman rubbed her face with nicotine-stained fingers. 'Bit of a night of it last night. Burns Night. You know how it is – downed a few too many.'

'I can tell,' Sam said, manoeuvring her back out onto the landing. 'Whisky, was it?'

She laughed. 'Whisky might have come into it somewhere. Are you Sam Falconer?'

Sam looked at a letter that the woman was holding. 'Is that what it says there?'

'Oh yes, yes.' She handed the envelope over. 'Sorry, I met the postman on the way in and said I'd give it to you. Could I have a word with you?'

'If you make it quick.' Sam was standing in the doorway; she didn't move an inch backwards. This woman might be fat but there was nothing slow about her; she'd moved into her flat with the nimbleness of a Fred Astaire.

'Could we do it inside?'

'No,' Sam said.

'It concerns Geoffrey Falconer.'

'Who are you?'

'I'm a journalist.'

'What's your newspaper?'

'*Daily Herald.*'

Sam still hadn't moved.

'I don't really want to talk to you about this on the landing,' the woman said.

'Well, you're not coming in here,' Sam repeated.

'We could go for a walk.'

'You look as if you can barely crawl.'

'Appearances can be deceptive. I'll wait outside.'

Sam closed the door and went back to the kitchen. She made no effort to rush. Twenty minutes later she came out of the block and saw the woman leaning against the railings, smoking another cigarette. As Sam approached her, she threw it into the road and a lorry roared over the top of it. It was bitterly cold but the sun was out and the sky was a blazing blue with large rushing clouds. 'There's a park at the end of the street,' Sam said. 'We can go there.'

'You look very like him.'

Sam tucked her scarf tighter round her neck and remained silent. Some things you could just do nothing about.

'Do you know where he is?'

'What's your interest in him?'

'When did you last see him?'

'I'm not telling you a thing until you tell me who you are and what your interest in him is.'

'My name's Kelly Webb. Geoff contacted me three months ago, telling me he had a story for me.'

'Why you?'

'He'd read a piece I did in the *Herald* which was sympathetic to David Shayler. You know, the MI5 whistleblower who ended up in prison. He thought I would put his story across sympathetically. We had opened negotiations.'

Sam thought of the thousand pounds sitting in her father's wallet and wondered if that was part of them. 'How far had the negotiations got?'

'Near the end. He had been due to deliver the information we'd discussed but he didn't turn up for the final meeting.'

'What date was the meeting?'

'Two days ago.'

The day he'd been shot. Final meeting. Maybe that's exactly what it was supposed to be. Maybe she'd set him up. Maybe she wasn't a journalist after all.

'You got some kind of ID?' Sam snapped.

Webb took her wallet out of her bag and handed Sam a small laminated card. It was an NUJ card in her name with a deeply unflattering photo of her on it. They walked on in silence for a few minutes. They entered Hurlingham Park, which was filled with tired-looking mothers, bundled-up babies and over-excited dogs. Webb suddenly stopped and grabbed Sam's arm.

'Look, is Geoff all right? Has something happened to him? The last time we spoke he was worried that they were onto him. He was moving around a lot and trying to cover his tracks. Is that why he didn't turn up to the meeting?'

Sam shook her arm free of the woman. 'You're going to have to do better than this.' She waved the card in the air before handing it back. 'How did you know about me?'

'He told me that if anything happened to him and I wasn't able to get hold of him I should speak to you . . . he told me you'd help me.'

'Well, he said absolutely nothing to me about you. I've not seen him recently. I can't help you.'

Webb flattened her chin into jowls that would have given Robbie Coltrane a good run for his money and dug her hands into the pockets of her coat. 'I realise you have no reason to trust me. But I am on his side in all this. I am aware of the pressures involved. It's a volatile time for a former SAS soldier to be claiming that he was involved in the murders of over forty Republicans. They will do anything to discredit him and to prevent him telling what he knows. He said that three of his mates in the same squad are no longer alive. It seems to me that his primary motivation is the desire to set the record straight. It's not financial.'

Sam laughed. 'How much are you paying him?'

'That's between me and him.'

Sam turned and began walking back to her flat. 'I can't help you,' she said. 'I need to be getting home.'

The woman was standing looking at her.'At least pass on a message. Tell him, Kelly says hi. That the deal's still on.'

'I'm not in a position to do that. I don't know if I'll see him again.'

Half an hour later Sam stood over the photocopier in the post office on the New King's Road, arranging the contents of her father's wallet on the glass. She made copies of everything and then made copies of the contents of the envelope. She bought a large padded envelope and some packing tape and put everything – the photocopies, the envelope containing the originals and the wallet – into the padded envelope and taped it up. As she came back into the block she met Edie struggling up the stairs with some bags of shopping.

'All right, babes?' Edie said when her eyes had come off her feet and the stairs.

'Could I come in for a second?'

'If you make it quick. I've got Denis coming round for some baccy.'

Sam followed Edie into her flat and through into her kitchen. Frank was snoring on top of Edie's fridge, a large opportunistic orange paw hung over the edge so that it could detect any movement of the door. Mind you, Sam thought, if a fridge opened in Tierra del Fuego, Frank would probably know about it.

'Oh, he's here,' Sam said.

'Yes, sorry, babes, I meant to tell you. But he's no trouble.'

Sam held out the padded envelope. 'I need a home for this for a couple of days, Edie. Would you mind? I'll be in Oxford, and after what happened the other day . . .'

'This what they were looking for?'

'Maybe. Could you keep it in the filing cabinet?'

Edie had a three-drawer dark green filing cabinet, which she used to lock up her cigarettes.

Her beady brown eyes scanned the outside of the envelope, as if she had X-ray vision and could read what was inside. 'Well, I'm not sure, babes.'

Sam held out a twenty-pound note. 'I'd really appreciate it.'

Edie took it. 'No trouble, babes. Pleased to help.' The note disappeared into the depths of her hairy cardigan.

'While I'm away in Oxford could you keep an eye on Frank for me?'

'Course I can. I've bought him a nice piece of chicken anyway.'

Edie was unpacking her shopping. 'Prices have gone up again at the post office. Do they think we don't notice?'

'Nothing gets past you, Edie.'

'I told him I was taking my business elsewhere.'

'Where to?'

'Budgens,' Edie said. 'It's more of a walk but I'll not be ripped off. They think they can hold us pensioners over a barrel because of our legs. Bloody euro's cutting into my profits as it is. All the fags have gone up. It's what happened with decimalisation. They think no one'll notice with the change of currency but it's a good ten per cent. People aren't that daft.'

'Well, you're not, Edie.'

'No, babes.'

'Do you have any dealings with Jackie on the top floor?'

'Why?'

'Just wondered.'

'Tight-fisted as they come. Always trying to knock me on the fags. Then says: "Oh, I've only got a fifty, Edie, can I pay you next week?" I'm onto her, though. Now I always have change for her. I won't be taken on like that.'

'Anything else about her?'

'Dodgy as a nine-bob note, babes.'

Sam smiled because this was a fairly accurate description of Edie. 'Why do you say that?'

Edie shrugged. 'You seen the locks she's got on that door of hers. It's like Fort Knox up there. What's she hiding?'

The doorbell went. 'That'll be Denis,' Edie said, herding Sam quickly out of the flat.

Back in her own, Sam wondered if Kelly Webb had been responsible for the break-in. Perhaps it was only when the burglary hadn't turned up what she wanted that she had rung on the doorbell. But then the burglary had taken place before her father was shot, before the meeting, so that didn't make sense, unless Webb wasn't who she was claiming to be. Unless there was never going to be a meeting and the deal was pure fiction.

Sam rang the *Daily Herald* and asked the person on the end of the line how she could check if someone worked for them. She was put through to a harassed-sounding man.

'Can you confirm that a Kelly Webb works for you?'

'Why?'

'I've been approached by her concerning a story and I want to know that she is who she says she is.'

'Hang on a minute.' Sam was put on hold.

A few minutes later the man came back on the line.

'No one here's heard of her.'

'Are you absolutely sure?'

'You asked – I've told you.' The phone went dead.

Sam stared at the silent receiver. If Kelly Webb wasn't a journalist then who exactly was she?

CHAPTER THIRTEEN

Sam stood in Christ Church Meadow in Oxford with her back to the college boathouses looking across the river at the graffiti-covered ruin that had once been the Oxford University Boat Club. She'd checked with Tom King where the squad would be. Usually they trained at Wallingford, which had the longest lock-to-lock stretch of water on the upper Thames, but the snowfall had brought flooding and that had forced them back to Oxford and the busy stretch of water between Iffley Lock and Folly Bridge, which all the college eights used.

The clouds were grey and louring and the vicious wind blowing off the river was just beginning to spit rain that felt like tiny slivers of glass against Sam's face. As she ducked her chin inside the collar of her coat and looked along the river to her left, an eight with dark blue oars came into sight and Briony Flint began to shout instructions to bring the boat in to the bank. The wind, however, had switched and was now hitting the eight side-on, pushing it away from the bank, and she was having difficulties getting the boat correctly manoeuvred.

Tom King skidded to a halt, dropped his bicycle on the towpath next to Sam and jumped down onto a wooden pontoon. 'Any news?'

Sam shook her head. 'Not about Harry directly, but I wanted to run some things past you.'

Tom grabbed hold of the tip of an oar and began pulling the boat up to the bank. 'Give me a hand, could you?' he said, indicating that Sam should do the same. 'It's the wind – it's a bugger to get them in when it's blowing like this.'

Sam took hold of an oar a couple down from the one Tom was

182

holding onto, squatted down and threw her body weight into pulling the boat towards the bank. When four oars lay over the top of the pontoon she stood up.

Briony Flint was the first out of the boat.

'Bit cold today,' Sam commented.

Flint touched her hair. 'At least it's not frozen.'

Sam watched her go into the boathouse and carry out a plastic box filled with the largest pairs of trainers she had ever seen. The oarsmen were taking their feet out of the shoes fixed in the boat and undoing the gates that held their blades in place.

'I need to talk to them about the outing,' Tom said. 'Then if it's all right with you we can walk back to Folly Bridge and you can tell me what's going on.'

Sam nodded. 'Fine. I'll wait for you here.' She moved out of the way as the eight men bent over and, on the barked instructions of Flint, lifted the boat clear of the water, hoisted it effortlessly onto their shoulders and loped into the boathouse.

There were a few other eights out on the water, their ragged catches and lack of balance indicating that they were a lower species altogether than the crew that had just finished their outing. Twenty minutes later, by which time Sam was frozen solid, Tom came out of the boathouse, picked up his bike and told her he was ready.

'Did Mark tell you what's happened?' Sam asked.

Tom pulled his dark blue woollen hat down over his ears and nodded. 'Poor kid, that's all we need – his mother being murdered. Any sign of him?'

Sam shook her head. 'Obviously the police are extremely eager to trace him and his brother.'

'It's odd, you know. Mark told me about David but Harry never talked about a brother. Never talked about his family much at all.'

'David was in prison and came out at the end of his first term, so I don't think that's very surprising. Harry wouldn't be talking about that in a new environment. That's the kind of thing you only tell people when you know them well.'

'Does David row?'

Sam laughed and shook her head. 'Apparently not at all interested, although Eric tried.'

'I bet he did. You don't get many physical specimens like Harry turning up all that often, but to have two of them . . . frankly, the thought's mouthwatering.'

'Coaches . . .' Sam said.

'Opportunists – every single one of us. So do you think they're aware that their mother's dead?'

'We're not sure.'

'What kind of stuff was his brother involved with?'

'Drugs, a bit of dealing, a bit of possession and petty thievery. It seems likely that he turned up at Oxford at the end of last term and was responsible for getting Harry into trouble with that girl.'

'It's ridiculous. No way was Harry involved with that.'

'I know, everything I've heard about Harry seems to make that completely impossible.'

'So how do you explain it?'

Sam sighed. 'If you rule out Harry there are only two possibilities: David did it or the girl lied and wanted to set up either one of them for some reason.'

'Are you certain David was in Oxford at the time?'

'No.'

'Have you traced the girl?'

'I know who she is but I haven't spoken to her yet. Have you heard of the Mad Hatter?'

'The bar?'

'Yes.'

King grimaced. 'Me and Theo go way back.'

'What, Carter – the man who runs it?'

'Yup.'

'What's the connection?'

'We were exact contemporaries, went to the same college.'

'Friends?'

He laughed. 'Hardly. He rowed, you know, but didn't make it into the Blue boat. Don't think he ever forgave me for that.'

'What did it have to do with you?'

'I was president that year. It was my decision not to risk him. There were quite a few who thought we should have.'

'Why was he a risk?'

'You've met him, right?'

Sam nodded.

'Well, he was a moody bastard even as an undergraduate. Either he'd get in the boat and row like a genius or he'd be completely crap. He had no consistency whatsoever. You never knew which Theo you'd be rowing with. I decided we couldn't risk that. I told him he had to be more consistent in training. He wasn't, so I dropped him to Isis and then he walked out of the squad.'

'Did you make it up?'

King shook his head. 'No, and a few months after he quit the squad he was sent down.'

'What for?'

King laughed. 'He hit his tutor.'

'Did you win that year?'

'Yes, but it's not to say we wouldn't have won by a larger margin with him in the boat. I don't know if it was the right decision or not. When he was on song he was fantastic. It's just that he was completely unpredictable. Nowadays he'd probably be diagnosed as bipolar.'

'So you wouldn't be the best person to ask him about Siobhan?'

'Is that the girl who said she was attacked?'

'Yes.'

He laughed. 'No, I'm not the man for that. I wouldn't be surprised if he didn't try and punch my lights out, even now.'

'How's Holden getting on?'

'Better than last time we spoke. There's no doubt he's a first-class oarsman. We're lucky to have two such talented men to choose from. He's settled down since Harry went missing. Harry was blowing him away in the head-to-heads and he wasn't taking kindly to it. He was trying too hard and tensing up and it was affecting his performances.'

'Any bad feeling between the two of them?'

'I think Holden's nose was pretty much out of joint last term. If we hadn't had Harry he would have expected to walk straight into the stroke's seat. And he's only here for a year.'

'Don't tell me – Social Sciences.'

King laughed. 'Yes, as it happens. But it's now or never. And he's as different to Harry as they come. Likes the ladies and the good life – I'd guess it's a long time since he last stuck *his* head in a church.'

They had almost reached Folly Bridge when they heard shouting behind them and the squad came pounding past.

Tom grinned approvingly at their disappearing backs. 'Gave them a bit of a bollocking in there. They're showing they took it on board. We don't have an enormous choice but we work hard with what we get here. They're a good bunch of lads.'

'And if Harry was back?'

He shrugged 'I don't know, but I'd probably put him back at stroke. Off the river he's a quiet boy and very unassuming. You wouldn't think of him as being a leader because he doesn't say much, but as soon as he has an oar in his hands it's like his whole personality changes. That boy's an absolute tiger. He doesn't know the meaning of the word "quit" and that's what you want in the stroke – the guys respond to him. You've no idea what fucking agony rowing can be. The stroke has to be able to take himself and the whole crew through pain barrier after pain barrier. Especially in this race. It's not like any other. Harry's remarkable – so steady and so brave.'

'What are the politics of having an American stroke as opposed to an Englishman?'

'There are none. There have been some fantastic American oarsmen who've stroked the Blue Boat over the years. Ultimately it's a question of which one makes the boat run faster – that's all anyone's interested in.'

'You realise Harry may get in touch with you?'

'Me?'

'Well, you're someone he trusts and respects.'

'He's only known me a few months, Sam. If I were to hazard a guess I think he'd go to Eric. He's coached him since he was a boy and was more *in loco parentis*, especially with the father he's got. It was Eric who got him involved in rowing in the first place.'

'Maybe, but if he does contact you, Tom, it would be a good idea to get the boy to hand himself in to the police. The mother's been killed and the longer they're missing the more suspicious the police'll be.'

'You think Harry was involved in her murder?'

Sam shook her head. 'I just don't know.'

'But if he wasn't, why hasn't he turned up?'

'His brother's in trouble – I don't think he'll leave his side.'

'He'll have to eventually.'

'I know, but he's only eighteen, Tom, I don't think he knows what to do.'

They had left Christ Church Meadow and were now walking up St Aldates. 'Where are you off to next?' Tom asked.

'Next stop, this same conversation but with the vicar of St Silas's. I'm trying to cover the people he might go to and fill them in on what's happened to his mother.'

Tom got onto his bicycle and spun the pedals into the right position.

'You're sure you still want me to continue? I mean it's not as if the police don't have a good reason for looking for him now. They're much more likely to turn him up than I am.'

'I was thinking it would be good for Harry if you could find him first.'

Sam sat in a pew at the back of St Silas's waiting for Emma Hodge to finish a wedding rehearsal. She'd gone looking for her at the vicarage but been told she was in the church and that the rehearsal had almost finished. Sam looked at a large stained-glass window of the crucified Christ, blood spurting from the gash in his side and from his hands and feet. She looked at the plaster on her finger. What was happening to her? The crucifixion represented sacrifice. Giving your own life so that others could live. Self-mutilation was pure narcissism. She felt sick and ashamed and frightened.

The rehearsal broke up and a couple of tiny rumbustious bridesmaids freed from the constraints of good behaviour tore past Sam, screaming like banshees pursued by *Buffy the Vampire Slayer*. Emma shook hands with the couple and then, catching sight of Sam, walked over to where she was sitting. This time she was dressed in a black cassock that fell to her ankles and had a dog collar round her neck. The effect was to make her look ludicrously young.

'So,' Sam said, 'are they going to defy the statistics?'

Hodge smiled somewhat wearily and sat down next to Sam. 'Why not? They share the same faith and they love each other – it's as good a start as any.'

'Have you heard about Harry's mother?'

She nodded.

'And that the police are looking for him?'

Again she nodded.

Sam was puzzled. 'How did you know?'

Emma Hodge folded her hands in her lap, sighed heavily and looked down at them.

'Did my brother, Mark, get in touch?'

She shook her head.

'You've seen Harry, haven't you?'

'I'm sorry but I can't—'

'Grace Cameron's face was beaten to a pulp and the back of her skull smashed to pieces. The same people who did it may well be looking for David. You know about David?'

'Yes.'

'You know everything, don't you?'

'I can't—'

'Surely you can tell me that.'

She shook her head and remained silent.

'Harry could be in serious danger,' Sam said. 'This isn't just about him going missing any more. His mother's been murdered.'

'I realise how serious it is. I've tried to—'

'Look, I'm on his side. I'm not aligned with the police. To be honest, since I've been on this case Harry's got under my skin. Everything I've heard about him has been good. His coach says he's the best he's ever had. I can't bear the thought of all that being thrown away.'

Hodge looked surprised. 'You really care about him?'

'Of course I do. I want to see him rowing in the Boat Race. If he's got it in him I want to see him rowing in the Olympics.'

'But you've never even met him. I thought he was just a job to you.'

'Is that what this is to you?' Sam gestured at the church.

Hodge smiled. 'Well, no, but it's generally accepted that being in the church is more vocational then being a private investigator.'

'I don't want him lost,' Sam said and then quite unexpectedly felt herself starting to shake, the tears pricking her eyes.

Hodge reached over and touched her arm. 'Are you all right?'

To her horror, Sam felt a sob burst out of her throat. She scrabbled in her bag and found a card. 'If he calls you again, will you get him to phone me?' A drip from her nose fell on the card and she wiped it off on her sleeve.

Hodge took the card and held it in her hands, turning it round and round.

'Sam . . .' she said.

'What?' Sam was standing up and slinging her bag round her shoulder.

Dear God, Sam thought, don't let her be sympathetic.

Hodge stood up. 'I just wanted to say that I'm sorry you're so upset. If you want to talk—'

'It's nothing,' Sam said and bolted for the door.

Sam sat in the Lady Chapel of Christ Church Cathedral. She'd been charged for the privilege, which came as something of a shock. It wasn't the money she minded; it was what it represented, the fact that she no longer belonged and was a tourist in what had been her home town. She had told Mark she would be at his rooms in St Barnabas's in half an hour's time for a family conference with Jean and Peter, but before that ordeal she sought peace and quiet. As a child, she had walked in and out of Oxford colleges with her stepfather or her mother but now the colleges were much more difficult to penetrate. More likely than not, you'd end up being challenged by an unimpressed porter and told the times of a guided tour.

Peter had been a student at Christ Church (which at that particular college meant a don) before becoming Warden of St Cuthbert's College and they had always come to the carol service that was held here every Christmas Eve. Occasionally they had come to other services as well. Sam stood up and walked through into the chancel, gazing up at the intricate star-shaped patterns of the vault spreading over her head. Behind her the choir was practising and the pure ethereal voices drifted down the nave towards her. Sam had always loved the cathedral, the feel of the place and the smell, the solemnity. While words she was largely indifferent to floated over her head, Sam had gazed at the *memento mori*, the stone-winged skull attached to the wall near the pulpit, and imagined herself floating free from her body and up and around the giant columns that held the cathedral in place, up into the vaulted ceiling and then along the chancel to browse up and down in front of the magnificent circular stained-glass windows above the altar. People had worshipped on this site since the eighth century. Even if you were an atheist you couldn't help but feel it and be calmed by it. Sam wasn't sure what she was. She suspected that belief had crept under her skin like a splinter when she was a child and as an adult she'd never quite had the courage to cut it out. It sat there itching from time to time, especially when she was in a cathedral. Her finger throbbed and she massaged it with her thumb.

I don't want him lost.

Sam put her face in her hands. Lost. Although she'd been talking about Harry, the grief she'd felt was all for herself.

The choir had finished practising and she followed them outside. No longer angelic and ethereal but earthy mischievous little boys, angelic only in looks. As she stood looking across the quad at Tom Tower, the sun burst from behind the clouds, flooding the college with bright sunshine. Sam walked over to Mercury and watched the fat white and gold fish circling in the sun. She looked back at the cathedral. In the old days churches were places of safety. If you got inside and claimed sanctuary there was nothing the secular authorities could do about it. Sam wondered where sanctuary would be for Harry. In a church? In a boathouse? With his coach or a priest? Or had he sought it with his mother? Everyone needed a place of safety. Sam stepped out of the main entrance of Christ Church into the secular roar and rush of St Aldates and, conscious of the fear fluttering in her stomach and that she was in much too fragile a state to face her family, she headed reluctantly towards St Barnabas's.

Mark opened the door.

'Mum and Peter are already here,' he said.

'Right.' Sam kissed him.

Her mother and Peter were seated next to each other on Mark's leather sofa. Sam made no attempt to greet them physically. She put her bag down, leaned against the wall and folded her arms. 'Hi,' she said.

'Do you want anything to drink?' Mark asked. Sam shook her head.

'OK,' Mark continued. 'The purpose of this meeting is to update each other fully on what's been going on with Dad.'

'Well, I doubt he's going to be standing outside your front door any more,' Sam said.

'Shut up,' Mark snapped and Sam felt almost physically assaulted by the savagery of his tone. He turned back to his parents. 'Mum. Why don't you go first.'

'The last couple of days he hasn't been there but yesterday evening we were contacted by a journalist called Kelly Webb, who wanted to know if I'd seen him and if I could tell her where he was. She said he had some information for her and he'd disappeared. I just put down the phone. I didn't know what to say to her.'

Sam groaned. It hadn't occurred to her that Kelly Webb would go after the rest of the family. It hadn't occurred to her that she'd know about them. 'Has she phoned again?' she asked.

'Yes,' Peter said. 'A few times this morning. I've started putting the phone down on her as well.'

Her mother looked at Sam. 'Do you know something about this?'

'The same woman doorstepped me yesterday, wanting to know where Dad was and if he'd left anything with me for her. I'm sorry, I had no reason to think she'd bother you. Apparently he'd told her that if he disappeared she should get in touch with me.'

'Why?' Peter asked.

'She seems to think he left something with me to hand over to her.'

'And had he?'

Sam nodded.

Silence filled the room and everyone stared at Sam. She was trying to work out how much she should tell them. Someone clattered noisily down the staircase outside Mark's rooms.

'Sam?' Mark said.

'Look, to start with he kept phoning me. I didn't answer or anything. Didn't pick up the phone. Then he put an envelope through the door and left a message asking me to look after it. I hid it under the floorboards. Then I got burgled. I presumed they were looking for what was in the envelope. The whole place was completely turned over but they didn't find it. Then a few days later I went back to the flat and there he was bleeding all over my sofa. He'd been shot through the shoulder. I phoned Max because he wouldn't let me take him to hospital – he was worried about the police. Max got him seen to at Charing Cross. I refused to have him back at my place. He's at Max's now, recuperating. Then Kelly Webb turns up and starts asking me where he is. I haven't told her anything.'

'What have you done with the envelope?' Mark said.

'Put it somewhere safe.'

'Have you read the contents?' Peter asked.

'No,' Sam lied. She didn't want to get into that particular conversation at the moment.

'Perhaps you should hand over the envelope to Webb,' he said. 'That'll get her off our backs.'

Sam didn't say anything. One thing she knew was that she wasn't going to do that. Not before talking to her father at any rate. Since talking to Webb he'd been shot. That might well change how he felt about handing over more information.

Peter continued. 'That's what the woman wants, isn't it? Once she gets it, then surely she'll leave us alone.'

'I don't think that's a good idea,' Sam said.

'Why not?'

'I don't know if that's what he wants. I don't know if she is who she says she is. I phoned the paper she claimed she worked for and they said they had no record of her. I'm worried about putting him in danger.'

'What about us?' her mother said. 'What about us being in danger?'

'I don't think he wants to hurt you.'

'You've read what's in it, haven't you?'

Sam shook her head.

Her mother crossed her legs and folded her hands in her lap. 'Still lying. You're still lying to us.'

Sam felt a bomb of anger explode in her stomach and start to spread upwards through her chest. Then it hit her vocal cords. 'Lying,' she shouted. 'How many years did you lie to us about Dad? How many fucking years was that – twenty-eight years' worth of lies?' She could feel the adrenaline sparking in her hands like hundreds of tiny electric shocks.

'Sam . . .' Mark warned.

But Sam wouldn't be stopped. 'You've got no fucking moral high ground to occupy. None whatsoever. So don't get on your high horse and get all so fucking snooty about who is or isn't lying.'

Her mother got to her feet.

'Yes, that's it,' Sam said. 'Whenever you're confronted with the truth you just run away from it or slap it.'

Her mother ran her hand through her hair. 'I didn't tell you the truth about your father because I didn't want to upset you. Maybe I was wrong not to. I didn't know he would come back after all these years. I wasn't to know that.'

'But even if he hadn't, don't you think we should have known the truth about him?'

'You never wanted to know the truth. You wanted to worship a dead hero.'

'How do you know what I wanted? You never asked me and you never gave me the choice.'

'So you think you want to know the truth, do you?'

'Jean, no—' Peter was scrambling off the sofa to reach her.

'No, Peter, Sam says she wants the truth and maybe she's right. Maybe I should have told her a long time ago.'

'But not in anger, Jean,' Peter said softly.

But she wasn't listening to her husband. She looked at Sam and continued. 'Your father had a horrible temper, especially when he'd been drinking. When he came back from a mission was always the worst. One time he came back and raped me. You were born nine months later. I tried to make it mean nothing but I'd be fooling myself if I said it made no difference to the way I felt about you. I so hoped that it wouldn't. I didn't think that it would, but you were so like him.' Sam's mother shook her head in exasperation. 'Why did you have to be so like him? You were fighting as soon as you could walk. If you'd been a boy I'm not sure I could have kept you. I thought because you were a girl . . .'

Sam knew her mother was still speaking because she could see her mouth moving, it was just that she couldn't hear anything that she was saying. She had heard nothing after the words 'nine months later', just the pounding in her ears. She was drowning again, the smell of chlorine in her nostrils. Down and down she spiralled … She looked at Mark and Peter and saw similar expressions on both their faces. It was as if they were all underwater and bubbles should be rising from their mouths towards the surface. The surface. Where the hell was that? She was hyperventilating, gasping for breath. She had to get out of this room. She had to get away from them all. She picked up her bag and made for the door. She felt as if she was moving in slow motion. Still she couldn't hear. Mark took hold of her arm and she saw his lips move; she pushed him away and walked slowly down the stairs and out into front quad.

In the High Street she found a bit of wall that didn't have a bike leaning against it, sat down on the pavement and put her head between her knees. As she waited for her head to clear the noises of the street gradually began to filter into her consciousness – the bikes going past, snatches of conversation, laughter, horns blaring out in the High – but finally it was the familiarity of the multitude of church bells beginning to strike the hour that returned Sam to herself.

She stood up, at a loss what to do. It wasn't as if what her mother had said came completely out of the blue for her. Max had suggested as much in a conversation she'd had with him before meeting up with her father. But being told it by her mother. That was a different thing altogether. Not in anger, Peter had said. But the expression on her mother's face had been one of profound weariness and sadness. Sam would have found anger easier to deal with.

A number 5 bus drew up outside Queen's with Blackbird Leys as its destination, a familiar number, travelling a very familiar route. Without really thinking clearly about what she was doing, Sam jumped on board. The bus went over Magdalen Bridge, swung round the roundabout in the Plain and set off down the Cowley Road, a tattered ribbon of a road leading to a less picturesque part of the city. A couple of miles further on, Sam got off and headed into the Blackbird Leys housing estate. A few minutes later she was standing outside a house, ringing the front door. The man who opened it was in his fifties but had the hard, tough body of a man in his thirties and a shaved head. He took one look at Sam then stepped forward and wrapped her in a huge hug.

The smell of him brought back overwhelming memories for

Sam. One thing you knew if you fought someone enough was what he smelled like. Fighting created intense physical intimacy. She had fought this man, her coach, Tyler, a lot – day after day after day. The first time she'd tried to throw him, she'd been ten years old and had broken a toe on his broad, tree trunk-like legs. It had taught her the crucial difference between kicking and sweeping. He smelled of home to her, of fighting, of practice. Of routine and discipline and security. Of a life she had loved but no longer lived. Of course, she thought, he's my place of safety. How could I have forgotten that?

This is what it must mean to people to come home. This feeling. She'd been away far too long. And suddenly she realised why she'd been crying in the church. Harry had someone looking for him. Someone who knew he was missing. Sam had been missing a long time, ever since she'd stopped fighting, and no one had come looking for her. No one had even noticed. Lost, she thought, I'm utterly, utterly lost. Sobs juddered through her body and she pressed her face against his chest. Tyler held onto her until she had stopped.

CHAPTER FOURTEEN

Sam sat in Tyler's cramped front room, nursing a mug of tea between both hands in an attempt to stop them shaking. On the wall were two black and white photos. One was of Tyler wearing a suit and tie in a group shot taken at the Kodokan in Japan in the 1960s; his was the only western face there. The other had been taken at the Budokwai in London and was of him in a *judogi*. It was before the era of washing machines that softened and whitened jackets and his appearance was noticeable for the black stains around the collar of his jacket where opponents had gripped it, and the black stains on the knees of his trousers from doing groundwork. His mantelpiece was covered with trophies and pictures of the people he had coached over the years, amongst them Sam.

Sam stroked Django, his ageing mutt of a dog, who he'd bought from the gypsies years ago. She'd known him as a piddling puppy but now he had white hairs round his muzzle and arthritic back legs. The dog had settled his large bulk against Sam's leg and was quite happy as long as Sam kept scratching his head. If she stopped he began to whine and claw at her knee.

Tyler came into the room with his own tea and sat down opposite Sam. Django immediately sidled away from her, threw himself against Tyler's leg and put his head on his thigh.

Tyler ran the dog's silky ear between his finger and thumb. 'Nice to see you, Sammy.'

She looked into her cup of tea. 'You still coaching?'

'Bits and pieces. Come along later, if you like. I'm teaching up in Headington at seven. It's been a while since I saw you.'

He had not said it accusingly but she felt guilty all the same.

'I find it hard being around it. It reminds me how much I miss it.'

He nodded.

'Did you find it hard, Tyler, to give up fighting competitively? How did you cope?'

'I wasn't nearly as good as you, Sammy. It wasn't the same at all.'

'But you must have missed it?'

'Of course I did, but it wasn't as if I had so much to lose.'

'When I was fighting – that's when I felt most alive, most like myself. I don't know whether I'll ever get that with anything else.'

'Maybe you should feel happy that you ever had that feeling in the first place. Lots of people go through life never finding the thing that'll make them feel that way. You found it really young. You worked on it. You became the best you could be. Isn't that enough?'

Sam blushed. She felt embarrassed. As if she was demanding too much.

'I don't say it to shame you, Sammy. But you must see you're one of the lucky ones. You're not going to be travelling in the back of a cab with Rod Steiger mumbling, "I could have been a contender." You can say, "I was a contender and I won. Not just once but four times." You're the best I ever had. I've got a girl now who reminds me of you. Karen Lewis. Fearless. Willing to have a go at anyone. Like a little sponge. Anything I tell her goes in and stays there and then she wants more.'

'Has she kicked you yet and broken her toe?'

Tyler laughed. 'It's only a matter of time.' He pulled up the trouser legs of his tracksuit and showed Sam a number of large black bruises on his shins. He stood up. 'I need to get ready. Fancy a trip up the hill?'

'Sure. Why not?'

An hour later Sam was sitting on a wooden bench in a community centre in Headington watching twenty little boys and girls doing forward somersaults.

Tyler, bare-footed and wearing a white *judogi* and black belt, walked over to where she was sitting. 'Spotted her yet?' he asked.

Sam nodded as she watched a girl with a long plait of hair

somersault in the air and land, bringing both arms down hard on the mat. Even Sam winced. 'God, Tyler, was I like that?'

Tyler shook his head. 'No, you were *much, much* worse . . .'

Sam rubbed her face. 'It's not surprising some days when I wake up I feel as if I've been flattened by a steamroller.'

She stood up.

'You off then?'

'Yup.' She'd only managed about ten minutes. She opened her mouth to begin to thank him but he cut across her.

'Give yourself time. It'll become easier to let go. You'll lighten up around it and then you can come back.' He ruffled her hair as if she were the seven-year-old he'd first started coaching and then turned his attention back to his class.

As Sam pushed open the door, she looked back and saw Karen Lewis, standing with her hands on her hips, staring after her.

After a few minutes walking, Sam reached the London Road that cuts through Headington and runs down into the centre of Oxford and found a bus stop. Headington was a depressing place, filled with charity shops and cheap supermarkets, and if that wasn't depressing enough the Co-operative Funeral Parlour was there to remind you that it was only ever going to end one way. It was dark and beginning to rain. Sam huddled down in her coat and sat staring ahead of her. Rape. The word ricocheted inside her head like a bullet that wasn't going to stop until it had torn up everything in its path. Like the explosive bullet hitting the watermelon in *The Day of the Jackal*. While she'd been at Tyler's she'd forced it somewhere into the furthest recesses of her mind but now it was all she could think of. Rape. That's all she could remember. What had anyone said after that? She had no idea. She hadn't heard a word. She saw the faces of Mark, her mother and Peter all staring at her. She saw the expression of pity on their faces and felt sick. A gust of wind whistled under the bus shelter, rattling the plastic top and making her jump. And what did that make her? Her mind answered, implacable in its accusations: evil, dirty, tainted, beyond redemption, worthless, unlovable, shameful. She closed her eyes. Tyler hadn't asked her what the matter was, but he wouldn't – it wasn't his style. That's why she'd gone to him, because he'd be there but not ask. But there was a bit of her that wanted something else, that wanted someone to ask.

You can phone me, Sam, any time.

How does that work?

You pick up the phone, you punch in the numbers and you speak to me.

Sam fumbled in her bag found her mobile phone, brought up Reg's number and dialled. She hoped he wouldn't pick up and in the same instant she prayed with all her might that he would.

'Reg Ellison speaking.'

Sam didn't say anything.

'Hello?'

Sam started to cry.

'Who is this?'

Tears poured down Sam's face.

'Can you tell me what's happened?'

Huddled in the corner of the bus shelter, Sam continued to cry. She didn't tell him who she was. She didn't speak. She just cried and he listened. Telling her that everything would be all right. That she was quite safe. That they could talk about it at the next session.

'Sam?' he said and she cut him off.

Sam wiped the tears off her face. I'm just like my father, she thought. I have the courage to phone but not the courage to say who I am. I'm a coward. I'm becoming everything I despise.

A bus came and Sam got on it. She felt slightly calmer now, less as if she was going to fly apart into tiny pieces, but she also felt utterly drained. She leaned her head against the window and looked at the smear of the car headlights coming up Headington Hill, reflecting off the rain-spattered glass on the front of the bus.

As Sam was stepping off the bus outside Queen's, her phone rang.

'Sam?' It was a woman's voice that Sam couldn't place immediately.

'Who's this?'

'It's Emma, we spoke earlier today at the church.'

'Oh yes.'

'It's just...'

'Yes.'

'Harry may phone you.'

'You've seen him?'

'He phoned. I gave him your number, so I wanted to warn you that he might be in contact.'

'Where is he?'

'I'm sorry, that's all I can say. I promised.'

'You realise the boy could be in danger? His mother was killed. Suppose he knows who did it? Suppose he was a witness? Whatever happened, we need to get him sorted out, get him back to college, back to his life.'

'I'm sorry,' Emma said. 'That really is all I can say. I told him you had his best interests at heart. I think he'll phone you.'

'Hold on—'

The phone went dead.

Sam looked at the screen on her mobile and realised that the answerphone symbol was flashing, indicating that she had messages. There were two. The first one was from Mark.

'Sam, where are you? Are you all right? It doesn't mean anything, Sam. Phone me. I'm worried about you. Please phone. It's not your fault. We're all so worried about you.'

The second message was from Max. 'He's gone, Sam. Thought I should let you know. And he seems to think you've got something that belongs to him, so expect him to be in touch.'

As Sam was digesting the messages, a car drew up alongside her and two men got out and walked towards her. Sam didn't like the look of them. There was something about the way they were approaching her that seemed too studiedly nonchalant. She backed away from them and as she did so they increased their pace. When one made a grab for her, Sam didn't wait for them to introduce themselves; she sprinted across the High and bolted down Queen's Lane, hearing her footsteps mixed with those of her pursuers, ricocheting off the blackened medieval walls. Up above her, attached to the side of New College, the gargoyles looked down on her, stonily indifferent to her plight.

The two men were gaining on her.

A diminutive don with a luxuriant grey beard and gnomish demeanour was wheeling his bicycle through the electronic gates that gave access to the back of Queen's College. Sam increased her pace and just managed to squeeze between them as they slammed shut, almost taking the fingertips of her closest pursuer with them.

She glanced at the top of the gates and was relieved to see sharp spikes and razor wire that would have made any further pursuit extremely foolhardy. The astonished don stared at her as she bent over, gasping for breath.

'I'm sorry,' he said, 'but this is private property. You're not allowed to come through here.'

'No, I know,' Sam said. 'But there are some people out there I'd prefer not to meet. Could you let me out into the High?'

'I don't—'

'I'm Peter Goodman's daughter,' Sam said. 'My brother's an English don at St Barnabas's – Mark Falconer. Perhaps you know them.'

'Oh really?'

'I was brought up in St Cuthbert's. I'm sorry to ask it of you but isn't there an exit through Drawda Hall?'

He smiled. She waited while he locked up his bicycle and then followed him across a courtyard and a small garden and then through two black metal gates, the second of which opened out onto the High.

'Thank you very much indeed,' Sam said.

'Say hello to Mark for me. I'm Professor Beckmann,' he said, holding out his hand. 'Felix Beckmann.'

'I will,' Sam said, taking it.

Thank God for the old-boy network, Sam thought, as the metal gate crashed shut behind her.

She looked in both directions along the High but saw no sign of the two men who had chased her. She was just deciding what to do next when her phone rang. It was Phil.

'Sam, could you come to the station? I've got Skinner here and he'd like a word.'

'What's he doing in town?'

'Following up some leads on the Grace Cameron murder.'

'Can't you just put him on the phone?'

'It'd be easier if you came in.'

Sam looked at her watch and sighed. 'I'm in the High. I should be there in about ten minutes.'

It was only after she cut the connection that she stopped to wonder how they knew she was in Oxford at all.

*

Skinner ran his hand down the same repulsive tie and sighed. He seemed distracted, bored even.

'Have you traced Harry?' he asked.

'No.'

He fidgeted with the tie from hell. 'Any closer to finding out where he might be?'

Sam shook her head. 'And you?'

He didn't reply. Sam was puzzled; there had seemed little urgency to the questions he was asking and nothing he'd said to her explained why it was so pressing that he talk to her.

'Has Harry been seen in Oxford?' she said. 'Is that why you're down?'

Before he could answer, the door opened and one of the men who had chased Sam came in.

Sam stood up. 'Hold on,' she said. 'Who the fuck is he?'

Skinner also stood up and walked to the door. 'Sorry, love. It's over my head.' He pushed the door open and left.

The man who had just entered pulled back the chair Skinner had vacated, sat down and placed a beige folder on the desk. He took out a handkerchief and wiped it over his sweating face. 'So, Miss Falconer, enjoy giving us the run-around, did you?'

'Yeah, your boss phoned, said it was either the fat farm for you or a bit of exercise. I said I'd see what I could do.'

'Sit down. I want to talk to you about your father.'

'Who the fuck are you? I was told they wanted to ask questions about Harry Cameron.'

The man didn't offer his name. 'We've lost track of your father over the last couple of days and thought you might be able to help us.'

'I don't know what you're talking about. My father died in Oman in 1974.'

'We both know that's not true. We understand he may have been injured—'

'You can understand whatever you like.'

'We also understand he may have come to you for help—'

Sam shook her head. 'I don't know what you're talking about.'

He nodded at the chair. 'Why don't you sit down, Samantha, and we can have a chat.'

Sam did sit down, although she had no intention of chatting.

'When did you last see him?'

'When I was four years old.'

The man opened the folder and pulled out a couple of photos and tossed them across the table at Sam. Sam picked one up. It was of her coming out of the café where she had met her father. She felt winded, as if an unseen hand had just delivered an uppercut to her stomach.

'So what?' she said. 'I'd been in a café. Drinking tea's not a crime, is it?'

He threw another one at her. This one was of inside the café. Of Sam and her father gripping each other's wrists. *Flesh of my flesh.* Before she could help herself, Sam was rubbing her wrist.

'Hurt you, did he?'

Sam pulled her jacket sleeve back over her wrist and folded her arms but didn't respond.

He leaned back in his chair. 'You don't think we'd let someone as dangerous as Geoffrey Falconer walk around without keeping tabs on him, do you?'

'I've got nothing to say to you.'

The man shifted his position in his seat. Sam stared at him, noticing how pale blue his eyes were and how his irises had narrowed to pinpricks.

'We know that he's phoned you. We suspect that he came to you for help and that you did help him. We also suspect he left something with you for safekeeping. Now you need to tell us where he is.'

'If you're so clever and you know so much already, go find him your fucking self.'

The man's hand shot cross the table and grabbed Sam's face. She felt his nails digging into her cheeks.

'Don't mistake me,' he snarled, 'for someone who plays by the rules.'

She jumped up, breaking his grip, and kicked over her chair. It was as if a switch had been flipped in her that transformed all the upset and misery she'd been feeling into red-hot rage.

'Come on,' Sam said. 'Just try me. I'm really in the mood.'

The man stood up, his hands hanging loosely at his sides. And Sam saw his eyes deaden. He took a step towards her and that was all Sam required. She flew at him, grabbed hold of his coat collar and threw him fast and clean onto the hard floor of the interview room. Then she was on top of him, hands fastened around his throat, choking the life out of him. She heard someone come into the room behind her then felt an arm round her own throat, pulling her away, and she let go of the man on the floor, driving backwards towards the wall, taking whoever it was with her. She heard the air come out of his lungs as he hit the wall with her elbow in his stomach.

She whipped round and saw Phil doubled over, holding out his hand. 'Steady, Sam, that's enough.'

'What the hell is this, Phil? Why did you get me to come here? Thought I deserved a bit of roughing up?'

'Skinner asked me to. I'm sorry, I don't know anything about this one.' He pointed to the man who was on his hands and knees coughing his lungs up. 'I thought it related to the Cameron case.'

The man slowly got to his feet, gingerly feeling his throat.

'Time-out, all right, mate?' Phil said.

'We haven't even got to the first round,' he croaked.

He picked the contents of the file off the floor and left the room. Phil righted the two chairs.

'Jesus Christ, Phil. Who the hell is that?'

He shrugged. 'I'm sorry, Sam. Like I said, Skinner asked me to get you in. He told me it was about the Cameron boy.'

'So what made you come bursting through the door just now?'

'That bloke's been around the station most of today and I was curious. Saw him come in here with you and thought I'd see what he was up to. I didn't think you'd take to him somehow, so I thought I'd keep an eye on how things were progressing.' He nodded at the mirror on the wall.

'You heard what he was asking?'

'Yes.'

Phil took a deep breath then winced and placed the flat of his hand against his ribs.

'Sorry, Phil, I hope I didn't hurt you. I thought—'

'Don't worry. Just didn't want you killing him.'

Sam's hands were shaking. If Phil hadn't come in, God knows what she would have done. She hadn't lost her temper like that in a long time. 'So what's the situation now? Can I go?'

Phil looked round the room. 'I can't see anyone stopping you.'

Sam shook her head. 'I've had the most fucking awful day. You haven't got time for a drink, have you?'

He ran his hand down the back of his head but didn't say anything.

She saw the hesitation and came to his rescue. 'Look, don't worry about it – you've got work to do. It's fine.'

'No, no, it's OK,' Phil said. 'Let's go.'

The Red Lion again, but this time Mark wasn't slumped in the corner.

'What can I get you?' Sam asked.

'No, let me,' Phil said. 'The usual?'

Sam nodded and sat down near the window. Now she felt empty, as if all the anger had drained out of her and left just despair. Phil came back with a pint of Guinness for her and tomato juice for himself. Sam frowned at his glass.

'You're not drinking?'

Phil shook his head.

'Since when?'

He shrugged.

'That why you knew about AA?'

'Maybe.'

'Well, you're as talkative as a clam.'

'I don't know how to talk about this with you, Sam. I have good days and bad days. Today's not been so good.'

'What happened? Is this about me?'

'Don't be so bloody vain.'

Sam laughed. 'Sorry – it's not been a good day for me either.'

'But you can say, God, let's go and have a drink. That's not an option for me any more.'

'Sorry.'

'No, that's not what I'm saying. I'm not saying it's your fault. I'm just saying it's not been a good day, that's what I'm saying. It's been the kind of day when I would have said the same.' He picked up his glass and twisted it in his hands.

'We don't have to stay here,' Sam said.

He nodded at her pint. 'You've got that to drink.'

'But do you want to leave?'

He shook his head. 'I have to get used to this. Finish your beer.'

'Are the meetings . . .' Sam paused, not sure what to say –
'. . . useful?'

'Some days I think they're the biggest wankers in the world,
other days – my guardian angels.'

'I thought you were seeing someone.'

He grunted. 'More like trying not to see myself.' He stared into
his tomato juice.

'I feel ashamed of myself. I haven't attacked someone in anger
since I was about six years old and shoved Georgie Stubbs's head
between the railings in the school playground and they had to put
soap on his ears to pull him out.'

'It was self-defence. He touched you first.'

'I wish that were true, but Georgie was as sweet-tempered as
they come.'

'Don't be an idiot. I meant the man in the station.'

Sam laughed. 'Not true there either. I made the decision to go
for him. If you hadn't come in I don't think I was going to let go
of him in a hurry.'

'Your father seems to be creating a whole lot of hassle for you,'
Phil commented.

'It's a horrible mess,' Sam agreed.

She drank the beer quickly and without much enjoyment. As
they were parting outside the pub, Sam touched his arm. 'You
look really well, Phil. You're thinner, your face is clearer.'

'Some days I feel as if I've lost my skin.'

'However it feels, it looks like it's working. That's why I
thought you were seeing someone. You know how people can
look when they've just started a new relationship. Like they're
well loved.'

Phil smiled. 'The running takes the edge off.'

'I'm seeing someone, by the way.'

He began to turn away from her. 'I hope it works out for you.'

'No, no,' Sam said, realising he'd misunderstood her. 'Not that
sort of someone – I mean a therapist.'

Phil looked dumbfounded.

Sam laughed. 'You should see the expression on your face.'

Phil shook his head. 'I . . .'

'Come on, Phil. It's not *that* surprising, is it?'

'Well, yes, Sam, it is.'

'Surely it's no more startling than you going to AA meetings?' Sam's phone rang. 'Sorry,' she said. 'I have to take this.'

She reached up, grabbed the lapel of his jacket, pulled his face down to her level and kissed him on the cheek. He squeezed her arm and headed back in the direction of the police station.

Sam took the call.

'Hello.'

'Sam Falconer?' The voice was tentative, young and male.

'Yes.'

'Emma Hodge gave me your number.'

'Harry?'

'Yes. She said you might be able to help.'

'Are you all right?'

'Could we meet?'

'Sure. Where are you?'

'I'm in the St Barnabas's boathouse in Christ Church Meadow.'

'I don't know which one that is.'

'I'll be waiting out front.'

'Isn't the meadow locked at night?'

'There's a gap in the railings next to the Folly Bridge entrance.'

Sam glanced at her watch. 'OK, I'll be there in half an hour.'

'Thanks.'

Harry had been right about the railings. Sam squeezed through the space and headed into the meadow. It was very dark in here and Sam took care with her footing because she didn't want to end up in the reed beds, which extended outwards from the bank into the Thames. It was also very quiet. Only a couple of hundred feet away was the bustle of central Oxford but here in Christ Church Meadow it was like being plunged into the deepest and darkest depths of the countryside. Enormous trees loomed over her as she hurried towards the boathouses.

When she was a child, Sam remembered walking round the park the day after a hurricane had torn through, ripping up trees by the roots. She'd jumped down into the craters left by the toppled trees and picked up pieces of blue and white china and white clay pipe. But then, looking up at the roots dangling over her head, she'd imagined she could hear them screaming and scrambled out of the crater, terrified. Looking up at the black branches above her head now, some of that fear returned.

Trying to calm herself, she paused and looked up the wide tree-lined path at the end of which stood Christ Church, bathed in floodlights. Thirteen of the twenty-three prime ministers Oxford had produced had gone to that college – Sam could never make up her mind whether that was a good or a bad thing. It was a grand college with a liberal tradition, and the only Oxford college whose head had to be a clergyman – maybe as good a place as any to educate leaders. She jumped as something scuttled across the path in front of her. Hoping it wasn't a rat, Sam continued on her way.

The moon emerged from behind the clouds as Sam crossed the bridge that led to the college boathouses. She had no idea which one was St Barnabas's but as she came off the bridge and onto a sandy path she saw the tall figure of a man about twenty feet ahead of her. She waved but at that moment the moon was obscured again, plunging the path ahead of her into darkness. She kept walking but when she reached the point where a stream ran into the main body of the river, creating a natural dead end to the path, she realised she had come too far.

She turned round and began walking back the way she had come.

'Harry?' she called.

A tall man stepped out from the side of one of the boathouses and walked towards her. He held out his hand and she took it.

'Thanks for coming,' he said.

Sam looked up at him, towering over a foot above her, and studied his face. Blond stubble covered his cheeks and his hair was greasy. He didn't seem to be able to stop shivering.

'I brought you this,' Sam said, handing over a bag containing a burger and chips. If he were anything like Mark had been at that age, he'd be starving.

Harry opened it and looked inside. 'That was thoughtful of you.'

'Do you know about your mother?' Sam asked.

'Yes.' Harry's face contorted. He looked down at the ground and hugged himself.

'How did you find out?'

He didn't reply.

'Do you know what happened on the boat that night?'

He gnawed on his lower lip.

'Were you there?'

Still he didn't say anything. Sam heard what she assumed were his teeth chattering.

'You know the police are looking for you and David?'

His head snapped up. 'Dave had nothing to do with it. It wasn't his fault. I want you to tell them he had nothing to do with it.'

'Why did you walk out of the trials?'

'Dave was in terrible trouble. He phoned. He's my brother. I had to go.'

'What happened?' Sam repeated.

'He owed a lot of money from before he went into prison. As soon as he was out they came after him for it. He didn't know what to do. He was frightened even before he came out.'

'Did they threaten him?'

'Yes.'

'Did he come to Oxford at the end of last term?'

He frowned. 'What do you mean?'

'I know you were arrested. I know Siobhan identified you and I know you had an alibi. Was it David who attacked her?'

Harry looked puzzled. 'He would never have done anything like that – ever. He wasn't even here.'

'Are you sure?'

'Absolutely.'

Sam frowned. 'So how do you explain it?'

'I can't make head or tail of it. Maybe she was put up to it. She was lying. I think they set her up to do it.'

'To get at you?'

'I don't know.'

'Maybe someone wanted to discredit you.'

He stared at his feet for a moment. 'I can't think of anyone who dislikes me that much.'

'You're absolutely sure it wasn't him?'

'Yes.'

'Have you ever been to the Mad Hatter?'

'Oh, yes – the squad used to go there. It wasn't really my kind of thing but I'd go to be sociable. I was there the night she said but

I left around nine-thirty and came back to college. I had a tutorial the following day.'

'Harry, did David kill your mother?'

Harry looked genuinely appalled. 'Emma said you were on our side.'

'I'm on *your* side, Harry. Addicts are desperate people. They'll do anything. Is he in that kind of state?'

'There is no "me" in this. It's "us". You can't separate us on this.'

'Were you there on the night she was murdered?'

Harry walked away from Sam towards the river and she followed him.

'Do you know where David was that night?'

Harry opened the bag and took out some chips.

Sam decided on another tack. 'Who do you think might have done it?'

He shook his head. 'Mum was so . . . gentle. She didn't have any enemies.'

'Could the person David owed money to have come after your mother for it? Could it have been a warning? Had they warned David? Maybe they didn't intend to kill her. Maybe it got out of hand.'

'I want you to tell the police we had nothing to do with her death. They need to be looking for someone else.'

'Why don't you come down to the police station with me now? You can tell them yourself and get the whole thing sorted out. You can go back to college and the rowing. Tom says they're really missing you.'

He smiled at the mention of rowing.

'He says you're a star.'

He shook his head. 'No, that's rubbish. There are nine in a boat; it's a team. There are no stars.'

'That's not how Tom sees it.'

'He's a good coach. I think it is. Anyway, they seem to be doing fine; Holden's having a whale of a time at stroke. I've been watching him. The guys are finding their rhythm behind him.'

'Tom says he'd have you back at stroke any day.'

Harry's face lit up. 'Did he?'

'He's the one that hired me to find you. What shall I tell him?'

He shook his head. 'I don't know.'

'What happened?' Sam said softly.

'It's all my fault,' he said. 'My arrogance, my naivety . . . I killed my mother. I might as well have loaded a gun and fired it.' He had spoken so quietly Sam barely heard him.

'What do you mean?'

Off behind the boathouses, a dog barked. Sam turned her head in the direction of the noise and thought she saw someone moving in the undergrowth. Her stomach lurched.

'Where's David?'

He shook his head. 'I'm not sure.'

Sam reached over and took hold of one of his hands. It was dark but she felt along the line of skin that lies at the base of the fingers and at the top of the palm, then ran her finger up the surface of each finger.

He frowned but didn't pull his hand away. 'What are you doing?'

Sam let go of his hand, having felt the rough skin and blisters. 'Just checking to make sure who I was talking to.'

'You think I'm my brother?'

'I've not met you before.'

'Are you going to tell the police where I am?'

'No.'

'Why not?'

'Because they're not employing me.'

He looked close to tears.

Sam felt helpless. 'I want to help you but to do that you've got to tell me what you know. At some time you're going to have to come back and get on with your life. At some point you're going to have to go to the police. Why not now?'

'I can't. Not yet. It's too dangerous.'

'What needs to happen?'

'It needs to be safe – for both of us. Otherwise there's just no point.'

'And how can things be made safe?'

He shook his head.

'Could your father help?'

Harry looked alarmed. 'No, please don't tell him you've seen me.'

'Is he involved in some way?'

'You mustn't say anything to him.'

'Could he have done this to your mother?'

'Dad? Of course not.'

'Who then? Who does David owe?'

'You must go now,' Harry said.

'Do you know anything about the burglary at your dad's?'

He shook his head. 'Look, it's not safe for Dave. If he goes to the police he'll go back inside and he won't be safe there. They'll come for him and we haven't got the money yet. I'm not leaving him.'

'And how are you proposing to get it?'

He didn't answer.

'Phone me,' Sam said. 'If you think I can be of any help.'

'Thanks.'

She turned and began walking back the way she had come. Harry had looked terrified at the mention of his father. As she reached the top of the bridge she turned round and looked back. She could have sworn that she saw two people walking back towards the boathouse but she blinked and they were both gone, lost in the shadows cast by the balcony.

CHAPTER FIFTEEN

Half an hour later, Sam ran down the steps to the Mad Hatter and pushed open the door. Tonight the club was even more crowded but the punters looked different to the last time Sam had been here in one crucial respect. They were all wearing fancy dress. Sam spotted two Mad Hatters, several Tweedledums and -dees, three Cheshire Cats, four Dormice and one Red Queen. In the corner, shrouded in smoke and above the level of most heads, two grubby white ears identified the position of the lone White Rabbit. Much to Sam's relief, the Mad Hatter was not behind the bar; instead there were two Alices – one male, one female. Sam, who had been hoping to blend into the background, stood out much more than she would have liked. As a couple of people entered the bar, a Cheshire Cat slid off his bar stool to greet them and Sam took his place.

She leaned on the bar and rubbed her face. God, she was tired. Meeting Harry had got her nowhere. As far as she was concerned the case wasn't over until Harry was back at college and back in the Blue Boat. Maybe if she could crack this bit of the puzzle the rest would fall into place. The male Alice, resplendent in long blonde wig and Alice band, blue dress and white pinafore, towered over Sam and in an American drawl asked her what she wanted.

'A Dormouse,' she replied. Sam couldn't remember what a Dormouse was but it was the first thing that came into her mind. She watched him as he squeezed, shook and poured; the resulting drink was swimming-pool blue and she wished she'd chosen something else.

'One Dormouse,' he said, placing it carefully in front of her.

'That'll be the full price because you're not in fancy dress. Happy hour only applies to those who take the trouble to dress up.'

Sam paid for the drink. 'That explains the hundred per cent turnout.'

'Ninety-nine point nine per cent,' the man said, eyeing her disapprovingly.

'Sorry, I didn't know.' She picked up the drink and sipped it. 'This is delicious,' she said.

The barman sniffed, as if to imply 'Of course it is – I made it.'

'Is Siobhan here tonight?' she asked. The female Alice looked sharply at her.

'Maybe,' the man said. 'What d'you want with Siobhan?'

'Just a chat.'

He turned his back to Sam, opened a dishwasher and was shrouded in steam. When he turned back round, one of his false eyelashes had half detached itself from the lid of his eye. 'Shit,' he said and poked at it with his finger.

'You've got a *Clockwork Orange* thing going on there,' Sam said.

The eyelash fell off completely and landed on his cheek. 'If she comes in I'll be sure to let you know.'

'Thanks.'

Sam took her drink and moved further into the club. Out the back there was a small courtyard, which contained a couple of pub tables with benches attached to their sides. Even though it wasn't warm, it was filled with Dormice and Cheshire Cats, who had torn open the Velcro fastenings of their costumes and were trying to cool off. Sam sipped her drink and watched the comings and goings. A Red Queen went into the toilets and, recognising her as the woman she had talked to when she was last here, Sam followed.

Waiting for her to come out, Sam leaned over a basin and looked at her reflection in the mirror. It was twelve days since she'd been doing this in the gym changing rooms but now that felt like years ago. The naked light bulb didn't help much but even in sympathetic lighting she would have looked terrible – emotional wear and tear was writ large on her face. Even when she hadn't been crying, her eyes looked as if she had, but when she *had* been, they turned the same colour as the flesh of a watermelon. She pulled down the lower lid of her right eye and stared disconsolately at the bloody tributaries that ran through the white. This day seemed to have been going on forever. Hearing the Red Queen come out of the cubicle, she turned away from her reflection with relief.

'Hello again,' Sam said.

The woman frowned, not appearing to recognise her, and began washing her hands.

'Could you tell me if Siobhan's in tonight?'

'Siobhan – yeah, of course she is.'

'Who is she?'

'She's behind the bar.'

'The Alice?'

The woman nodded.

'Where's the Mad Hatter?'

'Oh, he's around. He'll probably be in later.'

'Who's the hairy Alice?'

'Hairy who?'

'The dragged-up one.'

'Oh, some big-shot rower Siobhan's got the hots for.'

'Rower?'

'Yeah – Holden. They come in here quite a lot since he's been working here.'

Back at the bar, Sam spoke to the female Alice. 'Could I have a word?'

She waved her hand at the throng of people queuing for drinks. 'Give me a break. Can't you see how busy it is?'

'It'll only take a second.'

The hairy Alice came over. 'You being bothered?'

'It's all right.' She patted his arm and he went back to his job. Siobhan looked at Sam. 'If you're from the police I've had it with them.'

'No, I'm not. I'm a private investigator working for the Oxford University Boat Club. Just want to get clear in my mind what happened that night. Would you mind telling me what you remember? I'm puzzled because Harry says he left quite early that evening and went back to college.'

'He would, wouldn't he?'

'When do you finish?'

She sighed. 'Hold on a minute.' She said something to hairy Alice and then stepped out from behind the bar. 'Just a couple of minutes, OK?'

Sam followed her outside. Siobhan sat on the bottom of the steps just outside the door to the club and lit a cigarette.

'Were you working that night?' Sam began.

She shook her head. 'No, I'd just popped in for a quick drink. I knew the rowers were going to be here. I know some of them through Holden.'

'The guy behind the bar?'

She nodded.'

'Is he your boyfriend?'

She pulled a face. 'It's an on-and-off thing . . .'

'How did you meet him?'

'Working with him here.'

A gust of wind bounced an empty plastic bottle slowly down the steps towards them. 'So what do you remember of that night?'

'Not much.'

'Do you remember talking to Harry?'

Siobhan brought the cigarette to her lips. 'Not specifically, but I remember him being around with the guys earlier in the evening. The place was heaving – a bit like tonight. The whole squad was in here.'

'What's the last thing you remember?'

'Sitting at a table out back and drinking a Red Queen with Holden and some of the guys. Then I remember feeling dizzy and that's it.'

'Do you think you were drugged?'

'I don't know. All I know is that when I woke up I felt like shit. I've never felt that ill before and I had a terrible taste in my mouth.'

'But if you mix cocktails the effect can be pretty lethal.'

'But I hadn't. That's the thing – I hadn't drunk that much.'

'Did you keep an eye on your glass? Did you leave it at any point?'

'Come on – of course I left it. I thought I was amongst friends.'

'So someone could have spiked it?'

'Sure they could.'

'When you woke up, where were you?'

'I was in my flat – a couple of roads away.'

'But I don't get why you think Harry had anything to do with it. You don't even remember speaking to him. How come you think he was responsible?'

She sighed. 'There were witnesses.'

'To what?'

'They saw me leaving with him.'

'Who did?'

'Carter, Holden.'

'But you have no memory of what happened?'

Siobhan's jaw tightened. She took another cigarette out and lit it from the stub in her mouth. 'I know I had sex that night. I know I was in no state to consent to it.'

'Can you remember it?'

She shook her head. 'I could feel it the following morning.'

'Were there . . . I mean, surely you could have gone to the police and . . . what about DNA tests or blood tests to identify the drug?'

'Do you think I wanted to be raped all over again by the police? Anyway, there wasn't anything for them to test. He must have used a condom.'

'But there might have been pubic hair. Some kind of physical evidence—'

'Have you any fucking idea what it feels like to wake up and know that's happened to you? How disgusting and dirty you feel? How you want to scrub and scrub and scrub at yourself to feel clean but you never do? How much you want him off you and out of you and yet you can't get free of him because you don't even know who he is? So don't tell me what I should have fucking done.'

'I'm sorry. I wasn't judging you. I was thinking of preventing it happening again to someone else.'

'Yes, I know, and I'm thinking about *me*.'

'So then what happened? You decided not to go to the police?'

She nodded. 'Holden was really pissed off with me. But what could I say to him? I mean, I couldn't remember anything. Then, a couple of weeks later, I passed Cameron in Cornmarket. He walked right past me as if nothing had happened and I completely lost it. Thought I'd show him and phoned the police to report it. I knew he'd probably get off because there was no evidence but I just wanted to rattle him. To let him know I knew.'

'The thing is, Siobhan, I don't think it could possibly have been him. He's got a twin brother but there's nothing to suggest he was even in Oxford then. And you say it was definitely Harry that you knew?'

'I don't know anything about a bloody twin.'

'OK. But suppose it wasn't, suppose Holden and Carter lied to you. Can you think why they'd do that? You've only got their word to go on.'

Siobhan looked suddenly stricken. 'You're saying they used me to set him up?'

'Harry had an alibi.'

'Some silly bitch willing to defend him, who doesn't know what she's dealing with.'

'I've met her and she's not like that at all. She wouldn't have given a false alibi in a case involving date rape.'

'But why would Holden do that?'

'Was Holden jealous of Harry? He is the star rower.'

Siobhan bit her lip but said nothing.

'Siobhan?'

'Holden had his nose well put out of joint by Harry. He was expecting to swan in and be the big saviour but the first thing he saw was an article in the *Oxford Times* and the headline *Are these Oxford's Messiahs?*, with a photo of Tom King and Harry. And then Harry started blowing him away in all the training—'

'Well, well, well...' Carter stood at the top of the steps, his large frame casting a long shadow towards them. 'Who do we have here? I do believe it's the proverbial bad penny come back to haunt us.'

He swept down the stairs, put his arm round both of them and ushered them into the club. Sam noticed that his only nod towards fancy dress was a ticket attached to the side of his hat on which he'd written *10/6 in this style*.

He jerked his head at Siobhan. 'I don't pay you to chat.'

'Sorry.'

She got behind the bar and walked over to where a Dormouse was waving a twenty-pound note in the air.

Carter suddenly became cheerier. 'One for the road,' he suggested to Sam. 'On the house.'

'I'm not in fancy dress.'

'When you're the proprietor you can make exceptions to every rule.'

A few minutes later a green cocktail was placed in front of Sam.

'After this,' Carter said, 'I'd very much appreciate never seeing you again.'

Sam opened her eyes and saw her mother's face, then closed them again. This had to be a bad dream, one to add to the list. Her eyelids felt heavy and her eyeballs ached, her mouth felt like sandpaper. She waited a few seconds and tried again but her mother was still there and next to her Mark. She looked around, a mistake because it involved moving her neck and head, and saw enough to realise that she was in the spare room of the house in Park Town.

She tried to sit up. 'What the hell happened?'

'You drank too much,' her mother said.

Sam frowned. 'But I didn't.'

'You were found staggering around the centre of town, wearing that.' Mark pointed to a pile of fur on the ground.

Sam stared at it, puzzled. 'What is it, exactly?'

He held it up and Sam saw that it was a dormouse suit. 'Oh,' Sam said.

'Mean something to you?'

She closed her eyes and pressed her eyelids with her fingertips.

'You were picked up by the police and Phil phoned me to come and get you.'

'Poor Phil, he's been doing a lot of that recently.'

'What happened?'

Sam thought for a few seconds. 'I can't remember.'

Both Mark and her mother looked stricken.

'What's the matter?' Sam said.

Mark sat down on the side of the bed. 'When you say you can't remember, Sam . . .'

'Oh I see. No, no, not like then.'

'Are you sure?'

'Yes.'

'We've all been under a lot of strain recently.'

'No, Mark, not like that. I promise.'

'But then why can't you . . .?'

'I'd been in the Mad Hatter talking to Siobhan, the woman who got Harry arrested. I went back inside . . .'

The face of Carter swam in front of her eyes: 'One for the road . . .' She remembered the cool green cocktail on the bar in front of her, the dainty way he opened the cocktail umbrella and placed it against the rim of the glass.

'Oh,' she said.

'What?'

'They must have spiked my drink. He was warning me off.'

'Who?'

'The Mad Hatter.'

'She's talking gibberish,' her mother said to Mark.

'No,' Mark said. 'I think it's all right, Mum.'

Sam closed her eyes. The scene from the previous night swam in Sam's mind. Dormice merged with Alices, hairy and depilated, and Tweedledums danced with White Rabbits. Carter's face loomed towards her, deflating and then swelling until his features were obscenely stretched, a balloon on the point of bursting. Sam opened her eyes quickly before his head exploded. 'Better open than closed,' she said.

'You know your father does have a certain reputation in this town . . .'

God, how often had Sam heard that one? She'd had enough of Peter's reputation to last her a lifetime. She scrubbed at her eyes. 'At least I didn't dance naked on the Martyrs' Memorial like Mrs Wyatt and claim to be guided by the ghosts of Bishops Latimer and Ridley.'

'That's unfair, Sam,' Jean said. 'She'd come off her medication. You don't have that excuse.'

Sam sighed. Jean had always lacked a sense of humour when it came to that episode. It had struck Sam that there was an above average number of depressives and alcoholics among the wives of Oxford dons. It probably came from living with people who were far too intellectually arrogant ever to think there was anything the matter with them. Sam considered telling her mother that she was seeing a therapist, just to see how she'd respond, but she was also aware that, sober, the thought would never have crossed her mind. She knew Jean would be appalled. Seeing a therapist was definitely a betrayal of the stiff upper lip, a sign that Sam had drifted into the grip of the chattering classes. Therapy was close to anarchy as far as her mother was concerned, she might just as well tell her she'd joined the Communist Party.

'Are you . . . you know, all right?' Mark asked.

Sam lifted the duvet and stared at her clothed body. 'I can't remember. Last thing I remember is looking into that green cocktail. That's it. I think it was just a warning.'

'A pretty severe one.'

'He doesn't want me poking around any more. Probably pissed him off seeing me there again.'

Sam yawned. Her eyelids felt as if they were made of lead. She closed her eyes. 'Sorry but I think I need to sleep this off a bit more.'

That afternoon Sam sat next to her mother on the sofa in the living room. They were discussing her father.

'I loved him, of course.'

Sam didn't say anything.

'Well, you must realise that – and I was very young.'

'Did you know about his reputation?'

'Various people tried to warn me. I'd gone out with Max before your father. When I got engaged to Geoff, Max told me. I told him Geoff'd never be like that with me, that I was different. I was naive. I just couldn't imagine him hurting me. You can't before they do it. Then, once it's happened, you realise how stupid you've been.'

'Why didn't you leave?'

'Pride. Mark was tiny. What was I going to do with myself? Go back to my parents? That would have felt like a defeat. Mum had never liked him – maybe mothers have good instincts about those kind of things. If I'd gone back home I'd have felt that she'd won. I wanted my independence.'

'Even if you were being beaten?'

'Don't forget he was away a lot. That's why it lasted as long as it did.'

Sam nodded and looked through the window to where a squirrel was dangling from the end of a branch.

'I never intended to talk about the rape in anger, Sam. I'm sorry.'

'It's all right. I almost expected it. Max had told me something so . . . he told me Dad was violent. He knew that he'd raped you and I'd wondered if that was part of the difficulty.'

'I see.'

'But hearing it from you. Well, I suppose it confirmed my worst fears.'

'Yes. If he hadn't come back I would never have thought to tell you. I would have let sleeping dogs lie.'

Sam nodded. 'Well, maybe this is for the best.'

'It's because he's back – the old feelings rise up. It's surprising how fresh they feel, as if the scabs are ripped off and you bleed in the same way all over again.'

Sam looked at her finger and felt sick. 'At least I know the truth.'

'And the thing is, Sam, what you decide to do – I mean whether you see him or not – that's entirely up to you. It's got nothing to do with me, has it?' Her mother sounded as if she was trying to convince herself.

'Well, I wouldn't go that far.'

'Of course you don't have to have my permission. And before, when I slapped you, I'm sorry. I shouldn't have done that. But it was as if it was him taunting me across the years—'

'I see.'

'It's up to you, that's what I'm saying. Anyway, I dug out some photos of you and him.' She handed Sam a white envelope. Sam looked at the top photo. She and her father on a beach, golden sand, blue skies. Her hair was white blonde. She was about two years old. He was smiling, tanned. She felt as if someone had let off a flash bulb in her face. Her head jerked back and she dropped the photo. She felt dizzy and fumbled as she put the photo back in the envelope.

'Do you mind if I look at these later?'

'Of course not. Take them away with you.'

'Mum, why did you have me? You could have got rid of me.'

'I'd always wanted Mark to have a sibling.'

The pragmatism of her mother's reply took Sam by surprise and she laughed out loud.

'What?' Her mother looked puzzled. 'Once you were there, darling, I never considered not having you. I was glad you were a girl. I thought it would be easier—'

'Until you realised what sort of girl I was.'

She smiled. 'Maybe, but that wasn't your fault. Looking at it now, I can see that he was sick. After that first tour in Oman he changed completely. Nowadays I think they would have handled it differently but back then they just used to tell them to go off and get pissed with their friends in Hereford.'

'And then go home and beat up their wives? That must have helped a whole lot.'

'The trouble was they couldn't talk to anyone about where they'd been or what had happened. *I* didn't even know where he'd been. I knew it was somewhere hot because he was so tanned and his hair was bleached.' Jean stood up and walked over to the window. 'Has he told you why he's turned up now?'

Sam shook her head. 'Maybe he's ill. Maybe he's seeking some sort of absolution.'

'He asked Mark for forgiveness.'

'I know.'

Jean turned back into the room. 'I never, ever regretted having you, Sam.'

Saying that she didn't regret her, Sam thought, was probably as close as Jean could get to telling her she loved her. In the circumstances it seemed churlish to want anything more.

'No,' Sam said.

'I know it's not been easy between us at times but I would hate to think that we would ever lose contact.'

'Me too,' Sam said and was surprised to find that she meant it. Her mobile rang. 'Sorry, Mum, do you mind?'

'It's OK, go ahead.'

Sam took the call. It was Phil.

'How are you doing?'

'Not too bad. Thanks for calling out Mark.'

'Is this all to do with your father?'

'What?'

'You getting that drunk.'

'No, no, I wasn't drunk. I was at the Mad Hatter and they spiked my drink.'

'They?'

'Carter, I think.'

'I did warn you about that place, Sam. Can you prove it?'

'Come on, Phil, what do you think? This stuff doesn't stay in your body long enough and it affects your memory.'

'Why would they want to do that to you?'

'Carter saw me talking with Siobhan. Did she tell you that she personally had no memory of it being Harry? That Carter and Holden told her they saw her leaving with him?'

'She said what?'

'That she had no memory of it being Harry.'

'She never said that to us. She just swore blind it was him.'

'Tom King told me that Carter had a grudge against him going back to when they were contemporaries at college and Tom dropped him from the Blues because Carter was so inconsistent in his rowing.'

'For heaven's sake, do these guys never grow up? I mean it's just a bloody boat race. It's not life and death, is it?'

'Judo was life and death to me, Phil. Maybe it was similar for Carter. Anyway, he dropped out of the squad and was then sent down.'

'And you think that would be enough of a reason for him to set up Harry?'

'This is the first year Tom King's been coaching the OUBC and when Harry came up last term there was a piece in the *Oxford Times* about them both. That could have got Carter's goat.'

'But what's Holden's motive?'

'He's the one who'll stroke the boat in Harry's absence. He's a big-shot American rower. Any other year he'd think he'd come straight in and be doing that. But he didn't reckon on Harry Cameron. And apparently he's only here for a year. So it's now or never.'

'It still seems a bit extreme.'

'These guys are extreme, Phil. They have to be to do the race – it's an absolute ball-breaker.'

'I know but—'

'Siobhan says she definitely had sex that night and there's no way she consented to it because she was unconscious. It could have been Holden.'

'But if she can't remember then there's no case.'

'No, I know, but it lets Harry and his brother off the hook, doesn't it?'

'I might pull Holden and Carter in for a chat and see what I can find out.'

'Good.'

'Sam, Have you had any contact with Harry?'

'Why do you ask?'

'The church was robbed.'

'What?'

'St Silas's. The vicar, Emma Hodge, was badly beaten, forced to open a safe and had some personal effects stolen.'

'When did this happen?'

'Last night, while you were sleeping in your teapot.'

'What time?'

'Midnight.'

After Sam had left Harry. Perhaps that was how they'd decided to pay off David's debt – but by robbing a church? 'How is she?'

'Pretty shaken up.'

'Who did she say did it?'

'She's being pretty evasive. Have you seen him?'

Sam didn't say anything. She'd promised.

'Sam?'

'What hospital is Hodge in?'

'Sam – their mother's been killed and now Hodge has been attacked. If you know where they are you must say.'

'I don't know where he is,' Sam lied.

'Hodge says the boy was going to phone you.'

'Well, he didn't.'

'It was the call you took at the pub, wasn't it?'

Sam didn't say anything.

Phil sighed. 'You can't protect him forever, Sam. There's murder and now a serious assault involved. Skinner'll probably be in touch and he won't be so polite.'

'Phil, hold on a second, where's Hodge?'

'Back in the vicarage.'

*

Emma Hodge shifted her weight, trying to sit up straighter, and looked at Sam through her left eye, the one that wasn't swollen shut.

Sam winced in sympathy. 'How are you feeling?'

'Not too bad.'

'Was it David?'

'I assume so – he looked just like Harry and I don't believe Harry could have done this.'

'What happened?'

'I was surprised because someone who sounded like Harry phoned shortly after I phoned you. I thought he was arranging to meet you but he said he wanted to see me again and I told him to come over. He was worried about being seen so we made it late that night. He came to the vicarage at about midnight. I knew something was wrong as soon as I clapped eyes on him. He was very agitated and immediately asked me for money. When I refused he hit me, tore off my cross, took my watch and then forced me to open the safe. Then he made me give him access to the church and he took the cross and communion cups. Then he locked me in a cupboard and left.'

'Had you met him before?'

'No.'

'Had Harry talked to you about him?'

'Yes.'

'About the things that happened last term?'

'He came to see me after the police released him. He was very depressed and didn't know what to do. He was worried that David might have been involved but was adamant that he wasn't going to tell the police about his brother. If they found out, that was fine, but he wasn't going to be responsible for giving them the information.'

'Why did he come to you?'

'He wanted to discuss the moral implications with me.'

'Of not saying anything?'

'Yes.'

'And . . .'

She shook her head. 'I listened to him, really, that was what it amounted to. It was his decision.'

'You didn't tell him he should go to the police?'

'It's his twin brother we are talking about. He was convinced that he could persuade him to seek help. That he could influence him to the good. He thought it was important that David made the decision himself to come forward and clear his name.'

'He may have been responsible for killing their mother.'

Hodge didn't say anything. She closed her eyes and leaned her head against the back of the chair. 'You remember when we met before you said you distrusted people who were so certain. It's not as simple as that; it's not as if I don't have doubts. I do. I don't know that I advised him correctly. I'm not even sure Harry feels he did the right thing. It's not that simple. You do what you think is best at the time. That's all you can ever do. You encourage people to develop their own moral compass.'

Sam felt a flicker of sympathy for her. 'Do you know where they are now?'

She shook her head. 'But I would guess David's going to be looking to sell what he's stolen to get money for drugs. He was in a bad state.'

'He'll probably head for London. That's where all his contacts are.'

'And wherever David is,' Hodge said, 'you can guarantee Harry will be close behind.'

CHAPTER SIXTEEN

It was late that night when Sam got back to her Fulham flat. She set a bath running and threw in some Dead Sea salts and watched the water pouring from the taps. She didn't know where to go in her head. Nowhere seemed safe. 'Just don't think,' she said out loud, but found that even more difficult than obsessing over the information she had. She took off her clothes and slid into the hot water. Water to wash away sins. The sin wasn't hers but she was the end result, the embodiment, the manifestation. Logically, she knew she had done nothing wrong – but then why did she feel as if she was beyond redemption? She closed her eyes and inhaled the steam. She tried to take a deep breath but her chest felt weighed down, as if she could only take shallow breaths or it would hurt, like when she'd had bronchitis. 'Don't think,' she repeated to herself, 'Just try not to think.' She lay in the bath a long time, occasionally turning on the hot water tap with her big toe, drifting between sleep and wakefulness.

Suddenly Sam was wide awake. The water had cooled to blood temperature. Something had woken her – the quiet opening and closing of a door. She lay quite still in the water, frozen as if she'd just woken from a nightmare. Her mind was whirring and trying to rationalise, whereas all her body felt was terror. Edie, she thought. She had Sam's front door key so that she could let Frank in and out of the flat. Sam lay in the tepid water, holding her breath. Then she heard the boards in the hall creaking. It could still be Frank. When a cat with love handles like Frank's walked over broken floorboards it could sound uncannily like a person. She looked at her watch. But it was four o'clock in the morning – Edie wouldn't be up at this time. Sam was lying in the bath facing away from the door but in front of her on the window ledge was a huge mirror, which she'd propped there to block out draughts and make the room seem bigger. It was in this mirror that Sam saw the door to the bathroom slowly swing open. It could still be Frank, he could hurl open doors like Godzilla. Then a man's face appeared.

Sam was out of the bath and had a towel round her so quickly that she created a tidal wave, which slopped over the side and onto the floorboards. Her father was standing in the doorway holding out his hands in a gesture she assumed was intended to calm her down but which was doing nothing of the sort.

'Get out,' she snarled.

He stepped backwards and she slammed the door and pushed the bolt. She dropped the towel, pulled on her dressing gown, drew back the bolt and stepped out into the hall. He was leaning against the wall.

'I'm sorry I startled you.'

'How the fuck did you get in here?'

'Same way I did before. Milkmen can lose their keys and the lock you've got on your front door is rubbish. Anyone with a credit card could open it. You should put a dead bolt on it.'

He was very pale but he looked a lot better than when Sam had last seen him.

'What do you want?'

'I believe I left something here.'

'Edie's got it.'

He looked alarmed. 'Who the hell's she?'

Sam gestured to the wall she shared with Edie. 'Next-door flat.'

'She know what she's got?'

'Edie's OK – I gave her twenty pounds and she's not going to ask any questions.'

He shifted his shoulder awkwardly and flinched. Sam didn't offer him any sympathy. She wasn't going to ask him how he was.

'I need them,' he said.

'Well, I'm not waking Edie up in the middle of the night just for you – she's seventy-nine years old. You're going to have to wait.'

He began to say something but Sam cut him off. 'No,' she said. 'You can stay here till the morning and then I'll get the stuff from her. Or you can go away and come back later. She wakes up early.

Usually she goes off to get the papers at about six-thirty when the shop opens.'

Father and daughter stared at each other. Two hours to go with a rapist, a killer, her father, for company. Sam broke eye contact first and walked into the kitchen. Just to get away from him. He followed her. He leaned against the sink, undid the buttons of his army parka and took a packet of cigarettes out of the top pocket of his denim shirt. Frank, who loved men with the fervour of an animal who had spent his whole life surrounded by women, rubbed his whiskers against Geoffrey Falconer's black army boots and drooled.

'Place is in a bit of a state.'

'I got burgled.'

'What did they take?'

'Nothing – I assume they were looking for what you left with me.'

He narrowed his eyes in the smoke of his cigarette. 'Did they find it?'

Sam shook her head and switched on the kettle.

'Sorry.'

The word hung in the air between them. 'Sam—'

She cut across him. 'What the hell do you think you were doing hanging around in Oxford scaring my mother half to death? You're to keep away from her, do you hear, and Mark.'

He shook his head. 'I admit I was curious. I wanted to see them. I knew they wouldn't want to see me.'

'And what effect do you think you indulging your curiosity had on them? Leave them alone. You're not to go near Mum or Mark, do you understand? Stay away from Oxford altogether.'

He didn't say anything.

'Do you understand?' Sam repeated.

'Mark tell you what I talked to him about?'

Sam didn't say anything.

'I asked him for his forgiveness.'

Sam rounded on him. 'How dare you? Do you think that makes it all go away? You terrorised him as a boy and you scarred him for life. Then you turn up years later and expect it all to be OK. Well, it isn't.'

'Look at it from my point of view. If you wanted to say sorry, how would you go about it?'

'If you were genuine and truly remorseful you'd have realised that the best thing for you to do was to stay away from all of us.'

'You don't believe in forgiveness, Sam?'

'How dare you, you self-righteous bastard? It's not something you can demand.'

'I know that.'

'It's not something you can hold to someone's head like a loaded gun. Or criticise someone for not giving.'

He sighed and rubbed his face. 'I know that as well.'

The kettle boiled. Her hands were shaking as she poured the water into the teapot, put on the lid and swilled the water around inside. He was leaning against the cupboard with his arms folded, watching her.

'I'm not going to hurt you.'

Sam turned to face him. 'No,' she said. 'You're not.' She poured milk into two cups followed by tea. She didn't trust herself to pass it to him without spilling it. 'Here,' she said, nodding at the mug and he came over and picked it up.

'Who shot you?'

'Probably the same people as burgled you. I know what they've been up to, Sam. They killed all the others and I've got the evidence to prove it. They claimed Jo jumped out of a plane without a parachute, that he committed suicide, right. It's true he'd had head trouble but he was getting help, getting over it. Johnny's brakes were got at and Dave's body was found so badly burnt they couldn't tell what killed him. All three of them recorded as accidental deaths. Fucking cover-up – and I'm not going to let them get away with it. I'm not going to be the fourth. They're not going to get rid of me so easily. We were obeying orders, Sam, their orders. They can't just clear their consciences by killing us all off.'

'Kelly Webb came calling. Is she a journalist?'

'Yes, that's what she's telling me. What did old Kelly have to say for herself?'

'Like everyone else, she wanted to know where you were. She said you'd arranged to meet and you didn't turn up. She told me you'd told her to come to me.'

231

'What did you tell her?'

'Nothing. I told her I hadn't seen you. I said the same to some guy in Oxford police station who gave me these.' Sam indicated the bruises that had come up on her face where the man had grabbed her.

'He hurt you?'

'Not really. He gave me these and I almost killed him.'

He laughed. 'You're so like me it's uncanny. What happened?'

'They pulled me in on the pretext they wanted to ask me questions about a case I'm working on. Then the police officer dealing with that case leaves and another bloke comes in who starts throwing his weight around and asking questions about you.'

'What did he look like?'

Sam described the man and her father grunted as if in recognition.

'They really don't want me to say what I know. I may have to disappear for a bit.'

'Well, stay away from me while you're about it,' Sam said. 'You've brought nothing but trouble with you. Do you understand? After we've got the stuff from Edie, that's it.'

'I know I've fucked things up, Sam.' He began to move towards her.

'Stay where you are.'

'Come on, I just wanted some sugar.' He pointed to the packet next to the kettle.

Sam pushed it towards him. 'Knowing it's not enough,' Sam said.

Was it your hand reaching down through the water to grab me? The question hung suspended in the air between them but she couldn't bring herself to ask it. She was too frightened. Suppose he said yes. Where could they possibly go from there?

'You can have the couch in the front room.' She fetched him a duvet and then went back into her bedroom and locked the door behind her.

Sleep? Who did she think she was kidding? She lay on her bed staring into the darkness of her bedroom, listening to the tubes beginning to roll up the Wimbledon branch of the District Line. The trains started moving about four-thirty. Empty of people, they sounded entirely different in the early morning, rattling and bouncing much more than the trains weighed down by rush-hour passengers cursing the name of Ken Livingstone.

Why was she even allowing him to stay here? What was the matter with her? But once he had what he wanted then hopefully he'd be gone forever. She considered the word – forever. The trouble is she didn't want him to be gone. She never had, she'd always wanted him back. Even now, after everything that she knew about him, she was frightened of never seeing him again. She slipped into an uneasy, fitful sleep.

Her father stands over her. He reaches out his hand and touches her hair like you might touch the hair of a small child. He strokes it. Sam wakes up and feels his touch and it's the most soothing thing she has ever felt. She places her hand behind his neck and pulls him down towards her. And kisses him. The eroticism of the kiss is intense and grows. She wants him inside her. She pulls him onto the bed and they begin to make love.

Sam awoke with the eroticism of the dream registering in every cell of her body. Then the reality of what she had been dreaming hit her and the eroticism switched to revulsion in the split second it took for her to see her father's face contorted at the point of orgasm. She felt ashamed and disgusted with herself and utterly confused. Her heart was pounding so strongly that she felt dizzy and as if she might have a heart attack. Her breath was coming in shallow gasps. She sat hugging her knees, waiting for the shaking to subside, waiting until the sweat had turned cold on her body. Then she stood up and, on legs that felt like jelly, walked through into the front room. Her father opened his eyes when she came in, sat up and rubbed his face. She knew one thing for certain; she had to get him out of here.

'It's six-thirty,' she said. 'I'll try Edie.'

'You look sick.'

'Something I ate.'

Sam let herself out of her flat onto the landing, pushed open Edie's letterbox, whistled softly and then stood back and waved at the spyhole that Edie had in her front door. The door opened and

Edie appeared. She wasn't wearing her wig this early in the morning and her fine brown hair that had never seen dye and contained not a strand of white was plaited and lying against her right breast.

'What is it?'

'I'm sorry, Edie, but I need some of the things I left with you.'

'Come in, come in.' Edie took hold of her arm and pulled her into the flat. 'I'll get the key.'

Sam stood in Edie's hall, the mauve and yellow floral swirls of the carpet doing nothing to quell her nausea. Edie bustled back.

'Sorry it's so early,' Sam said.

Edie frowned. 'Early? This isn't early for me. I've been up an hour.'

She put the key in the lock of the dark green filing cabinet, turned it, pulled open the top drawer, reached down the back and drew out the padded envelope Sam had given her.

Sam ripped off the tape and took out the wallet and the envelope containing the papers her father had originally left with her. The photocopies she left in the padded envelope and handed back to Edie.

'Thanks, Edie.'

'You're welcome, babes.'

Sam walked back into her flat and handed the envelope to her father. He looked through everything, checking it was all there.

'Where's—?'

As she handed him his wallet, their hands touched and she jumped.

'You look inside this?'

'What do you think?'

'You haven't shown this to anyone?'

'No. Is that the name they gave you after you left us – James Parker?'

He didn't reply, just started counting the money.

Sam slapped the wallet out of his hands. It fell to the ground and notes fluttered in the air. Sam picked up the photo from the floor. 'Is that your family?' she asked, louder this time.

'Sam—'

'"You're the only home I've got." So that's not fucking true for starters, is it?'

234

'You don't think I had the right to start over? I couldn't come back for you.' He paused. 'I never willingly gave you up, Sam. They said I had no choice – either it was prison or Northern Ireland and I did exactly what they told me. What would you have done?'

Sam pointed to the photo. 'Do they know where you are or have you walked out on them too?'

He knelt down and picked some notes off the floor. Sam stood with her arms folded watching him as he continued to count the money.

'What are you going to do?'

Silence.

'Are you going back to them?'

He folded the wallet shut and put it away in the inside pocket of his jacket.

'Whatever I do, it's best you don't know what it is.'

'What shall I tell Kelly?'

'Tell her the deal's off. It's too dangerous.'

'Are you going to return the cash?'

'Tell her the deal's off, for the moment. I'll be in contact when things have calmed down a bit.'

He reached out to touch her cheek but, like a boxer swaying out of the way of a punch, Sam evaded him. And then he was gone. Sam looked out of the window to see if she could see which direction he'd gone in but the street was completely deserted; it was as if he'd vanished into thin air.

She almost hadn't come. Now she wished with every fibre of her being that she hadn't. She looked at Reg, feeling like a butterfly staring at a lepidopterist's pin.

'Did you phone me, Sam?'

She didn't say anything and Reg continued. 'I took a call on the number I gave you two evenings ago and I thought it might have been you. The woman was very distressed.'

Sam swallowed and gently touched the bruise on her cheek. She felt disassociated from her surroundings. Numb. She looked at the plaster on her finger, thought she should tell him about that. Didn't know how. So many things she should tell him.

'Look, it's your money. You can play games if you want to.'

She looked up, surprised. He'd never sounded that angry before. 'Yes,' she said.

'What?'

'Yes, it was me.'

'Can you tell me what happened?'

'Do you believe in original sin?'

'Sam, I don't think it's going to be of any help to have abstract philosophical discussions. You phoned me in a state of considerable distress but were unable to tell me what had happened. I think it would help if you could try and tell me what had made you so very upset.'

Sam blinked. Where to bloody start? Every bit of her ached. As she sat there she felt the places where she had broken her leg, the pain in her shoulder when it had dislocated, even the individual fingers she had broken over a fighting career that spanned fifteen years. And that was just the physical pain. She was lost and no one was looking for her. She looked across at Reg. Well, perhaps he was. When she'd been fighting she'd never felt this hopeless, this damned depressed.

'Sam?'

She cleared her throat. 'I'm having terrible nightmares.'

'Could you tell me about them?'

'Just the usual: snakes, incest, castration and death.' She hadn't said abuse.

'Do you always joke when you're upset?'

'Those are the good days.'

'And on the bad ones?'

Sam looked down at her hands. 'I come to standing over the sink, holding a bread knife, and see that I've made a good attempt at cutting off my finger.' Carefully she peeled off the plaster and massaged the cut. 'On the bad ones my mother tells me my father raped her and I was the result.'

Reg took a deep breath.

'She had accused me of lying and I returned the accusation and then she told me.'

'It's not your fault, Sam.'

Sam didn't say anything.

'What are you accusing yourself of?'

Sam shook her head. 'Evil, tainted, shameful ... being funda-mentally misconceived.'

'None of that's true. In a way it has nothing to do with you. You weren't even alive.'

'It's the origin of my birth and I can't move one step away from it.'

'Look, imagine yourself as a newborn baby.'

Sam didn't reply.

'Just humour me here – what do you see?'

'I'm screaming ... I'm covered in blood and muck.'

'And if you wipe away the blood, what do you see?'

'Reg, I'm not very maternal, so I don't think this is going to work.'

'Wipe away the blood,' Reg repeated. 'What do you see?'

'I don't know, I look like a prune, like Winston Churchill – I'm ugly.'

'It wasn't your fault, Sam. Newborn babies are completely and utterly innocent.'

'That's not what the church says. The church says we're born into sin. What about original sin?'

'But do you believe that?'

'I'm just saying there's another point of view.'

'But you can choose what you believe.'

'I feel it's my fault. I feel like I'm guilty. I fought my whole life to bring my father back to life. Now he's here and he's destroying my family all over again. That's my fault.'

'It isn't, Sam. Your father came looking for you for his own reasons. You didn't bring him back from the dead because he was never dead.'

'We were told he was dead. He was dead as far as I was concerned. I'd willed it my whole life. Every time I stepped out onto a judo mat to fight, I believed that I was fighting for him, that if I won it would make it happen, and then it did happen.'

'So, what are you saying – that you can raise the dead? What does that make you – God?'

Sam laughed. It was a relief to be doing something other than crying.

'Did the episode with your finger happen before or after your mother told you?'

'Before.'

'Have you ever cut yourself anywhere else before?'

Silence.

'Sam?'

'I think so.'

'You think so?'

Sam rubbed the scar on the side of her neck. 'There's this.'

'What happened?'

Sam stared to the right of Reg and down at the floor. 'It was around the time we moved from Hereford, about a year after Dad went. I remember Mum telling me we were going to move to Oxford and I remember telling her we couldn't because when Dad came back he wouldn't know where we were, he wouldn't be able to find us . . .' She pressed her thumbs against her closed eyelids, feeling the tears seep out and run down the side of her nose onto her lips. She tasted salt. Tears and blood; they tasted the same.

'So you never believed he was dead?'

She shook her head. 'Never.'

'What happened?'

'I remember telling her I'd never leave, that she couldn't make me. I ended up in hospital.'

Reg frowned. 'Can you remember what happened between your mother telling you and the hospital?'

'No.'

'You remember nothing?'

'Not really.'

'Who knows?'

She shrugged. 'My mother, Mark.'

'How would you feel about me talking to them?'

Sam looked up sharply. 'Do you really think that's necessary?'

'Yes, as soon as possible.'

'You're frightening me.'

'No, I think you're doing a pretty good job of that all by yourself.'

Sam sighed. 'My mother? No way. She'd probably never agree to it. Her idea of therapy is a small vase of gin at lunchtime and a complete *Times 2* crossword.'

'It doesn't have to be her.'

'Mark? Fine, as long as he'd be OK with it, but I don't want him upset.'

'Maybe he wouldn't mind being upset if it helped you.'

'Maybe he wouldn't but . . .' She ground to a halt.

'Sam?'

Sam felt a wave of emotion sweep over her. 'I just couldn't bear him being upset because of me.'

'Will you ask him to phone me?'

Sam couldn't speak. She put her face in her hands and wept.

As Sam came into the foyer of the Riverview building, Greg caught her eye and nodded to the man sitting in reception. It was Harry Cameron's father. He had seen her and was already on his feet walking towards her.

'Could I have a quick word?'

Sam doubted somehow it would be quick.

In her office Cameron sat down opposite her and looked around him.

'I'm so sorry about Grace,' Sam said.

He folded his arms. 'Even though we'd been divorced a long time and our relationship wasn't easy we had been married. There were the boys.'

'Yes.'

'I had to identify her.'

Sam winced. 'I'm sorry. That must have been awful.'

He placed his hands on his large, yellow corduroy-covered thighs. 'I know I was a bit of a prick last time you saw me.'

That was one way of describing it, Sam thought. 'Well . . .'

'I was wondering if you'd made any progress in finding the twins?'

Sam shook her head. 'I'm sorry . . .'

'The thing is, I wasn't altogether upfront with you before.'

'No?'

'The burglary – you know, the broken glass in the living room. I'm sure it was David.'

'How can you be so certain?'

'He came to me after he got out of prison. He was worried because he had a large debt owing from before he went inside. He was frightened they'd come after him. He wanted me to pay it off but I refused. I don't know how much money I've poured down the drain with that boy – rehab that doesn't work, and the QC set me back a bit. I decided I had to draw the line. It's not easy, you know, when it's your own flesh and blood.'

'How much did he owe?'

'I don't know. He asked for twenty thousand pounds.'

'Jesus!'

'You probably think I'm hard on him.'

'No, I don't. It's the tough love approach, isn't it? Anyway, I'm not in a position to judge. I've no experience of addicts.'

'The upshot was that we argued before I went away on holiday and I said I wasn't prepared to help him out. I told him he could come and work for me and pay it off gradually, but he said they weren't the kind of people to wait, that they'd had to wait while he was in prison and they weren't prepared to wait any longer. Then when I came back there'd been a break-in.'

'Didn't he have a key to the house?'

'He did but I think he wanted it to look like a burglary and so he smashed the glass in the back door. But the stupid little idiot smashed it from the inside. There was glass all over the patio but none inside on the carpet.'

'How can you be so sure it was him?'

'He took the dog. He'd adopted it. This was before he went inside. He'd been living rough for a while and the dog was good protection. He loved it. He made me swear to look after it until he came out. He was always asking about it. A neighbour was walking him and feeding him while I was away. But when I came back the dog was gone, and it didn't bark during the break-in or it would have woken the neighbours.'

'What else did he take?'

'My wife's jewellery.'

'How much was it worth?'

Cameron sniffed. 'A lot.'

'Didn't you have it in a safe?'

'Yes.'

'So the safe was opened?'

'Yes.'

'Did he know the combination?'

'Give me some credit.'

'So how did he get in?'

'Must have got someone to open it.'

Sam frowned. 'And you didn't tell the police?'

Cameron ran the flat of his hand over his forehead. 'There were items amongst the jewellery he knew I wouldn't want the police to know about.'

'Ah.'

'Look, he is my son. I didn't want the police knowing he'd breached his probation. I'd spent all that money trying to keep him out of prison in the first place. I didn't want to see him back inside. I thought I could sort it out myself.'

'What, get the jewellery back?'

'Yes.'

'Have you succeeded?'

He shook his head. 'I haven't seen him since it happened. And now Grace is dead and the police have been crawling all over me, all over my business.'

'The police will have been crawling all over anyone in any way connected with her. Family is always top of their list. An ex-husband with a history of domestic violence would be particularly high.'

He blushed. 'For God's sake, that was years ago when we were breaking up. You can't tell me you've never wanted to hit someone.'

Sam didn't say anything. She thought of Georgie Stubbs's head stuck through the railings and the time she'd once throttled Phil into a state of unconsciousness. She thought of the man in the Oxford police station and what might have happened to him if Phil hadn't intervened. Was that any different? All of them involved a loss of temper leading to violence. Perhaps she was kidding herself if she thought she was so different to this man sitting opposite her. The further away she got from fighting on a judo mat, the more violent she was becoming in her everyday life.

'Have you told the police about the burglary?'

'No, for the reasons I just gave.'

'Do you have any idea who might have killed her?'

He shook his head. 'Grace was . . .' He paused. 'Well, I suppose you could describe her as a very anxious person. Partly that was caused by her heart condition but she was also prone to periods of depression. She had been all her life. But she was a very gentle person. I can't imagine why anyone would want to kill her. But David could always wrap her round his little finger. If he stole the stuff from me, he may have asked his mother to sell it for him.'

'Couldn't he have sold it himself?'

'She had more contacts, a reputation in the market. People knew about David, knew he'd been inside. They'd have viewed anything he was selling with suspicion, but not if it was Grace. She'd have been a good cover.'

'And she would have done that for him?'

He shrugged. 'I don't know. Maybe she refused to and then they came looking for the goods.'

'Or she and David argued.'

'Perhaps. But I'm worried about the boys. As long as David's in trouble, Harry's not going to leave his side. Their mother's been killed. Suppose the boys are next? But I don't want the police involved.'

'It's a murder inquiry. Of course the police are involved – they're looking for them too.'

'Look, I'll pay you.'

'What for?'

'Bring the boys and the jewellery to me before the police find them.'

'Could David have killed her?'

'I just don't know. I can't believe it of him.'

'What if he was off his head? People can do all kinds of things, can't they?'

Cameron nodded.

'Who does he owe?'

Cameron didn't reply.

'They didn't find the jewellery on the boat after she was murdered?'

'I don't know, do I? I can hardly ask the police.'

'It could have been sold already.'

'I doubt it. No one in his right mind would touch it. And if that had happened they wouldn't have killed Grace. The debt would have already been paid off. If they kill her it sends a warning.'

'Surely rather an extreme one.'

He shrugged. 'Maybe they were going to rough her up a bit and it turned nasty.'

Cameron reached into the inside pocket of his jacket and brought out his wallet. He took out some cash and placed it on the table. 'Bring the boys to me and I'll double it.' Then he opened his briefcase and handed Sam a piece of paper. 'I've listed the items of jewellery which were stolen.'

A few minutes later Sam was looking down on Cameron walking out of the main entrance of the Riverview building. He'd certainly changed his tune since the first meeting with him. Did she believe that he was now the concerned father worried for his sons? Sam didn't trust sudden conversions. She didn't doubt he wanted his sons found but she wasn't altogether sure about his motives. One thing was clear: he wanted to find the jewellery and also wanted the police off his back. Maybe he'd just got desperate. Sam turned away from the window, picked up the cash and counted it thoughtfully. It was enough to buy her discretion. It was obvious that he'd had to tell her a lot more than he was comfortable with. But one thing worried her. According to Cameron, the dog was David's. At ten o'clock when Grace phoned Sam she had the dog. By the following morning there was no dog and Grace was dead. When she'd met up with Harry in Christ Church Meadow, she'd heard a dog bark and then seen two shadows. If the dog was with David presumably he'd been there that night before, during or after Grace was killed. Which placed him at the scene – unless, that is, Cameron was lying about the dog. She picked up the piece of paper lying on her desk. Her eye didn't move further than the first item: a triangular brooch of three gold fish inset with two fire opals, one of the items that Grace had been so careful to cover over with the *Antiques Gazette*.

Alan's flowers had died.

'Shall I throw these away?' Sam asked.

'Oh, do what you want.' Alan waved his hand airily. 'I don't fucking care.'

'So—'

'Don't ask me how I am,' Alan snapped.

'Is there anything I can do for you?'

'Get me out of here.'

'Come on, Alan, you're a grown man; surely you can just do that yourself? You're not strapped to the bed.'

'They're telling me I have to stay until next week.'

'Do you feel like you're ready to go home?'

'How would I fucking know? I'm not a doctor.'

'How's your stomach?'

'Sore. I'm probably going to get MRSA.'

Sam frowned. 'What's that?'

'Oh, you know what I mean, the thing that turns you black and then you rot and all your organs collapse.'

'Why should you get that?'

'The hospitals are filthy. It's all in here,' he tapped the newspaper that was lying on his bed. 'And I had an open wound.' His voice was rising in pitch. 'I want to be ill in France.'

'As opposed to lost?'

'Their hospitals, stupid. Much better than ours. You get red wine.'

'For heaven's sake, Alan. You sound like a hysterical queen.'

'I've been stabbed,' he shouted. 'What do you expect? I *am* a hysterical queen.'

'What's happened to Appendicitis?'

'He was discharged.'

'Maybe he'll visit you bearing food.'

'You're joking. Once out of here, no one in his right mind would want to come back. You look awful, by the way.'

'Shut up, you said that last time. Come on, let's go for a fag break.'

'I don't smoke.'

'You could do with some air.' She grabbed a wheelchair, which was sitting inside the door of the ward, helped Alan out of bed and set off with him along a corridor, down a lift and through reception to the entrance to the hospital.

Sam squatted down next to Alan, leaning on the arm of the chair, and lit a cigarette.

'My brothers are rucking about what happened,' Alan said.

'What's it to do with them?'

'*I'm* what it's to do with them.'

'The whole tribal thing?'

'Put it this way: they are not at all happy about their youngest brother being stabbed. I may be a poof and have done the unforgivable of joining the police, but I'm blood. Stab me and you stab the lot of them.'

Sam had an image of eight angry bulls charging around an arena with toreadors' spears hanging from their bloody backs. 'So what does that mean?'

'It means you've got eight men built like brick shithouses running around screaming blue murder, and it means Bert wants to have a conversation with Jackie to find out who knifed me.'

'Well, there's nothing stopping him, is there?'

'Perhaps it would be better if you were there.'

Sam groaned. 'That woman's been trouble ever since I stumbled into her on the staircase. She's almost got both of us killed.'

'Bert's been doing a bit of asking about and it seems Jackie was not being entirely honest with us.'

'She *is* an antiques dealer, Alan.'

He smiled. 'You know she said lots of people in that arcade had been attacked?'

Sam looked at the end of her cigarette. 'Yes.'

'Well, they haven't. It's only her.'

'What do you mean?'

'No one else but her has been attacked. Bert wants to know what the hell's going on. He thinks she probably owes the wrong person.'

'But what can your brother do?'

'My brother can set up a meeting with the person who's in charge of the man who stabbed me. Tell them he stabbed me – me being part of the tribe of Knowles – and see what they offer.'

'Blood money?'

'Yes.'

Sam sighed. 'Seems pretty arcane.'

'It's the way it works. If they discover who I am and who I'm linked to and my brothers did nothing, then that's a sign of weakness. They may start trying to muscle in on all kinds of things.'

'I've never been clear what it is exactly that your brothers do,' Sam said.

Alan laughed. '*All* kinds of things.'

Sam dropped her fag end amongst the thousand of others and

ground it into the pavement. 'We should get you in, it's cold out here.' She began wheeling Alan back into the hospital. 'I'm so sorry about this, Alan.'

'It's the last time I want to hear you say that.'

'But—'

'Shit happens,' he said, scratching his face. 'Could have happened on the Job, so happens it was now.'

Sam had barely been in her flat for five minutes when there was a tap on the door. She knew it wasn't Edie because there was no flat whistle. She opened the door to Jackie.

'Some bloke keeps leaving messages for me. Says he's a relative of Alan's.'

'Have you spoken to him?'

She shook her head. 'What's he want?'

'If you don't speak to him he'll probably come looking for you. He knows the arcade where you work.'

'But what does he want?' she repeated.

'He wants to know who you're in debt to and therefore who was responsible for stabbing his brother, who happens to be the youngest of a large west London criminal family.'

She frowned. 'But I thought you said Alan was an ex-police-man?'

'He is that as well.'

'Will you come with me, tomorrow?'

Sam groaned. 'What can I do?'

'At least you're friends with Alan.'

'Bert just wants information. He's not going to do anything to you.'

'Look, you're right, I do owe money and that means I'm still at risk.' Jackie held out two fifty-pound notes. 'Please.'

Sam took the notes. She'd been intending to go anyway, to see if Harry and David turned up there. This way she could do that and be paid.

'Five-thirty then?' Jackie said.

Sam nodded. 'Knock as you come down.'

She closed the door. Sam ordered a curry and sat in front of the television for a few hours not really focusing on what was on. Just watching to pass the time and to keep from thinking. She dozed in front of it, woke at twelve and went into the bedroom to go to bed properly. She pulled back the duvet and money fluttered into the air. She frowned and gathered it together and counted it. A thousand pounds. It was slightly damp and stained. This was truly blood money. Sam felt like a whore who'd been paid for services rendered. The dream came back to her vividly. Sleep suddenly didn't seem so inviting; she went into the front room and turned the television on again. She didn't want to risk another dream like the one she'd had last night. She stayed awake, staring blankly at the flickering images on the screen.

CHAPTER SEVENTEEN

When Jackie tapped on the door the following morning, Sam was fast asleep on the sofa, twisted into the kind of shape any corkscrew would have approved of. She blundered to the door. 'Give me a few minutes,' she said. 'I'll see you out front.'

Jackie rolled her eyes. 'The meters will all be taken.'

'Come on – five minutes.'

She put on her shoes and then passed the shower spray over her face and brushed her teeth. By the time she was walking down the street with Jackie, she felt as if she'd been shot from the barrel of a gun.

Sam delivered Jackie safely into Golding's Arcade and then wandered round the market. She had some breakfast at Freddy's and read the newspaper from front to back. Jackie would be finished at two, so she had a lot of time to look around for the twins. For the next couple of hours Sam slogged up and down Portobello Road. She was feeling decidedly footsore and considering grabbing a coffee when she saw him. Impossibly tall and blond with a blue holdall slung over his shoulder, he stood out like a lighthouse in the desert. He was a few metres ahead of her, in a heated discussion with a small, dark man wearing a black leather jacket that was several sizes too big for him. So, he had come to London. Sam walked into his eye line and made sure that when he looked up he saw her. No flicker of recognition, no response. Nothing. Just a dull stare that lingered on her for a second and then veered back to the man he was talking to. There was no doubt this was David. He was remarkably like his brother to look at, but the drug use was evident in the hollows of his cheeks, the black smudges under his eyes and the pallor of his skin.

Sam watched as he finished talking to the man and then followed him as he set off through the market. He went in and out of the arcades, stopping at various stalls and taking things out of the holdall to show to dealers. His lack of success was demonstrated by his increasingly frustrated gestures. Sam was just about to follow David into another arcade when a hand fell across her shoulders and she turned to see Bert standing next to her.

'Oh hi,' Sam said.

'Is she here?'

Sam was trying to keep moving forward but Bert had her in a friendly but firm grip that glued her to his side.

'Hold on a minute, Bert, I'll be back in a second.' She ducked under his arm and set off into the Admiral Vernon Arcade, but now David was nowhere to be seen. She swore and walked back to where Bert was waiting for her.

He raised his eyebrows interrogatively. Sam nodded towards the arcade that Jackie was working out in.

'Got a few things to do. I'll be catching up with you later.'

Sam retraced her steps to the small man in the leather jacket. 'Could I have a word?'

'Who you?' he said in an accent that Sam couldn't place but suspected was eastern European. 'Police? Social security?'

'No. I just wanted to ask you about a man I saw you talking to about half an hour ago.'

The man threw his hands in the air. 'Lady, how many people I see on a Saturday? Give me a break.'

'This man was very tall and blond. He was wearing a baseball hat and carrying a blue holdall. His name's David Cameron.'

'Ah, Grace's son.' He crossed himself and kissed his hand. 'Poor woman.'

'You knew Grace?'

He shrugged. 'Everyone knows Grace. She has been in the market many years.'

'What did David want?'

'To sell me things.'

'What things?'

'This and that.'

Sam looked into his showcase and saw a cross that she had last seen hanging round Emma Hodge's neck. 'Did he sell you this?'

The man's face hardened. 'I have this for many weeks. I get this from Tony, a Brighton dealer.'

'David sold this to you, didn't he?'

'Piss off – you begin to bore me now.'

'It belongs to a priest who was robbed. Other things were taken from the church; did he have those kinds of things on him? Church plates, communion cups, a cross . . .?'

'You go now.' He started waving his hands at her in a shooing gesture. 'Get away from my showcase; other people can't see.'

'That cross is stolen property.' She reached for it and his hand clamped over hers. 'How much?'

'Fifty pounds.'

'I'll give you twenty.'

'Fuck off.'

'See that policeman over there?' Sam nodded to where a policeman was slowly making his way through the crowds. She reached into her pocket and held out the note. He snatched it and let go of her hand. Sam pocketed the cross.

The man shouted something in a language that Sam didn't understand and spat on the ground near her feet and a large man, who'd been leaning against the outside of the Admiral Vernon Arcade smoking a cigarette and reading a paper, sauntered over. Sam didn't wait for the outcome of their conversation, which involved several vigorous head gestures in her direction.

As Sam and Jackie came out of Golding's Arcade ready to negotiate the crowds and walk back to the car, Bert came up alongside them.

'Thought I'd walk with you,' he said.

Jackie looked anxiously at Sam.

'OK, love – who d'you owe?'

Jackie didn't say anything.

He pulled her to a halt and put his face an inch away from hers. 'Look, I'm pissed off enough that my baby brother got stuck because of you and I'm pissed off enough that you haven't had the good manners to return my calls. I've got better things to do with my time than fuck about here on a Saturday morning, wasting my time tracking you down when my wife's nine months pregnant.'

Sam put her hand on his sleeve. 'Bert—'

'Keep out,' he snapped. He turned back to Jackie. 'So the word is you owe a lot and that's why they keep going for you. No one else in Golding's has been attacked. How come it's just you?'

Jackie's face was grey.

'Who?' Bert shouted.

Jackie looked at the pavement. 'Sullivan.'

Bert groaned. 'Jesus! How much.'

'Enough. I'm waiting for some money to come in from the States from one of the big department stores. When that comes I'll be able to clear it, or at any rate a large part of it.'

'When's that due?'

'Any day.'

'But he's not willing to wait.'

She shrugged. 'I've been able to keep out of their hands so far.'

Bert grabbed the front of her coat. 'Yes, and my baby brother's been stabbed because you weren't upfront about what was going on. If he'd known Eddie Sullivan was involved he might have been given a bit more warning. And Sammy here almost got her head smashed open with a baseball bat.'

'Look, I'd tried other people. They'd all refused to do it. Sam managed OK. I'm really sorry about Alan. I thought he'd be all right,' Jackie said.

'So you fucking should be.' Bert let go of the front of her coat as if it'd been smeared with dog shit. He strode away from them across the car park.

'What's he going to do?' Jackie asked.

Sam shrugged. 'I don't know. Use your imagination.'

Jackie groaned. 'I was trying not to.'

They got into the car and Jackie began driving back to Fulham.

'Nice business you're in,' Sam said.

'Most of them wouldn't piss on you if you were alight.'

'What are people saying about what happened to Grace?'

'It's what I said to you before. David owed money and once he was out of prison they wanted it settled. When he didn't come across, they came after Grace as a soft target because they knew she had goods they could sell.'

'Sullivan, the man you owe . . .'

'Yes.'

'Is he the same one David owed?'

'I don't know. He's a big lender. Everyone knows him.'

'Why?'

'He's the one to go to when you've run out of all other options.'

'David was in the market today trying to sell stuff.'

'Grace's?'

'I don't know, but there were definitely items he'd stolen from a church in Oxford. The man who bought some of it wasn't very impressed when I said it was stolen.'

'Who was that?'

Sam described him.

Jackie laughed. 'Most of his stuff's bent gear anyway.'

They had stopped at a red light. Sam looked in the wing mirror and saw a motorbike behind them carrying two people. 'Has this got central locking?'

'Come on,' Jackie said. 'Look at it, it's a rust bucket.'

Sam undid her seatbelt, reached into the back and locked the two passenger doors.

'What's the matter?' Jackie said.

Sam was still twisted round in her seat. One of the men had got off the motorbike and was approaching the car. 'Move,' she said.

'The lights are still red.'

'Get the fucking car moving,' Sam shouted. 'Now.'

A helmeted head loomed outside Sam's window; a hand tried the door handle. Jackie stamped on the accelerator and the car shot away from the lights. Sam heard a car screeching to a halt and then the blare of a horn. Behind them she saw the man run back to his bike.

'What's going on?'

'I didn't like the look of him,' Sam said.

They had driven a bit further when Jackie said, 'Something's the matter with the steering.'

'Shit,' Sam said. 'He's probably done your back tyre – keep driving.' She grabbed her phone from her pocket. I'll phone the police.' She was just about to punch 999 when she saw a police station. 'Turn in here,' she said. As the car lurched into the car park, the motorbike shot past them.

Sam turned to Jackie. 'Anyone you can go and stay with for a while?'

'What do you mean?'

'Come on – isn't it obvious? You're not safe.'

'What about my business?'

'What about your life?'

A policeman was tapping on Sam's window. She rolled it down and began to explain.

After getting the tyre changed and Jackie safely home, Sam crashed out and woke at five in the afternoon to the sound of her answerphone clicking off and Frank's claws digging into the side of her cheek. She removed his paw from her face, got up and played back the message.

'Wondered if you'd like to come over for supper tonight. Oh, it's Gerry here by the way. Gerry on the boat. Give me a call.'

Sam stared at the answerphone, puzzled. Was that someone asking her out on a date? It was such a long time since that had happened, she felt as if she couldn't decipher the evidence of her own ears. How sad was that? She played it again and then again and decided finally it was definitely someone who she found attractive inviting her out. Sam looked at the clock on her answerphone and wondered if it was too late to say yes. She phoned him back.

'Hi, it's Sam.'

'Oh hi, you on for supper?'

'I've only just woken up, I was at Portobello this morning, so is eight too late to come round?'

'Eight's fine.'

'Great.'

'See you then.'

Sam put down the phone and stared at it. Dear God, a date. What the hell did you wear on a date? All her dating with Phil had been done on a judo mat. It had given a new meaning to the expression of falling head over heels in love.

She opened her wardrobe and stared at her clothes: multiple pairs of jeans, T-shirts, jumpers and fleeces. There was more variety in her shoes – trainers, Doc Martens, Caterpillar boots and a pair of suede Campers. But as for date clothes, there were none.

Sam blamed Phil. He'd once told her what really turned him on was when she wore a scruffy old pair of paint-stained blue overalls. Sam suspected he was confusing lust with gratitude. She'd never come across anyone with such an aversion to DIY.

Whatever the case, Phil had never been a stockings and suspender belt sort of a bloke and there'd never been much incentive for a gal to doll herself up. Yes, Sam thought, it's all Phil's fault.

She threw her choices onto the bed: black jeans, black polo neck jumper, a pair of Doc Martens and a black leather jacket, then had a quick shower and washed her hair. There wasn't much she could do about the state of her face. In the end she applied a bit of red lipstick, hoping it wouldn't clash too much with her scars.

An hour later and the woman in black was walking up the gangplank to Gerry's boat.

Grace's boat was still cordoned off with blue and white police tape. The light coming from Gerry's boat looked warm and welcoming. Even more welcoming were the smells of cooking food filtering under the wooden door out in the cold night air. Sam knocked on the door and entered.

Gerry turned round in the tiny kitchen area and beckoned her in.

'Come in, come in,' he said. 'Take a seat.'

The boat was fugged up with the steam coming from a pan of water boiling on the stove.

Sam took the bottle she'd brought out of a plastic bag and placed it on the table. Gerry handed her a corkscrew and put two glasses on the table.

'Smells good,' Sam said.

Gerry opened a packet of spaghetti and handed it to her. 'How much do you think?'

Sam shrugged. 'I'm hopeless at this.' She slid about half the packet into her hand. 'This much?'

Gerry frowned. 'Bit more, maybe?'

Sam laughed. 'I always go through this and then end up doing all of it and throwing half away.'

'It's quite good fried the following day for breakfast.'

'Never heard of cereal and a banana?'

He shook his head. 'Nope.'

Sam dug the end of the corkscrew into the metal covering the top of the bottle and peeled it away. Then stood up to put the end into the cork. She popped the cork and poured the wine into their glasses.

'This looks good,' he said, taking hold of the bottle and turning it so he could see the label.

Sam looked round the interior of the boat. 'You have to keep things to a minimum in a boat, don't you?'

'Not a problem for me.'

'I'm a natural hoarder. Find it difficult to let go of anything. I could never live in a boat, not even one the size of Grace's. Maybe three boats moored side by side and one just for recycling.'

'You can't take it with you.'

'I never get that. How old are you? Not that old, right? My view is you can take it a hell of a long way.'

He laughed. 'I don't need much. In the job I do I've seen too many people eaten up by things being taken from them. You know, burglaries and stuff. Torturing themselves about what's gone missing, installing alarms, new locks, creating fortresses. And in the end it's just stuff and they'll be dead in their graves with nothing there with them but worms.'

'That's not what the Egyptians thought. They sent the pharaohs off with everything.'

'Yes, but they raided the tombs when they ran out of money.'

Sam laughed. 'A sort of major ISA – I let go very, very reluctantly.'

'I'll bear that in mind,' Gerry said.

For no good reason that she could think of, Sam blushed.

The meal was good: spaghetti, fried red onions, Parmesan and a tomato salad with fresh basil. Better than Sam would have managed. Gerry ate fast and pushed his plate away when he'd finished.

'I wondered if you'd heard anything else about Grace?'

Sam wiped her mouth and put down her fork. 'What kind of thing?'

'I don't know. How she died? Who they think killed her?'

'Have the police been back asking you questions?' She twisted the last bit of spaghetti round her fork and placed it in her mouth.

He nodded. 'They've been crawling over me like flies on shit. Getting me to go down the station for questioning, leaving me waiting for hours. You know, the usual thing. Making me sweat.'

'I suppose it's because you had the opportunity.'

'What do you mean?'

'Well, you live next door and you knew her.'

'I think their basic take on it is, if you know about locks you're only this far,' he held his thumb and finger about an inch apart, 'from being a burglar. If you're a burglar you're a criminal and if you're that you can do anything. They keep going on and on about what I was doing that evening.'

'And what were you doing?'

'Nothing – that's the trouble. I was here, wasn't I? Quiet evening in, watching TV. Not the kind of thing the police want to hear.'

'And you didn't hear anything?'

'No, and they kept going on about the dog. Did I hear the dog barking? They're obsessed with the dog.'

'Mr Cameron said the dog was David's.'

'He's been in touch with you?'

'Yes, and he was very keen to know where his sons are. Suddenly came over all friendly. Said David had stolen his wife's jewellery when they were away on holiday and tried to make it look like a burglary. He doesn't want the police involved because he doesn't want them asking where the jewellery came from in the first place. Also, he doesn't want David back in prison and he would be because he'd be in breach of his probation.'

Gerry laughed. 'How very paternal of him.'

'You don't think he's telling the truth?'

'He wants the stuff back, all right.'

'How well do you know the twins?'

'You know – to say "hi" to. I could never tell them apart. Used to assume it was David because more often than not it was. Harry was away at school, then college.'

He took the plates over to the sink and began to wash them up.

'Can I help you?' Sam asked.

'No – sorry, it comes from living alone. You eat – you wash up. I go onto automatic pilot.'

'Doesn't work that way with me. It's more: Eat. Leave it. Eat. Leave it. Try to eat. Oh dear, no clean dishes. Wash up one, pile rest in sink.'

He laughed. 'Coffee?'

Sam nodded and he put the kettle on.

'I saw David in the market today.'

He spun round. 'You're joking.'

'No. He'd robbed a church in Oxford and was trying to sell the stuff. Wasn't having much luck.'

'Where was he?'

'All over the place – I lost him in the Admiral Vernon.'

'Did you talk to him?' He was taking a cup off a metal hook.

'No.'

'How do you know what he was selling?'

'Talked to someone who he was trying to sell to. I recognised a cross in his showcase. It had been hanging round the neck of a vicar I know.'

'Any idea where he is now?'

Sam shook her head.

The kettle boiled and Gerry poured the water over some coffee grounds. Sam inhaled. 'Coffee is my drug of choice.'

He put the cups, cafetiere and milk on the table and sat down. Sam had been watching him as he made the coffee: long legs, flat stomach, broad shoulders. He was wearing camouflage trousers and a blue sweatshirt. He had a relaxed and comfortable manner in his body. She wasn't sure about the hair but felt she could be persuaded. He poured the coffee and then looked up and caught Sam scrutinising him.

'And?'

'Sorry?'

He smiled. 'Milk?' He pushed the cup and the milk bottle towards her.

She reached for the bottle but, distracted by thoughts of what he might look like uncamouflaged, she misjudged the distance and knocked it over, spilling milk all over Gerry's lap. He jumped to his feet and held the front of his trousers away from his skin.

'Shit,' Sam said. 'I am sorry.' She grabbed a cloth from the sink and began to mop up the table, the floor and the chair. Gerry was dabbing at himself with some paper towel.

'I think I'll change these,' he said. 'Won't be a minute.' He disappeared into a room towards the front of the boat.

Sam finished wiping up the milk and rinsed out the cloth in the sink. She was spreading it out on the washing-up rack when she felt a warm mouth on the back of her neck. It felt nice. And so did the warm mouth on her ear. And the front of her throat. And under her chin. And on her mouth. Mmmm, that felt especially nice.

'Want to try and warm up the parts you just poured freezing milk over?' Gerry asked.

Sam moved her hand onto the parts in question. 'Feels pretty warm already.'

'But,' Gerry said, 'they could be oh (he kissed her) . . . so (he kissed her again) . . . much . . . warmer.' His hand slid under Sam's shirt.

Sam murmured something.

'Was that yes?' Gerry said.

'Come on,' she said, pulling him by the front of his sweatshirt towards the bedroom.

It wasn't the earth that moved exactly but the boat was certainly rocking. It seemed to Sam to be rocking an embarrassing amount as she looked up at Gerry under the canopy created by his hair. She had never made love to a man with long hair before and found it a surprisingly sensual if rather ticklish experience. At one point she had gripped onto him so hard he had told her to let go, that she was hurting him. Holding on. And letting go. It was all a bloody complicated business. She tried to lose herself in the sex but couldn't, finding her brain whirring on all kinds of disconnected bits and pieces, but she tried to make the right noises. The pure physicality of sex was a relief, it reminded her of fighting, of groundwork. Gerry came and slid out of her.

'Have you?' he began.

'Yes, yes . . .' Sam reached over and pulled the duvet, which had fallen off the bed, back over their bodies and, enjoying the weight of him between her legs, fell asleep.

Her father moves towards her.

'Don't think you can escape me. You know it's always been you. Always. Since the day you were born. Since the moment I saw you. I knew we were meant for each other. You know it as well, I know you do.'

His hand touches her cheek, the thumb tracing under her eye.

'All the years I was away you were the only person I thought of. You can't get away from me, you know you can't.'

His face looms towards hers. His mouth is open and she sees the red inside of his mouth. He is going to swallow me, she thinks, I am going to disappear like Jonah into the whale but unlike Jonah I am never going to come back up. She feels his breath against her face. His mouth is on hers, the tongue forcing its way into her throat, and she is choking and can't breathe and bites down, feeling the blood pour out of his tongue, and as he pulls away from her his tongue comes away and she swallows it, feeling it move like a maggot down into her stomach, and when he speaks all she hears is his voice talking from deep down inside her.

'You're mine. Every man you sleep with, I'll be there, watching.'

She woke with the taste of blood in her mouth. Gerry's face loomed over her in the darkness. 'Are you all right? You were shouting.'

She pushed him away, still wrapped in the feelings of the dream. 'Was it a bad dream?'

'You don't want to know.' Sam touched her tongue with her fingers. It hurt; she must have bitten it in her sleep.

He ran his hand down her back. 'Suppose I do?'

Sam got out of the bed. 'I need some water,' she said and began feeling her way out of the room into the kitchen. She drank one glass, two glasses and was on the third when Gerry came in.

'Breakfast?' he asked.

'Isn't it too early? What's the time?'

'Seven.'

Sam stood leaning over the sink, her arms shaking. 'I should be going.' She brushed past him on the way to the bedroom.

'Sam?' He caught hold of her arm.

'Don't,' she said. 'I'm sorry, Gerry, but don't. Let go.'

He did. She pulled on her clothes and stepped back out into the main part of the boat. He was leaning against the sink watching her with his arms folded.

'Thanks,' she said. 'I had a really nice time.'

He burst out laughing. 'Yeah, right.'

'Look, just forget about this last bit.'

'Oh, what bit's that? The bit where you wake screaming, refuse to tell me what's going on, shut me out, refuse breakfast and rush out of here like an express train. Is that the bit you're talking about?'

'Well, yes,' Sam said. 'It's just I'm in no fit state at the moment.'

'For what?'

'For anything intimate.'

'What was last night?'

Sex, Sam thought.

'Very nice,' she said.

'"Very nice"?' he repeated.

'Well, yes. You know, I *did* have a nice time.'

'I don't want your gratitude.'

'I'll phone.'

'Sure you will.'

She pushed open the door and stepped out onto the top deck. It was cold and dark and she welcomed it. She walked briskly along the walkways up onto the street and set off along Cheyne Walk. Traffic was nose to tail heading into town. For a moment she stopped and looked at the black back of the swiftly flowing Thames. Wherever she went, wherever she sought refuge, he was there watching. However hard she tried, she couldn't escape him.

CHAPTER EIGHTEEN

As Sam fumbled in her bag for her keys, Kelly Webb got out of a car parked in front of Sam's mansion block.

Sam sighed. 'What's this, *Groundhog Day*?'

Kelly Webb leaned against the front door as Sam struggled with her keys. 'I've been doing a little research I thought you might be interested in.' Her breath reeked of alcohol.

'Alcoholic, was it?'

'My brother's birthday.' Webb began coughing and ended up doubled over and wheezing. Sam opened the front door and turned her body in the gap, blocking Webb from coming in.

'I've been doing some research of my own. The *Daily Herald* say they've never heard of you. So if you're not a journalist, who exactly are you?'

Webb frowned. 'Who did you talk to?'

'Didn't get a name. It was the person I was put through to.'

'Look, I'm freelance. You probably got some wee shite doing work experience who looked down a list and didn't see my name on it. If you want to check up on me, ask to speak to Andrew Hall. He's the man I'm reporting to.'

'I don't want you bothering my family.'

Webb searched in her bag, found an inhaler and used it. 'Not very friendly, are they?'

'Leave them alone.'

'Has Geoff gone to Oxford – has he holed up there?'

Sam didn't say anything and began closing the door on her.

Webb shrugged. 'Well, it's up to you. Don't blame me when you see the headlines.'

Sam stopped closing the door.

'Your stepfather's Peter Goodman, the mathematician. Your mother's Jean.'

'So what?'

'Did she know your father was alive when she married Goodman or did she just put that out of her mind?'

'What are you talking about?'

'They were never divorced, were they?'

'She had his death certificate. She didn't need a divorce.'

'But he wasn't dead.'

'What's your point?'

'Look, I'm not really interested in the domestic arrangements of your family. What I'm interested in is where Geoff is and what he has to say. But I've already paid out a substantial sum of money and if he doesn't deliver on that story, I'm going to have to come up with something to justify the expense to my editor. And that story will be the story of your family: your mother, your father, your brother, your stepfather and you.'

'Pretty boring story,' Sam said but she left the door open and Kelly Webb followed her up the stairs and into her flat.

Sam couldn't allow that to happen – Jean and Peter in an exposé and her responsible for it – no, that didn't bear thinking about. She heard her mother's voice: *Your father does have a reputation in this city.* Maybe she could toss a few snippets Webb's way in order to keep her happy.

They went into the front room. Sam didn't invite Webb to sit down.

Frank came rolling in after them.

Kelly stared at him for a moment in silence. 'Who's this? Fat Boy Fat?'

Sam sighed. 'It's a big-bone thing.'

Kelly laughed. 'Brontosaurus?'

'So,' Sam said. 'This is fun. You've come round to insult my cat.'

'When did you last see your father?'

'A couple of days ago. He came to pick up some stuff he'd left here. Said he might have to disappear for a bit.'

'Why'd he say that?'

Sam sighed. 'He'd been shot.'

Webb's face went blank with shock. 'Is he all right?'

'Yes.'

'When was this?'

'About a week ago. He turned up here and he'd been shot in the upper right shoulder. It had gone straight through. I got him treated and then he'd been recuperating with a friend.'

'Who did it?'

'He doesn't know – thinks the security forces don't want him talking about what he did in Northern Ireland.'

'Christ! What was he picking up?'

'Wallet he'd left here before I took him to hospital.'

'Who was he staying with?'

Sam shook her head. 'I'm not telling you that.'

'Where is he now?'

'No idea.'

'Would the person he recuperated with know?'

'No.'

'Why not?'

'Because if he's decided to go missing for a while, he's not going to tell anyone, is he? He's going to disappear without a word.'

'Do you know of any way I could get hold of him?'

Sam shook her head.

Webb considered Sam in silence for a few moments. 'How do you feel about your father?'

Sam took a step towards her and Kelly Webb took several hurried paces backwards.

She held out her hand in a stop sign. 'Keep your hair on.'

'That's all I have to say to you.'

'We have safe houses we could hide him in.'

'Come on! He's ex-SAS. Do you seriously think he doesn't know how to hide himself?'

'If he got shot he wasn't doing a very good job of it, was he?'

'You must see that whatever he agreed with you, it was before he was shot. That's changed everything. He's going to want to keep a pretty low profile. Before, he may have suspected he was in danger, but now he *knows* he is.'

'Did he say the deal was off?'

'For the moment, yes. He said he'd get back in touch with you when he could.'

After Kelly Webb had gone Sam listened to her answerphone

message. Eric: 'Harry's turned up and we need to talk to you. Phone me.' Then, two more calls from him along similar lines.

Sam dialled his number. 'Hi, it's Sam.'

'Where the hell have you been?'

'Good morning to you, too. Still off the fags?'

'Just. Harry's here. Can you come over?'

'Where's here? Three days ago he was in Oxford.'

'Well, now he's in Putney. Same place we met before.'

'Give me half an hour.'

As Sam reached the top of the boathouse stairs, Eric and Harry stood up.

'What's going on?' Sam said.

Eric sighed. 'Harry'd better tell you.'

'Dave's disappeared.'

'Was he with you in Oxford when I saw you?'

He nodded. 'But after you'd left he went and I've not heard from him since. The thing is, I've been trying to keep him off drugs. I've been with him twenty-four-seven and he'd been doing really well. But if he's gone there's only one thing he's aiming to do and that's score.'

'Had you told David about Emma Hodge?'

Harry frowned. 'Why?'

Sam didn't say anything.

Fear flitted across Harry's face. 'What's happened? Has something happened to her?'

'She was attacked on the same night I met you in Christ Church Meadow. She says it was him.'

Harry put his hands to his head and pulled at his hair. 'My God, is she all right?'

'Yes, but she was robbed and stuff was taken from the church.'

'It's my fault—'

'Did he know about her?'

He nodded. 'My phone's gone and her number was in it. He could have got it from there.'

'When were you aware of him going missing?'

'That night I spoke to you. He didn't come back.'

'I saw him in Portobello on Saturday morning.'

'Oh, shit.'

'Man I spoke to said he was trying to sell stuff from the church.' Sam reached into her pocket and brought out Emma Hodge's cross. 'I bought this back.'

Harry held it momentarily in the palm of his hand before returning it to Sam. He shook his head. 'I knew it.'

'It's a hell of a tall order to think you could keep him clean,' Sam said. 'He needs to get into some sort of rehabilitation programme, doesn't he?'

'And how easy do you think that is?' Harry said. 'They put him in prison and he comes out more addicted than when he went in and even more in debt.'

'Were you involved in the theft from your father?'

'Sorry?'

'Your father came to me and said that David had stolen your stepmother's jewellery from his home. He didn't report it because he said if he did David would be in breach of his probation. He wanted me to tell him when I found you.'

Harry's eyes narrowed. 'You're working for him now, are you?'

'I won't tell him if you don't want me to.'

He didn't say anything but looked relieved.

Sam went on. 'I have to ask you again. Was David involved with your mother's death?'

'No.' Harry looked horrified. 'No, I've told you. How could you think. . .? She was our mother. He loved her.'

'I'm not saying he didn't but drugs can make you do all kinds of things, can't they?'

He was shaking his head.

'Were you there when it happened?'

He shook his head.

'Was David?'

Harry didn't reply.

'Tell me, were you on the boat when I came and talked to your mother? I thought I heard someone moving around just before I left.'

He looked up, startled. 'No, I wasn't.'

'Who do you think might have killed your mother?'

'As I said to you in Oxford, Dave owed money. A lot of money.

265

He was frightened about coming out of prison because he knew they'd be waiting for him.'

'And the people he owed, they knew your mother?'

'She'd stalled out in the market for years. Dave used to go with her even when he was a little kid. He loved it. He'd done that since he was a boy. Everyone knew Dave and Mum were related.'

'Did he owe someone called Eddie Sullivan?'

Harry nodded.

'Where d'you think he is?'

'I don't know.'

'Any friends he'd go to – dealers, favourite places to score?'

'I don't know. Mum would have known.' He stopped and looked as if he was struggling to bite back tears.

Sam touched his arm. 'Isn't it time to go to the police?'

He shook his head. 'I have to find him.'

'What can't you tell them?'

He looked at her. 'If I go to them it's tantamount to pointing the finger at Dave and I won't do that. I have to persuade him to hand himself in. To get help. That's what I have to do first. He's in danger. I know he is. Will you help me? I can't do anything unless we find him.'

'But what then?'

'We have to get the money together to pay off the debt.'

'But your father said he'd asked for twenty thousand pounds. Where on earth are you going to get that sort of money?'

Harry looked horrified. 'That much?'

'That's what he said.'

'God, I had no idea.'

'You're also at risk.'

'What do you mean?'

'You look like him. Do you think they're going to waste their time on niceties? If what they're mainly looking to do is make an example of your brother because he hasn't paid up, they could just as easily make one of you. You should be careful.' Sam looked at Eric. 'Is he going to stay with you?'

Harry looked at Eric and Eric nodded. 'Will you help me find Dave?'

'OK, you need to draw up a list of likely places and then we can split it between us and go from there. We can start tomorrow.'

*

A couple of loud bangs that shook the building and the scream of splintering wood jolted Sam awake. She sat up in bed wondering if a lorry had crashed into the side of the mansion block. Then she saw shadows moving in her flat and smelled sweat. A torch shining in her face made her squint and a piece of paper was thrust at her. She put a hand over the light and tried to look beyond the glare of the torch at the person holding it, but couldn't.

'What the fuck?' She turned on her sidelight and squinted at the paper – a warrant to search her flat. Skinner was holding it.

'You should get your lights fixed,' he said. 'It's like a dungeon in here.'

'Dim light has its uses,' Sam said. 'And this,' she flicked the warrant, 'we both know is fucking ridiculous.'

Sam sat on the bed until they wanted to search underneath it. Then she sat on the sofa until they wanted to search under that. Then she sat on the floor until they said they needed to look under the rugs. In the end she sat on a stool in the kitchen, sipping a cup of tea, watching the men sneezing from the dust and bagging up her possessions and removing them in a van.

'Are you from that television programme that sorts out your clutter?' she asked one man who was pulling a chest of drawers away from the wall. And to another: 'This is a complete waste of your time.'

From the highest place in the flat, the top of the bookcases in the hall, Frank watched the proceedings with interest, occasionally scraping his claws across the top of a passing crew-cut.

'If that fucking cat does that one more time he goes in the bag,' a man said, carefully dabbing at his head and then examining his fingertips for blood.

'Try catching him,' Sam said. 'I'd really enjoy watching that.'

As the last bag was dragged from the flat, Sam patted the back of one of the men. 'Thanks boys, that saves me a trip to the dump.'

Skinner was the last to leave.

'Was this really necessary?' she said, nodding at her door, which was hanging lopsidedly from its hinges. 'If you'd knocked I'd have let you in. You know, I'm fairly conventional that way.'

He looked slightly embarrassed. 'Wasn't down to me.'

'This has got nothing to do with Grace, has it? It's that thug getting you to do his dirty work for him, seeing what he can dig up about my father? Who is he? Special Branch?'

'You should be careful who you decide to upset.'

'There's nothing there,' Sam said. 'It's all junk and this has been a complete waste of his and your time.' She gestured at the van. 'You can keep it all.'

As soon as the police had gone, Edie opened her door and surveyed the damage.

'You pissed them off, love, or what?'

'I suppose so, Edie, yes.'

'Nearly had a heart attack.' She nodded into her own flat. 'Thought it was Customs and Excise coming for my baccy.'

Sam smiled.

'What you going to do about your door?'

Sam shook her head slowly.

'Do you want me to get my friend Don over, love?'

'Would he do it?'

'He was in charge of all sorts, wasn't he – over in Wandsworth? Knows how to hang a door – for a fee.'

The idea of calling Gerry crossed Sam's mind but in almost the same instant she dismissed it. She couldn't. Not after how she'd left things the other morning.

'I suppose I could try Spence.'

'Spence.' Edie snorted dismissively. 'You'll have your door hanging off for a month. I'll phone Don in the morning.'

The following morning Don was outside Sam's door, toolkit in hand. He was tall, in his sixties with a very red face and wire-rimmed glasses. He was wearing pristinely white trainers, jeans and a denim shirt.

'All right, love? Edie said you'd had a few difficulties.' He patted the door. 'I see what she means.'

Sam was feeling exhausted. 'Could you rehang it?'

'No problem.'

'How much?'

'For a friend of Edie's, twenty-five quid.'

'Fine – thanks.'

Don dropped his bag on the landing and began to examine the side of the door. 'Looks like the hinges popped out, which makes it much easier for me. It's harder work when the hinges take large chunks of the frame with them.'

'Good – do you want some tea?'

'Thanks, love – three sugars.'

Sam came back with the cups a few minutes later.

'They find what they were looking for?'

'There wasn't anything for them to find.'

He smiled. 'Course not. Scared Edie half to death.'

Sam laughed and gestured next door. 'They wouldn't have a hope.'

'She's a great girl is Edie.' Don sipped his tea. 'She stays so active for her age.'

Sam considered the word 'active' in silence.

'You know she got married on the coach the other day?' he said.

'Married? She always swore she'd never do that again.'

'Not *really* married. We held a ceremony and the coach driver married them and she gave Albert a packet of condoms and some Viagra.'

Sam laughed nervously. 'It's a joke, right?'

'Keeps the customs boys distracted. If they come piling on the coach, we say, "Have a heart, boys, we've got newlyweds on board." '

'Does it work?'

Don shrugged. 'Sometimes. If it doesn't we've had a laugh, haven't we? They confiscate our gear and we just get pissed.' He put the cup of tea down and picked up his drill. 'You know, if she'd started younger she could have been a big player, Edie. She's a natural. I showed her the ropes but she's way outstripped me. Yeah, she really is something else. Runs her own show now.'

Much to Sam's relief, the whine of the drill cut off any chance of further conversation.

After Don had finished the door, Sam phoned the hospital to find out about Alan. She spoke to a nurse who told her that Alan had discharged himself the previous day, against doctor's instructions, so Sam phoned Alan's flat.

'Was that wise?' Sam asked.

'I don't care. I couldn't stand another day in that place.'

'How's the wound?'

'The wound is bloody marvellous.'

'Well, good for you, then,' Sam said. 'Can I go shopping for you or anything?'

'I have so much food in here you couldn't believe it.'

'Family's rallied round?'

'Eight sisters-in-law bearing gifts. I feel like the baby Jesus.'

'They still there?'

'No. I told them they all had to leave – that I needed my rest. They were doing my head in.'

'Do you mind if I moan and whine down the phone at you?'

'Carry on, love. It'll be respite from the inside of my head.'

'Got a visit from the police last night. Broke down the front door and ransacked the place.'

'What?'

'Warrant said it related to Grace Cameron's murder.'

'That's ridiculous.'

'I know, but Skinner came round here when there were bloodstains from my dad all over the sofa. Maybe that was all they needed. But I don't think it had anything to do with Grace, they were really looking for things about Dad.'

'Will they have found anything?'

'No. I've asked Edie to look after all that for me.'

'How's it going with the Cameron case?'

'Turns out David owes the same person as Jackie.'

'Sullivan?'

'You spoke to Bert?'

'Yes. Jesus, Sam. That's not good news. The debt's still outstanding?'

'Yes.'

'If the debt's not settled they'll be looking for the boy until it is.'

'I know.'

'I mean, anyone but Sullivan.'

'So, any ideas?'

'About what?'

'How to get him off the boys' backs.'

'You see how they've been with Jackie. No way are they going to let something like that go. You've got to pay him.'

'There must be something I can do.'

'Yes, get the hell out of there.'

'I can't do that.'

'Yes, Sam, you can.'

'No, Alan, I can't.'

'The mother's already been murdered, Sam, and as far as you can work out she wasn't even directly involved. She was incidental and they practically cut her face off. And, anyway, why are you still involved? Weren't you supposed to find Harry and that was that? Why are you still messing about in there?'

It was a good point.

'He can't go back into his life, can he? Not how things stand at the moment.'

'So? You found him.'

'I want him to be able to go back into his life.'

'Why?'

'I suppose I want him to be able to take part in the Boat Race.'

'Why?'

'Oh God, Alan, you're beginning to sound like Reg.'

'It's the sport thing, isn't it?'

'Well, yes. All the things they say about him – you know, Eric and Tom – it reminds me of the sort of thing people said about me when I was his age. I suppose I want him to fulfil his potential. That's not just about the Boat Race – it's about his future.'

'You're not thinking this through straight, Sam. You've become personally involved. Send in your bill and get out of there.'

'He wants to be a priest.'

'So what?'

'I can't just abandon him.'

'You're not his mother. He's not your responsibility.'

'He's an elite athlete. What else do I have to know?'

'Sam, he's eighteen years old and quite capable of making his own decisions. It's not up to you to save him.'

'Have you never needed a bit of saving, Alan? God knows there's been times in my life when I have.'

'Softy.'

'I suppose.'

They were both silent for a few moments.

'Do you think Bert could do anything?'

'What do you mean?

'I don't know, but presumably he's got something to say about the fact that Sullivan was responsible for you being stabbed.'

Silence.

'Alan?'

'I'll talk to him.'

'Thanks.'

'But in the meantime you're not to do anything without discussing it with me first.'

'Would I ever?'

'Yes,' Alan said, 'you would. But in this case, Sam, that could be incredibly risky.'

CHAPTER NINETEEN

Caffè Nero was seething. Sam sat opposite Harry watching the comings and goings on the streets of Soho. It was raining and people were jumping over puddles and trying to keep out of the way of cars and the savage spikes of umbrellas carelessly wielded by psychotic pedestrians, with murder lurking in their umbrella spokes. She had spent a dispiriting afternoon talking to junkies round Centrepoint, St Martin's in Trafalgar Square, and down by Waterloo. There had been no sign of David. No one knew anything or, if they knew, they certainly weren't saying. Harry carefully stirred in the top of his cappuccino and took a huge bite of the piece of coffee cake Sam had bought him. His knees kept banging the underside of the table they were sitting at.

'I don't know where else to try,' he said.

'Where could he go to sell stuff?'

'Kempton – twice a month on Tuesdays. Camden Passage on Wednesdays. Bermondsey on Fridays. Mum used to go to all those.'

'And he'd know about them?'

'Sure. He went there enough times.'

'Well, maybe we should give them a go.'

He nodded.

'Did your mother have any particular people she always bought from or sold to?'

Harry nodded. 'She used to. I'm not so up to date with her contacts as I was.'

'Tomorrow we'll try Camden Passage,' Sam said. 'What time does it kick off?'

'Mum used to leave around six.'

Sam groaned. 'It's not surprising antiques dealers are so bad-tempered, they've never had enough sleep.'

'I'm used to it,' Harry said. 'Early-morning outings, early-morning training.'

'Sadism,' Sam said. 'Pure and simple.'

'Did you never get up early to train?'

'Not that early. After I left school I was training full-time. It made things a whole lot easier.'

'You didn't go to college?'

'My parents weren't happy with me fighting. They never understood it. The deal was that as long as my schoolwork didn't suffer, they'd let me train. So I worked incredibly hard. But once I'd got the grades and the place at college, I realised all I wanted to do was train full-time and by then they couldn't do anything about it. Two years later I became World Champion.'

'Eric used to show us your fight.'

Sam sighed. 'He told me.'

'He said you were an example of someone who refused to admit they were beaten. That's what he wanted from us. Even with a dislocated shoulder you were trying to get back on the mat.'

'The power of denial,' Sam said drily.

Harry smiled. 'I don't know how I'd manage in a solo sport. I love the camaraderie of eights rowing.'

'I couldn't bear the idea that, however well you might row, you could be let down by the other guys in the boat. I always knew it was down to me. Win or lose, the buck stopped with me. No one else to blame.'

'It must be lonely.'

'There were always people to fight.'

He laughed. 'My father doesn't approve of my rowing – thinks it's a waste of time.'

'You should tell him that ninety per cent of the people taking part in last year's Boat Race ended up in the City. That it's a good career move.'

Harry smiled. 'He'd argue that he could have got a mate of his to get me into the City at sixteen. But, anyway, I don't want to go into the City. I'm afraid I'm a throwback. In the original Boat Race ninety per cent of them went into the Church and that's what I want.'

'Just something to keep him off your back.'

'Nothing will do that, I'm afraid.'

Sam drained her coffee and stood up. The rain had passed over and bright sunshine was making the pavements glisten. 'Are you going back to Eric's?'

'Not straight away. There's somewhere else I've thought of to check.'

Sam's phone rang. It was Alan telling her that Bert was coming round and could she come over. 'Hold on,' she said. Then to Harry: 'Are you going to be all right by yourself?'

'Yeah, no problem.'

Sam came out of the tube at Hammersmith and turned right. A twenty-minute walk brought her to the block where Alan lived. She pressed his bell and waited for the buzzer that would give her entrance to the foyer. From there a short ride in a lift took her to the twenty-sixth floor and Alan's flat.

He took a long time to come to the door. When he eventually opened it, he looked pale and was moving awkwardly.

Sam kissed him on the cheek and stepped past him into the flat. 'How are you?' she asked.

Alan walked slowly into the room behind her and sat down carefully in an upright chair. 'It's only when you get stabbed in the stomach that you realise how often you use your stomach muscles. If I sit in anything too low and try and stand up it hurts like hell. Also, all that lying in bed means my muscles have wasted. I'm going flabby and pale.' He pinched his bicep, mournfully.

Sam laid the flowers she'd brought on the glass coffee table. 'I can see you really need these,' she said, surveying a room that already looked like a florist's.

'Do you want anything?' Alan asked.

Sam shook her head. 'Had coffee in town. Picked up these.' She took two paper bags out of her bag and opened them so Alan could see their contents.

'Cake?'

Sam nodded.

He reached forward and then stopped, wincing.

'Don't move,' Sam said, standing up and handing it to him.

The doorbell rang. 'That'll be Bert. Do you mind?'

Sam went to the door and buzzed him up.

'How's the patient?' Bert said, walking past Sam into the flat.

'See for yourself.'

'All right, mate?' Bert said, patting Alan clumsily round the side of the head.

Alan grunted an acknowledgement.

Bert frowned. 'Don't like the look of you, you're all grey and sweaty.'

'I'm fine,' Alan said. 'And I'm not going back into hospital.'

Bert turned to Sam. 'What do you think, love?'

'I think he'll be OK, Bert. It's exhausting adjusting to being home at first. He needs to build up his stamina.'

Bert nodded and sat down next to Sam on the sofa. 'Alan said you got some kid you're worried about who owes money in the market?'

'That's right.'

'I've been doing a bit of sniffing around. Some of Sullivan's boys got to him in prison. Gave him a beating and told him payment was required pronto. When he wasn't quick enough with coming up with anything, they paid his mother a visit, told her they expected the debt to be paid one way or another. Word was the boy had got hold of a stash of stuff to settle the debt and then instead of settling up did a runner. So they came back to the mother a second time and this time they weren't quite so understanding.'

'Did they find what they wanted?'

Bert shook his head. 'Debt still outstanding; they're still looking for the boy.' He stood up. 'I'm thirsty. You want anything?' He nodded towards the kitchen.

'No, I'm fine.'

Sam heard the fridge opening and Bert came back into the room cracking open a can of beer. 'You sure?'

Sam nodded. 'Have you spoken to Sullivan yet about Alan?'

'We've been talking through middle men.'

'And . . .?'

Bert glared at her. ' "And"?' he repeated.

'Calm down,' Alan said.

Bert looked at his brother. 'Nosy, isn't she?'

'Come on, Bert, she's a private investigator. What do you expect?'

'Sorry,' Sam said. 'But what I was thinking was this. You need payback for Alan being stabbed. I need David Cameron let off the hook of this debt. Couldn't the one be used to solve the other?'

Bert slurped from the can and wiped his mouth on the back of his hand. 'Tell me what the fuck she's talking about,' he said to Alan.

Sam rubbed her chin. 'They let David Cameron's debt go and that's the blood-money payment.'

'So we get what, love? Precisely nothing.'

'But—'

'No, watch my lips, love – we get nothing.'

'But isn't it up to Alan? He's the one that got stabbed.'

Bert and Sam stared at Alan, who stared back.

Alan put up both his hands in surrender. 'Sorry, Sam, this is Bert's business. It's not my call.'

Sam stood up and walked over to the window. 'This kid's in trouble. He needs to pay them off, he's got a drug problem and he's going to need eyes in the back of his head until he does. He's not going to be able to do it. Last weekend he was in the market trying to sell stuff he'd stolen from a church.'

'Nothing else?' Alan said.

'I don't think so.'

'Everyone knows what happened to Grace. He'll be on a hiding to nothing. No one will want to buy from him.'

'Look, Bert, could you arrange for me to meet Sullivan?'

'No one meets Sullivan.'

Sam pulled a face. 'Well, one of his associates. Perhaps I can get the heat off the twins for a while.'

Bert frowned. 'Not such a good idea, love. Unless you've got some money on the table or a way of getting some quickly.'

Sam thought of the bloodstained money her father had left on her bed. No way she wanted to keep that. The money went to charity or perhaps to sort out his mess. 'Maybe I have.'

'How much?'

'A thousand.'

He shook his head. 'Not enough.'

'But can you arrange a meeting?'

'Sure.' Bert took out his phone and walked into the kitchen. Sam heard the murmur of his voice but not the detail of what he was saying. A few minutes later he came back into the room.

'All set. Tonight, ten o'clock, Battersea Bridge.'

Sam frowned. 'That's right by Grace's boat – why there?'

'That's what the man said.'

Alan looked at his brother. 'You going with her?'

He shook his head.

'Come on, Bert.'

'He doesn't have to. I can go by myself.'

'Shut up,' Alan said to Sam, then turned to Bert. 'You're going with her. I'd go if I could but I'm not much use if anything happens. If someone pushed me I'd just fall over. I can't run. I can't do anything.'

'But Mary—'

'You can phone her, can't you? She can get you on the mobile if she goes into labour.'

Bert shrugged.

'Well, that's decided then,' Alan said.

An hour later Sam was leaning over Battersea Bridge, looking down onto the top of Grace's boat. Bert was not with her. He'd got a call from his wife shortly after they'd left Alan's. He was now heading for Chelsea and Westminster Hospital and the birth of his fourth child. He'd tried to get her to call the meeting off but Sam had told him she'd be fine and he'd been too preoccupied to argue. Sam stared at the blue and white police 'do-not-cross' tape and tried not to think of the seagull's razor-sharp beak and bright yellow eye, of Grace's pulped face and the fact that she was going to meet someone who she suspected of killing her. The lights of the bridge cast wobbly smears on the dark, oily surface of the river. She shuddered and hunkered down further into her coat. She turned round. Behind her Albert Bridge, lit up with strings of fairy lights like the Blackpool illuminations, made the one she was standing on seem like a very poor relative indeed. She checked her watch, still five minutes to go. It was too cold to stand still. She walked into the middle of the bridge and looked along the length of the river, but here the wind was stronger, more biting, and she was struck full in the face by its force. She pulled the hood of her coat over her head and turned to walk back to where she had come from, to where a figure now stood, huddled like her against the wind.

The man was shaven-headed, wearing a three-quarter-length camel coat and what looked like a cashmere scarf. But the elegant lines of his coat could not disguise his bull-chested physique and the scarf could not conceal the width of his neck. If his exterior was sharp-suited, the man inside was decidedly blunt. His phone rang to the theme from *The Great Escape*. He prodded at a button, looked at the bright green screen and grunted before returning it to his pocket.

He dug his chin into his scarf and turned to Sam. 'Where's Bert?'

'Wife's about to give birth. Had to go to the hospital.'

'What do you want?'

'To talk to you about David Cameron.'

'And?'

'I understand he owes you money.'

'What's it to do with you?'

'I'm a friend.'

'Shit taste in friends.'

His phone went again. He took it from his pocket and by the light of the phone Sam saw he had long elegant fingers. He walked a little away from her, talking into the phone. Then snapped it shut and came back to where Sam was standing.

'You offering to pay the debt?' he asked.

'Was it your men who were involved in stabbing Bert's brother?'

The shift in the man's weight was almost imperceptible but it was enough to make Sam take two quick steps back and hold out her hand.

He laughed. 'Twitchy, aren't we?'

'Let Cameron's debt go and Bert'll let sleeping dogs lie.'

'Bert,' he sneered. 'You think I'm frightened of Bert. He's got no dogs to let loose and this is a fucking waste of my time. You owe it; you pay it – that's the way it goes. If you don't, you suffer. That's the only way to treat junkies. It's the only thing they understand.'

'But Bert could do a lot of damage. Do you want to go down that road?'

'Fucking amateur. You haven't got a clue.'

'It could save you a lot of trouble.'

'What's Bert got to say about it?'

'He says you'll be getting off cheap.'

'Well, that makes two unhappy men.'

'He won't let it go. You can't stab his baby brother and walk away from it.'

The man's face twisted into a snarl. 'If he goes after us he won't know what's hit him.'

'Oh, like Grace Cameron – how many times did you have to hit her before you killed her? Do you know what her face looked like when they fished her out of the river? Like the inside of a pomegranate, just bloody pulp.'

The man frowned. 'How do you know that?'

'I was there. I was one of the people who found her.'

'Is that why the police are crawling all over us?'

'Her head was half ripped off.'

He took hold of the front of Sam's coat and drew her face to within inches of his own. 'That had nothing to do with us.'

Sam broke his grip. 'What do you mean?'

'It must have happened afterwards.'

'But who'd do that to her?'

He shrugged. 'Maybe a lover's tiff.' He nodded down at the boats.

'What?'

'She had her toy boy next door.'

'What are you talking about?'

'Doyle – lives in the boat next to hers. They've been on and off for years.'

Sam felt as if a cold hand had been pressed down on the back of her neck. 'How do you know that?'

'It's never been a secret.'

He turned and began walking away from her towards the main road.

'What shall I tell Bert?'

He shrugged. 'If he wants to talk, fine, but he shouldn't send little girls to do a man's job.'

Sam remained, leaning on the parapet, looking down at Gerry's boat; no lights were showing. Gerry had been Grace's boyfriend. How on earth could she have missed that? It had never crossed her mind. Ageism, she thought, pure and simple ageism. It had never crossed her mind because there had been, at a rough guess, about twenty years' age difference between them. But what disturbed her most was that Gerry had never mentioned it to her and neither had Harry. Surely Harry must have known? What an idiot she'd been! Of course the police were crawling all over him. He was her lover and he lived next door. Someone had helped David get into his father's safe and steal that jewellery. Skinner had laughed when she described him as a locksmith, implying he was something else. Maybe they'd wanted Grace to sell it for them and she'd refused, maybe they'd turned nasty and killed her. She thought of his maimed hand. Suddenly she knew that there was no way he'd lost his fingers in an accident. No, he was in it up to his neck.

Sam walked swiftly off the bridge down to Gerry's boat and knocked on the door. She had no idea what she was going to say to him, but she didn't get to find out because no lights were on and no one answered. She made her way back up to Cheyne Walk but, before crossing the road and heading up Beaumont Street to the bus stop, she looked back. A light flared on the walkway next to Grace's boat. Someone was lighting a cigarette. Sam wondered what the person was waiting for. The only thing marking his presence now was the orange tip of the cigarette, glowing in the dark.

CHAPTER TWENTY

The phone was ringing as Sam opened her front door and she picked up.

'Oh hi, Kelly here.'

'What do you want?'

'I have a proposition to put to you. Suppose you have copies of or even the originals of information that your father was going to give to me. Things he'd discussed with me?' She paused but when Sam didn't reply she went on. 'And suppose you gave that information to me. It was, after all, what your father was intending to do.'

'Go on.'

'Well, surely once the story's out there, they're going to stop harassing you and won't they leave your father alone? I mean, there won't be anything for them to prevent happening, will there? Won't they go away?'

'They tried to kill him,' Sam said. 'I don't think letting him get away with it is on their agenda.'

'Do you see what I'm getting at, though?'

Sam bent down and scratched the top of Frank Cooper's head.

Kelly Webb continued. 'It would definitely take the pressure off you.'

'And your editor would stop complaining about the thousand pounds.'

'How do you know the amount?'

Sam ignored her. 'First, you don't know that I have anything for you to publish. Second, I don't know what my father's intention was. I only have your word for it. Third, I know you're desperate to have something to show for the fact you gave my father a thousand pounds and he has now disappeared. And, fourth, it will mean that forty Irish families will know that my father was involved in the murder of one of their relatives.'

'Forty! Does he name them all?'

'I have nothing else to say to you.'

'I think you have and while you do, you're at risk.'

'Do you know that if you smile at a Londoner they're even less likely to smile back at you than a Glaswegian?'

'What's your point?'

'Guess.'

Sam put down the phone, walked through into her front room and slumped onto the sofa. She knew that her father would not want anything coming out in the papers. He'd been shot and that had changed everything. There was no way she was going to hand anything over to Webb. She stretched out lengthways. Light spilled from the carriages of a train crossing the bridge, rippling along the black guttering of the houses on the opposite side of the road. A feeling of profound weariness washed over Sam.

Complication followed complication. The situation with her father was a mess and she had no idea how to go about sorting it out. Kelly Webb had a point, though. She didn't think that the people who were after her father would leave her alone. But sitting waiting for their next move was not a happy state of affairs. Then Sam thought of Gerry. How could she have been so stupid? He'd invited her over to pump her for information and she'd been all too happy to be pumped in more ways than one. Stupid tart! On top of that, David was still missing and she was no closer to finding the jewellery. And Alan had been right, she *was* personally involved with Harry. She felt it. All that possibility not yet fulfilled. She thought of Karen Lewis, the little girl with the plaits, watching her, hands on hips. She was starting to think like a coach and that meant just one thing, the competitor in her was dying.

The phone rang and Sam dragged herself off the sofa to answer it.

'Sam Falconer?' The voice was male and Sam couldn't place it.

'Yes.'

'Cameron here'

Mr Charm.

'Yes?'

'I was wondering how matters were progressing.'

'Rather slowly, I'm afraid.'

'Where are my sons?'

'I was with Harry this morning.'

'Why on earth didn't you phone me?' The change of tone was instantaneous; the bully was out of his box. 'Where is he?'

Sam felt caught on the hop. 'I'm sure he'll contact you when he wants to. He knows where you are.'

'I've paid you. Has he got the jewellery?'

'I'll give you the money back. I've told Harry you want to see him – it's up to him.'

'What about David?'

'I don't know.'

'You don't realise what you're involved with here. Tell Harry to call me immediately.' He slammed down the phone.

'Lovely man,' Sam said into the silent receiver.

Mind you, it was a good point – where the hell was that jewellery? She knew that Grace had had it. She knew the debt was still outstanding, so presumably Sullivan and his thugs hadn't found it. And if David had had to rob a church then presumably he didn't have it either. The phone rang again. This time it was Harry.

'That's weird,' Sam said. 'I've just had your father on the phone, asking where you and your brother were.'

'You didn't tell him?' He sounded frightened.

'No, I didn't. Well, I didn't know so I couldn't. I said you'd call him in your own good time. He didn't seem impressed.'

'Thank you.' The relief in his voice was transparent.

'Any luck?'

'Yes.'

'You've found him?'

'Yes, Dave's here with me now.'

'What are you going to do?'

'I'm in the boathouse. Could you come straight away?'

'Now?'

'I'm sorry. I know it's late.'

Sam glanced at her watch. Midnight.

'Can't it wait until morning?'

284

He lowered his voice. 'I don't know how long I can keep him here. I want you to talk to him.'

Sam rubbed her hand over her face. 'OK, I'll come at once.'

A couple of minutes later Sam stepped out of her front door and started towards the river. She didn't look behind her, so she didn't see two men get out of a car parked on the other side of the main road and follow her. It had been a windy, overcast day but now it seemed that the wind had blown all the cloud away and up above the level of the sodium orange of the street lighting, Sam could see the odd star. She walked under the bridge that carried the trains into Putney Bridge station and along past the car wash, then turned down the narrow alleyway that ran towards the underground station. A man was huddled halfway down the alley, covered in blankets.

'Sssspare sssome change . . .' he hissed, and Sam, thinking of the RIP on the wall of the fire station in the King's Road, dug in her pocket, dropped a pound coin in a plastic box and continued on down the alley. Hearing footsteps behind her, she turned. Two men stood in front of the man on the ground. One was handing him a cigarette, the other lighting it. Sam hurried on towards the bridge. She checked behind her again as she passed the entrance to the tube, and breathed a sigh of relief when she saw that no one was there. She was halfway up the stairs that led onto Putney Bridge when she heard footsteps behind her and then felt a crashing blow on the back of her head. She blacked out.

She came to feeling weirdly suspended. As if she were floating in space. Her head throbbed but when she raised her hand to touch where it hurt she realised that her arms were already above her head, dangling in the air. Something metallic fell past her cheek; she watched it drop into the rippling blackness. She opened her eyes wider. Where the hell was she and why couldn't she move her feet? They were trapped in some way, whereas her arms were free but hanging down by the side of her face. Gradually it dawned on her that she was suspended upside down, over the bank of the Thames, and someone was holding on to her feet. More metal fell past her cheeks, coins falling out of her pockets into the river.

If Winston had rats in Room 101, Sam had deep water.

She began to scream.

'Shut the fuck up,' she heard coming from above her. 'Or we'll drop you.'

Sam's coat had fallen over her head, covering her mouth, and she wrestled it away.

'Where is he?' a voice said.

Sam's head hurt like hell and she felt her eyes bulging out of her skull because of the pressure of being hung upside down. Who were these people? The boys in balaclavas looking for David? Henchmen of Cameron looking for his sons? Or people looking for her father?

'Who?' she gasped.

'Don't be clever with us.'

'Is it David?'

'We've got ourselves a joker here.'

Someone yanked hard on her legs. 'You really want to go for a swim, do you? That's OK by us. Looks a bit chilly, mind, but it's up to you. A dip in the Thames at this time of year looks like a death sentence to me.'

'I can't swim,' Sam screamed.

She heard laughter. 'Time to learn. Where's your father?'

'I don't know.'

'Not good enough.'

She felt a hand grab her belt and she was yanked back from the edge and dumped unceremoniously on the ground. The blood rushed out of her head and she saw stars. The man she recognised from the police station squatted down next to her and slapped her face. Sam tasted blood in the corner of her mouth. She felt dizzy and incoherent. 'I don't know where he is. Why would he tell me? He doesn't trust me. He's got no reason to. I hate him. If I knew where he was I'd tell you.'

The man stood up and she heard him talking to someone. 'Let's put her over the edge again.'

Sam started screaming. Hands grabbed her and again she was suspended over the edge. Sam closed her eyes and flashed back to being four years old. Then the water had looked so inviting, so beautifully blue, so tempting – until she was in it, until she was sinking, until she was gasping for air and drowning and going down and was going to die. I don't care if I live or die, she thought. Fucking drop me. The water didn't get me that time, it's

286

been waiting ever since. But this water wasn't blue, it was black and rippled, as if a mass of eels were slithering just beneath the surface. There was nothing she could do. It was going to happen to her all over again.

Up on the bridge she heard the wail of a police car and the screech of tyres. 'What the fuck do you think you're doing?'

She was dragged back and dumped and she heard the sounds of running feet. She was shivering uncontrollably and only vaguely aware of people talking near by. A young uniformed policeman squatted down next to her and touched her arm. 'You all right, love?'

Sam gasped for air. She tried to stand but she was shaking so much she couldn't get to her feet unaided. 'I can't swim,' she said.

The policeman took hold of her arm and got her to her feet. Behind him, up on the bridge, a police car's blue light turned round and round. The two men who had attacked Sam were nowhere to be seen.

'What happened?'

Sam couldn't stop her teeth from chattering. 'They attacked me.'

'Do you know them?'

Sam shook her head.

'You don't know who they were?'

'Drunks out for a bit of a laugh. You know how they get on a Saturday night round here.'

The policeman didn't look convinced. 'Bit extreme for that, love. Do you need hospital treatment?'

Sam shook her head but winced as she did so.

He turned her round and looked at the back of her head. 'Maybe we should take you to casualty and let someone have a look at that.'

'No – I'm fine.'

'Well, can we give you a lift?'

Perhaps the men were still out there waiting for her, waiting outside her flat. Suddenly a lift seemed like a really good idea. 'Could you run me down to the boathouses.'

'At this time?'

'My boyfriend's been working on one of the boats and is staying over.'

The police car stopped outside the boathouse and Sam got out.

'You sure he's there?' the policeman said. 'There aren't any lights on.

'Yes, it's fine, thanks.'

'We'll wait to see you in.'

'Don't worry, he's probably just having a nap or something.'

She ran up the outside steps and banged on the door. There was no response. She tried again with the same result. She was about to admit defeat and head back down to the police car when the door opened and Harry stood looking at her.

'Sorry I'm late,' Sam said. 'Something came up.'

She followed him through the door and he turned on a light.

'David's gone. Saw the police car outside and that was it—'

Sam put a fist to her forehead. 'Shit. I should have thought.'

'Why were you with them?'

'Ran into a bit of trouble and they offered me a lift.'

'He thought you'd called them in.'

Sam shook her head. 'I wouldn't do that.'

'I know, but I couldn't persuade him.'

'Where did you find him?'

'Back at Waterloo.'

'How is he?'

He gnawed on his lower lip. 'Not in good shape.'

'Did he kill her, Harry?'

The boy rounded on her, eyes blazing. 'How many times do I have to tell you?'

'Tell me about him, then.'

'He's my twin, what do you want me to say?'

'What's he like?'

'Is or was?'

Sam shrugged. 'Whichever.'

'As a kid everything came easy to him. He walked before me, read before me. Was better than me at everything, really. I was always bowling along, trying to keep up. He was much more extrovert and confident than me. But then he failed his eleven-plus. I still don't know how that happened. He shouldn't have done. It was as if he just decided not to try, decided to opt out. Then everything fell apart for him. My parents started arguing and ended up divorcing. We were separated for the first time. Things changed. I saw him in the holidays but it was like I'd betrayed him – I felt the separation was my fault.'

'Did he?'

'He'd never have said so, but I think we both felt this tremendous loss. I felt enormous guilt.'

'Guilty? Why?'

'I'd left him, hadn't I?'

'Or he left you. You're saying he chose to fail. Maybe he needed to separate.'

'I feel him as my responsibility in every bone of my body. It's up to me to sort this mess out. I'm all he's got left now Mum's dead.'

'What about your father?'

'He's just worried about getting his jewellery back. He doesn't care about Dave, he never has.'

'Why didn't you tell me your mother was having a relationship with Gerry Doyle?'

He looked surprised. 'You didn't ask.'

'How long had they been together?'

'They weren't exactly together. You wouldn't call either of them exclusive.'

'Did he sell her things?'

'Sometimes.'

'Stolen stuff?'

Harry shrugged.

'Do you know what happened to your mother's stock?'

'I've not been able to find out.'

'Has David got it?'

'He wouldn't have robbed St Silas's if he'd had something to sell.' Harry stood up. 'I'm going to make us some coffee.'

Sam followed him into a small kitchen and watched him fill the kettle. 'You're certain it wasn't David.'

'In every fibre of my being.'

'This thing with your father.'

'Yes.'

'He said David had stolen your stepmother's jewellery. But that involved getting into a safe. Was Gerry involved with that?'

He shrugged. 'Maybe. Dave and Gerry have been friends for a long time and Gerry prides himself on being able to get into anything. I think it was Gerry who first introduced him to drugs, then told him who to go to for more. He's charming, Gerry, but, a bit like Dave, he likes the short cuts.'

Sam blushed. 'But why was your mum—'

'Mum liked to smoke and you have to remember she wasn't well. She wasn't good alone. Gerry was near by. He was there. She needed him.'

'What did your dad do after the burglary?'

'Well, you've met him. You know what sort of man he is. He went ballistic and phoned up Mum, threatening all sorts. He was worried that she'd end up selling the stuff for Dave. He came on really heavy about it all. Told her she had to get it back and sort it all out.'

'Why was it your mother's responsibility?'

Harry handed Sam a cup of coffee and they walked back into the main room and sat down. 'It wasn't, but he knew Dave would bring it to her to sell. She'd be able to get better prices for it. And Dave could always get her to do things for him.'

'So your mother was caught between her ex-husband and her son and the loan sharks.'

He nodded.

'So where do you think the jewellery is?'

'Dave thinks it may still be on the boat.'

'Surely the police would have found it. They crawled over every inch of that boat.'

'Not necessarily. Mum used to hide things in some pretty weird places and Dad never reported the burglary. It's not stuff he'd want them tracing to him, so the police wouldn't know to look for it.'

'Do you think he killed her?'

'He's got a bad temper,' Harry said softly, 'always has had. And they had terrible rows when we were children. He put her in hospital once, but I can't imagine he'd kill her.'

'What are you aiming to do now?'

'Finding the jewellery's the only answer. If we've got that we've got a chance of getting Sullivan off Dave's back.'

'Have the police still got the boat sealed off?'

'Yes. They must take the tape down soon, though.'

Sam thought of the man standing smoking in the darkness. 'There are going to be a few people interested in searching it.'

'I know.'

Cameron, Sullivan, Gerry and David – all of them had an interest in what might be on the boat.

Sam went over to the balcony window and looked out at the river. The two men could still be out there. She didn't want to walk home. She turned back to Harry.

'I think I'll stay here for the night. I don't want to bump into some people I met this evening.'

'Sure – no problem.'

Harry turned off the light and they sat down next to each other on the floor with their backs to the wall.

'Thank you so much for your help,' he said.

'It's nothing,' Sam said.

'No, it's everything. For me at this moment the truth is, it's everything.'

Sam felt embarrassed and changed the subject. 'Eric told me you should enter *Mastermind* with the Boat Race as your specialist subject.'

Harry smiled. 'It's amazing how easy it is to retain information about something you're truly interested in. One of my favourite quotes on rowing is by Wittgenstein.'

'You must be joking.'

'I know it sounds unlikely but he was taken down to the river by Bertrand Russell, his mentor, to watch a race and afterwards he said, "The manner in which we have spent the afternoon is so vile, we ought not to go on living." '

'Those Cambridge men are such terrible drama queens, aren't they?'

Harry laughed. 'The thing is, it's not as if I haven't had days when I've thought the same.'

'But in the end you keep coming back for more.'

'Yes. I think Wittgenstein misunderstood. He thought sport was just something irrelevant and trifling.'

'He'd obviously never met an Australian.'

Harry smiled. 'I'm going to try and get some sleep.' He stretched himself out on the floor and curled up on his side.

Sam sat next to him, watching him sleep. She felt ridiculously protective of him. Golden youth – God, what a joke! Sometimes she thought it was a miracle anyone survived into adulthood at all.

CHAPTER TWENTY-ONE

Sam returned to her flat early the following morning. A couple of hours later her bell rang. She picked up the intercom phone. 'What?'

'Meter reader.'

She buzzed him in and was halfway down the hall to the kitchen when there was a knock on her door. 'The meters are downstairs,' she shouted but the knocking persisted and she walked wearily back the way she had come and opened the door.

Ten people were standing on the landing and none of them looked remotely like meter readers. She quickly slammed the door as a camera went off in her face. Someone opened her letterbox and a newspaper was shoved through it. She picked up the *Daily Tribune*.

'Do you know where he is, Sam?' A man shouted through the letterbox. Sam looked at the headline: *SAS soldier admits to murder of forty Republicans*. Underneath was the picture of her father coming out of the café.

'Oh fuck,' she groaned.

She tore open the paper and read the article, her alarm growing with each sentence. This certainly wasn't her father's version of events. According to this article, her father had been part of a maverick unit, operating without the knowledge or consent of the British authorities. He was a cold-blooded killer, operating outside the law, who had murdered Republicans. She was puzzled. Had her father gone to them and sold the story anyway? Had they twisted his version? But then why was it in the *Tribune* not the *Herald* – had they offered more money? The phone rang and Sam walked back into the hall to hear who was leaving a message.

'You don't know what you've done.' It was her father. 'How could you? I left those papers with you on trust. Was a thousand pounds not enough? Did they pay you well? I hope you can live with what you've done.'

Sam froze, unable to pick up the phone, and it went dead. He thought she'd betrayed him. Sam found Kelly Webb's card and phoned her but she wasn't answering. Then she tried Max.

'Do you know where he is, Max?'

'What the hell's all this stuff in the papers?'

'Look. I didn't do it. I didn't sell him out. I don't know how they got hold of it.'

'I'm not saying you did.'

'Do you know where he is?'

'No. We spoke briefly on the phone but he didn't say.'

'Well, if he gets in touch again, tell him it had nothing to do with me.'

'I don't think that will do much good, Sam. He says no one else could have.'

As she put down the phone, the letterbox opened again. 'Sam, do you know where your father is?'

'Fuck off,' she shouted.

She slumped down on the sofa. She should warn her family, but she couldn't face them. She needed to go out because she had an appointment with Reg. But how could she get rid of the journalists? Sam called Edie and explained her predicament.

Ten minutes later, as agreed, Sam heard Edie's front door open and the murmur of conversation. 'No, no, love,' Sam heard Edie say, 'I'm not doing it on my doorstep. It's too cold. I'm too old to stand in a draught. It's bad for my legs. You all have to come inside.'

Sam stood poised by her front door. As she heard the door to Edie's flat close, she saw the welcome sight of a number 22 bus driving past her window. She shot out of her flat and ran down the stairs to the main door of the block. She heard a shout behind her but didn't look round, she threw herself through the door and ran down the road after the bus, jumping onto the back of it as it slowed at a pedestrian crossing. It accelerated away and Sam looked out of the window and saw, with satisfaction, a man standing outside her block, looking after her. She took the bus for a couple of stops and then got off and caught one going the other direction back towards her flat and beyond.

'Sorry I'm late,' Sam said, taking a seat opposite Reg. It was only five minutes but to Sam, who was always early for everything, it felt like half an hour.

'What held you up?'

'Bunch of journalists on my doorstep.'

Reg gestured to the paper lying on his desk. 'I saw the paper.'

'Ah.'

'How are you?'

'I feel hunted.'

'What do they want?'

'To know where he is.'

'Do you know?'

'No, but he phoned. He thinks I sold him out. He'll be looking for me.'

'Did you speak to him?'

'No.'

'Why not?'

'I was frightened.'

'Why?'

'Isn't it obvious?'

They sat in silence for a few moments.

'Did you manage to ask Mark if he'd be willing to talk to me?'

Sam shook her head. 'I haven't got round to it yet.'

Reg sat forward in his chair and slapped his hands down on his knees. 'Let's go for a walk.'

Sam frowned. 'Is that normal?'

'Walking? I do that most days.'

Sam laughed. 'OK then.' She stood up and pulled her jacket off the back of the chair.

Richmond Park was a ten-minute walk from Reg's flat. They walked in silence round the outer perimeter road. The flock of parakeets, squawking and swooping over their heads in a flash of bright green feathers, seemed more deserving of palm trees, sandy beaches and blue skies than a grey English winter.

'Do you use the park a lot?' Sam asked.

'Fair bit – helps loosen things up sometimes. I've been very busy recently. All the television coverage of the war in Iraq and its aftermath triggers things off for lots of my clients. And it's all over the papers. They can't get away from it – bombs, soldiers, casualties, helicopters ... they go through a hell of a time.'

Sam felt the anxiety building in her. Why were they walking? What did he want to say to her? She glanced across at him. 'Spit it out, won't you?'

'Isn't that my line?'

She didn't reply.

'OK, Sam, I suppose I'm feeling frustrated. I get this feeling you're holding back. There's this thing you're coming to and then you veer away from it. Do you know what I'm talking about?'

'What the hell is this?' Sam said. 'Are you sacking me as a client?'

Reg grunted in amusement. 'I'm quite happy to keep taking your money, Sam. But if we don't progress, I guarantee you, it's you who'll sack me because you won't be able to see the point of what we're doing any more.'

'How do you know how fast I'm supposed to go?'

'Look, I don't. I'm just telling you what I'm sensing.'

'I feel like you're sacking me.'

'Well, I'm not. I'm inviting you to take risks.'

Reg stopped walking and Sam did as well. 'Your favourite throw in competition was *tomoe-nage*, wasn't it?'

'How do you know that?'

'It's a sacrifice throw, isn't it? You sacrifice your own balance in order to win. It's a risky throw but it works particularly well for a small opponent against a taller one. You almost sit down, put your right foot in their abdomen and throw them over your head in a full circle.'

'Yes, all that's true, but I don't see—'

'You were such a courageous fighter, Sam. You were willing to take big risks. This takes courage too. Maybe you need to allow yourself to sacrifice your balance in our sessions in order to get a larger gain.'

Sam felt she was being accused of cowardice. She felt exhausted and frightened and her head hurt where she'd been hit the night before and she felt really pissed off with Reg; she lapsed into a sullen silence.

'From my point of view, it's like watching a horse charge at a fence. At the last minute it veers off into the woods. It blunders around there for a while and then comes out further along the course until it charges at the next fence, which it then avoids and so on. So this is an invitation to try jumping next time.'

'Maybe I'm better on the flat.'

Reg sighed but didn't say anything.

'I think I slept with a murderer.'

'Woods.'

'How can you tell?'

'A guess. Am I right?'

'Perhaps.'

Twenty minutes later they were back at Reg's front door. Sam reached into her pocket and took out her purse.

'No, it's fine – we went for a walk.'

'We talked while we walked.'

'Look, it's fine—'

Sam held out the money. 'Don't be stupid,' she said. 'Therapy on the hoof's still therapy.'

'Will you phone Mark?'

'Yes.'

'Come in then and make the call.'

Feeling the pin skewer her to the board, Sam followed him reluctantly inside and rang Mark. He wanted to talk to her about the article in the paper but when Sam told him what she wanted from him, he became anxious and asked her if everything was all right. Sam reassured him and handed him over to Reg. They talked briefly and Reg made a note in his diary and put down the phone.

Sitting in the bus afterwards, Sam thought about what Reg had said. She felt humiliated, as if she'd been found wanting. Fuck him; she'd quit. How the hell did he know how fast it should go? As it was, nothing seemed to be getting any better. She'd had more horrible nightmares during these few weeks of therapy than in the rest of her life put together. And all this boring dredging-up of stuff was just narcissistic navel-gazing. Maybe her mother was right and the best course to take was the stiff upper lip, a small vase of gin and a complete *Times 2* crossword. Yes, she'd quit before the next session and then he could dedicate himself to his braver clients. Fuck him, fuck therapy, I'm out of there. Next stop – repression.

Footsteps clattered up the stairs behind her, then approached where she was sitting. Sam sighed. She was the only person on top of the bus. Why couldn't they sit somewhere else? It was like people who came and sat right in front of you when the whole cinema was empty. If she saw someone sitting at the front of the bus, she moved to the back. Her preference was always to keep as far away from people as possible. A hand grabbed her shoulder.

'What the—?' She turned. It was her father and he looked furious. 'Christ, you scared me.'

He sat down next to her and took hold of the collar of her coat and pushed her back against the window. 'Satisfied, are you?'

Sam shoved him away from her. 'Take your fucking hands off me.'

'How much did they give you?'

'Who?'

'The *Tribune*.'

'What are you talking about?'

'Kelly didn't offer you enough, so you had to go to another paper?'

'That article had nothing to do with me. I didn't sell the *Tribune* anything.'

'Where'd they get it, then?'

Sam frowned. 'I don't know.'

'What about that woman who lives next to you? You left it with her, didn't you?'

'Edie? She didn't know what it was and was happy to take the twenty pounds to look after it. That was much simpler.'

'I don't believe you.'

'Who else knew?'

'The government.'

'Exactly. Suppose they think it's just a matter of time before you sell the story, so they decide to leak the story to the press on their own terms. Then they put their spin on it and they hang you out to dry. They discredit you before you can give evidence. They control the story and forty Irish families have a good reason to want you dead. They hung me over the side of the Thames to encourage me to tell them where you are and I've got the press crawling all over me.'

He seemed shrunk in his clothes and utterly exhausted.

'What are you going to do?'

He shook his head.

'You could still put your side of the story to Kelly.'

'I doubt she'd be interested. It's no longer exclusive, is it? Who's that bloke you keep visiting?'

'What?'

'Bloke just now.'

'Nobody,' Sam said. 'He's nobody.'

He sighed and put out his hand to brace himself as the bus swung round a corner.

'What will you do?' she repeated.

'Disappear for a while. You're going to have to watch out for yourself, Sam. They've named you in the article. It may not just be the press who come after you.'

'What do you mean?'

'Payback time. Old Republican tactics. If you can't get the man, go for his family. Get him where it hurts. You'd hurt.'

'You barely know me.'

He didn't look at her. 'You'd hurt,' he repeated. 'And you don't want to get on the wrong end of a punishment beating. Last bloke I know that happened to, they broke his legs so badly he ended up in a wheelchair.'

'You really think there's a risk?'

'Yes. They've printed the list. Now forty Republican families know I killed their relatives.'

'Well, I can't just disappear. I've got my life to live.'

'Not much longer if they get hold of you. I'm warning you, Sam – this is serious. If anything odd happens, anything at all. Get the hell out.' He stood up. 'I'm going to get off here.'

'How will I know where you are?'

'I'll be in touch.'

'Where will you go?'

'Best I don't tell you. Then you'll have nothing to hide.' He reached round her neck and began to pull the dog tags over her head.

She grabbed his hand. 'What the hell do you think you're doing?'

'Give me these.'

'No.'

'I might need you. If I send them you'll know it's me.'

Sam let go of his hand and the tags swung free of her neck and disappeared into his coat pocket. She watched him step off the bus and walk briskly along the road. As the bus overtook him, he looked up at her and waved. Sam held the open palm of her hand against the glass and wondered if she'd ever see him again. Then placed her hand against her neck. She'd carried them since she was four years old; what was going to protect her now?

Sam got off at Putney Bridge and phoned Edie. 'They all still there?' she asked.

'Yeah, love. A couple of the diehards are waiting for you. Sold 'em quite a few fags. Couple of bottles of gin. Got myself a few more feeds. You should have seen them when I opened the filing cabinet. Those boys like their fags and drink.'

Sam laughed. That sounded like journalists, all right.

Sam couldn't go home so she went to the office. As she came through the doors into reception it was to the sight of Kelly Webb doing a duet of 'Love me Tender' with Greg.

'What's this?' Sam said. 'Karaoke night at the Dog and Duck?'

'He's good,' Webb said, advancing on Sam.

'You better come up,' Sam said and Webb followed her towards the lift.

In Sam's office, Webb stood staring out of the floor-to-ceiling windows down onto Putney Bridge. 'Why'd you go to them?' she asked.

Sam sat at her desk and ran both hands along the length of her face. 'I didn't.'

'Who then?'

'Look, I've been over all this. Everyone thinks it was me who sold the story but it wasn't. I had nothing to do with it.'

Webb frowned. 'Did Geoff change his mind, then?'

'He says he didn't do it. I didn't do it. That leaves you or the government.'

'It wasn't me – I didn't have anything to tell. I didn't have the kind of details in that article. *You* had those.'

'I think the government leaked it deliberately because they knew he was thinking of telling it anyway and if they did it first they could take the moral high ground and also land him in the shit.'

Kelly Webb whistled. 'I wouldn't like to be in his shoes.'

'He'll not be around for a bit,' Sam said.

'That's one way of putting it. Have you seen him?'

'No.'

'You just said he told you he didn't do it.'

Sam didn't say anything.

Webb walked round Sam's desk and sat down opposite her. 'They talk about you in the article.'

'I know.'

'What are you going to do?'

Sam shook her head. 'Suggestions gratefully received.'

'Fancy a pint?'

'You don't believe in giving your liver much of a holiday, do you?'

Webb stood up. 'I'll be dead soon enough. It can holiday then – with the worms.'

'I like your optimism.'

After an hour in the pub with Webb, trying to match her drink for drink, excluding chasers, Sam was pissed and Webb looked as if she would hit the bull's-eye every time.

Webb twisted a glass holding a whisky chaser round and round and eyed Sam. 'Fathers, eh.'

'Yours?'

'Pub landlord in Glasgow. Good bloke – gambler, drinker.' She laughed. 'Full of shite.' She stared into the bottom of her glass. 'Dead.'

'Thought you looked right at home.'

Webb looked around and grunted dismissively. 'Way too poncy for me. We had a panic button behind the bar linked to the nearby nick.'

'Get pressed often?'

'Aye, fair bit when the chairs started flying.' Webb drained the whisky and put down the glass. 'Look, why don't you give me some kind of statement to keep the others off your back?'

'What do they want to know?'

'Is the article true? Where is he?'

'Well, I'm not telling you any of that.'

Webb smiled. 'I'm sure we could work something out.'

At that particular moment Sam felt she wouldn't have been able to work out where her lips were, let alone anything more complicated. She shook her head. 'No deal.'

Webb got to her feet and nodded at Sam's glass.

Sam handed it to her. 'Doesn't make me garrulous, just mean.'

Webb smiled. 'Dearie, you don't know the meaning of the word. No pun intended.'

Sam stayed in the pub with Webb until five o'clock and then went to Alan's; at least that was a journalist-free zone. She spent the evening sleeping off what she'd drunk and regretting how much she'd drunk. At eleven that evening, after Alan had gone to bed, Harry phoned.

'They've taken down the police tape. I'm sure Dave'll go back to the boat.'

'To look for the jewellery?'

'Yes.'

'Does he know where it is?'

'He knows where Mum used to hide things.'

'So what do you want me to do?'

'I'm going to watch the boat. I'm sure he'll come.'

'Want some company?'

'Thanks.'

An hour later Sam was on the bridge, looking down on the boat. There was just a bit of broken police tape left, snaking out from the railings on the upper deck in the brisk wind that had blown up. There were no lights on in Gerry's boat. But there was light coming from Grace's boat, an orange, flickering light. The wind changed direction and Sam smelled smoke. With a jolt of alarm she realised what the light was.

The boat was on fire.

She sprinted off the bridge. The front door to Grace's boat was banging back and forth in the wind. Inside the air was filling with smoke.

'Hello,' Sam shouted into the boat but no one replied. She heard something downstairs and ran to the door, which opened onto the steps leading to the lower deck. Here the smoke was even thicker. As Sam felt her way down, someone pushed past her in the opposite direction. She tried to catch hold of whoever it was but he shoved her against the wall and barged past. Downstairs the table and chairs were overturned. Sam saw a body, lying sprawled face-down. She ran to it and rolled it over. It was Gerry. He was unconscious. The smoke was so thick down here she could barely breathe. She picked up a tea towel and ran to the sink to wet it. She ran back to Gerry and dragged him into a sitting position and shook him. He groaned. 'Come on, Gerry,' she shouted. 'Wake up.' She squeezed water from the towel down his neck. The smoke was thickening and flames were moving towards the stairs. 'Gerry,' she shouted again. 'Come on, you've got to give me a hand here.' She knew she wouldn't be able to carry him. He was too heavy and it was too narrow. Hearing someone coming down the steps, she turned and saw Harry.

'Oh thank God,' she said. 'Help me get him to his feet.'

'I'll drag him,' Harry said. He picked him up under the arms and began to pull him towards the stairs. Between them they managed to manhandle Gerry up the stairs but the door at the top was jammed. Harry let go of Gerry and threw himself against it. The door splintered and then gave way. Harry turned round, took hold of Gerry again and they staggered through the smoke towards the open deck. Harry managed to get Gerry off the boat and onto the pontoon but Sam had her hands on her knees and was doubled over, gasping for air, when she felt as if an enormous and invisible foot had kicked her in the back. An explosion ripped through the boat, propelling her in a cloud of splintered wood and shattered glass into the river. Gas, she thought, the fire's reached the gas cylinders.

The water was freezing.

Sam struggled to pull down the zip of her sheepskin jacket but couldn't. The jacket was getting heavier and heavier, dragging her under. A wave slapped Sam in the face and she took a mouthful of river water, making her cough and splutter. As she rose and fell in the water, she saw that the boat was completely ablaze now. But where was Harry? She clung onto a piece of wood and began searching the water around her but all she could see was debris from the explosion. 'Harry, Harry,' she shouted. And then she went under again.

Another explosion. Bigger this time, lighting up the night sky. Sam registered the flash then felt a tremendous blow to her head. She sank beneath the water. Everything was black now, there was just welcoming darkness and oblivion. It was over. This is what it felt like to die. It was as if a hand had reached up from the bottom of the river and latched onto her ankle and was pulling her down and down. It was her father's hand. She struggled briefly then gave up all resistance and sank. This is how she had imagined it – that they would go down together. She was not afraid to die. Death suddenly seemed easier than remembering. Reg's voice rang in her head. Surrender, she thought. Yes, that's it. I surrender. She opened her mouth, breathed in the black water of the Thames, felt her lungs bursting and passed out.

But the river gods didn't want Sam Falconer that day, maybe because she gave in to them so easily and they were more in the mood to tear life from a reluctant soul. No, they didn't want Sam that day, so they spat her back up on the end of a hook held by Mike Brown of the Thames River Police. A man approaching retirement, who deserved to hook a live one after twenty years of pulling floaters out of the water. He had seen her go down and hooked her as she went.

First noises. Then hands on her body pulling her up and laying her out. A mouth on hers, the heel of a hand pressing hard into her chest again and again and, with the spout of a whale, Sam lay coughing her lungs up, coughing and coughing herself back to life. She sat bolt upright and latched her hands round the throat of the startled policeman who had saved her.

'Steady, love,' he said, peeling her hands away from his jugular. 'That's no way to say thank you.'

She let go, feeling something sticky trickling down the side of her face. She put her hand up and touched it and it came away dark red with blood. Her head hurt like crazy. She remembered now; she'd been hit by something from the explosion. She looked around her. She was on a boat and a man wearing a uniform was kneeling next to her. He handed her a towel and told her to hold it against her head. Suddenly she remembered Harry and Gerry.

She grabbed his arm. 'There were three of us. Did you get the others?'

'Where?'

'Near me – I think.' But they'd been ahead of her. Had they got off the boat? Maybe they hadn't even ended up in the water.

'We haven't pulled anyone else out, love. Just you.'

'You must keep looking,' Sam said, gripping onto his arm. 'You've got to.'

He tried to move his arm away from her. 'I'll tell the boss.' But she wouldn't let go of him. 'Please, you have to find him.'

'Let go, love.' He prised her hand off his arm and stood up. 'Keep the pressure on that cut.' He disappeared round the side of the boat.

Sam sat holding her head, staring at the bonfire that had been Grace's boat. She had surrendered but she hadn't died. What was she to make of that? The flames had caught the creosote on the roof and were leaping into the air and touching the underside of Battersea Bridge. Firemen up on the bridge were starting to unravel hoses. The surface of the river around the boat Sam was sitting in was covered in debris. People were lined up on the bridge, looking at the burning boat. Sam scoured the bridge and the bank and then she saw him, his height holding him well above the heads of the crowd. Sam stood up, staggering as she did so. Her head throbbed and she felt as if she might faint. She waved her arm vigorously back and forth above her head and shouted, 'Harry!' But he didn't respond. He turned away and vanished into the crowd.

The officer came back. 'You should be sitting down,' he said. 'We have to get you to hospital. You'll need stitches.'

'No,' Sam said.

'Yes, I'm afraid so. I don't know what it was that hit you but it's made a right mess.'

'No fucking way,' Sam said. 'I'm not having stitches.'

'Calm down, love,' the man said. 'Here, take a whiff of this,' and he handed her an oxygen mask.

Sam looked into the eyes of the young doctor who was examining her forehead and said with the sort of manic certainty, disguising terror, that she usually reserved for dentists, 'No needles, right?'

She looked at Sam and said, 'Sorry, it's a mess. We need to sew it up otherwise it could scar quite badly.'

'What about those butterfly things?'

'No good in this case, I'm afraid. Shall I show you?

Sam held out her hand. 'No, and for God's sake don't show me the needle or I'll pass out.'

Skinner appeared in the doorway. The doctor began to wave him away but Sam stopped her. 'No, he'll do. I'm not going to have stitches without holding someone's hand. Sit here.' She indicated the chair next to her bed.

Skinner had blanched at the sight of her head. He swallowed and did as she asked.

'Hand,' Sam said, holding out her own, and he took it. 'Boxer, right?'

'Long time ago.'

'That'll do.' Sam closed her eyes as the doctor bent over her forehead.

When Sam opened them again twenty minutes later, it was to see Skinner with his tightly shut and looking decidedly green round the gills.

Sam let go of his hand and his eyes sprung open.

'I haven't experienced pain like that since I made the mistake of holding my wife's hand when she was giving birth.'

'Sorry.' Sam sat up, felt faint and lay back down again.

Skinner massaged his hand. 'The boat's completely toasted.'

'Fire seemed well set when I left,' Sam said.

'Do you know what happened?'

'I'd arranged to meet Harry.'

'And you didn't think to tell us?'

'I don't owe you any favours.' She was trying to work out what she should and shouldn't tell him but her head felt so fuzzy it was a struggle. 'He was sure his brother would come to the boat once it was no longer sealed off.'

'Why?'

'David had stolen some jewellery from his father. The boat had been off limits since Grace died but he thought he could find it.'

'We know he was beaten up just before he came out of prison.'

'Yes, he owed the wrong people from before he went inside.'

'Cameron never mentioned a burglary to us and he had plenty of opportunities.'

'That's up to him. You don't have to report a burglary if you don't want to – especially if you think your son may be involved and he's only just come out of prison.'

'Begs the question, though, doesn't it?'

'Ask him,' Sam said.

Skinner smiled. 'So you turned up at the boat?'

'It was on fire when I arrived. As I was going down the stairs, someone brushed past me but I couldn't see who he was because of the smoke, then I found Gerry unconscious. I was trying to get him out when Harry came down. We'd just got out onto the deck of the boat. The other two were slightly ahead of me and were on the pontoon when there was an explosion and I ended up in the water.'

'Who do you think was on the stairs?'

'Cameron? People David owed? David? Take your pick.'

'Why didn't you come to us with all of this?'

'Because there's not much of it and I presumed you probably knew most of it anyway.'

Skinner yawned and stretched his neck.

'One other thing,' Sam said. 'When they left Grace, she was alive.'

'Who?'

'All I know is that they say all the damage to her head and face – they don't know anything about that.'

Skinner nodded. 'Fits.'

'What with?'

'With the post-mortem report. The cause of death was a heart attack.'

Sam frowned. 'That's ridiculous. Her head was practically ripped off.'

'The thing is, there was no blood on the boat. If they'd done that sort of damage to her there'd have been blood everywhere. I've seen it – blunt instrument to the head and the blood goes on the ceiling, floor, walls. You can't believe it, but basically there's no place the blood doesn't go. Also there wasn't any blood on her clothes.'

'So what are they saying?'

'That the damage was done to her in the water.'

'But—'

'They think it was some kind of cutting blade – probably a propeller. She could have been hit by the bow of a boat and then been dragged underneath and got torn up by the blades. You've seen the size of some of the things that go down the Thames. If you bumped into one of those—'

'So let me get this straight. You're basically suggesting a Maxwell?'

'Yes. She has a heart attack and falls overboard. Then she gets hit by a boat and the trauma to her face and head happens then. She had a history of heart disease. Her doctor said it could have happened at any time.'

'So is it still a murder inquiry?'

Skinner didn't answer the question. 'We still need to talk to her sons.'

Sam put her hand up to her head and touched the place she'd been hit and instantly regretted it. 'Does this look terrible?'

'Don't go entering any beauty contests.'

Sam laughed. 'I'd need to double my leg length.'

'Who do you think set fire to the boat?'

Sam shook her head and then groaned and brought her hand up to her forehead.

'You sure you didn't see the person on the stairs?'

'Absolutely.'

Skinner stood up.

'Have you found the others?'

He shook his head. 'You think Harry'll contact you?'

She shrugged. 'He'll be looking for his brother.'

'Brotherly love.'

'I suppose so. Find anything incriminating in all that stuff you carted away?'

Skinner scowled. 'I'm not the one who's been going through it.'

'It was you who took it.'

He pulled on his raincoat.

'Before you go, could you tell me about Gerry Doyle?' she asked.

'What do you want to know?'

'He didn't lose his fingers because he was a lumberjack in the aftermath of the 1987 hurricane, did he?'

Skinner laughed. 'That what he told you?'

Sam stared at him.

Skinner was still laughing. 'That's a good one actually, just enough true information in there to make it possible. That's a good bluff.'

'Well?'

'He is a locksmith but he's also a burglar. He chose the wrong house one time and instead of phoning us they took offence and whacked his fingers off with a butcher's chopper.'

Sam winced.

'Kept him straight for a bit, but probably not that long . . .'

Sam groaned and sat up gingerly.

'What are you going to do?'

'Go home.'

'I think they want to keep you in overnight.'

'I'd like to see them try.'

CHAPTER TWENTY-TWO

Sam got home, took some painkillers and fell fast asleep. She woke at midday with her head throbbing, feeling sick and dizzy, turned over and went straight back to sleep. When she woke in the evening, she felt weak but in less pain. She lay in the darkness, struggling to clear her thoughts. Trying to focus on whoever it was who had pushed past her on the stairs: Cameron, David or one of Sullivan's henchmen. But why burn the boat? Sam considered the expression. Burning your boats. Cutting all ties. No going back. When she thought of it in those terms, she felt sure it had to be David. He'd have a good reason for attacking Gerry, especially if Gerry had got to the jewellery before him. But there was only one way to be certain.

She phoned Cameron.

'Did you hear about what happened?'

'Police told me.'

'Have you talked to David or Harry?'

'No.'

'Were you there?'

'What on earth are you talking about?'

'On the boat.'

'No.'

'You didn't think the jewellery might still be there? That it might be worth taking a look?'

'I didn't even know the police had allowed access to it.'

There was a knock on the door and Sam opened it. It was Jackie.

'I have to go,' Sam said and put down the phone.

'What are you doing here?' Sam said. 'I told you to keep out of the way—'

'It's all right. I got paid – all debts paid off. Jesus! What the hell happened to your head?'

'Life – you know how it is. Hits you on the head now and then.'

'I'll know who to come to if I'm ever in trouble again.'

'Count me out.'

'Look, I wanted to thank you. I'm sorry for all the hassle.'

Sam nodded and began to close the door.

'One thing.'

Sam raised her eyebrows.

'I thought you should know for insurance purposes.'

Insurance – there was that word again. It was like saying the word pension. It made her want to put her head in a vat of fat and not come out until the word had been erased from the English language. Pension? Sam was like Edie in that respect, more a money-under-the-mattress sort of person. She'd always assumed that she'd work till she dropped.

'Can I show you?'

Jackie barged past Sam into her front room. She looked around her. 'Ah, yes, here we are. Do you mind if I have a look?'

She picked a small ivory figure of a water buffalo off Sam's mantelpiece. It was one of the few things to have resisted the ferocity of the burglary. Jackie tapped it gently against her teeth and then turned it over. 'I thought so – see here?' She pointed to a carved oriental symbol. 'It's signed. This really is a fantastic piece. You see how its feet are carved. They didn't just carve the bits that are visible. They carved it in the round. It's a *netsuke*, the Japanese hung them from their belts.' Sam had never seen her look so enthusiastic before. 'You should insure this for about three or four thousand pounds.'

'What's this, *Antiques Roadshow*?'

Jackie laughed.

'It was my gran's.'

'Well, she must have had a good eye. I could sell it for you if you want.' Jackie handed it back to Sam.

Sam rubbed her thumb over the nose of the water buffalo. 'Thanks,' she said.

'You're welcome.'

'How's Alan doing?'

'He's out of hospital – doing OK.'

'Good.'

After Jackie had left, Sam stared at the water buffalo she was holding. Maybe this could replace the dog tags. She opened a drawer in her desk, found a bit of black ribbon, ran it through the hole, placed the *netsuke* in her pocket and tied the ribbon to the belt loop of her trousers. If the Japanese could do it so could she.

The following day Sam went into the office and to her horror found Alan there. She had phoned him the previous evening and told him what had happened but he'd said nothing about coming back to work.

'What the hell are you doing? You were just saying the other day you couldn't even stand up without it hurting.'

'I'm bored.'

'But—'

'I can't stay at home any longer, my sisters-in-law are driving me mad. They know where I am. I decided to give them a moving target.' Alan ducked his head from side to side like a snake. 'Harder to hit. Anyway, I knew everything would have fallen to pieces without me. Look at this post.'

'Paperwork was never my strong point.'

'To have paperwork, Sam, you have to open the envelopes first. This isn't paperwork this is piles and piles of envelopes.'

Sam sat down and stared at her desk. 'Maybe I could enter this as an installation at the ICA. You know, a sort of Tracey Emin's bed.'

'If you put bloodstained underwear anywhere in this room I'm quitting on the grounds of health and safety. There's only so much a man can stand. This has absolutely no artistic merit. It's just a mess, Sam – sort it out.'

'Jackie's been paid by the Americans, so she's no longer going to be a target.'

'Bully for her.'

Sam slumped at her desk, picked up an envelope and began tapping it against the fingers of her other hand.

'Are you going to bill the OUBC?'

She shook her head. 'They haven't got him back, have they?'

'Give me a break. You tracked him down, you advised him to go to the police—'

'Yes, and he's still out there somewhere and so is his brother and a debt is still owing and somewhere someone has a pile of stolen jewellery, unless it went down in the boat.'

'David,' Alan said, 'is in deep, deep shit.'

'I know.'

'Have you got a picture of him?'

Sam nodded. 'I've got one of Harry – it amounts to the same thing.'

'I'll give it to my brothers, see if they can track them down.'

'Thanks, Alan.'

The phone rang on her desk.

'Hi, it's Tom. I need good news.'

'What's happened?'

'Holden Webster's gone back to the States.'

'Why?'

'Said there was some sort of family emergency. First thing I knew about it was when he phoned from there.'

Sam doubted there'd been an emergency – thought it was more likely that Phil had pinned him against a wall and scared the living daylights out of him.

'I'm sorry, Tom – there's nothing I can tell you that'll help at the moment.'

'Shit,' he said. 'Who the hell am I going to get to stroke the boat?'

After she'd finished talking to him, she put a call in to Phil. 'Did you speak to Holden?'

'Yes – why?'

'Tom King's just been on the phone and said he's gone back to the States. I wondered if you might have had something to do with that.'

'I might have.'

'Tom's not very happy. He hasn't got anyone to stroke the boat now.'

'Frankly, Sam, that's not my problem, but having some arrogant sod who thinks he can rape women while they're unconscious loose among the student population is. I told him in no uncertain terms it would be a good idea for him to leave. I told him we had evidence that would tie him to Siobhan and that he had a couple of days to go, otherwise we'd come looking for him.'

'But there was no evidence.'

'No, but he didn't know that.'

'Did you talk to Carter as well?'

'Mad Hatter was raided last weekend. It's been temporarily closed down.'

Reg sat down opposite Mark and crossed his legs. 'Thanks for coming. I'm sorry it had to be so early.'

'I was in town. I thought it'd probably be better to do this face to face and I can't deny a bit of curiosity.'

'About me?'

'Definitely.'

Reg smiled. 'I can understand that.'

'So what was it you wanted to talk to me about?'

'Sam can't remember what happened between your mother telling her you were going to move from Hereford and her ending up in hospital. I was wondering if you could fill in the gap.'

'Oh.'

'Is that all right?'

'She's not ... I mean, you don't think she's going to—'

'It would be really helpful if you could tell me what you remember.'

Mark swallowed. 'When Mum told her, she became very upset. She screamed at her and told her she wouldn't go and she couldn't make her, that when Dad came back he wouldn't know where to find us.'

'How did your mother handle it?'

'Well, she tried to calm her down. You know, the usual sort of stuff. Told her it'd be all right once we got to Oxford and had settled in. It'd be a new start.'

'And then what happened?'

'Sam went very quiet, very withdrawn, for a couple of days. Then Mum took us to the cinema. It was supposed to be a treat but the film she chose . . .' Mark paused. 'This is probably going to sound ridiculous—'

'Try me.'

'Well, she took us to *The Railway Children*.'

Reg opened his mouth and then closed it again. There was a moment's pause. Then: 'Good grief,' he said.

'You know it, then?'

'Yes.'

'Well, Mum obviously didn't. I mean, if she had ... I mean, she just can't have done.' Mark pressed his fingers against his eyes.

'What happened?'

'Well, it reached *that* point, you know, on the platform when Jenny Agutter looks round and sees her father coming out of the steam of the engine.'

'Yes.'

'It's ridiculous, but to this day I can't watch that scene without being affected by it. Well, from that point on Sam was inconsolable. That night she was curled up in her bed, rocking backwards and forwards, saying the line from the film, 'Daddy, my daddy,' over and over again. In the morning she was gone.'

'Gone?'

'She went missing for the whole of the following day. The police found her that evening at the railway station. She said she'd gone there to wait for him. She said if he came back that's where he'd be.'

'Was she seen by anyone?'

Mark frowned. 'What sort of someone?'

'A doctor, a child psychiatrist?'

'Not then, no. I don't think my mother realised it was that serious.'

'But Sam was obviously a severely disturbed child?'

Mark looked startled. 'Do you think that's what she was?'

'Well, yes,' Reg said. 'What happened next?'

'Sam tried to kill herself. The second night she was home, she took Dad's old cut-throat razor and tried to cut her own throat. That's the scar she's got on her neck. I asked her afterwards about the razor and she said it had been so close to my father, literally scraped over his skin, and she thought that killing herself with it would bring her closer to him.'

Reg took a deep breath. 'And then she got some help?'

'Yes. Mum obviously couldn't pretend there wasn't a problem and I think Sam did have a few sessions with someone but we moved fairly soon after that and I don't think she saw anyone once we were in Oxford.'

'And how was she after you moved?'

'Quiet, withdrawn – furious with Mum. She was always getting into trouble at school for fighting. Once she started the judo that all calmed down. It saved her really, I think. She was all right as long as she could fight. It was something that she was very good at and a way for her to feel close to Dad.'

'But she can't fight now?'

'No, and I'm so worried about her. I mean, I would be lying if I didn't say I was surprised that she was seeing you. She's never been very introspective. So I was surprised but incredibly relieved.'

Reg nodded. 'Well, thank you very much for coming, that's been a great help.'

'Do I need to pay you?'

'No, I'll sort that out with Sam.'

'She's very upset at my father's return.'

'Yes.'

They were at the front door. Mark turned round. 'Is she going to be all right? She's not at risk, is she?'

'There are no quick fixes, no guarantees in my line of work, but I can assure you I'll do everything in my power to help her.'

Mark held out his hand. Reg considered it for a minute. 'Forgive me but—'

He smiled. 'It's nothing like hers,' he said.

'Ah, good,' Reg said, taking Mark's hand in his.

The following day Reg sat, watching the minute hand of the clock on his wall tick past the hour of Sam's appointment. She'd only been late the one time and then only by five minutes. He swore under his breath. He'd lost her. He'd pushed too hard, too soon, because he'd been worried about her, and his conversation with Mark had only compounded that worry. A client of his had killed himself a month ago and it had made him jumpy with his other clients, concerned that he'd miss the signs. And when Sam had mentioned the cutting that had *really* got to him. Half of all suicides had harmed themselves in the year before they died. He padded across the wooden floor and looked out into the street at the bus stop. She usually arrived early and then sat there waiting for the right time of the appointment, but today the bus shelter was empty. It had been a tightrope from the beginning. Just keeping her in the room for a whole session had been hard. He sighed. *Tomoe-nage.* He'd been trying to draw an analogy that she would recognise but he knew she'd taken it the wrong way, she'd seen it as giving in, losing power, surrendering. God knows, that's how he'd been – stubborn, obnoxious, defensive. He punched his fist into his open palm. Shit – she'd bolted and it was all his fault.

A couple of days passed in which nothing happened other than that the stitches on Sam's face started to itch and the piles of envelopes she hadn't opened got bigger. Sam and Alan were again in the office when Alan's phone rang. He stared at Sam.

'If it's the shrink, what do you want me to say?' Reg had phoned her and left messages at home and then at the office. Sam hadn't spoken to him and had not phoned back.

'Tell him I'm not here and you don't know when I'll be back.'

After a brief conversation he put the phone down. 'The twins have been seen in Oxford.'

'Who was that?'

'Bert.'

'How do your brothers know that? They never set foot out of London, do they?'

'They were showing the picture around and a dealer who lives in Oxford and goes to the market in Gloucester Green recognised him. Said she hadn't seen him around in Oxford before. That everyone was talking about him because of what he had.'

'Did he describe it?'

'It didn't mean anything to Bert but apparently it's very rare.'

'There were two of them there?'

'Yes.'

Oxford again. This time Sam took Alan with her. They spent the night on Mark's floor then early the following morning let themselves out into the Turl and walked up the Broad to Gloucester Green. It was cold and the damp clung to their clothes. Another early morning and another antiques market, with dealers stamping their feet and rubbing their faces to keep awake and eyeing the punters over the top of white polystyrene cups in the same way tigers eye steak, their breath creating unwelcome clouds in the air in front of them. Sam and Alan moved between the stalls looking at the mixture of books, watches, jewellery, old photos, old clothes, china and glass. Sam was just contemplating getting a hot drink to warm her up when she heard a shout from Alan. She saw him running and set off in pursuit. They ran past the cinema and turned left into George Street. It was as they turned into Cornmarket that she saw them both, Harry and David, running straight down the middle of the empty street, a small white dog with a brown face and a docked tail bounding at their heels. As they turned down the High, Sam passed Alan, doubled over, holding his stomach.

'I can't,' he said.

'Call Phil,' Sam shouted over her shoulder. 'Tell him they're going down the High. To send a car to Magdalen Bridge.'

Leg length was prevailing. The two men were well ahead of Sam and getting further away. Halfway down the street Sam heard the wail of a police car somewhere in front of her and then as she passed Queen's Lane saw the cars parked across the end of the street just beyond the bridge blocking access to the Plain and beyond. Two policemen got out of the car and David and Harry stopped.

Sam came up behind them. 'Harry,' she shouted and the one on the left turned round and stared at her. The other one ran at the police car, skipped out of the way of the grasping policeman, scrambled over the bonnet and ran onto the roundabout.

Harry turned his attention away from Sam and back to his brother. 'Dave,' he shouted and his brother turned briefly and raised his hand, as if in farewell.

Sam saw the coach accelerating on the roundabout behind him. 'Look out!' she shouted. He glanced at her and turned. The coach caught him full on and Sam heard a noise she hoped never to hear again in her life, the noise of a body being slammed to the ground and run over.

Sam covered her face with her hands and then wished she'd put them in her ears, wished with all her might that she had not heard the noise that came from Harry – the half scream, half howl. As if he was the one that had been torn up, as if it was his body lying bleeding and twisted in the road. One of the policemen grabbed hold of him.

'It's his brother,' Sam said. 'Let him go.' And he did.

Sam followed Harry to where the coach driver stood, hands to his head, staring down at David's body and the dark puddle creeping ominously across the tarmac.

Three gold fish swam in the pool of blood.

Almost before she was aware of what she was doing, Sam had leaned over and pocketed the brooch.

Harry was bent over his brother's body, rocking backwards and forwards. The dog was standing staring at David's body. It looked at Sam and began to whimper. Sam squatted down and called it to her side. In the distance the wail of an ambulance could be heard but Sam knew it was already too late for David, maybe it always had been.

CHAPTER TWENTY-THREE

Sam sat in the Oxford police station talking to Phil.
'When are you going to let him go?'

'Skinner needs to talk to him.'

'Can I see him? He's not under arrest, is he?'

Phil nodded. 'OK, just a few minutes.'

Phil held the door open for Sam, who was holding two cups of tea. Harry was alabaster white; it was as if he, not his brother, had lost all that blood.

Sam put the cups on the table and sat down. 'Try some of this,' she said. 'I've sugared it – it's good for shock.' But Harry made no move to pick up the cup.

'I always thought I'd feel something physical. You know, that I'd know if he died. But I was there and saw it happen and felt nothing.' He looked bewildered.

Sam didn't know what to say. 'It's the shock,' she said. 'It numbs.'

Harry bunched his hands into fists and pressed them against his eyes.

'Will you tell me now what happened on the boat?'

'They came that night.'

'The people David owed?'

He nodded. 'It was late. Mum couldn't sleep and neither could I and we were chatting upstairs so as not to wake up Dave. He was downstairs in the back bedroom. We were having a cup of tea. I think they just assumed I was Dave and I let them. They tied me up and started demanding to know where the stuff was.'

'The stuff he'd stolen from your father?'

'Yes. Mum wouldn't say anything. She could be very stubborn and I honestly didn't know.'

'What was David doing?'

'I don't know – I presume he was downstairs, sleeping.'

'Did he know what was going on?'

Harry shrugged. 'I've really no idea. Then they got out this thing. I didn't know what it was at first. It was metal and like a big razor. But I knew what it was when they touched me with it.'

'What happened?' Sam said.

'I was electrocuted. Just felt completely scrambled.'

'Probably a stun gun.'

'I suppose, but it wasn't in the shape of a gun.'

'Some of them aren't.'

'And what did your mother do?'

'She started having difficulty breathing. I told them she had a heart condition. I think at first they thought it was just a way to get them to back off but when they saw the state she was in they panicked. They left but said if the debt wasn't settled they'd be back and do the same to her.'

'After they'd gone Dave came up. He didn't say so but by the look of him I think he must have heard what had been happening. I was really worried about Mum but then she took her medication, calmed down and got some more colour back in her face and she said she was all right. She'd had that sort of spell all my life. But Dave was in this really weird mood. He said he had to go out and I knew what that meant. I tried to argue with him but he wasn't having it. He insisted. I spoke to Mum and she said I should go after him, so I did. But when we got back, we saw the police were crawling all over the place and Dave was frightened. He was worried about going back inside. He still owed Sullivan the money and he was really frightened of what they'd do to him. I presume they came back and started in on Mum again. I blame myself, I should never have left her, but she told me to, she was worried about Dave as well.'

'I don't think they did come back.'

'What d'you mean?'

'Skinner, the police officer in charge of the investigation, said she died of a heart attack. They think she had a heart attack and fell overboard. After seeing what happened to you, that wouldn't

320

be particularly surprising. Seeing someone you love being tortured must register pretty high on the Richter scale of most stressful events. The damage to her face and head could have been done afterwards.'

'Damage?'

Oh God, she'd forgotten he didn't know that. 'No, nothing,' she said.

Much to Sam's relief the door opened and Phil came in. 'Time's up.'

Sam stood up. 'Was it David who attacked Gerry and set fire to the boat?'

Harry nodded. 'He'd gone to the boat like I said to look for the stuff and found Gerry there doing exactly the same. He lost it completely – it was Gerry who first got him involved in drugs. He was clever enough not to take them himself, of course.'

'So he found the jewellery?'

'Yes.'

'And then he set fire to the boat?'

'That's right.'

'Do you want me to let Tom King and Emma Hodge know what's happened?'

He nodded.

'You just need to tell the police what you told me and they'll let you go. It's over now, Harry.'

He looked up. 'It's only just beginning.'

Sam went from the police station to St Silas's and bumped into Emma Hodge coming out of the main entrance to the church. She told her what had happened to Harry and David and was about to leave when she remembered. She put her hand in her pocket and brought out the cross.

'Yours, I think.'

'Where did you find it?'

'David sold it to someone at Portobello. I bought it back.'

'Why?'

'I knew it was yours.'

Emma Hodge hadn't taken it from Sam's hand.

'That's so kind of you.' She took it and looked at it, then handed it back. 'I'd like you keep it.'

'No, no . . . I don't even . . . it wouldn't be appropriate.'

'I'd like you to.'

Sam's hand went to her pocket. The dog tags were gone but now she had the water buffalo; he had vicious horns. And like judo he was Japanese. She'd stick with him.

'No,' she said firmly. 'It's yours, you should have it.'

Emma smiled and took it.

'I'm afraid the chain's broken.'

'That doesn't matter.'

'How are your injuries?'

'I'm feeling better, thanks. And you?'

Sam shrugged her shoulders. She didn't have a clue.

Sam stood in the doorway of the hall in Headington, looking at the class kneeling in an orderly group around Tyler. It was a dream that had brought her here, one she'd had a couple of days before. She had seen her blue *judogi* spinning and throwing, executing all the movements of a *judoka* but without having any body occupying it. It had looked beautiful, balletic almost, but Sam had woken with a feeling of tremendous sadness. It was as if the suit was telling her to let it go, in order that it could fight again. So here she was, clutching a plastic bag containing the suit. Karen saw her immediately. Tyler, noticing the distraction behind him, turned and smiled at Sam. 'Come on in,' he said. Sam took off her shoes, stepped on the *tatami* and knelt down next to Tyler, facing the group.

'Do you know who this is?' Tyler asked.

Karen's hand shot into the air. 'Sam Falconer.'

'Yes,' Tyler said. 'I started teaching Sam when she was about your age now and she became a World Champion.'

'Four times,' Karen said.

Sam smiled.

'Want to tell them how you did it?'

'I listened to everything Tyler told me and I trained hard,' Sam said.

Tyler smiled.

'Do you teach?' Karen asked.

'No.'

'Why not?'

Sam looked at Tyler. He replied for her. 'She needed a bit of a break – a bit of a change. Sometimes we need to do different things with our lives.'

'Yes,' Sam said. 'A change.'

Sam helped the class put the mats in the back of Tyler's van. Then she sought out Karen. She opened the plastic bag and pulled out her blue *judogi*. 'This was the *judogi* I wore when I first won the World Championships.'

The little girl stared at it.

'I want you to have it.'

'Aren't you going to use it any more?'

'No,' Sam said, squeezing the blue arm of the *judogi*. 'And I want it used.'

'It's too big for me.'

'You'll grow into it.'

The child took a book out of her bag titled 50 Great Judo Champions and started flicking through it. She found the page she was looking for and held it out to Sam. 'Will you sign?' she asked.

Sam looked at a photo of herself.

'*Tomoe-nage*,' she said. 'It was a favourite of mine.' She signed her name at the bottom of the photo and handed the book back to her. She turned and walked towards the door.

Tyler was outside sorting out the back of the van. 'What did you give her?' Tyler asked.

'Just an old *judogi* and a signature.'

Sam kissed him on the cheek.

He closed up the back of the van. 'Can I give you a lift anywhere?'

'No thanks. I'll walk. It'll clear my head.'

A week later, Sam climbed the stairs to Jackie's flat and knocked on the door. She'd stayed up in Oxford for a few days to keep an eye on Harry and then, when she was sure that there were enough other people doing that, she'd come back to London. She'd asked Alan to check through Bert that Sullivan knew that David was dead, to check that his death erased the debt. Her main concern was Harry's safety, but a couple of days later the reply came back that the debt was still owing.

Jackie opened the door. 'Oh hi,' she said. 'Want to sell it?'

'Not that,' Sam said.

In the front room she handed Jackie the brooch. Jackie didn't say anything at first, she just stared at it and frowned. Then she got out a small, glass, cylindrical object, which she held to her eye like a tiny telescope, and looked at the brooch. She turned it over and examined the back for a long time.

Then she looked at Sam, scrutinising her with much the same intensity as the brooch. 'I'm not going to ask you where you got this.'

'Can you sell it?'

Jackie sighed. 'Yes.'

'Privately?'

'Yes.'

'Quickly?'

She nodded.

'Go ahead then.'

'I would require a larger commission than usual in the circumstances.'

'Agreed. This is obviously not the kind of thing that should be put out in a showcase in Portobello.'

'No kidding.'

A fortnight later and Sam was counting the largest pile of fifty-pound notes she'd ever seen. In the end she decided to give the money to Bert. He could hand it over. He could negotiate with Sullivan's henchmen. He could keep back some as blood money. It was up to him. All she wanted to know was that they wouldn't come looking for Harry.

A couple of days later she took the call. Debt settled.

It was over. Harry was safe.

Sam told Harry none of this. She couldn't see the point.

EPILOGUE

Two months later. On the day of the Boat Race, Sam hadn't been sure what to do. She could have stayed at home and watched it on TV or she could have staked a claim against the green metal railings in Bishop's Park, if she'd been willing to get there early enough. Chiswick Bridge was another option if she'd wanted to see the finish. She might have stayed at home, if Mark hadn't phoned and told her he could get her onto one of the launches that followed the race down the river. That had been too good to resist.

As she was leaving the block she bumped into Edie. Edie had a short red biro wedged between her teeth. She took it out of her mouth and tapped it on the paper she was holding. Sam saw it was the racing pages of the *Sun*.

'Two-forty at Ayr – Tipsy Mouse. Good each-way bet.'

Sam, who knew absolutely nothing about betting, nodded her head and smiled inanely.

'Jumps?' Sam said, thinking of the conversation she'd had with Reg.

'Jumps?' Edie's voice was heavy with scorn. 'Scottish Grand National, love.'

'Oh.'

'Where you off to, anyway?'

'To watch the Boat Race.'

'Used to make up rosettes as a kid. My dad used to take me and we'd sell them up on the bridge.'

'Who did you support?'

'If I sold a light blue one, Cambridge. A dark blue one, Oxford.'

Sam laughed. Edie was nothing if not pragmatic.

She set off for the river. During the last couple of months there'd been no word from her father and no threats from any other source. Ever since Mike Brown hooked her out of the river she'd been feeling, well, bizarrely much more optimistic. Reg had stopped phoning and it made her feel like getting in touch with him. Maybe she'd do that tomorrow. The cherry trees by Putney Bridge station were in full bloom. Sam sat on a wall and stared at them; the smell of spring and the pink of cherry tree blossom were surely as effective as any sort of therapy. With her father out of the picture she felt more on an even keel. But she couldn't help worrying about him. Fear and fascination twined around each other with equal force. Had he changed? Was he the violent abuser of her childhood or a man seeking reconciliation with his family and the families of the men he had murdered in Northern Ireland? Suppose he was the latter? There were no easy answers, no trite resolutions, but for the moment Sam didn't care. Spring was coming and with it came hope.

She stood up and joined the streams of people walking towards the river. Up on the bridge it was impossible to walk along the pavements because of the crowds. Light blue and dark blue balloons tugged at the strings attaching them to the lampposts on the bridge and a young man waved a programme under Sam's nose. She bought one, opened it, found Harry's picture and read his biography. He had dedicated his participation in the race to the memory of his mother and his brother David. The wind had picked up and was chopping up the surface of the river. Oxford's was the heaviest crew in the Boat Race's history. If the river were rough, surely that would favour them? A man was pushing a shopping trolley filled with rosettes and flags through the crowds. Thinking of Edie, Sam stopped him and bought an Oxford rosette for three pounds. She found Mark outside the OUBC boathouse.

'God, you look sick,' Sam said.

'Nerves.'

'You're not even rowing.'

'Makes no difference.'

'Do the rough conditions favour them?'

'I don't know.'

'God, you're a complete basket case.'

Eric came up to Sam. 'You on the same launch?' Sam asked.

He nodded. 'Tell me you've got a cigarette on you.'

'I haven't but if I had I wouldn't give it to you.'

He scowled at her. A man was walking past with a cigarette dangling from his mouth. Eric left Sam's side and followed him. Sam saw him bum a cigarette and a light off him. Eric came back to where Mark and Sam were standing, drew the smoke deep into his lungs and then exhaled luxuriantly. 'God, that's so much better,' he said. He looked at Sam. 'How's the boy been doing?'

'It's been difficult to tell,' Sam said.

The launch took off into the middle of the river, turned under Putney Bridge and drew up behind the umpire's launch with a flotilla of other boats. The eights were already on the stake boats but both coxes had their arms up, indicating they weren't yet ready. The sky had darkened and heavy drops of rain began to fall. Thunder crashed overhead and suddenly Sam wasn't so sure about being out on the water.

The umpire's gun went off and with it came a huge roar from the people thronging the side of the river. The race was evenly balanced all the way, neither crew managing to get any further than half a length ahead, along all the twists and turns of the course.

With twenty metres to go Oxford were just ahead, with Cambridge coming back at them. Could Oxford hold on? As the two eights crossed the finishing line, Sam wasn't sure who had won. She looked at Mark and Eric, whose faces were tense and uncertain.

Then a voice rang out: 'Oxford – the winners.' And the tension melted into the smiles and laughter of celebration.

Sam didn't join in. She was looking at Harry. He was not standing in triumph. Neither was he turning round and embracing his number seven. He was leaning over the side of the boat being violently sick. Sam watched him and wondered what the TV cameras were doing with that. Sometimes victory looked like a man who had given his all to the point where he was throwing up the contents of his stomach, not particularly glamorous or telegenic, but victory none the less. Harry wiped his mouth and straightened up. He looked up at the launch circling near by and caught sight of Sam. He held his clenched fist in the air. Sam nodded. He'd given everything he had to give. Sam knew all about that.

Eric threw his arm round Sam. 'The boy's got the heart of a lion.'

Sam nodded but couldn't trust herself to speak.

It was a beautiful morning, the morning Harry took his brother's ashes to the river. The storms of race day had cleared away to leave clear blue skies and the mildest of breezes. He squatted down, removed the lid of the urn, took out a handful and let them run through his fingers, letting the wind take them, scudding across the surface of the river like pollen in the springtime. He took some more out, sunk his hand under the water and watched them sit on the surface and float away from him. He wanted to smear the ashes on his face, to stick his fingers in his mouth; he wanted to rub ashes in his eyes so that he'd never see again. He wanted to tear his face and punch holes into the condensed solid grief that sat in him as hard and immovable as stone. But instead he took another handful and then another and let the ash run through his fingers. The wind changed direction and, as if responding to his wishes, blew a fine dusting against his face. He coughed and blinked to clear his eyes.

He wanted Dave here in the river. Even though his brother had never rowed he wanted him somewhere that meant something to him and the river meant everything, especially the last couple of months when the discipline, the routine and being part of the squad had saved him. He hadn't been in a church since the funeral. For the first time in his life he'd been unable to pray and in the absence of prayer, training had become his religious practice. And the physical pain of the training was almost a relief. It was better than the grief that sat in the nerve endings in his teeth and took the taste of food from his mouth and cast a grey misery over his every waking moment. He didn't know if he had been rowing to save himself or beat Cambridge but had come to the conclusion it didn't matter. All that had mattered was having somewhere to go and something to do. He held the urn upside down, watching the last of his brother's ashes float across the river, and stood up. His body was sore from yesterday's race. They had won but he did not feel celebratory. He thought of the end of Wittgenstein's quotation . . . we ought not to go on living . . . But that was the one thing he had to do, he had to go on living without his mother and his brother. He turned and walked to where Sam Falconer stood waiting to take him to breakfast.